The Runes of War

Jane Welch was born in Derbyshire in 1964. For several years she and her husband taught skiing at a Pyrenean resort in the Principality of Andorra. This is her first novel.

Voyager

JANE WELCH

The Runes of War

Book One of
The Runespell Trilogy

HarperCollins*Publishers*

Voyager
HarperCollins*Publishers*
77–85 Fulham Palace Road,
Hammersmith, London W6 8JB

A paperback original 1995
5 7 9 8 6 4

A catalogue record for this book
is available from the British Library

ISBN 0 00 648025 X

Set in Linotron Goudy by
Rowland Phototypesetting Ltd,
Bury St Edmunds, Suffolk

Printed and bound in Great Britain by
Caledonian International Book Manufacturing Ltd, Glasgow

For Richard
whose magic fills my
life as much as it has shaped
this story

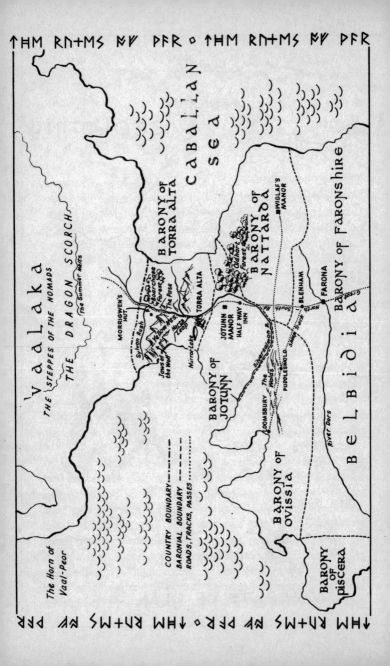

Prologue

The last scaly beast lay dying on the canyon floor. A pennon, bearing the Belbidian colours, fluttered from the hilt of the lance that pierced its chest and, with the dragon's final breath, the pass was won. From the floor of the canyon thrust a commanding tor, and at its summit yawned the cavernous nest from which a dynasty of dragons had once disgorged into the air. But now, over the slaughtered monster's empty lair, the proud men of Belbidia constructed a mighty fortress. They named the fortress Torra Alta and dedicated its power to the Mother Goddess, invoking the Primal Gods for their blessing.

For a thousand years Torra Alta had enforced its tyrannical rule over the pass through the Yellow Mountains. From high on its rocky throne it could lash out to protect the peaceful lands from the bloody hordes to the north. And so absolute had been its power that in three hundred years there had been no call to raise its might, for the fortress sat back needing only to glare down at the valley.

Now it happened that a great plain of ice encroached on the dread lands of northern Vaalaka, eating at pastures and freezing over the vast hunting grounds of the people. Tribes were forced southward into the harsh landscape of bare rock and parched soil that was the enduring monument of the ancient Dragon Wars. Here every summer the ice-cap receded and the meltwaters poured into the wasteland of the Dragon Scorch. The Vaalakan nomads grazed their herds along the banks of the seasonal rivers. When the Summer Melts dried out, they returned northward to the thin belt of green steppes on the fringe of the tundra, which was all that was left of their hunting grounds.

But as the millennium drew to a close, the tundra gained in power and ate steadily southward until one year the spring never came and the ice no longer melted. The Dragon Scorch remained permanently and inhospitably arid in the fast clutches of unyielding winter.

Imprisoned within the thin belt of the steppes the Vaalakan tribes squabbled amongst themselves, competing for food. The desperate struggle for survival twisted their souls and made them brutal and depraved, so that neighbours murdered each other to ensure food for their own families. They seemed doomed to a barbaric extinction, until one year there arose out of their number a leader, a man of great strength and pride in his people, and he was known to them as Morbak. He prayed that a God might hear him and help his people; but none would answer. When finally Morbak was near despair he heard a howling cry born on the ice-north wind, and the cry became wailing words. Believing the words, he took them to his people:

'Forsake all other Gods but Vaal-Peor. Turn away from the Great Mother because she no longer feeds us from her mantle. Turn to Vaal-Peor. He wants not prayers but sacrifices. Let blood pour onto the earth to feed Him and He will give me strength to lead you southwards through the Dragon Scorch into a new land beyond.'

Morbak was consumed by these words and he became as dark and treacherous as the land, naming himself the High Priest of Vaal-Peor, pouring evil into the hearts of his people.

He marched them south, spilling the warm blood of children in the name of his cold-hearted God. At the head of the united tribes, Morbak rode upon the back of a gargantuan troll, an ugly creature with coarse hog-like bristles and yellow fangs. He adorned his helmet with the skull and horns of an ibex; over his naked chest, on a string of pig-gut, hung the teeth and claws of a troll. And as he assumed this demonic form, a swelling number of his followers believed he was the God incarnate.

As the tribes of Morbak poured southward, following the course of the dried out Summer Melts that were frozen as hard as stone, they heard tales of a Belbidian fortress built upon a tower of rock that guarded the gateway through the mountains to the promised pastures. As Morbak drove his army onwards, goading them with his double-edged axe through the harsh and inhospitable lands, the rumours of an impassable fortress grew to terrifying proportions. Its garrison was said to be captained by the last living dragon and in times of threat its warriors walked abroad as sabre-toothed tigers, prowling the pass for any trespasser daring to enter Belbidia. The power of the fortress, so the local legends told, was a gift from the ancient Gods; the Primal Gods of Sun, Moon and Mother Earth, and the castle was blessed by their protection. Many of Morbak's people believed these tales of magic, and the legendary power of the Fortress at Torra Alta struck fear into the hearts of the Vaalakans. In their dismay they rebelled against Morbak, saying they would not march on such a fortress. But he took the youngest of his issue and drained the life-blood from its veins until the earth turned muddy red. He hurled his voice at the sky.

'Great God of Ice, Lord of the Tundra, how may we crush the might of Torra Alta?'

The tribes heard the icy howling of the wind and Morbak heard the words of Vaal-Peor. He told his people:

'The Fortress of Torra Alta is but a shell and her people are grown fat and slow on peace and plenty. They have forsaken their true Gods and worship those of the cities of the southland. Their worthless faith will be no defence against our own great Lord, who will show us how to smite at her roots and deliver us into Belbidia.'

The tribes of Morbak drew comfort from their leader's words and marched on to make their attack.

Chapter 1

The first Caspar knew of the unrest was when his father, the Lord Branwolf, Baron of Torra Alta, bellowed out orders for supplies to be brought up to the castle. For weeks a struggling procession of carts, wagons and pack-mules picked their way through the jagged rocks and fallen boulders that lay strewn across the rough-hewn road up to the fortress.

The threat of the encroaching hordes of Morbak made the boy feel *alive*. Men pulsed through the corridors and halls of the fortress. Outside, there was rushing to and fro with supplies and stocks for the armouries; the hammering of repairs; shouts of help for tools or building materials; yelling of orders and the rallying of the castle's people – united all as one entity. They were preparing for siege, as if slapped awake from a doze.

The heart of Torra Alta beat again and Caspar's blood raced with the thrill of it. Perhaps if he had been a little older he might have measured his excitement with apprehension, but the brutality of war meant nothing to him. At fourteen years of age, the boy clung to the glory of the heroes that filled the books and ballads he knew: war was the stuff of legends. Besides, Caspar had no reason to feel fear; he had absolute faith in the invincibility of his home.

Beside him, stretched up on elongated hind legs with its pendulous front paws dangling over the side of the parapet, a great deer-hound nuzzled up against his master, allowing the scruff of his neck to be kneaded and ruffled as the boy pensively twisted his fingers through the hound's coarse grey fur.

'What do you think then, Wartooth?' Caspar addressed his silent dog. 'Nothing, but nothing can touch us up here, can it? We're on top of the world.'

The auburn-haired youth hung over the battlements, drinking in the scene of scrambling animals whose hooves slithered over the stones in their efforts to haul their loads. It would be impossible to climb the Tor under the fury of Torra Alta's garrison. He thought back to ancient tales from the time of the Dragon Wars, in the millennium long past, when the fortress was raised upon the lair of a slain beast; since that day no army had successfully assailed the peak on which the citadel perched. It seemed to Caspar that the spirit of the dragon still cast a haunting eye from her lofty nest, as if scanning the valley for prey.

He had often studied his home from below, when returning from hunting boar in the scrubland and forests just north of the canyon. Entering the square-sided valley was always a proud moment: after the wildness of the hunt, it was grand to be met by the sight of the angular block of the keep, encinctured by the buttressed towers and pinnacled turrets of his father's fortress. The fortress dominated the pass from the height of the majestic Tor. The treeless pillar of rock, left standing by some great elemental force of nature, thrust up like the core of a volcano out of a calm sea. The flat valley floor stretched away on either side before washing against the canyon walls that framed Caspar's view.

A curving river, sluggish and tired from its hectic tumbling down the ranges of the Yellow Mountains to the north, idled through the centre of the valley and lapped around the foot of the Tor. In springs gone by, when the meltwater gushed off the mountains that divided Belbidia from the Dragon Scorch of southern Vaalaka, it had swelled the river to a roaring spate. In its haste the river cut into the stalk of rock on two sides, creating an overhang. Much of the fissured rock was sheer, though in places it would be possible for an athletic man to climb it, with luck on his side . . . after he had scrambled painfully over the steep acres of unstable scree that slumped around the base of the rock. Caspar knew how difficult that was.

Caspar's gaze plummeted to the remote canyon floor, catching sight of the long shadow of the Tor crowned with the bastions and barbicans of the castle. He fancied it looked like the shadow of a giant warrior-king reigning over the pass. The road to the fortress had been blasted and chiselled out of the western approach, which rose less steeply. On the lower slopes of the scarp the road cut back and forth, twisting through gorse and heather and then spiralled up encircling the pinnacle. Near the summit the road steepened into a stretch which Caspar and Hal had named the 'Slide', because in winter cruel ice glossed over the stones and the horses skidded and slipped.

Caspar jumped as he felt a sharp prod in the ribs, bringing him back from his reverie. It was Hal.

'Look. Over there.' Hal pointed at an uncovered wagon that seemed, at this distance, to be carrying barrels stacked two layers high. 'I'll bet you a hunting knife they won't make it with that wagon.' Caspar did not reply. He had learnt from long experience to avoid betting with his uncle.

Hal was Branwolf's much younger brother, in fact his half-brother. Their father, Baron Brungard, had remarried late in life and Hal had been born twenty years after his brother and only three years before Caspar. After their father died, young Lord Branwolf had raised Hal alongside his own boy, and because of their closeness in age he came to treat his young half-brother as his eldest son. However, by law and birthright, Caspar was Hal's superior and stood to inherit all: the Barony, Torra Alta and the power that went with that mighty fortress. Hal was an uncle treated as an elder brother: it was a relationship that the two boys both found awkward.

They watched together, Wartooth's grey muzzle pointing between them, as the wagon set off. Other carts were offloading cargo at the foot of the crag. Milled flour and grain, for the animal stock kept within the castle, were slung in sacks over the backs of mules. Ropes threaded the beasts together

3

and, driven by a short man with a hard voice and a hard stick, they snaked up to the castle. Unsuitable for transferring onto the mule train were: the wooden crates of laying hens that squawked in outrage at their journey, barrels of ale, pallets of salt beef wrapped in muslin cloth, bundles of saplings and caskets of arrowheads for the castle fletcher, battle axes, mail-shirts and barrels of tar. All these siege supplies and trappings of war remained on the wagons for their journey up.

The two youths had found a good vantage point on the castle wall just beyond the guard room. Unafraid of the dizzy heights they leant over the battlements, straining forward to gain a clear view of the miniature scenes far below. Caspar pressed his toes into the solid walls to balance himself as he stretched forward to take a look at the half-finished cathedral far below. Work on the sacred building had ceased with the news of the Vaalakan threat. It was the first time in his life that Caspar had been unable to see the ant-like masons crawling over the walls to chisel out the gargoyles and holy symbols. He liked the gargoyles.

Hal teasingly nudged his precariously balanced nephew and the younger boy swung down to a more stable position and grimaced at his grinning companion. Neither was worried by the height. Being born and reared in the castle, the surrounding drop was as normal to them as a swaying eyrie to an eagle. Indeed, Caspar used to dream he was a bird of prey and could step out of the top tower and soar into the heavens. However, it had given them much entertainment over the years when any stranger to the citadel swooned at the sickening drop.

Caspar signalled toward a stretch of road below them. 'There's your wagon.'

It was emerging from behind a spit of rock, an extra pair of cart-horses hitched to the team, their heads hung low as they leant forward into their collars, straining against the weight of the load. The body of the wagon rested between its four wheels, which stood as high as the wagon itself. The solid discs, with their hubs bulging out at shoulder height to a man, looked like mill wheels for grinding corn. The huge diameter of the wheels made it easier for the cumbersome vehicle to roll over the rough ground, though even then, as they clattered over the stones, a boulder or time-worn rut would trap them. A shout of warning from several voices and the terrible sound of wood under massive strain told Caspar and Hal that the wagon below them had met such a fate. The wagoner lashed his whip over the heads of the horses and a man at each wheel gripped the rim, hanging his weight from it in an attempt to manhandle the wheel round. With a final lurch forward, the vehicle crashed down from the obstacle and rumbled on.

'My bet still stands,' said Hal.

'Hey! I never agreed to any bet,' protested Caspar.

'Dear Nephew, where's your sense of adventure?' mocked Hal. 'Of course, I forgot you're still a boy and not big enough to bet yet.' The sarcastic words had the sting taken out of them by Hal's broad smile and were designed to tease rather than hurt. But they still dug at Caspar, who tried desperately, and as usual failed, to think of some witty retort. He knew Hal was only trying to bait him into taking up the challenge by using one of his old tricks out of their early childhood. Caspar hated being called 'nephew' and when small had always flown into a tantrum when Hal teased him with the title. But he had since learnt that he lost fewer quarrels with the older boy if he bit back his temper and behaved with infuriating dignity. He decided to parry Hal's challenge by changing the subject.

'What do you suppose is in those barrels anyway?' he asked calmly, still looking down at the wagon.

'I for one hope it's ale, or even Caldean wine,' Hal replied, putting on a voice slightly deeper than his natural tones. 'Otherwise we'll all be reduced to that boiled well water.'

Caspar groaned inwardly. He might have guessed that Hal was in one of those moods that had become all too frequent lately. He was forever trying to prove himself as a full-grown man and Caspar wished he would hurry up and grow out of the phase.

'There's nothing wrong with the well water.'

'Dragon's piss!' sneered Hal.

Caspar gave up on his companion. The promise of battle was evidently making Hal more difficult than usual.

The wellhead was housed within the deepest cellar of the central keep, which had been erected over the entrance to the dragons' ancient den. The mouth had been sealed over, except for the seemingly bottomless well, which plummeted into the caverns and labyrinth of tunnels honeycombing the core of Torra Alta. A cable, as thick as Caspar's wrist, was drawn through a system of pulleys by a winch. Attached to the cable was a line of buckets that dragged up water from the underground streams at the very roots of the Tor. The water smelt foul and wisps of yellow vapour floated off the surface of the buckets as they slopped up from the pit below, but the water was boiled in vats and sieved through purifying hunks of carbon to extract the sulphurous poisons.

Suddenly the Baron's clear voice boomed out from the courtyard below: 'Over here!'

Caspar spun round guiltily and dropped down behind the low wall on the inside of the parapet. For a second he thought he had been spotted and that his father must be summoning him to help with more unloading.

'Over here with the flour,' Baron Branwolf called, and Caspar sighed with relief as he realized that his father was gesturing to the mule-driver arriving at the gates. The man towed his melancholy beasts over to the Baron, leaving behind a thin, powdery trail across the cobblestones from one of the flour sacks that had split. The Baron was standing, feet astride with hands on hips, and looked, as always, ready for action. He was a vigorous man of solid build, carrying no spare flesh, and with the same sharply contoured features, raven hair and olive eyes of his younger brother, though Hal was a few inches shorter and had not yet broadened across his chest.

'How many more trips can you make before sundown?' Branwolf asked the mule-driver as he approached.

'Well, my Lord, it'll not be for want of trying, but the beasts are tiring.' The short man wiped his sleeve across his brow. 'Aye, tiring, that they are, but, daylight willing, Sir, I might get another couple more trips out of them, maybe three . . . Aye, three – if the packs are lighter. They don't take well to these heavy loads, Sir, that they don't.'

'Yes, yes.' Branwolf sounded as if he was trying to disguise his impatience but then he softened. 'All right then, let's keep it moving. I'll give you a hand here.' The Baron pushed up his cuffs to expose the tight cords of sinew and tendon, which striped his forearms, and heaved a sack of flour off the leading mule. 'We haven't got time to waste, Driver.'

'No Sir, so I've been told.' The mule-driver leant against the flank of one of the animals to draw his breath for a moment. 'And one of the carters too, Sir, he was telling me a most horrible tale. He'd been up north not ten leagues beyond the head of the canyon to fetch in pine logs, and he swore he'd not go back that way again, not for logs and not for gold neither, he said.' The mule-driver dragged another flour sack off the back of the mule and let it slump to the ground. 'He saw shadows moving in the Boarchase Forest. Aye my Lord, and heard tales of strange beasts roaming thereabouts. Evil beasts.'

'Huh!' Branwolf was dismissive. 'Savages that's all, an outlying group of worthless spies no doubt. We have to expect them. They adorn themselves in animal carcasses.' He grunted under the weight of a flour sack. 'There's no need to fear a small party of heathens – unskilled warriors, no match for any fellow of Belbidia. You don't need to worry about them, Driver. It's Morbak's central force, the main army, we need to be ready for.'

'This army then, as you say, Sir, it's mighty close then?'

'We've got a few weeks yet.' The Baron's voice was reassuring. 'My own spies tell me that Morbak and his main force are still deep in the Dragon Scorch. But we need this fortress fully provisioned and secured against siege by the beginning of the Fogmoon, no later. It will be difficult to get the wagons up the frosty road even during the month of the Wolfmoon . . .' He glanced back at the road.

A guilty feeling spread over Caspar.

'Don't you think we'd better go and help again?' he asked Hal.

'We've been lugging crates and sacks around all day,' grumbled the older youth. 'Five more minutes and then we'll go down again.'

Caspar watched his father pace over towards the Captain of the garrison, who was checking through the cargo of the wagon halted beneath the fang-like prongs of the portcullis. Baron Branwolf immediately climbed up on top of the wagon and started handing down the crates. Caspar reflected that his father hadn't stopped unloading or dragging sacks into the storerooms for the last four days, working alongside and harder than all the soldiers and servants within the walls of Torra Alta.

A shrill cry from below cut through the noise within the castle. Hal was still leaning over the battlements.

'It's that wagon. There on the Slide.' Hal's voice was urgent. He was already leaping down from the wall and tearing across the cobbled courtyard towards the storerooms, Wartooth's long legs racing alongside, when the Baron's voice rang out. 'Rope!'

Hal acknowledged his older brother with a wave of his hand as he disappeared through the nearest door.

'You four –' Branwolf pointed to a group from the garrison '– follow me.' He continued to hurl out orders whilst running towards the gates.

Caspar hesitated for a moment, not knowing whether to run after Hal or go straight to his father. Hal was already sprinting through the gates with a coil of rope over his shoulder, followed by a dozen men from the guardroom and nearly tripping over the excited hound who was weaving about his feet. Caspar dashed after them. By the time he got to the wagon Hal had lashed the rope to its front axle and the Baron was directing men to haul on the wheels, rope and harness to save the floundering vehicle. It teetered on the steep pitch of the track. The wagoner must have attempted to rush the section, relying on momentum to carry him through – but the horses' strength had faded midway and they were now wrestling to stop the weight of the loaded wagon dragging them backwards.

The men jostled each other for space around the wheels and leather strapping of the harness. Caspar found room by a dun mare, on the inside of the ledge, and twisted his forearm through the leathers to get a firm grip. The horse's coat was matted and dark with sweat, her muscles quivering with the strain. Facing the wagon, with one foot braced against the rock-face, the boy leant back and pulled with all his strength. But the wagon was still slipping, hooves grating against the rock in a frenzied battle for grip. A caustic smell of burning arose from the brakes as they smouldered against the iron wheel rims.

'You, soldier,' shouted Branwolf. 'Get out from behind that wheel. If she rolls back, it'll take your foot off.' The man leapt aside and found a new position.

'On the count of three we all pull together,' commanded the Baron. 'Get yourself a firm footing. Ready? One, two-' His words were snatched away by the cracking of the whip as the slightly built wagoner lashed out at the horses.

'Steady there, lad. It's all in the timing,' explained the Baron, raising his voice above the excited barks of the deerhound. 'Wait for the count of three.'

'We're going to roll over that cliff.' The wagoner's voice was thin and barely audible. His eyes gaped down at the distant valley floor, eyelids frozen open. A greyish hue deadened the glow of his smooth cheeks and his lips were dry with fear.

'You haven't made the climb up to Torra Alta before, have you?' asked Branwolf, trying to calm the young man.

The man's lips formed the word 'no' but no sound came out.

'Don't look down; think only about what you've got to do,' urged the Baron. 'Concentrate on the leading pair.'

9

The youth spoke softly. 'My father was ill. I said I'd take the wagon up for him. I didn't realize it would be like this.' But he couldn't drag his eyes away from the precipitous drop and his voice tailed off.

'He's frozen up,' the Baron said flatly.

Using the hub of one of the great wheels as a step, Hal swung up to sit beside the young wagoner.

'It's all right, you know. The height does that to a lot of men.' Hal's generous attitude surprised his young red-haired nephew: the dark youth so rarely missed an opportunity to tease someone. 'Now give me the reins. We've got to get these horses moving.'

Hal was forced to prise the whip and reins out from the man's rigidly closed fists.

'Right, I'm ready,' he announced.

Baron Branwolf tried again: 'One, two, three, *heave!*'

On 'three' Caspar drew in a deep breath and on 'heave' exhaled sharply, releasing a cry as he kicked back against the rock-face. A similar grunt came from all the men around the wagon except for Hal's excited 'Now!'. It made up for his inability to make the whip crack. He had thrust it forward with enough force, the leather whistling as it sliced through the air, but he mistimed the wrist action that should have snapped the leash taut. The anticipated crack became a mere sigh but the horses responded and the wagon surged up a full foot.

'Hold it now, men. We'll take a rest for a second,' ordered the Baron.

The great belly of the dun heaved in and out, like the smith's bellows.

'Heave!' cried the Baron again. But this time the wagon advanced them only a hand's width before it stuck fast.

'And again, men. One, two, three, *heave!*'

Caspar felt the joints in his shoulders and arms stretching and in his fingers his grip was beginning to fade. He fixed his eyes onto his whitening hands and concentrated fiercely on keeping his knuckles tightly closed around the leather harness.

'We're up against a rock,' a soldier called out from beside one of the wheels.

'Relax a moment and let her run back a bit. Let's take another run up,' ordered Branwolf.

The wagon creaked on its axles as the strain was released. Caspar took the opportunity to wipe the sweat from his palms and flex his fingers to regain some of their strength.

On the next count Hal managed to produce an ear-splitting crack from the whip. It lashed across the broad back of the lead horse and a line of red beads sprang up across its quarters. The animal squealed and, when the wagon still remained anchored to the rock, the great cart-horse panicked. Unable to bolt, it thrashed at the ground, sparks flashing from its iron-shod hooves as they struck the rock, and it kicked out backwards desperately trying to break from its burden. The Baron grabbed its bridle, pulling the tossing head down to calm the beast, and suddenly with a jolt they cleared the obstructing rock and gained another foot.

'Not too harshly!' admonished the Baron.

Hal grunted in acknowledgement; his face furrowed with concentration. He gave a quick glance at the ashen face of the young man beside him.

'It's not as easy as it looks – using a whip,' Hal said to him, gesturing with the leather goad. The man didn't seem to hear.

On the third heave the wagon reached smoother road and rushed forward at a pace. Caspar fell backwards and rolled to the side, catching a fleeting glimpse of the wheels as they crashed past his shoulder. By the time he got to his feet the wagon was thundering away, the hocks of the six heavyweight horses thrusting in unison beneath their quarters. The long-legged deer-hound snarled at the wheels of the cart, tripping up soldiers as he darted back and forth in his excitement. Caspar paused to catch his breath and then sprinted after them.

Panting heavily, with his speed now exhausted, Caspar trotted into the courtyard in time to see Hal standing tall on top of the driving seat, pulling back hard on the reins to balance himself. He looked for all the world as if he had just won a chariot race, whooping with delight and punching the air with his free arm. The horses stood four-square with white foaming sweat smearing their shoulders and flanks. Finally, Hal sat down looking pleased. The young man next to him quietly climbed down, looking almost worse than he had on the road. Feeling sorry for the wagoner, Caspar went over to him, trying to think of something appropriate to say, but his father had got there first.

'Don't worry, lad; that's not the first time someone's been stricken by the heights.'

'I'm sorry, my Lord, I feel such a fool,' the wagoner mumbled, unable to look the tall, raven-haired man in the face.

'Forget it. Just go and take care of your horses.' The Baron smiled kindly at him and then turned to his son. 'And, Spar, it's about time you and Hal got back to work. Get him down from there and start unloading the barrels.' Branwolf looked despairingly up at the dreamy expression on Hal's face.

Later that day, when the swollen globe of the sun sank towards the jagged peaks in the west, spilling its blood in a wash of red across the sky, the floor of the canyon was already shrouded in the black pall of night. The citadel of Torra Alta caught the last rays of red-gold and flashed like a bronzed shield as it reflected the evening sun off the whinstone walls.

In the very centre of the courtyard a smooth round slab was embedded in the cobbles, featureless except for a ring of pagan runes engraved around its circumference. The once sharp etching was barely visible, worn by the passage of feet over the centuries. Caspar stood in the middle of the heartstone and raised his weary arms to catch the last drops of the day's warmth.

'Can't you feel the magic, the ancient power of this very spot?' he asked in an awed voice.

'No, I can't. Come on, Spar, we'll be late,' replied Hal.

Caspar didn't move. It seemed to him that the night crawled

up from below, stealthily slinking over the walls like a black panther, stalking low on its belly.

'Don't you see, Hal? Right here on this stone, it's like a gateway between day and night.'

'It's just a heartstone, Spar. Our ancestors worshipped it, but it's a heathen thing. They were primitive,' Hal reasoned sensibly.

'It's not just a stone,' Caspar objected. 'In front of me the sky is red, it's daytime, but behind me,' he turned and pointed to the east, 'everything is black night. Here where I stand it's twilight. The sun catches my head, my face, my arms – they are in the light; but my feet are in the shadow of night. Right here it is dusk.'

'Take my word for it, Nephew, you won't get too many wenches interested in you if you talk like that – Baron's son or not. Sunsets, I ask you!'

Caspar ignored him. It didn't matter that Hal could not sense the magic of the place and time; he could, and it seemed to concentrate his thoughts. As the sun touched down to rest, the sky was a blend of mysterious colours, from black behind him, through to purple and lilac overhead, spreading to pearl and pale salmon pink and finally the rich colours of blood, burnt orange and gold, in the west. In that one moment, when day met night, the world stood still, holding its breath, as if in reverence for the ancient God, mourning the lord of the heavens in his magnificent death throes.

The clear peal of a bell shattered the moment, echoing back from the canyon walls, clamorous and sharp in the chill air of evening. Hal grew restless.

'Stop dreaming. It's Evensong.'

'I know, I know,' replied the younger youth, but his sapphire-blue eyes, still hazy and unfocused, remained staring at the sunset. 'I was just thinking how beautiful it all is. Our lands. Our fortress.'

'Yours maybe, but not mine,' quipped Hal, with what could have been bitterness but sounded more like a matter-of-fact attitude. 'You're the one who gets to inherit it all.'

'No, it's our Torra Alta,' Caspar said firmly. 'It's always been home to you as much as to me.'

'I know. It's just sometimes it feels strange that we've been brought up as brothers. I really do feel I'm your brother, your older brother, but yet you're the one who will become Baron one day.'

Not knowing how to reply to Hal's unusual frankness about his feelings, Caspar dropped his head to avoid his uncle's eyes and traced his foot over the strange indistinct runic lettering.

The bells pealed out again.

'Come on. The Chaplain will be peeved if we're late and we ought to be praying for the safety of our Torra Alta.' Hal emphasized the 'our' and smiled with resignation at his companion.

Father Gwion and his curate, Dunnock, nodded frostily at the two youths as they crept into the back of the Chapel. Their lateness had not gone unremarked. Dunnock had just returned from the northern frontier of the Barony. He was the only preacher who took the good news of the one true God so far north to the simple woodsmen of the Boarchase Forest.

'Dear Lord, protect us from the idol-worshippers, who come to rape our land.' The Chaplain's voice was solemn.

'Almighty Father help drive out the pagan from our Barony,' Dunnock implored passionately.

Caspar bowed his head and prayed fervently.

Chapter 2

'Draw up the portcullis, in the name of the King.' The cry came from beneath a proud plume of feathers, sprouting from a bronze helmet. The messenger sat impatiently on his caparisoned steed, which was blowing heavily, hard pressed from the climb. It tossed its head nervously and the lavish tassels, hanging from its bridle, swung and sprayed out like the full skirts of a spinning dancer.

Caspar wiped the stickiness of sleep from the corner of his eyes and crawled into the narrow slit of his chamber's window to get a clearer look. The portcullis was still down from the night and mist hung listlessly in the valley. The agitated messenger cried up again to the night watchman:

'Raise the portcullis. I must see Baron Branwolf immediately.'

A screech of metal on metal and the rhythmic clanking of a chain moving over the cogs of the winch, and the portcullis snarled open and drew up its teeth. Still buckling his belt, the Baron was striding purposefully across the open courtyard. Caspar, eager not to miss any news, struggled to get his arm through a sleeve and fumbled with the laces on his calf-skin breeches. As he burst through the door, he nearly collided with Hal, who was still wrenching up a knee-length boot with his thumbs, having been too impatient to loosen the laces. Together they raced out into the courtyard, their leather soles slapping the rounded stones. The two youths drew up short, at an almost respectful distance from Branwolf, and listened intently.

The Baron turned to glare at them with his olive-coloured

eyes. That look, Caspar knew, was meant as a warning for them to withdraw to a more respectful distance while his father received important news from the King's messenger, but all the same Caspar's curiosity was too compelling to allow him to obey just a look. Hal, too, stubbornly stood his ground.

'My Lord, I bring greetings from the King's Frontier Patrol,' the messenger formally announced as he dismounted smartly from his sweat-soaked horse. He smoothed straight his yellow, red and black tabard then gave the Baron a perfunctory bow of the head. His manner, though polite, by no means showed the respect owing to a high baron of Belbidia. Hiding behind the royal colours of his livery, the man evidently felt entitled to display the arrogant airs of the King's court.

Branwolf looked back to the messenger. Caspar hid a smile as the King's servant wilted visibly under the Baron's imperious gaze.

Then the messenger looked suddenly more serious. 'Lord Branwolf, Morbak has moved fast and the Vaalakan tribes are massing in the central wastelands of the Dragon Scorch where the rivulets once flowed off the ice-cap and joined to form the one river. We have news of enemy spies probing the line of the Silversalmon River as well as in the western Forests bordering your own lands . . .' He paused to add weight to his words. 'The enemy may be here by the mid-winter festival.'

Branwolf's face was grave. 'Before the end of the Wolf-moon, by God!' He chewed on his lower lip and tilted his head from side to side just fractionally, as if calculating the cargo deliveries that were possible in the time available to him. Not long since, King Rewik took many of the castle's supplies for his wars against the heathen in the holy lands. Even now they were scarcely re-stocked, let alone ready to withstand an invasion.

Less than two months, thought Caspar, then war!

'If you two are going to stand there gawking, you might as well be useful.' Branwolf turned towards the youths again. 'Hal, go and fetch the Captain. Tell him to bring his maps. Spar, get me some parchment and a quill.'

Caspar found his father and the others already seated in the watchtower, around a bare table on which he placed the parchment. The Captain spread the scrolled maps and held them open with two empty ale tankards. His plain studded hauberk was covered by a heavy bear-skin cloak slung across his rangy shoulders to keep out the early morning chill. His coarse eyebrows met over a beaky nose to give a fierce, hungry look as he peered intently at the messenger. Like most men, the King's servant was intimidated.

A soldier brought in a flagon of ale and put it squarely in front of the messenger who drank deeply. Caspar opened a pot of deep red ink and set it within reach of his father alongside two quills, his own rather mis-used ones he hoped would cause no comment . . . nor difficulty in their use.

'How many are there now? Do you yet know the size of Morbak's army?' demanded the Baron.

'There remains some doubt about their number,' replied the messenger, wiping the froth from the stubbly beard that had grown in the harsh weeks in the Dragon Scorch. 'They have divided into two bodies. The number still advancing to the west of the Summer Melts, we estimate between seventy and eighty thousand. The other fork of the army, probably forty to fifty thousand strong. Heading south along the Melts and then veering east towards the head of the Silversalmon and the entrance to the Pass.' As though awed by the seriousness of the information he imparted, the messenger was reduced uncharacteristically to brevity.

In a moment of silence, everyone in the room counted the figures and understood the combined force to be one hundred and twenty thousand.

'God have mercy,' Branwolf muttered.

Rallying, the King's messenger continued: 'They are however a ropy lot. Staves, pikes, pitchforks even. Only a few have axes, though they all carry knives. Thieves' weapons if you ask me – I mean, no self-respecting soldier fights with a knife. Hyenas, I'd call them, scavenging carrion.'

'Messenger, no fool-soldier would attempt to lead an army

like that past Torra Alta,' scoffed the stern-looking Captain.

The messenger showed no emotion at the Captain's scorn. 'My Captain believes that Morbak is sending one fork directly through the heart of the Dragon Scorch to the head of the Pass. They are taking the short route because they are dragging with them huge siege engines.'

'And the larger section?' asked Baron Branwolf as he scratched out a rough map of the area to the north. He wrote some numbers down at the head of the Pass between the Yellow Mountain ranges, with a large arrow next to the figures pointing towards Torra Alta.

'My Captain believes that the large part of the army is taking the longer but easier route along the coast west of the course of the Summer Melts before turning east back towards the Boarchase, skirting the northern foothills of the Yellow Mountains before rejoining with the other half of the army and the siege equipment.' Again the messenger's composure broke and he became impassioned. 'It's a terrible sight, my Lord Baron! That creature Morbak on his devilish troll, slaying his own men to drive the army on. Slaying their women and children, if they slow them up. By God, even their own helpless children. Hell's too good a place for these barbarians. God help us, Morbak's like the Devil himself.'

'Be sensible man. He's not the Devil.' Branwolf was irritated by this emotional account.

'No, my Lord, you haven't seen them.' The messenger was serious. 'These people are a starving, wretched, half-clad people, but to eat the bodies of their own dead. It is the work of the Devil. At least now King Rewik has driven the last of the heathen from our own lands.'

Caspar felt faintly sick. His father's face was red with anger and he took a few deep breaths to compose himself.

'No man in Belbidia has ever worshipped Vaal-Peor. You can not compare these barbarians to the ancient pagans of Belbidia. Now let's look at this.' He picked up one of the Captain's maps and tapped it determinedly, then traced the line of the Summer Melts. The Baron had command of his voice and his words were steady. 'So your superiors believe that this western fork of the Vaalakan army will turn east here towards the Pass when they draw level with the Boarchase?'

'That's our best guess, Lord Branwolf. His main army will march parallel to the northern foothills of the Yellow Mountains,' replied the messenger, running his finger along the map from the Summer Melts at the coast until he reached the head of the Pass. He jabbed at it to indicate the spot. 'Unless of course he intends to take to the sea but we don't believe that, otherwise why would he be sending the other fork with the siege engines?'

'Sir, it doesn't make sense,' the Captain butted in emphatically. 'These siege engines: Morbak must know that a siege engine is worthless against Torra Alta. It would be impossible to drag them up the Tor. He couldn't get them anywhere near the walls to even start to try and breach them. So why waste these men on dragging useless equipment through the wastelands? If he's prepared to waste the men why not keep his army together and drive them all directly at Torra Alta and attack before we are ready? He is stronger with his army all together. Morbak's chief weapon is the sheer size of his army. Splitting it up doesn't make sense, Sir.'

The Baron nodded at him pensively. 'Go on.'

'So what good is this forty thousand coming directly towards the head of the Pass going to do Morbak? Even that number, Sir, we'd hold them off indefinitely because, by the sounds of it, these mangy weasels are so ill-equipped. No siege engine can get near to breach the walls and battlements of the fortress; nothing like that could be dragged up the Tor. Their only chance would be to sneak past – and then we'd pick off every one of them from this height. Only got to spit at them, by the sound of it.'

'They know that,' agreed Branwolf. 'He's smart though; this cur Morbak. He's sending enough men to keep us here though, isn't he?' The Baron slammed his fist down on the oak table spilling ale from the tankards. 'That's it. He's planning to pin us here so he only has to worry about the King. He's going to damn well pin us here with one fork and then storm through towards the King in the west. The siege engines are merely a decoy to make us think he is preparing the way for the rest of the army.'

'West, Sir!' The Captain sounded astonished.

Wide-eyed with excitement, Caspar was too caught up in the thrill of being with the men in the thick of planning for battle, too intent on the glory and the strategy to contemplate the vulnerability of his country or the seriousness of their situation. He had no doubt that somehow today, in this room, they would form a plan that would overthrow Morbak. Caspar chanced a look at Hal whose elbows were thrust attentively forward on the oak table, rolling the empty tankard back and forth between his palms. He's trying to look like he's got all the answers, thought Caspar, and returned his attention to his father.

'Yes, west,' continued the Baron.

'No, we don't think so.' The messenger shook his head. 'He has no ships. The Vaalakan coast has been frozen for many years now and he's not equipped to strike across the sea.'

'I didn't say that,' the Baron corrected the King's messenger. 'It's impossible for him to cross the sea. He's sending forty thousand men to pin me here in Torra Alta to defend the Pass and he's sending the siege engines just to make us *think* that the rest of the army will be turning east towards the Pass. Morbak thinks King Rewik will send his reinforcements to me while all along he's planning to drive his men through here.' Branwolf pointed angrily at the map, his finger scoring the very western edge of the Yellow Mountains. 'He's going to invade *here* while we are impotently pinned *here* in Torra Alta. Impotent. Damn well impotent, that's what we are.'

'Never, Sir. Not my men, Sir,' objected the Captain. 'Nor any Belbidian. But it'll take Morbak, um . . . well at least the reckoning of two new moons to reach the coast, and they'll be hungry, barren weeks. If you're right they'll not be strong enough to make it through the mountains.' The beaky-nosed soldier picked up the Baron's quill and sketched the map onto the sheet of parchment.

'The shoreline itself is impassable. The mountains drop in sheer cliffs to a deep raging sea without beaches. And though the mountains there are slightly lower they are densely forested. They could never get through. They will be forced slightly east up the mountains. There's only one pass through there, and at this time of year it'll already be under several feet of snow, Sir.'

'The Jaws of the Wolf,' said Branwolf, giving the Pass its name. 'It's a treacherous route, could take thousands, maybe tens of thousands, of their lives. Let's hope so.'

'Maybe you are right, my Lord, but I think that when he sees that terrible pass he'll turn east and join up with the other half that's aiming to lay siege to Torra Alta. That's it, no doubt about it, Sir. I don't think we should be underestimating this Morbak, not underestimating the Devil at all. He can still head east. He might want us to guess that he's heading for the Jaws of the Wolf when all along he will be heading for Torra Alta. Any way you look at it, it might all be an elaborate trick to prevent us from being fully prepared for him. He sends the engines, knowing that we'll know it's a trick and hoping then that we'll think he's going for the Jaws of the Wolf. So King Rewik prepares for him there and then suddenly he turns east and makes a full attack one hundred and twenty thousand strong on our garrison of one thousand before pouring into Belbidia, Sir.'

'Tricks? Decoys?' The raven-haired nobleman was either asking a question or expressing his disbelief at the idea – Caspar was not sure which. 'But maybe he just doesn't know how difficult the Jaws of the Wolf will be. Perhaps he thinks he'll suffer fewer losses battling with the elements there, rather than facing the wrath of Torra Alta?' He grinned arrogantly in a way that for a moment reminded Caspar of Hal, but then the edges of the Baron's mouth flattened into the heavy lines of grave responsibility.

'I wouldn't like to bet on it, Sir.' The beaky-nosed Captain frowned thoughtfully. 'He's trying to out-smart us, I reckon. He's gambling we'll go west to stop him at the Jaw of the Wolf, hoping maybe that we'll even weaken Torra Alta to reinforce the King's army, who'll be desperate for our help, Sir,' reasoned the Captain. 'So that it's easier for him to pour through the Pass here.'

'One hundred and twenty thousand men against our one thousand,' echoed the Baron. 'Hungry people. I'm sure Morbak would be very pleased to feed their bellies on food from the farmsteads and ranches of the Belbidian plains before facing the King's army, aren't you, men? But we're not dancing like puppets to his tune. We're not budging from Torra Alta. Never. If the fortress falls, we fall with it.'

Caspar felt rather bewildered by his father's speed of thought. He listened to the imposing man guessing and reguessing what the enemy might do, and planning counter strategies. How did the Baron know what to do after centuries of peace? Caspar only knew his father as a huntsman who loved the chase. Stags, wild boar and the occasional mountain lion were his sport, and the thrill of his hunting parties had enticed many noblemen to be his guests at Torra Alta. Within the castle walls the chase continued, only here the sport was of a more lascivious nature. Caspar did not even remember his mother, the Lady Keridwen. He had been told very little about her death, except that it was soon after he was born . . . and for a reason unknown, or one that no one would talk about. She had ridden alone into the mountains. The spring snows were very unstable that year: it was believed that she was claimed by an avalanche. All Caspar could remember was an ever changing stream of female faces smiling next to his father's.

His father's face – suddenly it was so imposing. The Captain had always seen to the garrison and now, within a month of reports of the Vaalakan invasion reaching him, the Baron was behaving as if he had been a general all his life. Caspar felt proud.

Shortly, the parchment was covered with numbers, lines,

arrows and cryptic inscriptions. Baron Branwolf gave it a last inspection before rolling it up and tossing it with great accuracy into the unlit hearth.

'This isn't going to help us. We have no option but to stand fast.' He turned to the messenger. 'Take a new horse and ride to the King. Tell him that he can depend on us to hold Torra Alta and secure the Pass.'

The group of men rose up from the table and the Captain led the messenger away in search of a fresh mount.

'Now, boys, don't just stand there,' said Branwolf.

Hal indignantly puffed out his chest, balking at the term boy.

'You two had better get down to the well. You'll be of more use there than anywhere else and the Wellmaster will keep you out of trouble. Catrik won't stand for any of your nonsense.'

'But that's not fair. We can't see –' Caspar began.

'Spar! Don't cross me at a time like this. The more water we draw now, the more hands will be free later. Besides, I want the sulphur.' The Baron swung the oak door open and the chill breeze of morning swept in from the airy courtyard. The Chaplain, a gleaming silhouette in his black satin cowl of office, stood just outside the door. He raised his hand, with its glittering rings, and revealed the more practical homespun jerkin he wore beneath, which was necessary for survival in the rarefied air of Torra Alta. He greeted his kinsmen with ice-blue eyes and a smile that could have belonged to a fleeting ghost.

'My Brother, there is news this morning?' he anxiously addressed the Baron. It sounded to Caspar as though the Chaplain over-played the anxiety in his voice.

'Indeed, indeed, Gwion, I will discuss it with you shortly, but first I must scribe a note to King Rewik ready for his messenger to take.'

Caspar looked up reluctantly at the shaved head of his uncle, trying to hide his scowl but curious to see the priest's face. He didn't like to look the Chaplain in the eyes. From his earliest days those eyes had glared down from the pulpit transmitting the fear of God straight at Caspar. He was surprised to find the mirror of his own scowl on the holy man's pale face.

Though Gwion called the Baron brother he was in fact the brother of the Baron's long-departed wife. As a young child, Caspar had often cocked his head on one side and squinted at his wiry uncle as he tried to imagine what the man's sister would have looked like. He never worked it out. The man was slightly built but with hard sinewy muscles and austere lines to the face, which the boy had imagined had been achieved through hours of soul-searching prayer. His mother could never have looked like that, but of course she was a woman and Gwion was a man. The Chaplain's lack of hair also gave the imaginative youth very little to conjure with: his polished white head was partially shaved sprouting only a wispy tonsure of dull brown hairs that stroked the man's ears and neck. He couldn't believe his mother's eyes had been like the priest's, either. Sometimes he thought he remembered them, but maybe that was only his imagination when he looked into the mirror and saw the startling deep violet of his own eyes. Hal of course had always teased him about his colouring. It was unusual in Belbidia and Hal had said he had the eyes of an elf.

'Gwion, would you be so good as to use your influence over these wayward boys, and make sure they report to Catrik in the wellroom? I don't want to hear that they've been skulking off.' There was that conspiratorial note that the adults used to keep the youths in their place which Caspar deeply resented. He glanced at Hal whose skin had flushed a deep crimson with his ready anger at being referred to as boys. 'Oh, and, Hal, see you both take the charcoal down with you. I promised Catrik extra help and you two will be as good as any.' Branwolf gave them a satisfied smile and left the watchtower.

The two youths trailed out after the Chaplain, Hal grumbling quietly under his breath. Caspar stopped at the open door to the watchroom and turned back to see the discarded parchment lying curled up in the fireplace. He darted back for the souvenir and within seconds he was again in step with his disgruntled uncle, the parchment stuffed into his leather pouch that was strapped beneath his linen shirt.

Father Gwion delivered them to the stores just inside the portcullis where the charcoal was heaped to the ceilings in large grimy sacks. In haste he pronounced a sharp word of warning that he and God had their eyes on them. 'The Vaalakans are moving on us and this is not a game. You must study your consciences and take your responsibilities a little less lightly.' He sighed, looking heavenward and moving his lips as if in prayer. 'Branwolf tells me the enemy is in the Dragon Scorch and don't forget it! You must behave accordingly.'

Then he was gone, mercifully. Caspar turned to look at the mountain of sacks, instantly dismissing the thought of his Uncle Gwion from his mind. The man was always lecturing them and he presumed it was because, in gratitude to Branwolf, he was trying to see their souls were guided along the right path. But for once his words rolled ominously through Caspar's mind. He pictured the vast and relentless body of soldiers marching through the northern wastes to hammer on the gates of the castle.

He hefted one of the sacks. 'At least they're light,' he said, not wanting to talk about the enemy. He didn't want to admit to himself, let alone Hal, that, now the novelty of being privy to the warriors' war strategies had worn off, he was frightened by the sudden discovery that the enemy was on the move – and the numbers were so vast. And he did not want to think about his uncle, who had not been present when the messenger disclosed this latest news of the Vaalakans – but had been, evidently, outside, listening, his shining black back curved as he stooped to lean his ear to the door of the watchtower.

'Don't we even get to have breakfast first?' complained Hal. 'I'm hungry and it's disgusting down in the wellroom. The smell!'

'Oh stop complaining. It doesn't make it any better.'

'Don't be such an *adult*, Spar. It doesn't suit you,' retorted the older youth.

Caspar changed the subject, as he gripped the neck of two sacks, one in either hand, and bumped them over the cobbles.

'What does he want sulphur for?'

'Don't you know anything?' Hal seemed to brighten up at the prospect of showing off his superior knowledge. 'It's to make explosives with. Catrik explained it to me.'

'I thought you didn't like going down there,' interrupted Caspar.

'I don't, but a man needs to know how these things work, so I went to find out.'

'Saltpetre,' said Catrik, when they reached the wellroom. Caspar nodded as he examined the broken crystalline weave and the glassy shine of the white rocks that Catrik pointed at.

'We crush them up into a powder – they're very brittle. Then the sulphur. We get that from the water. The water is boiled off, leaving the sulphur behind as a residue in the cauldron. The water vapour is cooled and collected into these funnels,' he explained, tapping a vertical cylinder. 'Where it is poured through a mesh of crushed charcoal. The charcoal extracts the remaining toxins from the well water. And it is also the last ingredient in our explosive. Simple but effective.'

'How powerful is it?' asked Caspar, intrigued.

'Very. It's dangerous stuff and could blow a hole through these walls, if we used the right amount.' Catrik slapped the stones. 'But we won't have any at this rate, if you two don't get a move on. Fetch the rest of the charcoal down and then I'll show you what to do.'

It was a long way down to the wellroom. The old spiral stairway curled round and round and the steps steadily became more slippery with condensation, imbued with the stale smell of mildew. The wellroom itself was uncomfortably humid and smelt strongly of sulphur. Saturated solutions of mineral salts dripped persistently from pale yellow stalactites clinging to the ceiling and formed slimy yellow puddles on the floor; crusty stains patterned the walls; indeed everything was tainted with sulphur. The sweaty temperature was maintained by a roaring furnace that heated the vats.

It's a picture of Hell, thought Caspar, hell-fire and brimstone. A dungeon of flames; churning, groaning engines; the cauldron spitting lumps of undigested sulphur and hissing steam; a mechanical dragon, he mused.

'Now, hang your cloaks behind the door so that you can get to work. Here, take one of these each,' said Catrik, handing them a palette knife, 'and start scraping the sulphur out of the used cauldrons. Scrape it into this barrel here, and when you've done one, start on the next one.'

A cord of massively thick, twisted metal, strong enough to moor a warship, rose out of the well and looped over a giant wheel. Attached to this cable a continual line of buckets, brimming with the discoloured well water, slopped into the wellroom. The wheel was rotated by a treadmill, which was worked by teams of mournful-looking donkeys, who trudged on and on, resigned to walking away a lifetime and never going anywhere, adding the smells of animal and dung to the ripe atmosphere. Caspar felt sorry for them.

He surveyed the room, tracing the water's journey as it was tipped from the buckets, by a strategically placed beam, into a cauldron suspended over the fire. From there it was a complex work of engineering, funnelling off the vapour, and the boy wondered which one of his ancestors had designed it. He examined the neck of one of the vats where it was plugged by layers of coarse meshing stuffed with carbon, watching with fascination as the water percolated through it. A tap at the bottom released the water, ready to drink and tasting almost as if it had rushed clear and sparkling straight off the mountain side: Caspar thought so anyway, even if Hal did not.

By manoeuvring a winch and tackle over the cauldron, Catrik was able to swing the excessive weight of the giant cast-iron pot into the midst of the flames where he left it to boil. He had exchanged it for one that had simmered dry, the last remaining drops of water sizzling on the scorching metal, and now he swivelled the arm of the lifting tackle away, to allow the sulphur-coated cauldron to cool. Beyond the furnace, behind the donkeys' imprisoning treadmill, a row of these cauldrons, encrusted inside with the yellow flowers of sulphur, waited to be cleaned. The two youths attacked the first one vigorously, rasping away with their knives.

'It looks like pollen,' remarked Caspar.

'I don't think it would make very good honey, but perhaps,' chuckled Hal, 'it'll give those savages a bee-sting they won't forget.'

The air smelt stale and an occasional whiff of putrid gases seeped up from the wellhead.

'Ugh, that's revolting,' exclaimed Hal.

'Don't stand too close to the well when it does that. It's not good for you,' Catrik called over to them. 'A backdraught sometimes draws up those noxious fumes but it'll clear in a minute.'

'Eggs, rotten eggs, that's what it smells like to me,' Caspar stated disgustedly, burying his nose in his sleeve to try and block out the stench.

The following hours taught Caspar more about honest hard labour, than all the previous week's work unloading provisions. The shirt on his back clung to the skin between his shoulder blades. When he gingerly pulled himself upright after spending an hour with his head plunged into a cavernous cauldron, the sweat trickled off his forehead and stung his eyes. He abandoned the scraped out cauldron to wait its turn again in the endless rotation and wearily leant into the next one.

When Catrik called, 'Bring over those sulphur barrels,' Caspar stood up readily. For a moment his head spun and he had to clutch at the cauldron until the dizziness faded.

'The Baron's orders are that we make up as much explosive powder as possible. He wants a score of caskets,' explained Catrik as he finished breaking the lumps of saltpetre into powder with a rolling stone.

'What does he want them now for? I thought it was dangerous to store it premixed,' said Hal knowledgeably.

'Questions, questions. No respect – the youth of today. You don't ask what the Baron wants things for, you just jump to it, my boy.' The deep furrows on Catrik's face softened and he seemed to change his mind. 'Ah, but you've been working hard so I'll tell you. He wants them for mines – mines to encircle the Tor. If the enemy advances on us an archer will shoot a lighted arrow into the casket and – *boom* . . .' The old man threw up his arms. 'And that will fix a few hundred of the accursed dogs.'

The Wellmaster allowed Caspar and Hal to measure out appropriate quantities of the powders, following his strict instructions. But they were only permitted to watch as the old man poured the concoction carefully into diminutive barrels and knocked the lids on firmly.

'Stack these up neatly over by the stairway,' directed the Wellmaster.

Caspar was greatly relieved to be given a different task. He looked over towards Hal and thought that his uncle seemed surprisingly content. Perhaps the responsibility of handling the explosives appealed to his military aspirations.

'Shhh! Stand still,' ordered Hal suddenly.

'What?'

'Shhh. Listen.'

'I can't hear anything.'

'It's gone now,' said Hal. 'No. There, listen. It's a sort of tapping sound.'

Caspar stood quietly, straining to hear anything above the clunking of the treadmill and the hissing and groaning of the furnace. Finally he heard something.

'Is it rats?' He considered the tapping sound that came faintly up from the well. 'Could be the buckets catching down at the bottom or maybe one's come adrift.'

They could still hear a distant knocking sound that had an intermittent metallic beat.

'A pound to a pinch of snuff, it's not my buckets. I only checked them over yesterday.' Catrik looked concerned and pulled at his grey beard. 'Besides, loose buckets make a hell of a din. And it's not rats either: it's not a scratchy enough noise for them.' He continued to hang over the wellkerb, staring into the pitch black, his head tilted to one side listening intently. Without moving from his crouched position he ordered: 'Hal, stop those wretched donkeys. Spar, go and find the Baron.'

The well was black. It stared back up at them like the pupil of a giant eye, hiding its secrets in the utter darkness. The cable was visible for just a few feet before it dissolved into the gloom. An involuntary shiver ran through Caspar's spine: there was nothing quite so unnerving as looking at nothing and listening to silence.

Another gust of air swept up from the well, forcing the men gathered around it, including the Baron, the Chaplain and the Captain, to recoil reflexively from the fumes.

'We used to call that the dragon's belch,' the Wellmaster said.

Then the disturbing noises came again. A rhythmical chime reverberated through the tunnels before fading away like the dying tones of a gong, as the peal was absorbed by the rock and silence returned.

'It's not possible,' exclaimed Catrik, 'but it sounds like mining.' The old man's face dropped into long, pendulous jowls as he looked towards his liege.

'It can't be. It must be your old buckets, Catrik. One of them's cut loose and is swirling in the pools down there and crashing against the rocks,' the Chaplain objected. 'No spies could get down there.'

'I agree with Father Gwion, Sir,' the Captain added.

'Ah,' said the Wellmaster, apparently insensitive to the import of what he said and intrigued by the scientific questions posed by the situation. 'They may have been alerted to the whereabouts of our caves by those heavy rains earlier this moon. Many of the underground streams are in spate. Any damage to a channel roof might leave tell-tale signs of subsidence, showing the Vaalakans where there might be potholes or caves.'

'But even if they do break through, Sir, they could only get one man up at a time, Sir,' observed the Captain.

'Even if Catrik is right and there are men down there,' the robed priest added sceptically, 'they will starve to death in the labyrinths, God rest their souls.'

'A good point,' conceded Baron Branwolf. 'The number they could force through those narrow channels could never be a military threat – they'd be like snakes trapped in a pit. But I don't think they need numbers for what they intend to do: I think they're here to spit venom into our water.'

Poison the well, thought Caspar horrified, but then brightened as he looked at the equipment around him.

'Surely our purification could-' he began but the Wellmaster curtailed him.

'I'm afraid not. This is designed for very specific impurities. Some poisons would evaporate and condense with the water and so still remain in it.'

For the first time, a tiny spark of insecurity began to flicker within the boy, but this was rapidly extinguished by the Baron's authoritative commands.

'Catrik, bring ten barrels of explosive over here. Captain, fetch two of your men. Whatever is causing the noise will have to be investigated and you can lead our party down.'

Gwion was stripping off his silk robes revealing his practical clothes underneath. Without the swirling robes, which normally surrounded him, he looked much younger and more athletic.

'My Brother Branwolf. I will lead the party. The Captain has very much more pressing tasks, organizing the castle defences. After all it's probably only a matter of a few buckets.'

Branwolf smiled gratefully and placed a hand on the man's shoulder. 'Thank you. Yes, I think you are right; after all it's only a matter of investigation at this stage and you do know the labyrinths better than any other. I need the Captain to help me with the old ballistas on the west wall.'

Within a few minutes, the men had strapped a casket of explosive powder to either hip. Hal twisted his belt round so that his dagger made more room for the barrels and then tested the leashes, to make sure his cargo was secured firmly. Caspar watched and waited patiently for his turn to have the powder barrels harnessed to him as well.

'No, Spar.' His father's voice was kindly but firm. 'It's too dangerous. You're not old enough for this yet.'

Caspar felt the corners of his mouth drop. Why should Hal go and he be left behind? He raised his hand to hide the disappointment written across his face and from behind the cover of his tousled fringe glared resentfully at his young uncle. Hal was composed and grim-faced, ready for action. How was he managing to conceal his excitement at going down the well and being treated as a warrior, wondered the disgruntled boy.

Branwolf spoke. 'Trace the noise. If it's not the buckets, assume it's enemy spies. I want you to find which tunnel they are trying to break into. Then get the men well back and leave the rest to Catrik.' The Baron turned to address the grey-haired Wellmaster. 'With the powder, blow the rocks so that you completely seal off the tunnel and then lay some mines. Make sure that only you organize all the explosives.' Branwolf paused for a second to see if his men were prepared. 'If Catrik is right, we need to move fast before any barbarians manage to break through into the network.'

'We need torches, of course, to see by, since the well is not blessed by God's light,' the Chaplain said.

'No, take the stones.'

'The stones, Brother Branwolf? Are you sure. Nobody has touched them for a decade.'

Over in the far corner of the wellroom squatted a low oak chest, black with age and coated with the ubiquitous yellow crystal like spawning fungi. The chest was lined with lead and filled with a clear viscous oil. His father had explained that the liquid stabilized the stones and kept them cool.

Caspar had been shown the stones many years before and he had been sure that he had sensed their pulsating energy. But Hal had insisted that he was imagining things as usual.

'Where do they come from?' Caspar had asked, longing to hold one. But his father had angrily told him never to touch them, saying only, 'They've always been here, but since the coming of the true religion, they have been kept away from places where people might meddle with them.'

'I've kept them for emergencies like this,' said Branwolf now. 'Their light is better when working down in the well and doesn't burn out like the flames from the torches.'

Caspar thought he could feel again that strange excitement associated with the stones: a mixture of fear and power he couldn't quite explain. The Baron rolled up his cuffs and plunged his arm into the liquid to draw out a smooth white stone the size of a goose egg. At first it was opaque, like hard, cold marble but, gradually, its surface took on a translucence, seeming to melt as the swirling silvery patterns moved over it like floating clouds, though it still remained perfectly solid and spherical. The pearly stone gradually began to glow, emitting a soft, pale light, which had given it the name of moonstone.

Branwolf slipped the first of the moonstones into a net pouch made of a lattice work of leather strands which the Captain took from a hook on the wall and held ready.

'Here you are, Catrik, tie this to your belt.'

The man looked at the Chaplain.

'I'm not sure that I like this,' he said nervously. 'They're ancient things, said to be filled with magic and I'm a God-fearing man, my Lord. I'd prefer to take a torch. To carry a heathen thing like that doesn't seem safe.'

'Let me feel them,' the Chaplain demanded. With intense concentration he cupped a stone in his hand and peered into its depths. 'If it has the spirit of the heathen and the work of the Devil in it I will know.' A pulse beat visibly in his throat and his pupils blackened with fierce emotion as he sought to disclose any remnants of paganism in the heart of the castle. 'There is nothing sinister about these stones,' he declared calmly after a long moment of silence. Caspar thought he sensed a touch of regret and suspected that the man would

33

have secretly liked to have unearthed a relic of the Old Faith so that he could have the glory of exposing and destroying it. The Chaplain had preached that destroying the heathen brought one's soul closer to God and he had always been very vehement about such matters. 'Catrik, you are a man of science, you must know an explanation for their glow.'

The old retainer didn't answer but looked disgustedly at the spherical white stone that the Baron handed to him.

'There is merely a luminous gas inside them,' said the Baron, holding out the leather net. 'You're not going superstitious on me, are you – a man of your learning?'

The Wellmaster took it tentatively and retreated back, muttering just out of Branwolf's earshot: 'I don't know of any such gas. It's not in any of the tables or lists of properties. We shouldn't be touching these pagan things. Who knows what devils it might bring, like it did to that poor sweet Lady? She was fond of these stones, Lord bless her soul.'

Caspar was electrified by the old man's unguarded mumblings. The moonstones and the lady had something to do with him! But the feeling quickly passed. The ghostly light of the moonstones must be bewitching my thoughts, he decided, as he watched his father net the remaining four moonstones. He was mesmerized by their light.

'You need a flint-box to light the powder,' the Baron remarked.

'Yes, Sir, I have one,' Catrik replied smartly, then made one more attempt to rid himself of the moonstone. 'Sir, but we don't know enough about how these stones work. Surely it would be safer to use torches.'

The Baron replied with astonishing patience and complete finality. 'No, those oil-sodden torches spit and drip, and with them so close to the powder, it would be far too dangerous. Good luck, men. God be with you.'

The Chaplain adjusted the strapping that embraced the barrels and then tapped the lids, as if to reassure himself that they were secure, before swinging his leg over the wall that surrounded the wellhead. The cold light of the moonstones, steady and unflickering, fell on the inside of the well walls and lit the way down.

'Men, let's go!' he said cheerfully, in a voice that was too ready for action for a man of the Church and a thought flickered into Caspar's mind that his uncle's enthusiasm for activity was why the man had been overlooked for promotion within the Church. He remembered many years ago when the Baron, his two uncles and himself had made a state visit to the capital, Farona, and how Branwolf had begged King Rewik to look on his brother-in-law with favour, asking for the Chaplain's promotion to a bishopric. But the King's archbishop had taken one look at the man and had refused him. Puzzled by this the young heir to Torra Alta had decided that the priests from the soft heartland of Belbidia cast aspersions on the necessary rough life and less sophisticated way of the men from the northern barony. His Uncle Gwion, who possibly lacked the grace and dignity of Farona's priests, had been denied promotion, since the Church preferred the more staid, sombre and inactive personalities. But a soft-spoken man with no understanding of the harsh life of the mountains would never understand the spiritual needs of the tough men of Torra Alta's garrison and Caspar dreaded the thought of a lowlander eventually becoming bishop of the new cathedral that his father was building.

One by one the men disappeared down into the bottomless pit and Caspar looked on with disappointment. The well was the only part of his father's lands that he had never seen and he desperately wanted to know what it was like down there in the dragons' lair.

'Spar, you stay here and scrape out some more sulphur. We'll need even more of it now.' The Baron swivelled on the heel of his boot and left to see to the ballistas.

Caspar paced in frustration round the well, running his hand along the brim of the wellkerb until his palm was hot with the friction. The same sharp, angular lettering was engraved around the top of the circular wall as adorned the slab in the centre of the courtyard. This time he didn't give the runes a second thought.

A faint halo of the pearly light glowed around the head of the grey-haired Wellmaster far below, before he too faded away into the dark.

'Damn it!' Caspar grabbed his own cloak, swung himself over the wellkerb and stretched for the first fret of the ladder. 'I won't be left behind.'

The very top section of the well was a narrow chimney lined with brick, just as Caspar had expected. The plummeting well, however, had never been bored through solid rock. When the first men of Torra Alta had ousted the dragons from their nest, they had discovered a gaping entrance that led down through the rock to the monsters' den deep in the bowels of the earth. Caspar's forefathers had floored over the yawning hole, leaving only an opening for the cylindrical mouth of the wellhead. Great joists, overlain with trunk-like beams and buttressed by archways of stones, suspended the wellroom floor and domed over the upper chamber of the dragons' lair. The ladder, cable and line of buckets dropped through the centre of it.

Caspar lowered himself down a dozen or so rungs. The orange light of the furnace above no longer fell on the walls of the well and he could hardly see an arm's length from his nose. He knew that he must be in the cavern but it was too dark for him to ascertain the extent of the space around him. He continued to lower himself down towards the light of the moonstones shining below. It was a peculiar feeling knowing that he was suspended in mid air a hundred feet above the cavern floor, but Caspar wasn't the least concerned about falling. His arms soon ached hideously. He reflected that it was much easier to climb a ladder than descend one, because his toes constantly had to search for the next secure foothold. He stopped to look down but still could not make anything out except for a soft globe of light encircling the others some distance below. In a momentary lapse of concentration his foot slipped and, for a heart-stopping second, Caspar found himself dangling by one arm.

When he felt a shiver run through the ladder, he knew the others were getting off at the bottom. And once the stabilizing weight of the party below was gone, the ladder moved in a gentle bounce, keeping rhythm with his step. Shortly, his own foot reached solid rock and the ladder ended in bulky reinforced bracketing, which bolted it into the ground.

During his schooling, the boy had spent many hours browsing through the castle's library, and had found dusty old tomes that catalogued the plans of the well and its construction. He knew that the well was drilled through the rock until it broke into another chamber, falling freely again until it met the floor. This pattern of bore-hole followed by cavern continued down through three more levels until finally, the well found its source. At the point where the boy stood, the ladder was no longer necessary because it was possible to thread a route down through the tunnels, which interconnected the various chambers, until it too led out by the underground streams.

The buckets were quite clearly all properly intact as Catrik had asserted and the metallic chime still vibrated through the hollow rocks. Caspar's heart thumped excitedly against his chest. The others had moved away from the well, tracing the source of the unnatural noise – the sound of enemy activity.

The muffled echo of the padding footsteps spoke back in hollow whispers from the cavern walls and Caspar followed, treading soundlessly, hidden by the endless night of the caves. It was a heavy blackness that shrouded this sunless world and kept its secrets from the small eyes of surface dwellers. He kept his own eyes focused on the light of the moonstones, hoping that he would not run into an unseen rock and kept his arms outstretched in front of him as feelers to warn him of anything unexpected. The halo of light finally touched rock; bouncing off crevassed, gnarled shapes, dipping into niches and reflecting back from the icicle-smooth stalactites. A tunnel, Caspar deduced.

The uneven floor made progress difficult so the boy hurried

forward to steal a little of the stones' light, risking getting closer to the Chaplain and his party. The tunnel led steeply down and was littered with loose flints that had tumbled from the walls and ceiling. The sides were irregular, receding away where a seam of soft rock had been gnawed at by the seeping water, or in places jutting out into the pathway, where a knot of hard rock defied the hunger of the water. The formation of alternate bands of hard and soft rock repeated itself and Caspar got the irksome impression that the protruding ridges of rock were like the ribs of a flesh-picked carcass; and that he was walking within it.

After a while, the passageway narrowed and the floor and sides felt polished smooth and perfectly flat to Caspar's touch as he ran his fingertips along the walls. He was curious as to what had made the sudden change in the rock structure. When the waisted section widened out again he realized that it must have been scoured smooth by the dragons. The passage of generations of the fat scaly lizards, squeezing their way through the constricted tunnel, dragging their grey bellies over the ground had eroded the harder rock into a shiny gloss. He shivered as it dawned on him how big the monsters must have been: he was unable to touch both sides of the tunnel at once with arms fully outstretched. When his ancestors first captured the Tor, it must have been a brave man that led the way to oust the dragon's brood from these black, crypt-like caves.

The tunnel continued to fall away steeply, curling constantly downwards. Slippery, pebble-smooth rocks were followed by sharp foot-snatching scree, all of it percolated through by seeping water, trickling down the sides, dripping from the roof. Occasionally the pearl-white light of the moon-stones illuminated a grotto, each one different from the last, crowded with stalagmites and stalactites and as old as time. Caspar didn't know what the stalagmites were called, but their strange shapes fascinated him. The conical statues varied in height, one tall and king-like in the centre and the others, courtiers perhaps, encircling their liege – and on the outside of the group they were kneeling, Caspar fancied. All of them were arrayed in splendid colours of scarlet and emerald robes; salts of iron and copper. He was spellbound by their unearthly beauty.

Still trailing behind the others, Caspar trod carefully, endeavouring to keep outside the pool of light, making it too easy to trip or stumble on unseen rocks. After the heat of the well room, the caves had a pleasant coolness and the temperature stayed constant as they kept winding down into the bowels of Torra Alta. He had expected it to get colder the further they descended, but it did not. He could still see nothing around his feet and continued to rely on the touch of his fingertips. At last an unexpected rock, projecting into the pathway, caught his foot, throwing him off balance and, unable to catch himself because of the slippery surface, he fell heavily to the ground with a thud, letting out a short sharp cry.

'What was that?' Caspar heard one of the men exclaim and his heart sank.

'Go and take a look, soldier.' The Chaplain's sharp voice echoed back up the tunnel. It wasn't long before the moonstone's light swept across Caspar's guilty face.

'Oh, it's you, Spar.' The soldier sounded relieved.

'What is it, soldier?' shouted the priest.

'It's Master Spar, Father. He's followed us down here.'

'Bring him here! On the double!' Father Gwion was mightily indignant. For a moment Caspar felt like bolting back up to the well room. But now he had been caught and would have to face the holy man. It was too late now to retreat.

'Caspar,' groaned the Chaplain. He always called the youth by his full name as if it were unseemly to use his nickname. 'I can't believe you could disobey the Baron at a time like this. Hear that.' Gwion paused to listen to the rhythmical metallic beat whose chilling peal echoed through the tunnels. 'That is the sound of the enemy. I am disappointed in you, Caspar. God will frown on you and Branwolf will be bitterly disappointed that you have broken his trust.'

Caspar had expected anger but the thought of his father's disappointment was much harder to bear. Perhaps satisfying his curiosity was not going to be worth it after all.

'You'll have to remain with us now, Caspar,' continued the Chaplain. 'Keep out of trouble. I don't want to have to report any more of your childish antics to the Baron, do I, young nephew?' The man's eyebrows raised threateningly above eyes that looked a ghostly blue in the light of the moonstone.

With head hung low, Caspar fell into line in the middle of the group. It was a relief to walk with the full aid of the moonstones' light glowing around him, but otherwise the excitement had evaporated from the adventure. Every hundred paces the Chaplain called a halt so that they could listen for the enemy. The peal of pickaxe and hammer on stone was becoming more distinct and the harsh guttural tones of the enemy gabbled on in unintelligible grunts.

'Sound travels a long way through these rocks but I still can't make out where they are,' said Catrik, 'except that they are beneath us.'

They kept on burrowing downwards, through the maze of tunnels as they curled and twisted, sometimes breaking into yawning caverns, like being swallowed into the belly of a whale. The tonsured priest selected another tunnel burrowing downwards and finally they reached the lower levels. The air was fresher, washed by the spray of the splashing streams that distorted the echoes of the enemy's mining activities with their unrelenting babbling. Finally they located the tunnel where the reverberating metallic tolls were the clearest.

'I think it's this one, men.' Father Gwion indicated a tunnel entrance by swinging the light of the moonstone towards it.

Catrik was shaking his head. 'Permit me, Father, but it's the next one. Listen again.'

The Chaplain frowned.

'He's right,' Hal agreed. 'Catrik is definitely right. It's the next tunnel.'

The priest conceded the point. 'We'll go a little way in to check that there are no forks or junctions that they can re-enter by. Moreover we want to put as much distance as possible between the explosion and the well.'

'Very wise, Father. It wouldn't be good to have the blast go back up through the well into the well room,' said Catrik. 'But why don't we just kill the varmints?'

'Yes,' added Hal enthusiastically. 'Why don't we kill them?'

'Unfortunately, Catrik, young Hal, we can't risk it. We don't know how many there are and it's more important that we seal off their approach than kill a handful of them. And I do not wish to have any unnecessary deaths,' declared the man of God.

Caspar thought that his father had made a mistake in letting Gwion lead the men down and looking at Hal's face he realized that his young raven-haired uncle thought the same.

'Our duty, men, is to protect the well,' the Chaplain continued. 'Torra Alta must have water. Moreover I have Master Caspar to think about now. We can't enter into any skirmishes when we have the Baron's young son to protect. Branwolf would never forgive me.'

Catrik was nodding in thoughtful agreement while Caspar scowled angrily at being treated like a young helpless child.

The Chaplain looked stiffly at his sister's child. 'And you don't, young Caspar, look repentant enough to me after your disobedience. You are too young to be down here and now we have to nursemaid you too rather than concentrating on the job,' he added viciously.

How dare he treat me like this, thought Caspar, outraged by the Chaplain's condescension. He glared straight back, eyes brimming with rebellion, careless of how many passages from the scriptures he would later have to copy out as punishment.

They marched into the tunnel, with hands fingering the hilts of their swords as they listened to the growing sounds of the enemy.

'Can't they hear us?' whispered Hal.

'No, the fools are making too much noise,' the Wellmaster replied and then added with a sinister intonation, 'but those are not just human voices, you know.'

The sound travelled easily through the hollow rock as if it were amplified by a drum-like chamber. Mixed in with the clink of steel hammering at the rock and the patter of boots scurrying back and forth, there was the rattling tap of clawed toes. A large animal, Caspar thought. Heavy with long slow strides, perhaps a bear. He shuddered. They turned a sharp corner and the sound of hammer splintering rock became distinctly louder. Caspar thought that at last they had traced the enemy's tell-tale echoes through the interwoven tunnels to just one entrance, where the sound was not distorted by junction, fork and cross-roads.

'This is far enough, men,' hissed the Chaplain. 'Unfasten your powder barrels. We'll check the tunnel carefully for any side passages before Catrik arranges the explosives.'

He sent the two soldiers and Hal to check every recess and grotto along the tunnel walls to ensure that there were no passages leading out at the back of them, leaving Catrik to arrange the caskets of powder. The old Wellmaster carefully examined the rock structure deciding how best to lay the explosives so that the blast would bring down an overhanging rock, running for a goodly distance along the roof, and so block the tunnel completely. Caspar waited patiently, wondering why he was not sent to search for any hidden passages. Then he remembered that he did not have any light of his own by which to search. He watched the domes of white light float up and down the tunnel as Hal and the soldiers methodically searched the rock-face. Hal returned shortly.

'I think there's a small opening further up.'

'Right, Hal,' Catrik called to him. 'I'll put a barrel in it just in case. Keep checking.'

It seemed to take ages for the old Wellmaster to arrange the powder caskets. With an impatient voice the Chaplain insisted on helping him lay out the kegs, though Catrik said it was too dangerous a task for a man of the Church to perform. Even though Gwion insisted on helping to speed up the process, Caspar was concerned that they were taking too long.

'Won't they tunnel through soon?'

'We've got enough time yet; don't worry, lad,' Catrik's comforting deep tones echoed through the tunnels. 'Sound travels a very long distance through this porous rock. I'd say they have several feet of rock to axe out and that'll take them a long time.'

The boy relaxed and then began to fidget as he watched the others work and found that he could do nothing to help. The two men had arranged the explosives several times, continually arguing about how the kegs should be placed in order to produce the most effective blast. Caspar began to look around him: he saw nothing but cold plain stone until he wandered a short distance down the tunnel, as far as the light from Catrik's moonstones would allow. Here he found an apse-like recess floored by a rippling pool into which a miniature waterfall cascaded from a crack in the rock-face above. The droplets that sprayed into the air sparkled like diamonds and sapphires as they danced in the white light of the moonstones.

How extraordinary, thought Caspar. There were many waterfalls tumbling from the Yellow Mountains and in the daylight the spray captured the natural light in a myriad of fragmented rainbows. But there were no warm colours of the sun in this spray, no reds and oranges, only cold blue and white.

The ghostly light reached up to the rock-face above the waterfall and, glinting brightly and as beautiful as the sparkling sapphire droplets, he saw a cluster of crystals. Perhaps they're precious or maybe they have magic like the moonstones, he thought eagerly and started to climb up alongside the waterfall towards them. Their colour was certainly bewitching, like the rich turquoise of a peacock breast, and their sharp-edged, hexagonal shape looked too perfect to be natural.

The transfixed boy found another foothold to assist him in his climb and then he had to stretch his fingertips to reach up to a ledge for his next purchase. The gushing sound of the waterfall coming from behind the wall of rock filled his ears and he was lost to the miniature world of the crystal-crowned grotto. Forgetting all else, he struggled to climb higher; the ascent itself becoming an absorbing challenge, and the sound of water flowing behind the rock swelled to a roar. He thought to himself that there must be some sort of river flowing behind the rock-face and that the waterfall was escaping from it.

Another ledge helped him nearer to his goal and finally he grasped the crystals in his fist. The moment of triumph, however, disintegrated as his beautiful prize began to crumble into worthless dust. For just a second he had a comic vision of Dunnock the curate preaching at him of the folly of worshipping false idols, but this image was viciously torn away when his thoughts were burst into by somebody, or something, grabbing the scruff of his neck, as if meaning to strangle him. He was wrenched backwards off the rock. Still locked in the stranglehold he plunged into the pool, deep down into the black bottomless depths, icy cold and shocking.

Fighting panic, he found himself dragged deeper. He thrashed violently to free himself from his attacker, his lungs screaming for air, but he was not strong enough. The pain in his chest was crushing. He began to twist and wriggle, tearing at the arm that was still locked around his throat.

God, please help me, he prayed, as weakness crept into his muscles and his brain began to numb. For a second he thought he saw a bright red light flash across the surface of the water. He was trying to force back the strange enveloping sleep that dulled his eyes and his hearing.

No! I must keep on fighting, I must. Spar, fight, you must keep on fighting, he frantically urged himself.

And at last the throttling grip around his neck broke and he was free to kick upwards, desperate to gasp in air.

Chapter 3

'It's rotted right through,' the Captain complained, as he wriggled back out from underneath the supporting platform of the war-engine. 'The teeth on the winding gear aren't ever going to bite again. I doubt Catrik will be able to repair it; and if he can I'll eat my hat – as he would say.'

Branwolf looked in frustration at the old ballista, his eyes angrily narrowed to dark slits. For a moment he wanted to kick the machine, but he quickly regained his composure. 'Well, Captain, we'll just have to manage without it. Have this dragged away. We'll smash it up for firewood. And bring one of the newer ballistas over here from the north wall: that'll even up our defences a little.' He sighed at the rotted war-engine. 'I don't suppose these old contraptions had much fire power anyway. What we really need are more men.' His thoughts ran to the exorbitant cost of the new cathedral, on top of King Rewik's burdensome Church taxes. These had forced him to cut back on the garrison numbers. He lowered his voice and muttered confidentially to his trusted Captain. 'I have only a thousand men; my great-grandfather had three thousand men. Times have changed – and fast.'

The two dark men in their heavy bearskin cloaks swirled round, alerted by a cry from the watchtower above.

Though a little shorter than his rangy captain, Branwolf's stature dwarfed the other man. The broadness of his chest and the sense of proud authority emanating from him gave Branwolf a large and powerful presence. The once almost jet-black hair – which had been like Hal's – was now streaked with grey at the temple. The clean lines of his face and sharp, determined set to the jaw were also shared by Hal, and at first glance they had the same secretive, dark olive eyes. But the gleam of the Baron's eyes was solemn, and the wisdom of his careworn gaze had etched the corners of his eyes with feathered creases that told of sadness. Hal's luminous eyes, beneath gently curving brows – which usually were raised arrogantly – held up to the world a stubbornly cheeky appraisal, as though he did not care a damn!

The Baron's dress alone did not immediately set him apart from his men. Like them he wore a coarse homespun shirt and a thick practical deerskin hauberk, which was worn and faded by the heavy demands of garrison life. A brown bearskin cloak slung over his shoulder protected him from the worst of the cold. However, his proud bearing declared to the world that he was a high baron from one of the wealthiest realms surrounding the Caballan Sea. Only King Rewik outranked him in the feudal hierarchy and only six other men in all Belbidia were his equal. Branwolf, however, chose not to decorate himself in gold amulets, flowing satins and ermines. He considered that such finery was only for women.

'There's someone else in trouble on the Slide,' the Captain shouted urgently, already running towards the portcullis. The Baron quickly overtook him to look in dismay at the scene below. A train of mules brayed in panic, struggling to save themselves from falling off the edge of the road. Sparks flew off their hooves as they struck and scrabbled at the bare rock. But gradually they slithered backwards, pulled by the weight of the last animal, which had lost its footing on the treacherous road. Still hitched to the mule train by the creaking straps of its harness, the animal dangled in thin air over the hundred-foot drop to the jagged points of the scree slope below.

The mule driver frantically lashed at the leading mule while garrison soldiers grappled with the rest of the team. Branwolf strode past the grunting men to the fifth mule whose hindquarters were a foot from the edge of the precipice. He pressed his back into its rump, dug his heels firmly into a notch in the sharply sloping ground and drew his skinning knife. The sharp blade glinted in the morning sun and with one quick flash he severed the taut leathers that held the dangling ass. The five mules on the Slide lurched forward, leaving the soldiers stumbling on their knees. Seconds later the sickening thud of the mule crashing onto the pointed rocks far below echoed back and forth between the valley walls.

The mule-driver swung round and for a second it seemed that his eyes dared to accuse his overlord of callously killing one of his animals; but hurriedly he averted his gaze. The Baron however didn't miss the look and he paced up the steep rock to stare the man levelly in the eye.

'If you had bothered to assess the situation rather than just beating the rest of your animals into strips of hide, perhaps you'd have realized its neck was already broken. You were risking those five for the sake of a few sacks of flour and the knacker's price for a dead mule.' He strode disgustedly back towards the castle, but then turned back on the man. 'It would never have happened if you hadn't over-burdened them. I don't want these animals abused. We'll get more out of them at the end of the day if they're not exhausted at the beginning.'

He stood feet astride and hands on hips staring at the heaped supplies that his men were unloading just inside the outer battlements. He immediately fell to delegating various tasks to his bustling soldiers, trying to create order in their unguided proceedings. Hal should be doing this, he thought in irritation. Then he remembered the clattering noise down the well and hoped Hal and his men had rooted out the worst. He hoped, of course, that Gwion was right about the disturbance. Surely it was only some mechanical noise. Spar could help here, though, he decided. Spar was young but the boy would have to learn some responsibility soon. He sighed at the thought of his young red-haired lad and shook his head. No, not yet; he was still too young.

'Get those arrowheads to the fletcher,' he ordered. His chief fletcher had grumbled for weeks that it was no good making shafts if he didn't have the barbs for the arrows.

A crate of squawking chickens slipped from a soldier's

47

hands. The wicker cage split open on the cobbles, releasing the flapping birds into the courtyard. The castle hounds leapt from their curled slumber where they warmed their coats in the morning sun and avidly chased the frantic birds, chomping tail feathers in their excited mouths. The mules added their raucous braying to the pandemonium while a tethered horse put all its effort into wrecking the wagon harnessed to it.

'God, have mercy,' Branwolf muttered. 'For God's sake, someone deal with the dogs! And fetch Spar; he can get those chickens.' The hounds, however, were far too excited by the prospect of fresh food in front of their noses to respond to the soldiers' efforts to control them. In exasperation Branwolf emitted a shrill piercing whistle through his teeth and flung open the door to the watchroom. The reluctant hounds slunk past him with their tails between their legs and cowered in the dark corners of the watchroom. 'Someone get the boy,' Branwolf ordered again, thinking that Caspar would probably enjoy catching chickens more than scraping out the sweltering vats. He'd been in that wellroom long enough.

The dark-haired Baron studiously ignored the rooster, as it perched on top of the crenellations crowing at him like a victorious general, and heaved the next crate off the back of the wagon and handed it down to one of the kitchen boys.

A soldier came running back out of the door that led down into the wellroom and sprinted across the courtyard. 'My Lord, there's no sign of Master Spar and there's cries for help coming up from the well.'

Branwolf dropped the crate, letting it crack open at his feet. He pumped his legs towards his chest in his efforts to move as fast as he could, leapt down the spiral staircase and thrust his head down into the well. 'Hello!'

The Chaplain's voice floated up. 'Set the mechanisms rolling. Catrik's injured. We have to winch him up.'

The Baron slapped the rumps of the donkeys tethered in the treadmill to send them lumbering forward. The slack on the pulley system snapped tight and the cable groaned into action. The metallic clank of the buckets was already echoing up from the black cavernous pits, sloshing their yellow stinking water into the troughed channels, before the Captain and several men came breathlessly into the room. Branwolf paced up and down impatiently thumping the rim of a sulphur vat every time he passed it, as he waited for Gwion and Catrik to be winched up to the surface. Catrik injured; and now of all times.

The shining crown of Gwion's shaven head poked up above the wellkerb, then the circlet of flat-brown hair fringing it. The lacklustre blue eyes were startled and concerned as he looked up from the groaning body of Catrik cradled in his arms. The Baron leapt forward and struggled with the dead weight of the old retainer as they eased him gently onto the floor and wrapped him in a cloak. Blood, splinters of rock and a powdery coating of explosive dust caked his face and his dark reddened eyes blinked up at his liege-lord.

'The lads . . . trapped,' he gasped in utter exhaustion. His eyelids flickered and closed and Branwolf pressed his head against the man's cracked lips to catch his words. 'I tried to get to them but . . .' He fell silent and Branwolf stood up with clenched fists, blood pounding in his head as he tried to think what the man was saying. Not Spar, no not Spar; he couldn't lose him too . . .

'I've left the other men down there, trying to dig them out.' The Chaplain clutched on to Branwolf's hand. 'Catrik's stone, it ignited the powder and there was a rock-fall.' The face of the wiry priest was white. 'God have mercy on them.'

'How many are trapped?' Branwolf coughed to maintain a steady voice.

'Just Hal and Caspar.'

'Just Hal and Spar,' Branwolf echoed. Just my whole life, he thought helplessly. 'Right, Captain, get someone to look after Catrik right away and get half a dozen men with picks and shovels. Father Gwion can lead us to the spot.' He steadied himself for a moment by clutching hold of the kerb stones as he tried to banish the picture of his son trapped, crushed, suffocating beneath tons of rock.

49

His brother-in-law's hand firmly gripped his arm, offering him reassurance and Branwolf gratefully took a calming breath.

'Right. We will dig them out. Now come on, let's get going. Let's get those torches lit and for God's sake everybody –' he stared thunderously at his men but spoke in deep level tones '– keep those torches up and don't let them spit. I don't want anyone blinded by spitting torches.' He turned to the Chaplain and spoke softly, 'You'd better say the appropriate prayers over Catrik before we go – just in case.' He wasn't sure whether the old Wellmaster could hear him or not but he stooped down over him to whisper in his ear. 'You don't look too bad now, old man. We've both seen worse. I'm going to get them back, so don't you worry. You hang on because we need you. I need you, old man.'

He took one last look at Catrik's ash covered face, the unnaturally pale lips and the mud splattered over him, before turning to lead his men downward, trailing smoke from their oil-soaked torches, into the tunnel that coiled beneath the mouth of the well. For a moment the tunnel was illuminated with spitting orange flame. Branwolf walked into the hectic light that bounced back off the close circular walls, light that failed to disclose the way ahead through the sinuous passage. The sick feeling in his stomach increased. He was stepping through the fiery gizzard of a dragon down into its cavernous belly. The last time he had ventured down into the well had been in search of his wife!

The haunting memory of her bright voice was drowned by the heavy footsteps rushing behind him. Her simple joy in life and how she had filled the castle with her laughter . . . He felt bitter, deeply angry and bitter that she had abandoned him and, worse, abandoned Spar. One day she had been there and the next day she was gone. No word, nothing. He hoped she was dead. It was a terrible thing to hope for and he prayed God would forgive him for such a thought but it was, after all these years, the only way he could think of her. If she was still alive, had just abandoned them, then he could only hate her . . . and yet he loved her, loved her more than he loved life. For years he had hoped that one day she would simply walk in beneath the portcullis and be there back in his castle again; but the years passed and with it his hope died.

So many women, he thought, so many smiling lifeless faces. He had dallied with their beautiful bodies trying vainly to fill the aching gap in his heart. So many women, but all their eyes were dead.

He had searched the castle and the valley for her, before finally climbing down in the well. He had ordered all his men, a thousand professional soldiers, down into the catacombs and he had kept them searching there for three days. Then with only the help of his brother-in-law, he had continued to search every day for a month but they had found no sign of her. Rejecting the dark labyrinth below the castle, he had spent a year scouring the Barony, even reaching into the heathen villages that persisted in their heretical worship deep in the heart of the Boarchase Forest.

In despair, he had tried to fling himself into the New Faith, but the mercy of the one true God offered little solace. The Chaplain had also sought comfort in the scriptures and had chosen to dedicate his life to the new Lord. Branwolf envied him the comfort of faith but was glad of it – in an obscure part of himself, he hoped that Gwion's faith could act as proxy for the whole family. So it saddened and angered Branwolf that Rewik's archbishop always preferred to select for each new bishopric a smoother, more cultivated priest from the lowlands. The energetic Torra Altan had been denied promotion within the Church. Only the Baron's influence had ensured Gwion's promotion over Dunnock, his sparrow-like curate.

He prayed this wouldn't become another dreadful search like the one twelve years ago. Looking up towards his brother-in-law's boots tapping against each new rung of the ladder he realized he was being illogical. Gwion knew where the boys were. Of course they could dig them out. The boys were strong, tough, healthy lads; they would survive a few cuts and bruises, he told himself firmly. They weren't old like Catrik. For the first time he thought guiltily of Hal and remembered his father's dying plea to protect the boy. He had brought Hal up as his own son; but Spar was all he had left of his beloved Keridwen.

He stumbled as his foot touched solid ground unexpectedly. He paced anxiously back and forth as he waited for his men to catch up with him. Finally the last man was down and he turned to grunt at the small priest whose fringe of hair looked like flames in the light of the firebrands.

'Right then, Gwion, lead on at a pace. Captain, take the rear. And keep close, men – tight together. I don't want anyone straying. Keep the torches up and keep moving.'

They moved off at a steady trot, weaving through the tunnels. Long stretched shadows jogged along beside them, like hobgoblins moulded to the curved shape of the smooth, scale-worn tunnels. The Chaplain dodged left and right and paused once or twice at a junction before selecting the right tunnel. He was very flushed and red, his blue eyes darting back and forth as he anxiously decided which way to turn. Branwolf looked at his shaking hand and realized he was greatly distressed.

'It's not your fault,' Branwolf said, placing a kindly hand on his brother-in-law's shoulder as he wondered what he would have done without the man's spiritual support during the long years of the last decade. 'You mustn't feel responsible. I'm sure you did everything in your power.'

'But who else can I blame? I was in charge. I should have sent Caspar back the moment he appeared trailing after us.' There was a quiver to the man's voice but he never dropped those clear-cut clipped tones that he had worked so hard to achieve to disguise his peasant upbringing. 'If anything has happened . . . Come on; it's this way.'

He should have marked out the trail, Branwolf thought to himself but decided that his brother-in-law was already feeling too guilty to add to his remorse by basting him for it now.

They jogged on again through the still, cool world deep within the roots of the Yellow Mountains. The echo of their slapping feet on the damp bare rock wormed away in disorientating directions to come back at them from unexplored grottoes and side chambers swallowed in the shadows. Their firebrands touched on the hidden faces of the rock, seams of copper and threads of quartz blinking in the sudden light. The dank lifeless labyrinth entombed beneath the unimaginable tonnage of rock over their heads, drew them deeper into its oppressed depths. As Gwion picked his way through the coiling entrails in the bowels of the earth, he paused for only a moment before at last turning down into a low sloping tunnel. Abruptly he came to a halt, faced with a wall of scree. The remaining men from the earlier party were already frantically trying to drag away the fallen boulders but they had made little impact on the cave-in. Branwolf stared blankly at the tonnage of rubble. Dear God . . . have mercy on my boy, he prayed.

Dust-smothered men, streaked in sweat, ceased working as the Baron approached. As their panting eased Branwolf was aware of the oppressive silence. A fine, choking powder still clogged the air in the aftermath of the explosion and Branwolf glowered as one of the men coughed noisily. The man stifled his splutterings into the sleeve of his jacket rather than risk the wrath of his liege-lord – who strained his ears, listening intently, as he tried to reach out with every sense of his body to feel the presence of his son. All he could hear was a distant plop of condensing water dripping. The constant sound of drip following drip had inexorably measured the pulse of time since long before the reckoning of man. The relentless splash of falling water counted through forgotten aeons.

The Baron took a deep breath and bellowed with all his might: 'Spar! Spar!'

The sound of his voice echoed on and on through the tunnels. The howling resonance was ghostly and horrifying. He waited for the echoes to die down and listened for any noise, any tiny sound of movement from the rubble. He fell into a disappointed silence that held the stilled breath of everyone gathered in the cramped space.

'They might be able to hear us but we might not be able to hear them,' the Captain whispered gently in the Baron's ear.

Branwolf looked at his friend thankfully. He drew in a deep breath and bellowed again, more loudly than before. 'Spar . . . Hal . . . I'm coming to get you; don't worry. I'm coming for you.' He took two deep even breaths to steady himself as his voice threatened to trail away. He must not let his men see how afraid he was, not at a time like this, not when the vast numbers of Vaalakan hordes threatened to hurl their entire might against him. A leader must always be strong. Calm again, Branwolf listened vainly for any noise but was greeted mercilessly once more by a chilled silence. Suddenly he remembered why Hal and the Chaplain had been sent down here in the first place.

'Those clatterings earlier – they couldn't have been the well mechanism otherwise you wouldn't have gone so deep into the tunnel network. Did you locate the noise?'

Gwion nodded. 'The noise was definitely mining and it came from beyond this tunnel. Then it stopped, after the explosion.'

Branwolf wondered vaguely where the other moonstones had gone but dismissed the care from his mind. 'Get these powder kegs out of the way,' he ordered. 'Soldier, go back and store them well down the tunnel forking off this one. I'm not having any more mistakes. You, man, hold a torch for him but stand well clear of the kegs.' He looked closely at the mountain of rubble choking the tunnel and let his eyes trace down the jagged scree that stretched out towards his feet. He stared at where the men had been working away at the bottom of the pile as he carefully decided what to do.

'This will be like any other scree slope – wider at the bottom than the top – so we'll get through faster if we try and dig our way through up there.' He pointed at the roof of the tunnel where the rubble sloped up and away from them.

'But, Sir, we thought they might be buried at the bottom of all this,' a soldier muttered. The skin on his hands was already torn and blood oozed from small cuts inflicted by the splinters of rock.

'I'll have three teams and we'll rotate: three men at the top with picks, three at the base and the rest can take a breather. Then we can work fast for as long as possible.'

Branwolf led the first team of men, scrambling over the rocks until his head was pressed against the damp roof of the tunnel. There he wedged his torch into a crack between two boulders and raised his pick. The tunnels echoed with the sounds of tumbling boulders as he wrenched away a heavy slab of rock and heaved it behind him. It clattered below for the men to clear aside. They worked on in silence broken only by their laboured grunts and an occasional oath when tumbling rocks caused minor injuries. Their thoughts were too dreadful to utter.

The powdery film that covered the Baron's face blended with sweat to form a grimy slurry. He attacked the scree, every stroke designed to crush a Vaalakan skull and kill one of the barbarous enemy. How long had they been threatening to invade? And now that demon Morbak was about to lead his army through the desolate lands to march on *him*. He almost smiled as he thought of the boys' romantic image of the forthcoming war: they both thought they would become heroes. He laughed sardonically, hammering his pick into a crevice between two rocks and working it back and forth until he had prised one of the boulders from its nest. Heroes! But then he supposed that he would have felt like that once.

'Take a rest now, men,' he bellowed. 'And I want absolute silence.' The light of the flickering torches revealed an appreciable gap in the mountainous rock-fall but there were still no hopeful signs that they were about to reach the other side. He drew a deep breath and let his voice ring out: 'Spar . . . Hal . . . Spar . . .'

Once the hollow echoes dwindled away everyone held their

breath as they listened for the barest whisper of a reply. But they were met with silence, stony, hollow silence.

Branwolf sighed and picked up his axe. 'Right, we'll swap round. You three,' he pointed to his fellow team mates, 'take a rest and you, clearing the rocks at the bottom there, come up with me.' He didn't pause for a second longer before drawing the pick handle back and smiting it against the rock.

'My Lord Branwolf, I think you'd better rest too,' the Captain quietly advised. 'You won't do your son any good by exhausting yourself.'

'No!'

The torches were smouldering and thick black smoke curled up from their stubby remnants. Branwolf hadn't rested for two hours and now a sizeable hole gaped in the rock-fall. He was black with sooty grime except for where the runnels of sweat streaming from his forehead washed away the dirt to reveal his pale skin. He paused briefly to rip the shirt from his back, revealing the ridged muscles on his sweat-glistening back which were sharply defined by the shadows cast by the flickering light. He seized up his pick and returned with renewed vigour to his task. His chest heaved with the effort of each blow.

'The torches are nearly out,' the Captain whispered gently to him again. 'You must rest now.'

'No! Send one of the men back for more torches. And bring more men.'

Gwion was still there at his side and, though a smaller, slighter man, his taut furious muscles had worked almost as hard as his own. This was rough work for a Chaplain, but his face was set hard and determined. Though his sweat-soaked shirt clung to his lower back, he still kept it on and neatly buttoned at the cuffs. Gwion often preached about the sins of exposing flesh and how that led to sinful lusts and desires. Such sermons were generally embellished with frosty glances towards the Baron and withering looks at Hal.

'God have mercy on my sister's boy. Have mercy. Don't punish him for the sins of his mother. He is an innocent,' the priest muttered in prayer. His words were barely audible above the hammering blows of the picks.

Branwolf's senses were so strained, listening for any movement or even the pulse of an unconscious body from the rubble beneath him, that he instantly heard the breathed words. He looked at his brother-in-law. 'God cannot punish him: his worst crime is disobedience.'

'The Lord is merciful,' the Chaplain murmured in placatory tones. 'But I think Catrik was right: those pagan moonstones, we should never have touched them. We must find all of them and destroy them to show the good Lord that we truly worship Him alone.' Branwolf smote the rock again, grunting and groaning as much to block out Gwion's words as to ease his physical effort.

The night wore on and there was still no sign of breaking through the blocked tunnel. When at last he had to admit that the fresh soldiers worked harder and faster than he could after all his hours of labour, Branwolf dozed fitfully, giving orders to wake him the second they found anything – anything at all. He took satisfaction from seeing how other men worked with all their might to find his son as the soldiers toiled through the night, carting away the cleared rubble, digging deeper and deeper into the heaped rock. But tension prevented the Baron from sleeping properly, and though his muscles ached and the skin on his hands was raw and blistered soon he insisted on returning to his position at the front of the team.

He heaved at a boulder, shouting to look out below as it tumbled down behind him and crashed onto the tunnel floor, splitting in two. Suddenly he was aware of that same crashing noise coming from in front of him; he must have set off a rock-fall on the other side of the cave-in. He must be nearly through. He reached for his torch, thrusting the fire into the pitch-black hole that opened up before him. They were through but he could still see very little. He swallowed hard, trying to hold his breath and quiet his pounding pulse to listen for any noise. Running water, gushing, tumbling, drummed in his ears – but that was all! He hollered into the darkness but only the sound of the water splashing over rocks touched his ears.

He turned back to reassess the situation. 'Captain, send for more men. I want every last stone in this heap moved aside in case they are trapped under it. I'm going to search the other side. I hope Hal has the sense to keep still and wait for me to get him out. Give me a new torch.'

The Captain handed him a brightly flaring firebrand, freshly lit, which spat with excess oil.

'Wait!' Father Gwion, his face deathly strained, grabbed a fresh torch for himself. 'I'm coming with you.'

Branwolf acknowledged his brother-in-law's support as he grabbed his shirt then wormed his way forward over the jagged rocks. He felt nothing, no physical pain, only a sickening grief for his son. Thrusting the torch before him, he slithered forward on his belly until he was finally free on the other side and leapt down into the blocked tunnel. When he shouted again for the missing boys the echo came directly back rather than wailing on and on. He frowned to himself, realizing that there must be a dead-end not far ahead. Gwion was right behind him and together they searched the debris at their feet for any evidence of the boys on this side of the cave-in. Branwolf's heart was in his mouth as he thought he saw something that looked like a hand reaching out of the cracks in the rubble. As he leapt at it he realized with relief that it was only a pale splinter of wood from the exploded keg.

The Chaplain was waiting quietly and when Branwolf looked towards his hazy blue eyes he felt the comfort of the companionship. 'Come on, we'll search the tunnel. Maybe they are unconscious and that's why they haven't answered.'

He marched steadily forward, thrusting his firebrand into every recess on the left while the Chaplain scoured the right hand side of the tunnel. They passed a deep pool of yellow-stained water that was lapping up and spilling over onto the tunnel floor. Branwolf frowned at it for a moment. There was something slightly out of place about the pool, though he couldn't think what.

'You would think after all those months of searching down here I would remember every inch of rock,' he sighed. 'I must have covered every tunnel a hundred times – a thousand times.'

'The tunnels change,' the priest muttered. 'The heavy rains,' he added more firmly. 'As Catrik said, many of the underground rivers have spated and so perhaps they have opened up new ways. Besides, the labyrinth is so monotonous you could get lost down here and wander forever.' He looked quickly at the grief-stricken Baron. 'I'm sorry, I didn't mean to say that. I know we trod every inch looking for her. She wasn't down here, Branwolf. I know she wasn't down here.'

Now, again, they had found nothing, no trace of the young Torra Altans. He had prayed for one more turn in the tunnel, one more side-chamber where he might have found the two boys huddled together in fright. Maybe too hurt to yell for help, but alive, alive. But the tunnel was empty. He had to face the fact.

Gwion looked at him with big round frightened eyes and he clutched at his chest. 'I'm sorry, Branwolf.' He coughed to clear his choked voice.

The grief-racked Baron found his eyes were dry and his voice was level – though within the privacy of his skull he was screaming with anguish. Logic told him that Hal and Spar were crushed under the rubble. And so much rubble. They were buried under feet of rock – they had to be – there was nowhere else for them to go.

But he stared fiercely at the Chaplain. 'I know he's not dead! I know my son is alive!'

The tonsured, grime-smeared priest wasn't able to speak for a minute but then in a thin trembling voice, he muttered, 'I prayed we would find them here on this side. I prayed they would be here and safe.'

'You are certain that they weren't on the Torra Alta side of the cave-in?' Branwolf asked, leaping at the barest of hopes.

The Chaplain shook his head. 'Caspar was a long way down the tunnel. Why ever didn't I keep a more vigilant eye on him? But I didn't know the moonstone would just explode like that. He was ahead of us as the stone started to whine. We shouted for him to come back, and when there was no answer Hal just ran, ran like a hare to try and get the boy. But then there was the flash of the explosions and so much dust . . .'

Hal ran after him, Branwolf thought, slowly mulling the image over in his mind, imagining his younger brother, charging into danger to save Caspar's skin. Hal! I'm hard on the lad, I know I am, he thought regretfully. He is so loyal.

The broad-shouldered Baron turned back down the tunnel and stared at the rubble once more, wondering briefly if he was looking at his son's tomb. He shook his head, refusing to allow the thought into his mind. Maybe I am deluded just like everyone told me I was about Keridwen. Maybe it is too painful for me to face, but I *know* he's not under there.

'Gwion,' he barked fiercely, and as his brother-in-law leapt round, he softened his look, letting his eyes apologize for his gruff tone rather than wasting time with words. 'Get back to the other side. I want at least another fifty men down here. We can have teams working from either side now and get this all cleared away much faster. I want every last stone moved aside so that we can know beyond doubt. I'll have no uncertainty.'

'I'll get them,' came the Chaplain's reassuring voice. 'I'll get them, but what are you going to do?'

'I'm going to look again. I just think we've missed something.'

'I'll pass the word to the Captain and then look with you. Two pairs of eyes are better than one.'

Branwolf shook his head and dismissed the priest. 'No, go and help organize the men.' The presence of his brother-in-law there at his side reminded him too much of their search for Keridwen. The memory added to his anguish and he felt it was clouding his judgement. He needed to think. He was sure there was something out of place here and perhaps alone he would be able to fathom it.

Chapter 4

It was dark. The incandescent glow from the moonstones was gone, replaced by feeble shimmers of yellow light that sifted through the thick dust that blurred the ripple patterns on the walls and ceiling. A ball of feeble yellow light dimly glowed in the depths of the pool. Confusion curdled his mind and Caspar slumped his head and shoulders onto a slab of stone that sloped into the pool. Wheezing water from his lungs he gasped in deep breaths of dust-choked air, too exhausted to drag himself out.

Through the smoke-clogged gloom he couldn't see how much of the tunnel was blocked. The powder kegs, he thought. Something went wrong and I'm trapped. Then in the half-light he made out a black, heaving shape. Caspar called out to it: 'What's happened?' There was no reply. The man was heaving fitfully as if retching up the dregs of the pool. Caspar swung a knee onto the slab of stone, stood up and tottered unsteadily around the curving edge of the pool towards the man slumped at the other side. 'Are you all right?' Caspar sounded more urgent. 'Are you hurt? Answer me.'

The black shape began to moan. The hunched body shook, as raking coughs scraped his lungs to cleanse out the foul, sulphurous water, and when the coughing released him he slumped back into dolorous moans. At last he recovered enough to spit an angry stream of oaths out into the air.

'Of course, I'm bloody well not all right. Do you think I'm lying here coughing my guts up for the hell of it?'

'Hal!' But Caspar did not know what else to say. He stumbled through the dying light and fell to his knees next to his uncle, fumbling to loosen Hal's sodden mass of clothing so that he could breathe more freely. Hal pushed him away.

'Just give me a second, will you? I'll be all right in a minute. God, that water.' He talked in bursts as he tried to draw breath.

'What happened?'

In silence Hal uncoiled from his hunched position and looked dismally into the pool. 'Damn it. I'll have to go into that muck again to get the moonstone back.'

'But what happened?'

'You've probably got both of us killed, that's what happened.'

'Are we trapped?'

'Well, what do you think, Spar?' Hal's words bristled with sarcasm. 'What in God's name were you doing here, anyway? I was screaming for you.'

'I didn't hear anything.'

'You must have done.'

'The waterfall. Up there.' Caspar pointed into the arched recess over the pool. 'There's a noise of running water coming from behind the rock – I couldn't hear anything else.'

Hal peered up into the gloom.

'I saw some crystals: I thought they might be precious,' said Caspar as if that explained everything.

'Well, I hope they were worth it.'

Realizing how irresponsible he had been, Caspar felt ashamed and then angry – angry at himself and angry with Hal for being there, for being right and for making him feel childish.

'What did you do? Light the powder deliberately to kill me so that Torra Alta would be yours – but then found you were too much of a coward to go through with it?'

Hal's fist punched squarely into the middle of Caspar's face and they became a knot of flailing arms until Hal had the younger boy pinioned beneath him.

'You stupid, spoilt brat, I should have let you get blown

apart.' Hal released his grip and Caspar sat up gingerly prodding his nose.

'You've broken it.'

'Good.'

They sat, hunched over, brooding sulkily for a while. The acrid dust and pungent smoke were settling. The only sound was from the splashing waterfall and Caspar realized that the enemy noises had ceased. In fact he had not heard them since the explosion.

'Hal?'

'What?'

'Hal . . .' Caspar paused, not knowing how to put his feelings into words. 'I'm sorry. I just wanted to say . . . I don't know . . . just sorry, I suppose.'

Hal grunted in acknowledgement.

'Why did it explode? I mean the powder. Something must have gone wrong.'

'It was Father Gwion's moonstone. It started to whine.'

'What?'

'Whine,' Hal repeated and then added thoughtfully as he squeezed some of the water out of his clothes. 'Only his though.'

'I think they're all different. I think the old Druids used them for different things; they don't all behave the same,' guessed Caspar. 'Anyway, go on.'

'It started to glow bright red and the whine became, well, like a scream.' His eyes grew wide. 'It was pumping in and out like a heart! Catrik kept muttering on about devils, but anyway none of us could touch the stone because of the heat it gave off. It was obvious it was going to explode.' Hal shook his head sending out a spray of water from his hair that was clinging to his cheeks and neck. 'Then I couldn't find you. I shouted and shouted and when I did see you up there above the pool I thought we'd both be killed by the blast. I just didn't think there was enough time to run far enough for safety, but I hoped the water might protect us.'

'What happened to the others?'

'They bolted back up the tunnel when they realized it was going to explode. I hope Catrik made it. He stayed yelling for you until the last second and he was a way behind the others.'

'Oh.' Caspar felt subdued knowing that he had been abandoned by all but Hal. He reached out his hand and gripped his uncle's forearm. 'I owe you. Thanks.'

Hal placed his hand on top of Caspar's. 'You'd have done the same for me. Come on.' Hal pushed himself to his feet. 'Time to get wet again.'

Before Caspar could protest, Hal had plunged headlong into the pool. He swallowed more of that poison than I did, thought the younger Torra Altan. He should have let me go for the moonstone.

The once bright fire of the orb had diminished to dusky embers. It was like looking at the sun through the fog which choked the canyon at certain times of year. Caspar knelt over the pool, peering into the depths. He could just make out Hal's hand as he yanked the moonstone free from the fissure where it was lodged. His uncle burst through the surface of the water, holding the prize above his head for Caspar to take. The boy grabbed the leather leash attached to the net encompassing the stone, and stood up so that he could pull Hal out of the water with his other hand.

As soon as the moonstone began to dry, its lustre returned. Caspar felt a disturbing mixture of enthrallment and fear tremble through his body though the emotion passed so quickly that he wasn't sure it hadn't been his imagination. Hal's voice brought him quickly back to reality.

'Come on, Spar, give me the light. We've got to find a way out of here.'

'Why should you have the light?' the Baron's son complained.

'Because I'm older than you and I'm bigger than you,' retorted Hal with a smug grin.

'Well, that's not a good enough reason,' the younger boy replied defiantly as he laced the leash of the moonstone to the belt of his breeches. Somehow he felt possessive over the strange glow of light. He was sure his father was right when he explained that the moonstone must contain a gas that glowed on exposure to air, but all the same he was fascinated by its apparent magic. Hal was on his feet now, pushing back his sodden black fringe from his face. They both looked around deciding what to do next. Taking a deep breath, Caspar wiped his nose on the back of his sleeve, but then jerked his head away smartly.

'My nose, it really hurts. I'm sure it's broken.'

'It looks awful,' agreed Hal, somewhat unsympathetically, before striding over to examine the wall of rubble that blocked the passageway leading upwards to Torra Alta. Blocks of stone ranging from boulders to pebbles all smothered with a layer of powdery dust packed the tunnel to the roof. They vainly clambered up onto the scree and pulled at some of the looser hunks of rubble, but they knew it was useless before they even started.

'You know the enemy's stopped mining, don't you?' said Hal.

'Ages ago. The blast must have scared them off.'

'Ha! I bet they thought it was the roar of the dragon. Cowards! Miserable Vaalakan cowards,' mocked Hal trying to cheer himself up.

'Catrik certainly did a good job with his powder,' remarked Caspar ironically as he slumped onto one of the imprisoning boulders.

'As men of Torra Alta, we should be grateful,' said Hal grandly.

'But I don't want to be a hero – just yet.'

'Heroes don't have to die.' Hal pulled at his nephew's arm. 'Come on, we'll look down the tunnel. There might be a cavern or a shaft leading out of it.'

The tunnel snaked downwards with featureless stone walls staring blankly at them. Twice it widened out into vaulted chambers, but no fissure or fractured seam offered them any help. They turned one more corner and were confronted by a wall of rock.

'Dead-end,' announced Caspar flatly.

Hal angrily clenched his fist around the hilt of his dagger, raised his arm and beat the pommel of the weapon into the rock.

'There has to be a way out of here,' he screamed defiantly at the faceless rock, giving it a kick with the toe of his boot.

'Above the pool – you remember. I said there was running water.' Caspar sounded suddenly hopeful. 'There must be a channel or something.'

They tore back up the tunnel, the light from the moonstone casting strange shadows that loomed large and then shrank again as the stone bounced against Caspar's hip. Within moments they were back where they had started from, next to the pool. They scaled the rock into the recess, shinning themselves on the spray-soaked boulders in their eagerness to explore their escape route. Their ears were filled with the roar of unseen water gushing over rocks, so that they had to shout to one another. The gentle fall of water trickling into the pool seemed out of proportion to the clamour of that roar.

A narrow ledge provided just enough support for Caspar to balance on the toes of his boots. He clung to the steep wall with the fingertips of one hand while he stretched up for a knot of rock, which offered him his next purchase. Now he was able to swing up into the grotto from where the trickle of water spouted. The powdery grains of his once-coveted crystals were still mocking him on a platform of rock just to the left. He picked up a handful and let the grains run through his fingers into the water where they instantly dissolved. Hal had already drawn his dagger and was using the tip to tease out a loose chip of stone in the crack from where the water spilt.

'What?' Caspar shouted. He could see that Hal was trying to tell him something.

'It . . . bottom of a lake . . . might drown us.'

Caspar crawled closer to Hal's ear to ease the problem of communication. 'What?'

'I said, we might be underneath the bottom of an underground lake and it might flood out and drown us,' Hal repeated at the top of his voice.

Caspar shook his head. 'No. It's running; listen to it. And running fast.'

'Or a great big cascading monumental river,' added Hal, unhelpfully, 'which might drown us.'

Unsheathing his own dagger, Caspar wriggled further into the narrow space, letting the water pour straight onto his lap and soak his breeches. He examined the narrow fracture in the rock and noted that the waterfall escaped from near the bottom of it.

'We've got to try higher up. It might be above the water-line on the other side.'

'I hope you're right,' shouted Hal.

Elbowing each other for space, the two boys jammed the points of their daggers into the fissure and twisted the blades back and forth to try and entice a piece of rock free. An occasional splinter fell away but their progress was slow.

'God, look at that,' Hal exclaimed in disgust as he examined the tip of his dagger. The sharp point had snapped off where he had twisted it against the rock. 'Cruel way to treat a good dagger,' he muttered, just audible above the noise.

'This isn't working.'

'Give me some space, will you,' demanded Hal. 'And find me a stone.'

Caspar's knees grated into the sharp rock as he twisted round to cast about for a suitably sized stone.

'Here. Will this do?'

Hal took the stone off him and beat it against the crack.

'Yes. And get me another one. Smaller and with a point.'

The younger boy had to climb half way back down to the pool before his hand fell on a flint-shaped stone. He refused to admit they were trapped. This will work, he kept thinking.

As though reading his mind, Hal said, 'If this doesn't work, you realize that the only people who will rescue us are the Vaalakans.'

'Father will dig through,' protested the faithful boy.

68

'Sure he will. But how long? You saw how much rock came down. It'll take weeks and we'll be starved to death by then.'

After ramming the wedge of stone into the crack, Hal raised his other rock and pounded it repeatedly. The impact chiselled out a fragment of stone and at last a hunk fell away widening the gap. A trickle of water wriggled through; then as another slice of rock slid away, it swelled to a gentle stream.

'Move up higher,' urged Caspar excitedly. 'We're going to break through.'

'Yes, but to what?' Hal hammered again with the primitive tools as gradually the slit opened up. Suddenly a gush of water burst through, cleaving a gateway through the rock. The two youths flung themselves aside and clung onto the walls of the recess with tearing fingernails, expecting a damburst – which never came. The momentary flood subsided. A chunk of rock had broken away, creating an aperture leading through to the tunnel on the other side. A quiet rivulet slipped over the bottom of the enlarged fissure.

'Thank God,' shouted Hal.

'You first, and remember not to swallow any of the water,' reminded Caspar.

The opening was just big enough for them to squeeze through on their bellies. The hilt of Caspar's dagger caught fast and he twisted vigorously to free it. Using his elbows he pulled himself into the fast-running stream, craning his head backwards to keep his mouth well above the water. Once his feet were clear he was able to stand up but only as far as the low arch of the roof allowed. Thankfully the stream gushed up no higher than his thighs, but its bed was jagged and rocks twisted and rolled beneath his feet. Yellow slime coated the walls and the air was rank, contaminated. Now that they were no longer beneath the stream its pounding roar eased to a more bearable level.

'Upstream,' Hal declared. 'It's got to be the best way.'

'I'm right behind you,' the smaller auburn-haired boy panted.

Hal set off at a fast lope, his shoulders hunched, head held low to avoid the rocky ceiling.

Keeping pace with difficulty, Caspar for the first time wondered about his father. By now, the Chaplain would have told him they were trapped. Father might think we are dead, he thought with dismay. He felt immensely guilty for stealing down into the well against his father's orders. His imagination drew the face of his stricken father in his mind. The castle retainers would be muttering sadly, 'Not again. First his wife and now his son. The grief of it, the grief.' Caspar of course did not remember the day his mother had vanished, he had been only an infant but, ever since, he had been haunted by nightmares of weeping and wailing. Through his earliest years he remembered his father's face as long and drawn.

For years Caspar had harboured a secret fantasy, or perhaps just a desperate hope that his mother was still alive. He tried to remember everything that he had been told about her. She had to be beautiful that was for certain: the Baron was only interested in beautiful women. But Branwolf would never talk about her.

Caspar had asked his Uncle Gwion about her but the priest's thin lips were sealed. Latterly, Gwion frowned angrily at the mention of her name and silenced Caspar with the claim that it was too painful for him or the Baron to be reminded of the woman. When probed further, he would solemnly remind Caspar that it was Keridwen's own sinful ways that had brought the wrath of the good Lord upon her. Once the boy had even overheard his pious uncle say to his nurse, 'I've taught this boy to fear God's Word and I don't want any mention of that woman or what she was confusing him now.'

His nurse, however, had loved the Lady Keridwen and she would secretly tell the boy about her. She told him how much his mother had loved him and that she was the best mother that had ever been. He had drawn great comfort from that. The castle gossips had led him to believe that his mother had abandoned him and God had justly punished her with death.

'Can't you keep up?' Hal yelled back at him impatiently.

'Branwolf's trying to ready the castle for war, he shouldn't have to waste time looking for us. Hurry up!'

Caspar had forgotten all about the Vaalakans! He now felt even more repentant for his foolish behaviour in disobeying his father and stealing down into the well.

'Father's going to kill me.'

'Damn right,' agreed Hal. 'But we've got to get back and get back fast, otherwise we'll only make things worse.'

The uneven bed of the stream led them steeply upwards but its roof became lower, forcing them into an uncomfortable and ape-like crouch. Caspar's thighs ached with the strain of the constant climb. He felt cold, hungry, miserable and his injured nose throbbed. His soaked calf-skin breeches clung to his legs, heavy and restricting. The noxious stench rising from the water was beginning to make his head spin. He longed for fresh air. Instead, the low ceiling dipped and they were forced onto their hands and knees, crawling upwards against the current, along the line of the underground stream. Water splashed up towards his mouth and nose and he spat out mouthfuls of the leaping stream and wondered how much his body could stand before the water poisoned him.

Berating himself constantly, Caspar had given up hope of their escape when at last the channel opened into a chamber. The stream danced through the centre but to either side there was dry rock and headroom to stand. They rested for a moment, waiting for the light of the moonstone to swell and fill the chamber. The stream had dampened the moonstone's ardour and it was, once more, a dim hazy ball, its magic shrouded by the cooling liquid. Gradually the light revealed a wide, arching cave, its vaulted roof climbing into the darkness beyond the spread of the moonstone's glow. The black mouths of grottoes gaped out at them and a cluster of glinting quartz crystals reflected the white light onto bands of red iron-ore smeared across the rock-face. Gradually, as he looked around the outer walls of the cavern, his eyes focused on areas of darker blackness – perhaps some were not grottoes but tunnels. As the white glow spread across the open space, he focused on one low patch of shadow: it looked unnatural, too regular and sharply cut. It had to have been mined out of the rock.

Hal had seen it too. 'Come on, we'll try that one.' He grinned. 'When we get back, I'm going to stand on the watch-tower and be the first to shoot a Vaalakan.' Hal drew his right arm back, curling his fingers around the imaginary bowstring.

'No, you won't, because I'll get there first,' Caspar boasted.

'Ah! But you'd miss.'

The tunnel climbed steeply but then began to level out. When it started to dive back down again the two boys halted uncertainly.

Caspar swung the moonstone to the left. Its light bloomed into a side-chamber, which had been hidden behind a curving wall in the tunnel. 'There's another passageway and look, there's light coming from it. This must be the way out.'

They sprinted forward, Hal hurling himself ahead to the turning in the tunnel. But he stopped dead. A moment later, Caspar too stood in wonder at the entrance to a jewelled cave that came fully alive in the light of the moonstone he carried. A spectrum of blue, violet and indigo light danced on the stalactites, which unerringly dripped a yellow liquid. Caspar thought that the light of the moonstone had awoken the natural colours of a crystal cave, illuminating mineral seams sprinkled with reflecting gems and semi-precious sulphates like the turquoise crystals above the pool. Gradually his dazzled eyes took in the scene and he realized he was looking at a hoard of treasure . . . in the middle of which lay an oddly metallic tangle of broken bodies. The boys stared at these until the bodies, mercifully, resolved themselves into empty suits of armour, all of them far too small to fit a full grown Belbidian.

'It's all so *old*.' Caspar's voice was filled with awe, seeing the crusting of rust and the pitted decay in the metal of a blade. 'A hero's sword! From the glorious days of the Dragon Wars.'

Hal was dismissive. 'Old and rusty – about as much good as a woman's spindle.'

Caspar noted that his uncle's gaze caressed instead the jewelled pommel of the sword, its rubies and diamonds. He
noticed then that strings of priceless necklaces were tangled
up with the weapons, and there was a resplendent spill of
gems over the ground. These Hal scooped into his hands,
lustrous stones he gazed upon reverently, breathing deeply.

'These could win me the heart of the most beautiful princess
in the whole world . . . or buy me a kingdom!' Hal's voice
was choked with desire.

Caspar thought only that the wealth they had found could
pay for more soldiers, and pay to re-arm all the men defending
Torra Alta – and fit Firecracker with the finest plate armour.
But then his gaze fell upon a torc etched with moons that
rested on the very top of the pile of treasure. His dreams of
wealth were swept away: the torc enchanted him.

Beside him Hal dropped the jewels he held and stepped
backwards with a sound of disgust. Suddenly Caspar realized
that the object of his delight was crafted in pagan design, and
unwittingly he had yearned more for that heathen artefact
than for all the other priceless jewels.

'Don't touch it!' Hal warned before Caspar could touch the
beautiful twisted band of silver. 'We don't need bad luck –
it's pagan, all of it.'

Shocked, Caspar all at once became aware of the light that
had attracted them to the chamber in the first place. It was
not coming from a shaft that would lead them out of the
caves, it emanated from within the heaped hoard of treasure
itself.

'Let's get out of here,' Hal insisted. 'Where's that light
coming from?'

'From the treasure,' Caspar said simply, giving Hal time to
think on the idea. 'We're still trapped.'

'It can't be . . .' Hal started to object and then his voice
trailed away into despondency. 'Oh God!' He clambered over
the heap of metal and jewels that clattered and crunched
beneath his feet and scrambled to the top of the pile. He
angrily kicked the pagan torc aside with his booted foot, not

wanting to touch it with his bare skin, and its jangling descent echoed throughout the chamber. He plunged his hand in amidst the gold and silver chalices reaching towards the glow, which threaded through the diamonds and sapphires giving them life. 'Oh God, no.' The youth sounded bitterly disappointed. 'It's another moonstone.' He turned round to look at Caspar, his face thrown into weird shadows that blackened his eye-sockets as he held the moonstone aloft.

Caspar's skin was tingling. He gawped at the stone, drawn by its power. This one was bigger than any of the other five that had been kept in the oak casket in the wellroom. It was bigger, at least twice as big, and in some way stronger. The other stones had made him feel peculiar but this one was somehow compelling. Though he could hear nothing he felt, or at least believed, that it was singing to him, urging him to touch the surface of the brilliant gem.

'Let's get out of here,' Hal growled, letting the stone slip from his hand. It rolled over the treasure and came to a halt at Caspar's feet. 'There must be another way.'

Caspar did not hear Hal. Slowly he opened out his free hand and knelt next to the lucent stone, thrilled by it. He cupped his palm towards the glowing moonstone and gently, tentatively he reached to it. The shock of its touch forced him to snatch his hand away and he rubbed the burnt palm on his thigh.

'Haven't you played the fool enough for one day?' Hal shouted angrily.

But Caspar could not take his eyes away from the stone. It was changing and he followed its swirling patterns, looking for a logic in the bright clouds scudding beneath the now translucent surface.

'It's trying to talk to me, Hal.' Caspar's voice was slow and weary as if he was falling into a trance.

'For God's sake,' yelled Hal.

Again he edged the palm of one hand towards the ball of white light. As he touched it a shock hit his skin and sliced through the nerves, running up his arm until it bit into his brain. He gritted his teeth and slapped his other hand onto the surface of the moonstone to complete the circle. The jolt snapped his muscles ridged and a flash of jagged lightning seared through the dark, hidden depths of his mind.

'The pain will pass,' a soft lulling voice told him. 'Hold on. Fight the pain. It will pass.'

Demons with axes hewed at the insides of his eyes and shapeless fiends gnawed at the blood vessels that fed his brain, their upturned-fangs shredding through his flesh. You will lose your mind to us, they shrieked. Caspar screamed back a silent denial with all the strength he possessed. The images began to melt, their dying screams falling away into the oblivion of banished nightmares and his mind was released, free to stare into the heart of the white-hot crystal.

'Spar, what is it?' Hal sounded fearful. 'You're shaking.' But Caspar remained mesmerized by the ancient magic trapped in the stone.

'Clouds, clear for the far-seeing eyes.' He murmured the incantation, not knowing where he had found the words. Half certain that he knew what would happen and half in amazed disbelief, he watched as the swirling shreds of opaque patterns rolled aside and he gazed into the centre of the stone. It was as clear as the soft water in a shallow mountain stream.

'Spar, what's happening to you? Let go of it.' Hal's voice was on the verge of panic. 'Drop it. Your eyes! They're white. Drop it!' Hal's words struggled through the chasm between consciousness and oblivion. To Caspar it felt as if he were lost on a mountain and that the words were born on the wind from a faraway valley.

'A face,' the entranced boy whispered. 'I can see a face.'

Hal gripped his nephew's wrists, meaning to wrench them apart so that he would drop the moonstone, but the second he touched Caspar, he too could see the image and instantly fell under the spell.

'She's beautiful,' Hal sighed.

'She looks dead.' Caspar felt a deep loss, an unbearable

weight of sadness crushing his heart. 'Look, she is dead, crushed beneath the hard skin of the crystal.'

'Maybe, but it's only some sort of mirage in the crystal.' The image produced no emotion in Hal. 'Maybe it's a sort of memory of something that once happened here to the people who owned all this ancient treasure.' Hal laughed at the absurdity of his own idea.

Caspar looked deeper into the crystal at the colourless skin of the woman trapped in the stone. He felt as if his eyes could melt through the moonstone and touch her. The deeper he looked at her the more hope swelled in his grieving heart.

The colour flowed back into the woman's cheeks and the grey-blue lips warmed to a healthy rose-red. Even the reddish hue that streaked her brown locks curling in ringlets to her shoulders glistened in the thawing warmth of the moonstone, like hammered copper reflecting the evening sun. A flicker passed across her eyelids and slowly they opened to reveal eyes of deep cerulean blue. It was like searching the heavens on a perfect mid-summer's day. Caspar felt her returning gaze reaching out to probe his emotions – his wants, his fears, his needs – through the channel of his own tear-filled eyes.

The woman stretched out a slender arm as if trying to touch him and Caspar felt overwhelmed with love and happiness. But then his agony returned as he realized that she was imploring him for help. Her lips moved as if she was calling to him.

'I can't hear her,' cried Caspar in despair. 'She needs our help.' He felt desperate and helpless as he watched the crystal drag her down into its depths again and frost over her vibrant face. The frost dulled her lips and cheeks, and her hair stiffened into icicles. The brilliant eyes closed and her mouth opened into an agonized and silent scream just as the ice froze solid and trapped her in that perpetual pose of torture.

'No! No . . .' Caspar's voice trailed off into a sob and Hal jerked the stone away from his white-knuckled grasp.

'She needs our help,' Caspar found himself yelling inexplicably.

'It was just an image – a vision.' Hal struggled to sound

rational and put a comforting arm round his distraught nephew. 'It was a trick of the witch-craft that made the stones. It wasn't real. It was the fears in your mind.'

'You saw it too,' protested Caspar. 'The face was real.'

'I saw what you saw in your own mind. I was looking at your nightmare.' Hal fought to find a reasonable explanation of what he had seen. 'It was just an evil image created by black magic. Now pull yourself together, otherwise we'll be dead too like the woman. We've got to get out of here. Come on.' Hal firmly dragged the boy by the shoulder who was fumbling with the leather leash of the other small moonstone. He slipped the smaller egg-sized orb into his pocket and slid the larger moonstone into the leather pouch. He fastened it securely to his belt, twisting in extra knots to make sure it couldn't come loose, as he followed his uncle out into the tunnels again. All thought of the rest of the treasure was banished from his mind by the compelling force of the moonstone. Hal was already striding ahead as he descended into the darkness of the tunnel.

'Here, Spar, bring the light. Look; what's that?' Hal pointed to a white object that hung, like a shredded rag, from a point of rock.

Caspar raised the moonstone above their heads to get a better look. 'I don't know,' he replied, stepping closer to investigate, then exclaimed coldly, 'My God, it's a piece of flesh! Hal, it's skin!'

They examined the shard of hairless flesh but didn't touch it. The skin was torn and grey with decay and, where the blood had dripped onto the stone, it had formed brown congealed stains. Another shred of the carcass hung from a spiked rock just a little further on. Caspar looked at Hal, his jaw sagging in horror unable to speak.

'Well, all I can say is, I hope it's a Vaalakan,' said Hal sternly, trying to cover up his revulsion.

'Are you sure it's a man?'

'Well, it might be a woman, Spar,' he replied sarcastically, 'but yes of course I'm sure. That's human all right.'

77

'We'd better get out of here.' Caspar pulled at Hal's arm. 'There's got to be an over-sized predator down here somewhere. We've got to get out.'

They started to run back down towards the vaulted chamber. Maybe it's a mountain lion or a bear that's using this tunnel as a lair, he thought as he hurried after Hal. What kind of a gruesome flesh-eater would live down here?

Chapter 5

It came from in front. Their first warning was a deep, throaty grunt before the two boys stared full into its jaws, into the ribbed tunnel of its throat. The scaly bulk of the monster was of such gargantuan proportions that it blocked the tunnel leading back to the central chamber. All the colour seemed to have been sucked from its body except for the blue veins that protruded through the off-white skin beneath its throat. The veins pulsed visibly. It swung a clawed limb forward and then another, its low-slung belly rasping over the ground. Then it stopped and solemnly stretched out its neck, probing the air with its gnarly snout, nostrils flaring. It snorted as it caught their scent and a snake's tongue flickered from its mouth.

Caspar's vision was filled with the compelling sight of its curved fangs glistening with saliva. A yellow slime crusted its gums and clung to the sharp white lines of the tapered teeth. The rancid stench of decaying animals being digested within its gut belched out with feverish heat.

Caspar and Hal backed up the tunnel, terrified.

'Don't run,' breathed Hal. 'Nice and slowly now. He can't see us.'

Long imprisonment in the sunless pit had dissolved the eyes of the beast, leaving a layer of grey flesh that sealed over the rolling socket. It might not be able to see, thought Caspar, but it can certainly smell us.

They continued to step backwards. Every reflex screamed at them to run in panic but years of hunting wild boar in the forest had trained them to suppress fear in order to survive attack.

Two shrivelled stumps projected from behind the monster's shoulder blades, supporting a flap of withered skin that wagged feebly. A hooked talon hung uselessly from the tip of the appendage. He could not believe what confronted him: a huge carnivorous reptile with slicing teeth, grotesquely enlarged nostrils and what once must have been wings. However atrophied, it should not exist, not now, not after a thousand years.

The mutated dragon slithered towards them, its hooked claws rolled out sideways in a circuitous motion, swinging forwards from the elbow. It advanced slowly but inexorably.

Caspar found that Hal was dragging him backwards by the arm. His amazement had rooted him to the spot but now step by step he and Hal retreated down the tunnel. Not for one second did their eyes stray from the dragon. A crunching sound underfoot alerted Caspar to a change in their surroundings. To his dismay Caspar discovered that they had backed into a den strewn with skulls, disembodied limbs and broken carcasses. Most of the rotted meat was of deer but some of the carcasses were reminiscent of fox, or goat. There was even the sandy tail and hindquarters of what appeared to be the remains of a mountain lion. Most of the animals were half eaten, carelessly chewed and then discarded. This predator killed for pleasure not just for food. In desperation, he cast the light of the moonstone on to the smooth rounded walls of the lair. There was no exit. They had retreated straight into the dragon's larder. They were trapped.

Huge pointed fangs chomped in its jaw, the sharp edges of the teeth slicing against each other. A curious gurgling noise came from its throat, a growl but wetter, as if the snarl was drowning in an excess of saliva.

The boys stood shoulder to shoulder, daggers drawn, their faces ashen, reflecting the unnatural, bloodless colour of the dragon that had cornered them.

'We'll make a good stand,' said Hal uncertainly.

'Sure we will.' Caspar didn't sound convinced but he gripped his dagger in both hands with fierce determination.

'We are men of Torra Alta. Our forefathers drove out the dragons. We need not fear this worm.' Hal's voice became stronger and more defiant.

'Worm!' shouted Caspar at the mutant. 'Coward!' He, Caspar the first and only son of the great Branwolf, Baron of Torra Alta, would not be a coward like this monster. If this was to be his final stand he would die with his dagger buried in the dragon's belly and die bravely. He would die a hero and his deeds would be praised in ballads to be sung all across Belbidia.

The dragon's macabre gurgling became louder, bursting into a full-throated roar. The flaps of skin under its neck bloated like a bladder full of air and vibrated to amplify the horrendous thunder from its throat. Suddenly a blast of air gushed from its mouth and the sack of skin hung loosely in folds again. Its hot breath smelt at first sickly-sweet like something fermenting but as it belched at them they recoiled from the rancid stench of rotting meat and were forced to shrink back further into its lair.

'You decrepit lizard,' Hal laughed in its face, 'you're just a bedraggled bag of wind.'

'Where's your dragon-fire then?' sneered Caspar. 'Not much of a dragon without fire, are you?'

The dragon made an unexpectedly agile lunge at them, rushing forwards, but then stopped short and edged back as if it were toying with them.

Caspar fought a scream in his throat and tried to twist it into a defiant battle-cry, but his voice trailed off in the face of the leviathan lizard. In a trembling whisper he appealed to his uncle, 'What the hell are we going to do?'

'What can we do, Spar?' Hal sounded close to despair. 'Except . . . maybe . . . let's see. Give me that moonstone. Quick!'

Hal snatched at the leather strap, wrapping the end of the moonstone's leash tightly around his hand and swinging the weight of the stone like a pendulum, waiting for the dragon to advance.

The dragon's cumbersome bulk swayed from side to side, matching the rhythm of the swinging moonstone. The scales on its fleshy white belly rasped on the ground, cracking and splintering bones as its weight shifted on three-toed claws over the carcasses.

The worm reared up as high as the roof would allow, its massive frame dwarfing the boys as it prepared to strike.

'When I shout, dive sideways to distract him,' ordered Hal.

'Thanks a million,' murmured the younger boy, 'I've always wanted to go down in history as the decoy.'

'Just do it.'

The forked tongue flickered and the mutant dragon struck. Hal yelled and Caspar obligingly plunged to the floor amongst the decaying carcasses, drawing the dragon away from its original target. It twisted in mid-strike and Hal swung the moonstone like a mace at the creature's naked belly. An agonized scream pealed round the lair and Caspar thought the very noise would suffocate them. But the dragon reared up again for a second strike and Caspar quickly scrambled to his feet to make another sacrificial dive.

'Go for it, Hal: it worked.'

But this time as the dragon lunged at them its giant claw swiped sideways and wrenched the leather from Hal's hand. The moonstone hurtled aside to hammer against the wall, spraying out a spectacular shower of sparks. It lay out of reach behind the vast bulk of the monster, its ghostly light silhouetting the spikes of the dragon's spinal fins that ridged its back. The great beast shifted its bulk round so that the barbs of its arrow-head tail hooked into the moonstone's leash as if claiming the stone for its own. Dimly in the back of Caspar's panicked mind, he realized that the heaps of ancient jewels and armour in the other chamber were the dragon's prized hoard. The moonstone must be part of its precious treasure. The beast seemed no longer drawn by the light now that it lay behind it, beyond the reach of the humans. Its forked tongue flickered out towards them, feeling their presence by tasting their weak scent on the air. The monster towered above them, the flap of skin swelling beneath its throat as it bellowed out its triumphant, gurgling roar and prepared to strike.

Caspar's desperate fingers fumbled for the smaller moonstone, his trembling hand barely able to grip the smooth stone that felt cool to his touch. Unlike the larger moonstone it produced no more than a tingle through his nerves. Flinging it sideways, he prayed that the light would distract the monster. Its white rays scattered over the vault of the chamber, suddenly illuminating the dagger-like stalactites high up in the gloomy roof of the cave. The dragon twitched his cavernous nostrils, momentarily jerking its head towards the moonstone but then ignored it and reared up, coiling its neck back ready to make a final strike.

This is it, thought Caspar. He gripped his dagger in both hands so that when the monster fell on him it would first bite through the blade. He felt proud as he watched his uncle do the same, proud that neither of them would shame their ancestors in a cowardly death.

'Time for a prayer,' said Hal, almost in resignation. 'I can't think of anything else. Dear Lord and Father, deliver us from this creature of Hell and let my blade sink deep into its cold heart.'

Something dragged Caspar's eyes away from the dragon towards the bright glow of the larger moonstone. From somewhere deep in his subconscious his own unsolicited prayer formed into simple words.

'Help us.' He was surprised by his thoughts, not understanding to whom he had made the appeal. 'Help us,' he murmured.

An ear-splitting shriek howled from the monster. Where its moist and curling tongue should have been now projected a steel arrowhead. For a moment the sickly-pale monster reeled on its haunches, swaying and teetering like a gigantic old drunk as it lurched forward at them. Caspar thought its vast tonnage would, at any second, crush them to a pulp. Finally it slumped to the ground in a thunderous crash, its jaw shattering on the bedrock a mere foot from the boys' toes. Dark purplish blood gobbed in spurts where the crossbow bolt split the scales at the back of its neck and a pulsing stream of the puce fluid flooded out between the gaps of its serrated teeth. Its limbs convulsed in agony. The lengthy tail, thrashing violently, brought boulders down from the rock-face above, and its back arched into a rigid spasm of pain.

It all happened so quickly: Caspar had no time to think until the first of his rescuers scaled over the quivering mound of the dragon's body. Blond-haired men, scantily clad in rough skins, brandished double-headed axes. Four of them scrambled over the bloated reptilian belly, and although he had never seen one Caspar had no doubt that they were Vaalakans.

Their attention was concentrated totally on the Belbidian boys. More Vaalakans squeezed into the foetid space, bearing torches. Satisfaction spread across their bearded faces in the orange light of these spitting firebrands. One of them had a crossbow which he levelled at Hal's head while another spat some strange and ugly words at their captives. A fat ginger-bearded man clambered over the mountain of dragon belly, grunting, to grin at Hal and Caspar.

'He saying drop your knives, he say.' The Vaalakan had trouble forming the words.

The knuckles on Caspar's hand blanched.

'They're not knives, they're daggers,' the young boy replied defiantly. It seemed a pointless thing to say but Caspar thought that a simple 'no' would have seemed a little too blunt in the circumstances.

'Knives, daggers, it matter not. Just be dropping them.' The ginger-bearded man reddened as his voice grew angrier. 'You obeys me, you weak Belbidak boylings.'

Hal roared with rage and charged at the man. The crossbow swung to follow the youth's charge but the ginger leader raised an arm to stay the shot and prepared to meet Hal's attack himself. One quick blow with the handle of his axe caught Hal on the back of the neck and he collapsed to the ground. Caspar ran to help his friend but as he went to kneel beside Hal a boot caught him under the chin and he sprawled backwards.

'You do nothings now. No move, no talk, no breathings unless I tell.'

Caspar watched as Hal's fingers crawled towards his dagger, which had fallen just out of reach. The big man roared with laughter so that his belly shook before he stamped the heel of his boot onto the back of Hal's hand, grinding the fingers into the rock.

Hal screamed. It was a short yell, rapidly swallowed, but there was no disguising the pain it had expressed. Caspar realized that he had never heard his uncle scream out in pain before: it was too much for the young heir of Torra Alta. He dived at the dagger and in a blind rage stabbed wildly, his senses lost in the lust for battle.

He came to with the sound of Hal's voice urgently crying his name in his ear.

He lay still, hoping that the world would soon stop spinning. His hands would not move and gradually, in his befuddled state, Caspar understood that he was bound hand and foot. Hal's arms were also tied in a twisted knot behind his back but still he knelt protectively over his younger relative.

A thick hairy-backed hand grasped Caspar's collar and started to pull the boy to his hobbled feet. Hal rammed his shoulder into the Vaalakan.

'Just leave him alone! Don't you dare touch him, you grotesque excuse for a human, or else, or else . . .'

'Or else? Yes, or else?' sneered the Vaalakan leader. 'You is killing me on your little own, Belbidak? You not have enough beating for one day, or you wanting more? Easy more is. I enjoy.' He laughed from deep in his gut, knowing that the two Belbidians were conquered. 'I gives few more minutes so that boyling can walk. And then we go.' He returned to his vulgar native tongue, cracking out orders to the four men as well as shouting over the dragon's anguished body. Another blond-haired man sprang with more finesse over the carcass. He was similarly clad in boots made from hide, laced in a criss-cross pattern up to his bulging calves, and a ragged cloak made from black bearskin slung over one shoulder. He looked younger than the others, not much older than Hal, with a considerable bulk of lean muscle bunching into aggressive knots across his bullish shoulders. Once he had landed on his feet he pulled on a heavy chain and an animal followed him over.

'We haves time to be feeding our pets, now,' laughed the ginger-bearded man.

The animal was big, about the size of an ox, but it seemed uncertain whether to walk on two legs or four. The short back legs were solid with muscle that comfortably supported its weight as it reared onto its haunches, the easier to slash at the belly of the dragon with its long claws. It ripped a tear through the thick scaly hide exposing a coil of pulsating entrails. The axeman wrenched at the animal's chain, thumping it on the nose with the flat of his axe to prevent it from plunging its bulbous head into the wet maw of the dragon. The beast jerked its blunt nose backwards, shaking its head with the pain from the blow so that its shaggy mane flicked from side to side. From its shoulders downwards the beast was almost hairless with only sparse clumps of coarse bristle sprouting along the length of its hunched spine. They poked out between the rolls of baggage lashed to its back.

The putrid stench of the dragon's entrails rapidly brought Caspar to his senses and he looked up with revulsion at the sight of this Vaalakan beast that grunted so noisily. Its great claws rattled over the ground as it struggled reluctantly away from the bulk of the dragon and contented itself with the putrid leg of a goat, which it splintered between its fangs. It discarded the bones however for a juicier carcass and plunged its head into the maggoty cavity of a hind, wrenching out an internal organ that the dragon had left untouched. Perhaps it had been the rattling claws of this heavy animal they had heard earlier on the other side of the tunnel before the explosion, thought Caspar with repugnance.

The young, insipidly blond Vaalakan yanked viciously on the chain attached to a ring piercing the creature's pug-nose. The animal's head came up from the carcass dripping with gore and offal. But what revolted Caspar most was the shape of its face: hairless with big round eyes and a flat muzzle. If it had not been for the long canines that pushed out between its lips, he would have described it as almost human. The forehead sloped back too sharply, and the nostrils were splayed too widely, but otherwise it was distinctly human.

'Go now,' announced the leader. 'We, all. Now.'

'What do you want with us?' demanded Hal.

'You, not in position to makes question. Get up.'

'Why don't you just kill us now and be done with it,' continued Hal valiantly.

'No. Kill later. First we walk. Walk long way. Then you talk. Look. See, you have good knives, good clothes, you is someone's children and that someone is big in your fortress. You talks to us, because you have many things to tell. And you have white stones.' First he strode to the smaller moonstone lying near the dragon's head and stared intently into its heart. He dropped it carelessly. Then he crunched over the broken bones of half-eaten carcasses to reach the tail of the dragon from where he delicately lifted the moonstone by its leash. The dragon's tail thumped weakly and Caspar understood with horror that the beast was not yet dead. The bolt from the crossbow must have missed its brain. The Vaalakan's face lit up as he gazed at the mesmerizing light of the larger moonstone. 'You talks. You tells us about this. Master looking for this many long years. We finds this and we find boylings from big castle at same time. Most strange.'

'We aren't from the fortress,' Caspar burst out. 'My father is a smith and he made the daggers. We live in the east. We know nothing about the fortress. And we know nothing about that white stone.'

'So, why you is under the fortress? You say me why.'

'Because my father was delivering weapons and . . .'

'We got lost,' Hal finished for him.

'Yes, and why this other thing here this other stone? You bringing that with you to find the great sorcery stone.'

'No!' Caspar vainly objected.

'And this with writings on.' The Vaalakan waved a sodden and screwed up ball of parchment in their faces. 'Why, the little boyling is having this map thing? You say me.'

'Because, um, because we needed it to find the way to the fortress,' replied Hal hurriedly.

'And we don't know about the fortress you see,' added Caspar hopefully.

'You tells lies, and very bad lies too,' laughed the Vaalakan. 'Little childrens from important families in Belbidak is no good at lies. We go now.' Carefully he strung the larger moonstone around his neck and scrambled over the belly of the dragon.

A hand shoved Caspar from behind and his stomach turned as they were forced to grovel through the pool of dark sticky blood that had oozed from the dragon's wounds. As his foot touched the scales and he clambered over the springy ribcage he could faintly feel the slow double thud of two giant hearts. The grotesque beast groaned and the bladder of skin under its neck quivered and ruffled as they were dragged from the chamber. Ahead of him Caspar was drawn by the light of the moonstone strung around the Vaalakan's neck, shining pure and white in contrast to the evil horrors of the bloody chamber. The boy felt a sharp pang stab at his heart as he thought of the moonstone in the clutches of the enemy and for a moment he struggled against his bonds.

'Leave it, Spar! It's useless struggling with them here.'

'But I must have the moonstone.' Caspar knew that his words must sound demented to his uncle but somehow he couldn't stop them forming on his tongue.

Hal looked at him in shock. 'Are you mad, Spar?'

The younger, spry Vaalakan followed Caspar's urgent stare and looked towards his chief who carried the glowing orb. 'Is you warlocks as well as cubs of nobleman, with your black magics toy?' Caspar thought his tone was more sinister, edged with a touch of awe. 'The Big Priest of Vaal-Peor will be many pleased at our trophy today. A Belbidak trophy. And at me. I first heard you scratchings, scratchings like rats.'

The hobbles snatched at his ankles as Caspar shuffled

through one awkward step after another. His head was still dizzy from the beating he had suffered at the hands of these brutish men and he was beginning to feel sick. Hal looked bruised and none the better for a raw, swelling wound that marked his temple, but he held his head high and thrust out his chest proudly. Caspar made an effort to do the same, but he winced from the bruising around his upper torso. With every painful step the two boys wrenched backwards against their bonds, screaming abuse at their captors until they were red in the face and their throats burned with hoarseness. The Vaalakans ignored them, merely snarling angrily amongst themselves as they jostled for space in the tunnels. In helpless frustration, Hal and Caspar resorted to bickering with one another.

'I wish that dragon had eaten us,' the dejected boy grumbled to Hal, as they were dragged by their leather bonds back towards the vaulted chamber.

'Well, I don't. Otherwise, I wouldn't get a chance to kill these savages, these dirty weasels. I shall kill every last one.'

'How, Hal? Just tell me how.'

The older boy fell silent for a while, leaving Caspar to brood. Anger and fear were breeding together in his heart to conceive an unnatural, unbearable concoction of emotions.

'I'll find a way,' Hal began brightly, trying to raise their morale. 'All we need is a strategy. Like all pagans they are primitive and cruel and will use only their vicious and brutal instincts to lead them. We will be able to out-think their barbaric minds. Fear and pain are their chiefs: ours will be strategy.'

'You sound like you read that in a book,' observed Caspar, eager to grasp onto any thought that might distract him from the horrors of their predicament. 'I thought you said books were for women and churchmen only.'

'The ones *you* read are. You're the son of a baron and you don't bother to learn about the craft of war or what makes a man a leader.'

'I do so. I have read all the great legends. I know the tales of the Dragon Wars backwards.' Caspar dug his heels into the rock only to be yanked helplessly forward with such force that he thought his arms would be wrenched from their sockets.

'Stories, just stories.' Hal was scathing. 'I'm talking about real books – manuals, filled with instructions and the teachings of the tacticians through the centuries.' The dark-haired youth grunted with the effort as he too struggled to free his bonds. 'The ones with diagrams that show battle manoeuvres and how to build war-engines. Real books, Spar. Damn it; I can't get . . . it's impossible to get these bonds off. Proper books for men.'

'You're not telling . . . This is useless, the knots won't budge. You're not telling me that you've read such books.'

'Branwolf's library is full of volumes of battle plans taken from Belbidian, Salisien and Camaalian wars, as well as manuals on leadership and the logistics of command. They're very informative.' Hal's voice was full of pompous indignation.

'Well, it's a shame you haven't learnt to practise any of what you've read.'

'It's a shame you haven't even bothered to read any. You'll need the skills of leadership more than I will,' retorted Hal.

'I've read lots,' objected Caspar, 'but this is hardly the time to fight, is it?'

Hal laughed, his contrary mood dissolving readily into frankness. 'No, you're right. You're not often right but this time you are.'

'Thanks a lot, Hal,' Caspar grumbled. 'And my nose still hurts,' he added accusingly.

'Well, you deserved it at the time.'

'What words you hissing in the snaky voices?' The Vaalakan leader jerked forcefully on the leather thong strapping Caspar's wrists. 'I thinks we wanting to move faster.'

The stream, which had led them to this part of the cave system, flowed rapidly through the centre of the cathedral-like cavern. It looked all too familiar except that, in the firelight of the Vaalakan torches, the tainted water took on a sanguine stain. Caspar shivered involuntarily, hoping that this river of blood was not a dolorous portent. They forded the stream and entered a fresh passageway obscured from view by a water-sculpted pillar of stone.

The grating noise from the claws of the hairless beast, caught Caspar's nerves. The animal was awkward and unnatural. It seemed unable to pick its feet up properly and dragged the long spiked claws over the rough stone, with a fierce scratching sound. Every now and then the young powerfully muscled Vaalakan pulled affectionately at the animal's stubby ears and muttered away to it in unintelligible grunts.

'What kind of an animal is that foul creature?' Caspar asked his uncle.

'It's a Vaalakan. They're meant to be human beings.'

'You know exactly what I mean: that hairless hog with the face of a prehistoric man.'

'It's a troll.'

'How do you know?' demanded Caspar, uncertain that Hal had any real knowledge but was just pretending to be authoritative.

'I know everything, because I take the trouble to find out.'

'No, seriously how do you know?' coaxed the boy as he leant back against his ties to perplex the Vaalakan brute who was dragging him into the new-found passage.

'"The Illustrated Book of Animals from Northern Climes, Rare and Common" – so there.'

'Don't believe you. It would have to have game animals or hunting dogs in the title for you to look at it,' argued the younger boy, still straining against the bulky fur-clad warrior.

'All right, I give in. I made it up and I'm only guessing. But it isn't a bear and it isn't a hog and it isn't a man, so I reckon it's a troll.' Hal lowered his voice. 'Look, can't you put your mind to something useful and work out how we are going to break free rather than worry about stupid things like what type of animal that is?'

Caspar was silent for a moment. There must be some way, he thought to himself. A moment will come when they are off-guard: they must stop to eat or sleep. Maybe these primitive savages would fight amongst themselves as Hal had suggested. There was nothing for it but to bide their time. 'They look like they know where they're going,' he whispered to Hal. 'Let them lead us to the surface and then we'll make plans. I can't think of anything else we can do.'

The route that the Vaalakans had chosen was cramped. The tunnel roof gradually shelved until the troll was forced to crouch so that its elbows pushed up alongside its shoulder blades. Even the taller Vaalakans stooped to avoid hitting their heads. The tunnel could not have accommodated the albino dragon so if there were any more of its kind at least they were free from that terror, thought Caspar. But even that notion could not raise his spirits from the gloom into which he had sunk. It was all his fault, everything. How could he have been so churlish; how could he have allowed his selfish pride and childish curiosity to lead Hal into such danger? The remorse whipped his conscience mercilessly: if only he hadn't been such a fool and disobeyed his father. Preposterous hope suggested to him that maybe a Belbidian patrol would rescue them when they reached the surface. Hal deserves such luck even if I don't. Yes, and maybe the Vaalakans will turn into swans and fly away. How could he think such ridiculous things?

A curtain of clear light loomed ahead where a shaft dropped into the tunnel from above. Then the firebrands flickered in a rush of clean air that caressed Caspar's face and brought new hope to his defeated spirit. Perhaps once they were out of this evil place with its dragon, dungeons and contaminated water something would bring them luck. The chimney was sheer sided and rose five paces up above their heads, impossible to climb with their hands bound. Perhaps they will untie us, thought Caspar; perhaps this is our first chance.

But the grunting Vaalakans had other plans. They had obviously used this route before because they ascended the chimney with the skill of travelling tumblers performing a favoured act. First the troll reared up onto his back legs, then one of the Vaalakans clambered over the rolls of baggage to stand on its shoulders. He was followed by another who leapt up the living ladder to reach the outside world – from where he lowered a rope for the rest of the party. Hal and Caspar were left guarded by the crossbowman and the sneering bullish Vaalakan holding the troll.

'Well, are you going to cut these ties so we can climb out?' demanded Hal. 'Or are you too afraid now that your over-muscled nursemaids have gone?'

'Shut ugly mouth,' growled the young savage. His command of Belbidian was evidently limited, but he understood Hal's mocking tone. He gestured to the man with the crossbow who promptly shoved the tip of a loaded bolt against Hal's temple. 'Me Scragg, no afraid.' He smiled mockingly as he fastened the dangling rope to Hal's wrists and yelled up the shaft to the others above.

The rope snapped taut and Hal was wrenched up by his wrists into the air. His body slammed against the sides of the shaft, collecting another raw batch of grazes as his skin and clothing snagged on protruding rocks. As Caspar was dragged into the open air and bumped onto the moss-covered ground, his captors roared with sadistic laughter at his obvious discomfort. Hal was still swearing on the ground when Scragg emerged from the underworld and the Northman virtually danced with delight at Hal's pain. He placed the heel of his skin-boots over the Belbidian's head and pressed it firmly into the mud. 'Scragg, no afraid. Me likes your pain.'

The ginger-bearded leader spoke sharply to Scragg who reluctantly released the Torra Altan. Muttering away in his own language, he skulked off to seek his pet troll, which had been left to make its own way out of the labyrinth.

There was, of course, no Belbidian welcoming party to rescue the two boys. Caspar knew there wouldn't be but all the same it was a disappointment. The only compensation was the brilliant blue sky, common at these high altitudes, and the crisp, fresh air. Caspar's first objective was to find his bearings. It was impossible to judge how far or in which direction they had travelled underground. His legs told him they had come a long way but for all he knew it could have been in circles. However, he understood that the tunnels provided easier more direct routes through the Yellow Mountains since the surface of the range was mostly untracked and liberally scarred by ravines and precipices. They could be several days' ride from Torra Alta for all he knew and out of reach of any chance rescue. The ridge spanning two peaks to the north of them was vaguely familiar and he decided that they must be far to the west in the high mountains. The head of the valley rose steeply, finally soaring to a crown of sheer black-faced cliffs that stood in a crescent formation of protective rock. Caspar caught a glimpse of brilliant sunlight dancing on the still waters of a high mountain tarn. 'Mirror Lake,' he murmured.

Hal nodded. 'At least two leagues from Torra Alta – a good day's ride through this terrain.'

The two boys stared glumly around them at the pale golden hue of the distant peaks which gave the Yellow Mountains their name. The high concentration of sulphurous deposits in the land had fooled many would-be gold prospectors. Several had died of exposure as they sought the elusive gold. It was like chasing the source of a rainbow: the yellow hue was clearly discernible from afar and always faded to a mere dusky brown in the immediate valley. The vegetation was sparse. A huddled cluster of juniper bushes cowered in the lee of a boulder. Coarse grasses, bracken and the occasional dwarfed birch sprouted from the acid soil, but generally the ground was carpeted in scree and rubble that had tumbled from the encircling cliffs. We're above the tree-line, deduced Caspar. The sharp nip to the air reinforced his conclusion. Ravines in perpetual shadow cosseted fields of grey snow that had survived the summer months.

The craggy peaks above them gave Caspar the uncanny feeling that they were being held in the palm of a giant upturned claw. A tarn nestled at the base of the tooth-like peaks and a fresh stream slipped merrily away, draining water from the boggy marshes that languished around the mountain lake. The sun had passed its zenith and was now sliding down behind the peaks that glowered over them.

A large knuckled hand hauled Caspar to his feet. Like two stubborn pack mules the boys were forcibly pulled behind their captors along a narrow goat track at the edge of the freshwater stream.

'Keep your foots running, boylings,' ordered the leader, who had not spoken for some time. 'You keeps on pulling backwards and little Belbidak boys will be sorry, will be.'

Hal spat at the ground and stared defiantly at the big man, but did not say anything. He strained hard against the leash, digging his heels into the ground with every hobbled step until the leather cords around his wrists sawed through the flesh and a bracelet of blood adorned his forearms.

'Me say you be sorry.' The leader then returned to his native tongue, doling out rapid orders to his men. In no time Caspar and Hal found themselves lashed to the spiny back of the troll like two sacks of flour, wedged between the bundles of furs and clanking cauldrons. Ginger beard scratched Hal's nose as the Vaalakan thrust his face at him, choking the proud youth with stale breath. 'And now you is sorry. Troll make for bad horse. Very uncomfortable.'

'Parsley,' said Hal matter-of-factly, leaving Caspar completely puzzled as to what his uncle was talking about.

'Parzley, parzley, why you say parzley?' demanded the Vaalakan, enraged at not being able to understand the Belbidian words in case they constituted a grave insult.

'Because it's a little green herb and you need some for your foul breath, Red Beard,' laughed Hal, much too bravely for his own good, and Caspar winced at the sound of the resounding smack that hit his uncle across the mouth.

'Rudbardak, no Red Beard.'

Blood gathered in Caspar's head as he swung upside down to the rhythm of the troll's gait. Its knobbly vertebrae and sharp bones protruded from far too many places, stabbing Caspar and grinding at his ribs, while its perpetual rolling motion made Caspar feel sick. He imagined this was the type of sickness that people suffered at sea.

'Where do you think they are taking us?' moaned Hal.

'North.'

'How do you know?'

'Because of the sun.' Their shadows stretched away to the right and the eastern aspects of the valleys were already plunged into premature night. 'It'll get cold soon.'

It was difficult to communicate with the air being thumped from their lungs by the troll's awkward gait, but they managed to speak in short breathless bursts. Together, they guessed at their woeful fate in the clutches of the Vaalakans and vainly tried to plan an escape. Every once in a while the cumbersome beast twisted its neck around to stare at them with its human eyes. Threads of saliva trailed from the corner of its mouth.

Speaking in stiff Belbidian for the benefit of his prisoners, Scragg crooned softly to his pet. 'Later. When we be finishing with them, my little one, you cans be playing with them then.'

'What do you think he means by play with?' asked Caspar.

'I don't think we want to know.' Hal wriggled to relieve some of the cramp that stabbed at his muscles. His arms were trussed up tightly behind his back and his shoulder joints felt like they were dislocating. 'Whatever happens though, Spar, we must not tell them anything about the fortress unless it's lies. If you have to talk be as inventive as you can.'

'Of course,' Caspar replied after a moment's pause. He hadn't been listening to his uncle's voice and his mind had wandered away to fret over his father in Torra Alta. He would be grief-stricken by their disappearance. But even thoughts of his father were fleeting. His mind continually returned to the moonstone around the chief Vaalakan's neck. He fancied somehow that it was summoning him. When he closed his eyes he could see the image of its pearly glow in his mind.

Northward progress was slow, though judging from their distorted upside-down view, the two prisoners reckoned they were being taken steadily downwards. Twilight in the narrow steep-sided valley was a protracted phenomenon. It came early but lingered in soft pastel shades on the west-facing slopes which were not yet swallowed up by the shadows rising out of the valley floor. Eventually they were all stumbling through the dark and the Vaalakans called a halt. The leashes girthing the troll were unbuckled and Caspar and Hal slumped to the ground.

'We makes camp here,' announced the big Vaalakan somewhat unnecessarily since his men were already gathering kindling for a fire. 'And no thinking of taking yourself a little walking off now, because I have made you chained to the animal.'

'We is thanking you,' replied Hal with practised sarcasm.

The fire brought welcome warmth and the tantalizing aroma of a stew cooking in its flames. The two boys sat huddled together for comfort and warmth. Their arms were still pinioned behind their backs, hunger and cold now compounding their discomfort.

Hal suddenly burst out in a fit of rage at the Vaalakans. 'I shall kill you. Kill you all. My God will torture your toady souls and you will scream in Hell for eternity.'

At this point the troll decided to make a new nest for the night. It limbered up onto all fours puffing and grunting with the effort, then stretched and ambled over to the other side of the campfire dragging Caspar and Hal by their wrists, heedless of their protesting screams. The Vaalakans cackled hysterically, clutching at their bloated stomachs as they enjoyed the Belbidians' humiliation and helplessness. Caspar felt sick with anger and shame.

'I'll get them,' snarled Hal between clenched teeth. 'I'll torture them to death, especially that low-life Scragg. I'll mince him into a thousand pieces with his own axe and feed him to Wartooth.'

Caspar reflected fondly on their faithful hound. 'No, we don't want to poison Wartooth. I'd feed that milk-coloured weasel to his own pet troll. Much more fitting.'

The thought of revenge seemed to restore Hal's dignity and as the enemy settled down for the night he muttered to his shivering companion beside him, 'No need to give them an easy night, Spar,' and started to yell at the top of his voice. 'Hey, what about some food? Give us some food here.'

Caspar's nagging stomach urged him to join in the clamour. 'We're no use to you if you starve us to death.'

'Fat boylings not need flesh to eat. You be living off your own blubber for much days yet,' laughed Scragg.

'You can't starve us,' protested Hal.

'No?' Scragg's sadistic tone twisted into sly delight. 'Ah, but I, Scragg, such nice person. I give you my supper to show how big is my heart.'

The spiteful young Northman jumped to his feet, balancing a plate with feigned elegance on the tips of his fingers.

'It for you. An offering.'

Knowing that Scragg could only be planning some abominable trick, the two boys stared with expressionless faces. But Caspar found himself wanting to believe the cruel words of the Vaalakan. With a jolt he realized that his resistance was being weakened by fear and degradation. The Vaalakan extended the piled plate towards his prisoners but then stopped.

'Ah! but your hands is tied, yes? Ha! So you must be grovelling like dogs for your food.' He laughed hideously and spat into the stew before letting it slide from the tilted plate onto the ground and then spread it with the toe of his boot. 'My offering. You be eating that, you Belbidak brats.'

'Stop it, Hal. Ignore him,' shouted Caspar as his uncle tripped over his hobbles in a hopeless attempt to attack the sneering Vaalakan. 'At least don't give him the satisfaction of seeing us humiliated.'

Hal sat back unhappily. 'I'm starving, Spar. What are we going to do?'

'I don't know.' Caspar's voice cracked with emotional strain. 'I'm afraid.' He shuffled closer to his uncle. 'I'm afraid and I'm sorry and it's all my fault.'

Chapter 6

A lonesome howl split the silence of that chill cloudless night. Caspar started from a fitful sleep, his mind struggling to separate the cry in the darkness from the demons and banshees that had screeched through his dreams. As his irrational fears retreated to the esoteric universe of his dreams, he remembered his cold and hunger. His arms were numb. My fingers, he thought in panic, realizing he could barely feel them. He gave Hal a jolt with his knee.

'You awake?'

'No.'

'Hal, flex your fingers.'

'What?!'

'Move your fingers about quickly, or you might lose them to frostbite.' Caspar used his shoulder to push himself awkwardly up onto his knees and rubbed his lashed arms rapidly up and down his back. 'Mine are frozen solid: I can't feel them.' He frantically tried to pump blood through the tight tourniquets of their leather bonds to warm his fingers.

Hal immediately realized Caspar had a serious point and followed suit. 'We must keep awake, Spar. Keep moving.'

The blood started to feed back into Caspar's hands, but far from being warm and comforting it felt as if a thousand stabbing needles pumped through his arteries, piercing metal into every last capillary. He bent double and gritted his teeth with the pain until it subsided, leaving his hands hot and throbbing. When he looked up again the black shape of a Vaalakan brandishing an axe towered over him, grunting angrily.

'I think he's telling us to stay still,' suggested Caspar,

keeping his voice steady and dignified. 'Leave us alone, you fat ox, unless you're going to bring us some food,' added Hal with chattering teeth.

The Vaalakan only grunted again and continued his watch. He steadily paced the perimeter of the camp, stepping over the black snoring mounds cocooned in animal skins. Keeping half an eye on the prisoners, he periodically stopped to study the magnificent glow of the harvest moon.

'What's he looking at the moon for?' Hal was puzzled and any conversation filled the long hours of a wakeful night.

'To tell the time, I imagine.' The auburn-haired youth raised his head to follow the Vaalakan's line of vision. 'Isn't it an amazing colour? Do you think it could be an omen?'

'Yesterday it was the sun, today it's the moon – tomorrow what will it be? Fairies?'

'Shut up.'

The harvest moon was a dusky burnt orange, almost full, and its sombre light mirrored the dying embers of the fire. Or the setting sun, mused Caspar, disturbed by this wrongness.

'Bloody moon. And as for those moonstones, I reckon Catrik was right. As he would say, a pound to a pinch of snuff that's what's brought all this evil on us. It's got you talking like a heathen and I don't like it.'

The haunting cry of the wolf again echoed through the valleys. It was drawing closer. The unbearable loneliness in the howl left the younger boy feeling utterly abandoned amongst these wicked, brutal men. A couple of days ago the news of the imminent Vaalakan invasion had been exciting; a chance for adventure, glory in battle and heroic deeds. What heroic deeds? Just look at us, he thought to himself in disgust, trussed up like a boiling-fowl, pathetic, helpless and scared.

'What do they want with us, Hal? Why haven't they killed us? Information or ransom?'

'Information firstly, I would guess. A secret way into Torra Alta? Things about the tunnel, or the well, or the range of the weapons? I don't know.' He shrugged. 'But I can't help thinking . . . They seem obsessed with that wretched stone. But why?' Hal spoke quickly as if he had been thinking about these things for some time.

Caspar let his eyes slide towards the dim hazy glow escaping from the edges of a black bearskin rug that concealed the chief Vaalakan warrior. The red-bearded Northman was still clinging possessively to the orb. 'It's not just a stone. Its light is different from the others; so beautiful . . . and at the same time mournful as if it really were a part of the moon fallen out of the heavens.'

'It's no different to the others.' Hal was instantly dismissive. 'Just a little bigger. I can understand why these primitive barbarians are mesmerized by it; but you?' He shook his head and flicked back the lock of hair that fell across his shadowed face. They both fell silent for several minutes, fearfully contemplating their fate.

'Do you remember back in the caverns when they said something about the master?' Hal's quizzical voice finally broke the silence. 'That ugly, almost albino one, he definitely muttered something about the master.'

'Morbak, presumably.'

'But why would Morbak want the moonstone? It's ridiculous.' Hal fell to muttering to himself as if he were trying to work through the problem and Caspar drifted sullenly back into a world of half-dreams. His mind never wandered too far from thoughts of the moonstone's power and its image of the anguished woman. The moonstone was singing to him, calling him. Like the wolf out there in the mountains, crying for the moon, he wanted to throw his head back and howl for the white glow of the orb. The idea suddenly struck him as so absurd that he shook himself and dragged his eyes away from the stone's mesmerizing light. The horrified thought that some evil enchantment was bewitching him made his heart thump with fear. He started to recite the lines of scripture that the Chaplain had so often made him rewrite in an attempt to 'purify his spirit and bring him closer to God'. Perhaps Gwion is right, he thought, perhaps I do need help!

The long cold night stretched out interminably and Caspar's mind rolled over several outlandish plans for escape but he knew in his heart that they were all ridiculous. His last hope was that Hal would finally think of something practical and get them out of the hellish clutches of the enemy. Hal was good at plans.

'Hal? Can't you think of anything? I mean what are we going to do? You always think of something, Hal.'

'That's right,' growled the uncle, 'dump all the responsibility on me. How should I know what to do? I don't know any better than you.'

They sat propped up against each other. As sleep dragged on their eyelids they had to force themselves to remember to flex their hands. If they slept the cold would creep up on them and steal their fingers.

Feeling desperately alone and helpless he prayed that Branwolf would suddenly ride out of the night and rescue them. He had never felt so abandoned and vulnerable. At least he couldn't remember feeling like this, not since . . . No, he couldn't remember . . .

He had never been able to remember how he had felt when his mother suddenly vanished. In fact, he had lost all memory of her. His father always fell into an anguished rage when Caspar tried to question him. Often he would rant on about a row over the building of the cathedral, but that explained nothing. Only the castle's gossips would tell him anything. From them he learnt that the Baron had met Keridwen somewhere in a village along the edge of the Boarchase Forest. Her beauty had so enchanted him that he had immediately brought her home and married her.

A different Vaalakan was on watch, the smaller barbarian with the dirty blond hair who carried a crossbow rather than the customary axe. He curtailed their conversation with a well-aimed kick at Caspar's thigh.

In the silence, Caspar fell back into the world of sleep, and this time his dreams were peaceful, pleasantly caressing his thoughts. In his mind the woman from the moonstone was dancing in circles around the fire, her long rich hair glowing brightly in its light and her arms stretching towards the moon. She smiled at Caspar before loosening his bonds. She fed him bread, honey and warm milk as if he were a small child. Then she spoke in a bewitching, limpid voice but Caspar could not distinguish the words. When she saw this, her voice trailed off into a sad cry as though she called from afar. The boy awoke to the lonesome howl of the wolf.

The moon was now a pure silvery-white. An overhanging crag high above the valley floor was pitch black against the white of the waxing globe and for a second Caspar thought he saw something move. He was not certain but then it moved again. A black shape separated itself from the form of the rock and the distinct outline of a great wolf stood in the halo of the moon. It squatted on its haunches, stretched out a thickly-maned neck and threw back its long muzzle to bay at the moon, a long wailing cry. A howl filled with sadness, thought Caspar, as if it were calling to its lost mate.

Movement around the fire caught his eye. In horror he realized that the Vaalakan on watch had levelled his loaded crossbow at the wolf and was taking careful aim.

'No!' exclaimed Caspar. His cry brought groans of protest from the disturbed Vaalakans, and the man with the crossbow spun round. The troll snarled threateningly, revealing his curving fangs in the moonlight. It heaved its awkward body up onto its stubby legs and circled several times like a dog treading down its bed, dragging the two Belbidians back and forth with its movements. When peace was regained, the wolf had vanished.

'What the hell did you do that for!' demanded Hal.

'He was going to kill the wolf!'

'So?'

The boy felt confused and did not know how to reply. Wolves were dangerous, murderous thieves. But the cry from this wolf was so despairing, so abandoned, it had called to the sadness in Caspar, and he had answered.

In the peace that followed, the knock of a wooden spoon

against the sides of the cooking pot suddenly reminded the boys of their empty stomachs. The crossbowman was sneaking a few spoonfuls of stew from the previous day's leftovers to keep him going through the night.

'Hey, Vaalakan,' Hal called out softly to the man who gnawed appreciatively on a gristly piece of rabbit. 'Come on; it won't hurt you to let us have some.'

Caspar's stomach ached with hunger. 'Please.'

The smaller less muscled, Vaalakan looked thoughtfully at his snoring comrades and then with a shrug strolled over to the two Torra Altans. His knife flashed in the moonlight and Caspar involuntarily flinched away until he realized that the man did indeed have a soul and was going to cut their bonds so that they could eat. The boy flexed his fingers as the leather tresses fell away but his new found freedom was short lived. The Vaalakan retied his hands, but at least this time they were knotted in front of him.

'Kullak not stupid,' he grunted. 'Not let boylings loose. But I feel hunger many times.' He rubbed at his stomach. 'Not good to make man hungry.'

Jostling shoulders with his uncle, Caspar plunged his tied hands into the pot to scrape out some of the cold stew.

'Don't take it all,' Hal blurted indistinctly through his stuffed mouth.

After licking his sticky fingers, Caspar curled up next to his uncle, grateful for his companionship. He awoke to find Hal snugly wrapped in their fur-skin whilst he was left shivering and exposed to the damp morning air. Grunted orders from the ginger-haired Vaalakan sent two of the axemen scurrying around the camp to roll up the bedding skins and collect the scattered pans abandoned after last night's supper. Messy, disorganized people, the boy thought. Despite his imposing stature and commanding voice the Vaalakan leader was totally ignored by the young Scragg and the man with the crossbow. They were standing over the cooking pot, which Hal and Caspar had scraped clean, their faces black with rage as they shouted at each other. In disgust Scragg vented his anger on the iron pot, booting it into the embers and breaking a jagged chink off with his axe.

'Looks like Scragg's going to take it out on us now,' warned Hal as the Vaalakan pushed his countryman aside and strode determinedly towards them. 'Leave the talking to me.'

Near the dying embers in the centre of the camp an open sack of dry, unleavened bread lay across the axeman's path. He stooped to tear a sizeable hunk off the loaf and brought it over to them.

'You hungry? You hungry, sons of noblemen? I gives you bread if you tells me about the caves under your big fortress.' A sadistic laugh then cracked his mouth open. 'No, I changes my mind. You not so hungry now after rabbit meat. Bread is for my loved one instead.'

The troll gobbled up the bread in two mouthfuls without chewing and his master lovingly rubbed the leathery hide underneath its chin.

'I hate that animal,' said Hal bitterly.

Much to Caspar's relief, Scragg did not trouble himself to retie their arms behind their backs but merely examined the knot, checking its tautness. Unsatisfied, he poured water from the cauldron over the ties and snagged the knot tighter. 'There, Belbidaks. Leather dry hard. No undoings, I think.' He hitched their leashes to the troll's girth and then took up the animal's tether, which was knotted to the ring piercing its pug nose.

'You walks this day. You be more hungry at nightfall.' Scragg twisted his face up into a grimace-like smile.

The rope hobbling their ankles was only just long enough to allow the boys to take short sharp steps and the enforced march quickly became exhausting. The Vaalakans followed the course of the stream down through the steep-sided valleys. In places the narrow gorges were so sheer that their sides overshadowed the floor leaving it constantly in partial shadow. Here the air was chill with damp and a morning mist veiled the stream.

Scragg paced beside them, mimicking their hobbled steps.

'Very hard it is to walk like that. Very hard.' He took a long draught from a flask slung around his neck. 'Cool water. Good water, fresh from mountain. Ah!' he sighed with exaggerated pleasure. 'Too bad for Belbidak boylings, Scragg has no water for you.'

The pots and pans carelessly loaded onto the ungainly troll's pack jangled constantly, each rolling stride hurling the badly packed cargo from side to side. The girth looked as if it was slipping as the luggage started to lurch more onto one side and, when the ginger-bearded man left the front of the party to keep an eye on his prisoners, he critically eyed the wayward pack. He heaved gruffly on the buckles, drawing in the girth around the animal's bulging belly. It spat sideways at him with displeasure and the big muscular Vaalakan belted it smartly across the nose, before resuming his position at the head of the party.

When the narrow goat track levelled out for a stretch, the troll blundered up awkwardly onto its hindquarters and walked stiff-legged like a giant bear before crashing back down onto all fours again. Once more Caspar thought how strange a beast it was as it vacillated between the two gaits. It must be some kind of crossbreed, he decided. The foul beast craned its head round to stare at the two small strangers and strained its whip-like tail to the side to deposit a steaming line of stinking droppings. Hal and Caspar deftly side-stepped into the bracken, struggling through the undergrowth at the side of the track to avoid the troll's dung. The animal still fixed them with its round beady eyes, the humanoid face wrinkling up into a sneer.

'It did that deliberately,' declared Hal in outrage.

Scragg grinned happily and leapt up onto the troll's back to gloat down at them, facing the troll's rear. 'Alas for me, you is not for killing,' he said with feeling. 'All prisoners is for taking to Morbak. He question you, and the great God Vaal-Peor make you answer. Then will Scragg see your death.' Happiness lit his face at the thought and he slid down from the beast, turning his back on Hal's reply.

'My God is a greater God. He is the one true God. No false idol or demon will overcome his power.' Hal shouted the words after Scragg but his enemy ignored him and left the declaration sounding hollow and the Belbidian stumbling along helplessly behind the troll.

'Our God doesn't appear to be doing much for us at the moment,' observed Caspar tactlessly.

'*Blasphemy*, Spar!' Hal sounded half shocked and half amazed. 'These are heathens. The one true God will defend us from their devils.'

'But maybe not their axes?' suggested the younger boy grimly.

'I've never heard you speak like that!'

'I know.' Caspar wanted to explain, however inadequately. 'It was a dream I had last night . . . and a feeling I get from the moonstone – which Red Beard stole from us.' He felt a sharp surge of uncontrolled possessiveness the moment his mind reached towards the orb with its unexplained images.

The Vaalakans marched on relentlessly without stopping. By noon the two Belbidian prisoners were stumbling and parched with thirst. A stream sparkled tantalizingly close and Caspar veered off the track to wade through the shallows, hurriedly stooping to scoop up a mouthful of ice-cold water in his cupped hands. But the constant pull on the leathers around his wrist made the movement awkward. Hal followed suit, lunging for the water, and managed to catch a few quenching drops. Caspar stooped again but just as his hands reached down level with his ankles a smack from the flat blade of Scragg's axe across the broad flank of the troll set the animal charging forward. The slight youth fell into the shallows and was dragged and bumped over the rocks, with Hal running after him trying to pull the boy onto his feet.

It's the helplessness that hurts, Caspar thought to himself, when he at last found his feet again, with blood on his face and bruises everywhere. Being powerless like some dumb animal.

Before his eyes, swinging back and forth on the troll's hunched back, the sharp edge of the broken cooking pot moved . . . presenting possibilities. Another thing he was vaguely aware of – but had not yet focused on – was the strange prickling feeling between his shoulder blades. The occasional unexplained snap of a twig or a startled partridge flying up from the undergrowth long after their party had passed led him to suspect that someone or something was stalking them. He dismissed the feeling as imagination and returned to contemplate the possibilities of the cooking pot as a weapon or tool of escape.

The dark gorge channelled into a wide open valley carved by a fiercely tumbling river that crossed their path from west to east. But rather than follow the easier course of the meadow-lined valley the big red-bearded Vaalakan ordered them to ford the rippling shallows and then climb straight out of the valley, continuing due north. The climb was arduous and for once Caspar was almost grateful to be tied to the troll. He could lean back against the leather ropes and allow the powerful beast to drag him up the slope.

'I know where we are now,' Hal whispered between laboured breaths. 'That river has to be Hart's Leap. It joins the Silver-salmon about twenty leagues north of Torra Alta.'

'Too small,' objected Caspar.

'No. We must be some distance west, nearer to its source, where it flows from the Dragon's Claw Valley. It has to be Hart's Leap. Nothing else runs west to east like that through the Yellow Mountains.'

Caspar nodded in agreement, glad at least to know which way to run if they could make a break. He looked back towards the white running water, down the bracken and birch coated slope.

'What's that? I saw something move.'

'Careful; don't alert the Vaalakans,' warned Hal as he turned around slowly, trying to appear nonchalant. 'Where? I can't see anything.'

'To the right. Near the silver birches at the edge of the valley floor. In the shadows. Something moving. It's gone now. No, there it is again; higher up.'

'Probably just a deer. I can't see anything.' Hal was dismissive.

'Can't be. No deer would stay within ten miles of the racket produced by that troll, let alone follow us,' argued Caspar.

They reached the summit of the ridge and even the hard muscles of the Vaalakans were paying the price for the fast climb. The ginger-bearded leader raised his hand to call a halt and waved Kullak over to him. They surveyed the panorama from the valley below, pivoting through a full circle to spy out the land to the north and back again to look up the Dragon's Claw Valley. Caspar followed their gaze, noting a tired patch of slushy snow, which had shrunk back into the shadowed hollow behind an outcrop. A bright splash of red contrasted distinctly with the white ground. An eagle must have made a recent kill, he decided, noting the lack of large tracks in the melting snow.

The Vaalakans shielded their eyes from the bright glare of the sun that now climbed high into the blue heavens and shone deeply into the Dragon's Claw Valley. The full sun chased out the shadows from the pockets and hollows as it blazed onto the river's source. Rushing meltwater cascaded from a great slab of grey ice that clung to the side of the tallest peak. Caspar realized at once how the area acquired its unusual name: the mass of ice raked the mountainside, just like a giant claw. The glacier's surface coruscated with bright sunlight and Caspar was amazed when all the dazzled Vaalakans fell to their knees and opened their arms in a gesture of supplication.

'The glacier, Hal, it's part of their Ice-God religion! Perhaps the noon-day sun on the ice is some sort of sign to them.'

'Here comes our chance, then.' Hal's expression was grim with readiness. As the Vaalakans stepped into a horse-shoe formation for their pagan ceremony he and Caspar struggled surreptitiously and vainly to free their bonds.

'The cooking pot,' said Caspar urgently, causing Hal to look at him askance. 'Scragg smashed it with his axe and left a sharp edge . . .'

'Right, don't move. I'll get it.' Hal as always took immediate control. 'Don't do anything to attract their attention.'

'As if I would.'

The semi-circle of axe-wielding pagans began a slow tuneless chant, their chests now completely bare with the black bearskin robes discarded behind them. Caspar was astonished to see the number of white scars that covered the men's bodies. Only Kullak's skin was unblemished. Scragg had a raised purplish scar in the shape of a sickle that ran beneath his left shoulder blade. Despite the rush of adrenaline that jolted his heart into beating twice its normal speed, Caspar was aware of a vague sense of pity for these battle-scarred men so far from home. He hated them. They were cruel, sadistic barbarians who meant to slaughter his kinsmen before plundering the ripe harvest of Belbidia's heartland. But still they were human beings and to carry the wounds of so many blade thrusts seemed wrong for any man.

Just as Hal stretched his tied hands up towards the cooking pot, Kullak burst into a new chant that ran with discordant wailing moans against the monotonous drone of the general hymn. From the scabbard strapped to his calf, he unsheathed his long knife, raising the blade above his head and twisting it back and forth to catch the light. The dirty-blond Northman lunged in a strange trance-like dance towards the snow-filled hollow and scooped up an armful of slush. He cradled it on his upturned forearms before moulding it into a tight hard ball. The solemn dance continued and Caspar could now distinguish the repetitive words of his enemy's chant. 'Vaal-Peor, Vaal-Peor!' The chant grew louder as the men slapped their left arms diagonally over their chests to cover their hearts and held out their right forearms, pointing towards the glacier.

A cold, sickening feeling spread over Caspar's body as he felt a strong sense of evil surround the ridge on which they stood, as though the gods, if there were gods other than the one true God, were savouring the moment of worship. Kullak squatted low with his legs splayed wide apart swaying from one foot to the other, holding the ball of snow high above his head. From the corner of his eye the boy could just make out Hal's hands closing around the handle of the pot. Please, please, dear God, please help us to escape, prayed Caspar, but the strong sense of evil all around made him feel that his prayer had been swallowed whole and stolen by the enemy.

The troll grunted. Hal froze. The pot was in his hand and Caspar was unable to draw another breath until he was convinced that the Vaalakans were still engrossed in their worship. He felt sick as he watched Kullak sway back and forth with white up-turned eyes. He moved from one man to the next, slicing a slow cut into their out-held forearms and catching the trickles of blood onto the ball of snow cupped in his hand. He completed the full semi-circle of men whilst Hal hid behind the troll and carved frantically at the leather bonds with the rough edge of the pot.

'Just keep still, Spar.'

Caspar felt quite unable to move. He was repelled by the gruesome vision of the Vaalakan priest now facing the glacier with both arms raised above his head. Kullak sliced into his own arm with the sacrificial knife so that the blood spiralled down his arm and flowed over his shoulders. The steady mesmerizing chant droned on. 'Vaal-Peor, Vaal-Peor!'

'Spar, for God's sake.' Hal's urgent whisper broke through the spell and Caspar realized with a shock that his uncle had hissed his name several times. He shook off the awful compulsion that transfixed his eyes, drawing him into the dreadful, sacrificial rite before them. He returned with a jolt to real time, acutely aware of the urgency of the situation. Hal inched forward to stand beside him.

'I'm free. Walk slowly back to the side of the troll,' Hal ordered without looking at him. Caspar shuffled backwards, keeping his eyes focused on a spot in the centre of Kullak's back, willing the enemy to prolong the rite and not to turn around. He brushed the pot with his shoulder and inched round, raising his tethered wrists. The troll now formed a barrier between him and the enemy and he worked furiously to sever the bonds. First he struggled with his hands, sawing the ties back and forth on the broken lip of the cauldron. It seemed like an eternity before the first strand began to fray and then suddenly it snapped free. With renewed vigour he fought more keenly to tear the other straps apart, unheeding of the cuts that he inflicted on his skin from the ragged metal edges. With a snap the leather gave way. Caspar struggled to keep calm as he fumbled for the strands that hobbled his ankles. He held the leather taut as he sawed it back and forth across the ridge of jagged metal. He feared that the sound of his pulse thumping in his ears must be loud enough to alert the Vaalakans, but the droning chant continued and suddenly he was free.

'Hal, I've done it,' he whispered to his uncle's back. The dark youth took slow controlled, backward steps until he had glided alongside his excited nephew.

Caspar nodded and slid his foot back and began to creep down the slope. He itched to bolt as fast and as far as he could but he knew a sudden movement would signal their escape faster than anything else. The Vaalakans were dropping out of sight beneath the ridge and soon, he thought, they would be able to run. They slithered along, grasping hold of the heather to ease their descent, without making a sound. A patch of earth was slippery under Caspar's feet and he slid down the animal track for a pace or so before his toe caught on the root of a gorse bush. More carefully this time, he stretched his foot down for a more secure hold and continued the descent. The twisted cord of root beneath his foot suddenly snapped and he fell too rapidly, grasping at fronds of bracken that shredded through his fingers as he tried to slow his fall. A stone dislodged by his scrabbling feet started to roll inexorably down the hill, gathering pace as it went. It bounced onto other loose rocks, starting a small but audible landslide. Caspar heard its fall with dismay.

'That's done it, Spar,' warned Hal. 'Run for your life!'

The auburn-haired youth twisted round to face down into the Hart's Leap Valley and launched into a hectic, uncontrolled descent, leaping and skittering like a mountain goat from one ledge to the next, unable to stop. Hal was sliding, careering down the hillside as he grappled with his hands for the coarse vegetation to slow himself. Keep your feet out in front, willed Caspar, and you'll be all right. But Hal had not lived his entire life on the steep slopes of Torra Alta without learning the pitfalls of bolting like a hare down sheer-sided slopes. He kept his nerve, digging his heels in until they bit into the earth. As soon as he felt the first check from the ground he quickly bounced into his next stride so that he was not tipped head over heels. Then rapidly he ran into short quick bouncing steps, returning to the barely controlled rhythm of the descent.

Hoots and yells from the top of the ridge announced the Vaalakan pursuit and for the first time Caspar knew the panic of the fox at the sound of the baying hounds. The steep descent gave the light, nimble boys the advantage over the heavy men raised on the steppes of Vaalaka. The valley floor came rushing up towards them and once they had forded the river they pumped their legs hard to make for the cover of the silver birches. Hal was stretching ahead of him, his longer legs carrying him more easily over the ground. A hundred paces, thought Caspar, a hundred paces and we can disappear into the cover of the wood. The shouts from the Vaalakans grew louder and he pressed on hard, forcing his knees high up towards his chest. With each stride his lungs burst with the effort of the sprint.

The trees were all he could focus on. Vaguely he was aware of Hal waving him on, urging him to keep up. Beyond his uncle something moved, running out towards them from the leafy shadows. For a moment he could not recognize the bounding shape but suddenly, with a leap of joy, he realized that his faithful Wartooth was rushing to his rescue. The joy lasted a split second as an acute pain seized the boy's ankle, like a man-trap slicing through his flesh to crush his bone. He crashed heavily to the ground, rolling over and over.

Writhing in agony, Caspar clutched at his ankle. Blood spurted out between his fingers as he closed his hands tightly round his boot to try to stem the flow oozing out around the shaft of a crossbow bolt that skewered his ankle joint. The sight of the Vaalakans compelled him to his feet and he staggered a few more paces before collapsing again.

'Keep running, Hal. Go!' he ordered his uncle who had sprinted back and was trying to help him to his feet. 'Leave me. Make a run for it.'

'No, Spar, you can't make it,' Hal replied bravely.

'Please –'

'There's no time to argue; lean on my shoulder.' Hal gripped his nephew's arm and supported him as they tried to run. Another bolt whistled past them and penetrated deep into the ground.

Blood gushing from his wound, Caspar swooned to the ground, twisting round in time to see Kullak stop dead in his tracks and take careful aim. For a split second their eyes met and Caspar braced himself for the shock. He lay helpless on the ground despite Hal's efforts and, just as he knew Kullak had released the trigger on his deadly weapon, he heard a ferocious snarl from behind him. A grey shape leapt over his prone body into the path of the loosed bolt.

Wartooth crumpled into a flaccid heap after giving out a pitiful shriek. The bolt that had been aimed to maim his master stuck deep into his shoulder and the faithful hunting dog lay inert on the ground. Alive but in deep shock, his blood steadily drained out onto the injured boy.

For a moment Caspar was aware of Hal's reassuring voice close by his ear. 'I won't leave you, Spar. Don't worry, I'm here.' Then all he could see was the bare hairy legs of the axemen as they closed in and encircled them. There was no escape. Scragg's face loomed into his.

'No tries escape again. No tries never, Belbidaks.' The hideous grin on the Vaalakan's face warned that something awful was about to happen. Caspar could not contain the scream as the young Vaalakan gripped the crossbow bolt that ran right through his ankle and gave it a sharp yank. He could feel the weapon grinding against the bone.

'Leave him alone,' screamed Hal.

As Caspar lost consciousness he was vaguely aware of the living nightmare around him. The big axemen fell on Hal and hammered him down with the butts of their weapons. Caspar desperately wanted to help him but all he could do was scream under Scragg's torture. He knew he was still screaming when he swooned. Suddenly he could hear nothing, but he knew that the piercing noise was still shrieking from his lungs.

When Caspar came round, the big ginger-bearded leader was pulling Scragg off him. Red Beard smashed his bloodthirsty subordinate full square in the face with the flat of his own axe blade, knocking the younger man onto his back. The boy's first thoughts were for his uncle and the limp dog whose body still lay warm and wet over his legs. He prayed Hal was alive and was overwhelmed with a great wrenching grief as he realized his beloved dog was probably dying.

The ruddy face of the Vaalakan leader peered anxiously into his eyes.

'Is you alive, Belbidak? Is you alive?'

Caspar moaned but did not answer.

'Good. Keep breathings, Belbidak.' The Vaalakan seemed reassured. Caspar supposed that he too ought to be reassured. The Vaalakans obviously needed them alive but, right now, he was not sure that he wanted to continue with the nightmare that his life had turned into.

Straining his head round, he was able to see the Vaalakan stoop over Hal and repeat the same urgent message. Hal did not even moan. Instantly Caspar ceased to feel any more physical pain and his only concern was for his life-long companion. He dragged himself on his elbows across to where Hal's beaten body lay.

'Hal! Hal! Speak to me!' There was still no reply. Hal's face looked grey and his body lay completely still. In panic Caspar pressed his head to his uncle's chest, listening for a heartbeat. It was there, but fast and very faint.

'Don't leave me, Hal! You promised you wouldn't leave me.'

Then Kullak started to wail over the battered Belbidian in

a monotonous chant. He must be some kind of religious man, a witch-doctor or some kind of shaman, thought Caspar with horror.

'No, no. Don't call on your Ice-God,' he begged, petrified that such a God might really exist to answer the Vaalakan priest. 'He's too cold already. Can't you see he needs warmth.'

'We prays for healing not cold,' Red Beard replied for Kullak, whose eyes were completely white as if he was looking in on his soul.

The other Vaalakans, responding to shouted orders from Red Beard, brought kindling and set about creating a blaze to heat a cauldron of water. Kullak dipped his fingers into the tepid water and let some droplets trickle onto Hal's lips. They rolled off, untasted.

The water boiled and Caspar didn't resist as Kullak cut away the top half of his boot so that he could bathe the ankle. The boy no longer cared when the Vaalakan witch-doctor frowned at his injury. 'The bolt stays. It stops the wound. If no bolt there, you is bleedings to death.'

All Caspar's thoughts were concentrated on Hal, willing his friend's heart to beat stronger. He crept close to Hal, wrapping him in a fur-skin as he whispered reassuring words into his unheeding ear. Caspar hoped that, even though Hal could not respond, somewhere deep in that closed-off mind he could hear his voice and draw comfort from it. He tucked the fur-skin underneath Hal's body to keep him off the ground and rolled another to act as a pillow. Caspar then stripped the cloak off his own back and tucked it lovingly over the great hound, hoping the dog was still alive.

Suddenly, a girl and a mountain wolf stepped out of the shadows of the silver birches. Though limping heavily on one foot and leaning for support on the thick-maned neck of her companion, she approached confidently – and the men surrounding the injured Belbidians drew back, strangely cowed. As she drew closer, Caspar could make out her hideously distorted face, all swollen across the left side with one eye-socket bulging and closed over.

Kullak stared in horror, his tongue flickering in and out of his thin lips as he began to hiss, hooking his long-nailed fingers into ridged spikes. He flicked his hand towards the girl in a gesture to her ward.

Draped in tattered, mud-stained rags and swamped by a long hooded robe that trailed in the earth, the small figure clumsily approached, dragging her lame foot behind her. She made directly for the circle of men and fixed the ginger-bearded Vaalakan with her one good eye.

'You need my help,' she said simply.

Chapter 7

Barrows grumbled beneath the weight of the rubble as the men of Torra Alta worked hard and earnestly to clear the rock-fall. Meanwhile, the Baron frowned quizzically at tiny scratch marks in the rock-face that cut short the tunnel beyond. He raised his fist to hammer experimentally on the wall with the hilt of his knife. His blows made similar scratches except his were about six inches higher.

It might be a coincidence, he rationalized silently. The scratches might have been there for years, but then they look fresh and Hal was certainly prone to physically vent his frustrations. The height of the scratch marks would be about right. He strode back to examine the pool and looked at it quizzically. Surely the water level was higher than it had been a moment before? Not much, just a couple of inches. He stooped to examine the sulphurous waters at the very edge of the underground pool, fed by the babbling water above. Somewhere at the bottom, he deduced, it must seep away through cracks in the rocks down towards the water-table. But now, he judged, it wasn't filtering away as fast as it had done in the recent past. The stone at the edge was still black whereas six inches further in they were coated with sulphurous deposits built up over years. His hand shimmered in the golden water as he rasped his fingertips over the rocks, feeling the friction of clean bare stone at the edge of the pool. When he stretched further into the water, with his arm submerged up to his elbow, the rocks were slimy and his fingertips came away coated with a yellow residue. Either there's been a recent flood overhead or someone's tampered with the inlet, allowing a faster flow to fill the pool. He looked up at the waterfall before stepping around the pool and climbing above it, working his shoulders into the narrow recess. His mind was too intent even to notice the ice-cool water that gushed over into his lap and soaked his deerhide leggings as he crawled forward.

The sound of the men toiling below, with their rhythmic chime of picks on rock and the tumbling crash of boulders, was drowned out by the roar of fast flowing water rumbling over the rocks. This waterfall, he thought, is spilling out from an underground river. The opening was only about a foot across and he looked at it doubtfully. Surely it was too narrow for anyone to get through – even for Hal or Spar. Then he remembered once, when the cook had complained about some freshly baked tarts mysteriously vanishing from her locked pantry, how he had examined the grill above the doorway. It had been no more than a mere slit. Under the interrogation of Gwion, who had threatened them with the wrath of God if they lied, the two boys had eventually admitted to squirming their way through the grille. They're like mice, getting into anything and everything and a grin at last appeared on his taut, anxious face. He had found hope.

But what if only one had escaped the rock-fall? This could have been the escape route for one alone and the other might still have been crushed under the tonnage of boulders. It was possible but he didn't believe it. Those two might argue and fight but they were never a stone's throw from each other. And if one had escaped he would have stayed to drag the rocks away and dig the other out, however futile the task might seem. Yes, he was certain, that neither would ever have given up on the other.

The waterfall, gushing over the lip of rock, filled the bottom half of the opening, pouring down in twists, like mercury caught in a tumbling helical vortex, dragging the light down into its swirling depths. Branwolf thrust his broad torso forward into the rushing water, twisting his head sideways to keep his mouth above the flow. He squirmed his arm forward and thrust the torch through the gap, keeping the flames above the level of the dousing water. Above the brim of the waterfall he could see beyond into another tunnel in the honeycombed rock where the torchlight danced on the splashing surface of the stream. He judged there was a three-foot space above the water before the light of his torch reached the swirling patterns on the roof. This tunnel, he thought, had been bored by water alone and not by the worming dragons that had threaded through the roots of the Tor.

He worked his way backwards, feeding his body out of the small cramped recess and winced as his hand grazed a splinter. He looked at his palm and frowned at a fragment of metal embedded in his skin. It sparkled like burnished copper in the orange glow of the torchlight but as he turned it over he nodded to himself. Definitely! It had to be the tip of a steel dagger broken off in the boys' attempts to widen the gap in the rock.

He teased the splinter out of his skin and slipped and slithered back down the rock. He pounded back towards the Chaplain and his team of two dozen men who had now made an appreciable indent in the mountain of rock, piling the boulders in cairns stretching back up the tunnel.

'Gwion! Gwion! Quick!' he yelled excitedly and to a man the work-team dropped their tools in a cacophony of metal shrieks and clangs. They turned to look expectantly at the drenched Baron. He brought himself to a dignified halt and steadied his voice.

'Keep working, men. I still need all of this cleared – just in case.' He lowered his voice. 'Gwion, come with me and take a look at this.' He reached for a pick and turned quickly back towards the pool. He pointed up towards the mouth of the waterfall and shouted above the noise of the splashing cascade and the rumbling river above. 'They've squeezed through there; I'm sure they have. Look, I found this.'

'Oh, thank God,' the Chaplain responded immediately. 'They must be alive, or at least one of them is,' he added a little more uncertainly, his quick mind following the same track as his brother-in-law's. 'The Lord be praised; there is hope. Even Hal could get through that gap. Those two could get through anything. The good Lord knows I've had to chastise them enough about getting into places they shouldn't. Well, what do we do?' The pitch of his voice was rising with excitement. 'Follow them through?'

Branwolf nodded. 'We'll have to open up the fissure first. You go back and fetch a dozen men with torches and a dozen spares to give us more time in the tunnels. Tell the Captain that I want that rubble fully cleared before he returns to the surface to continue the siege preparations. If, of course, he finds one of them under that rubble while we're gone . . . well, we still have to find the other.'

He wedged the torch into a crevice at the side of the cascading rivulet and worked the hook of the pick into the mouth of the opening. Yanking the axe back and forth, he thumped his palm against its handle until a fragment of rock splintered away. They must have worked at this for hours, he thought. In the sunless world of the caverns he had no way of reckoning the passage of time except for the slow burning of the torches. He tried to quell his rising frustration at the cramped working space that didn't allow him enough room to swing the pick and crack open the wall of rock barring his way. He had to content himself with small sharp movements that only little by little chiselled away at the rim of the opening. Finally he placed the head of the pick across the mouth and rammed it repeatedly against the rock until it eventually gave way. Water poured over his body and he twisted his head sideways, working the points of his shoulders between the rocks. The earnest priest was right behind him urging him to be careful.

He held his breath as the foul-tasting water gushed over his face and he hauled his shoulders through into the new tunnel. While his body blocked the hole, he was plunged into utter darkness. He kicked his legs and worked his toes over the crevices in the rock until he was able to struggle onto all fours with his body floating in a shallow but fast moving river. He heaved himself upright, cracking his head on the lower ceiling, which reminded him to hunch his back. The dim glow filtered up through the hole that he had just scraped through and he reached his hand back to take a torch offered by the Chaplain.

It took several minutes for the rest of the men to worm through the gap and Branwolf waited, disguising his impatience as he looked up and down the cramped tunnels. Which way had they gone, up against the flow or downstream towards the depths?

'Which way?' he murmured.

'I would go upstream towards the surface,' Father Gwion offered.

Branwolf tried to put himself into the mind of his young reckless half-brother. What would Hal have done? The older, more impulsive youth would certainly have made the decisions. He thought of the weight of overbearing rock and the tonnage of the earth's mantle pressing down above his head. He felt trapped and claustrophobic down here, as would any man born and bred on the airy heights of Torra Alta. He knew from experience that it would be better to take one of the tunnels leading downwards. They brought better access to the main underground rivers that fed the springs near the foot of the canyon walls and swelled the waters of the Silversalmon. But Hal wasn't to know that and the boy would have certainly sought the most direct route to the surface.

'I'm sure you are right, Gwion. Without any knowledge of the tunnels I'm sure I'd have gone upstream too.' He led the Chaplain and his twelve men as they splashed through the underground river, with their cramped shoulders stooped over to protect their heads. The wet leather of the Baron's breeches dragged against his aching thigh muscles but his anxiety chased away his tiredness. He realized, though, that his men were feeling the pressure as they gradually lagged behind and only his brother-in-law remained doggedly at his heels. He wondered how the men born in an age of peace would stand up to the hardships of the inevitable siege. Oh Spar, how could you do this to me? Why didn't you just wait for me to come and fetch you? Didn't you know I would come for you? He tried to put himself in his son's position. Spar had always been difficult to understand. He seemed so whimsical and distant sometimes, staring out at the distant peaks or being drawn towards the glow of the moon. He wondered if his boy felt misunderstood, but he still must have known he would dig them out. Vaalakans or not, he would have put every last man down the well to dig them out. The boys must have looked at that wall of rubble and despaired. They had no way of knowing how much of the tunnel was blocked or if any of the Chaplain's party had survived the explosion on the other side. They must have known he would eventually come for them but they weren't to know how long that would take. It might have taken days and, to their tender years, days without food must have seemed like a fate worse than death. They couldn't even drink the untreated yellow water poisoned by the sulphur deposits.

At last the foul-smelling stream led them into an open chamber where Branwolf could stretch up his cramped neck. He held the firebrand high to illuminate a tall vaulted cave with half a dozen tunnels breaking away at different angles. He stepped round and his torch fell on the sculpted shapes of stalagmites and stalactites that groped out of the dark. He detected a stale foetid smell and underlying it another aroma – but he couldn't quite place it. His instincts told him to be wary. He felt somehow that he had stepped back in time; there was a sinister, ghostly atmosphere to these chambers and he did not like it.

'Spread out, men, but stay in pairs. Search the entrances to each of these tunnels and call out if you find anything unusual.' His brother-in-law remained closely at his side, thrusting the flaming torch deep into every crevice and behind every stone or stalagmite, searching frantically. Branwolf strode towards the first tunnel and plunged his torch into the darkness. He saw a snaking passageway with curved walls moulded with swirling tongues of rock that aligned with the churning patterns of running water. The channel probably only held water in times of high flood. He cupped his free hand to his mouth and bellowed out his son's name, then waited for the echoes to recede before hollering again. He was met with unrelenting silence. He studied the floor, looking for any discarded item or scratch marks and silently berated his son and half-brother for not leaving some spoor to trace them by. Nothing. A hopeless nothing.

'Sir! My Lord! Here; look.' One of the soldiers was waving his torch about and its swaying light instantly caught the Baron's attention. He splashed through the stream and sprinted to the man on the far side of the vaulted chamber. 'It's blood, Sir, look.'

Branwolf knelt and smeared his finger through the pool of dark thick liquid. He rubbed it between his fingertips, sensing a hint of warmth. It was still runny and not yet dry. He raised his smeared fingertips to his nose and sniffed. Instantly he flinched away, repelled by the smell, which reminded him of charred stale fish.

'Gwion,' he spoke softly. 'What do you make of this?' His brother-in-law knelt beside him and dipped his finger into the fresh blood. He sniffed it and frowned.

'Fear the creatures of the Devil; shun the creatures of the underworld, for their breath is foul and their blood is evil,' he muttered as if quoting from the holy scriptures. 'I fear we are too near the pit of Hell down here in this unnatural world beneath the earth.'

The men were looking anxiously about and someone with a vivid imagination was muttering about hobgoblins.

'There is always a logical explanation.' The Baron's steady voice filled the chamber. 'You are Belbidia's finest fighting men. Men of Torra Alta, be ashamed that you quake at superstitions and old wives' tales.'

'My Lord Branwolf!' Another excited cry came from the far side of the cavern. 'Sir, there's something over here.' As Branwolf hurried over, he stopped to see the trail of dark blood that marked out a direct line between the two tunnels. In places the pools were smeared as if something large had been swept through them. The passageway led steeply upwards and after examining the foul smelling blood, he rattled his fingers against the walls of the tunnel as he examined the smooth rock-face. It lacked the convoluted patterns of water-carved rock and instead was chipped with the tell-tale marks of a pick and chisel. A man-made tunnel leading up out of the earth, he thought; surely it was worth a try. Faced with all those other options, Hal could well have chosen the one that was different and led steeply upwards; it would have been the most obvious choice. He decided to explore the tunnel himself but, not wanting to waste any time, he thought it wise to send his men out to search the other tunnels just in case his assumptions were wrong. 'Right, men, I want you to search deeper into each of the tunnels, but don't go more than an arrow shot's length and then return to the central chamber. I don't want anyone getting lost. Father Gwion and I will explore this one.'

Though disconcerted by the stench of the blood, Branwolf suddenly felt hopeful. Hal must have chosen this tunnel: it was the most logical choice. His foot slipped in the thick blood and he grasped at the rock-face for support, grazing his hand. He looked at his palm and frowned at the silvery translucent scales that clung to his skin. The Chaplain was hurrying ahead of him, anxiously twitching his shaven head from side to side, peering into the shadows. It's just like before, Branwolf sighed; with the Chaplain searching frantically for his sister. He was quite certain, though, that they had never reached these tunnels. He knew that the catacombs under Torra Alta had once reached deep under the roots of the Yellow Mountains. Hundreds of years ago, however, his ancestors had sealed off any side-tunnels to protect the castle from underground attack. He suddenly realized that if Hal and Caspar had made it through to new unexplored channels then it was possible that Keridwen could have done the same. She could have been lost in a network of tunnels that he had failed to search. The thought sickened him. His mind swung from the thought of his wife to the strange clanking noises that Catrik had insisted must be coming from enemy spies trying to break through into the castle labyrinth.

He frowned inwardly as he thought simultaneously of Keridwen and the Vaalakans and gradually his mind began to link the two. Why was it that the year Keridwen vanished was also the first year of the Vaalakan border raids. Each subsequent year had brought a few skirmishes or the theft of a handful of goats but gradually the rumours of a greater threat developed. He had sent spies northward and had learnt of fast-spreading tales describing Morbak and his plans to unite the northern nomads.

He looked ahead and with a start realized that the Chaplain had vanished.

'Gwion,' he yelled but there was no reply. He started forward at a run but was relieved to see the warm glow of his brother-in-law's torch filtering out from a side chamber. He swung himself round the corner and his mouth dropped open in amazement as the torchlight coruscated off the bright angles of precious metals and polished stones. He gawped at the dazzling treasure of jewels, armour, amulets and weapons. The small angular priest sank to his knees, turning over the ancient pieces. His eyes sparkled with wonder. For a very brief second Branwolf thought that all this ancient wealth would pay all the taxes due to the King for his lifetime if not even for Spar's as well. He could relax the pressure on the loggers, the sulphur miners and the trappers who brought wolfskins to the markets. He could pay Torra Alta's contribution to the King's Church Tax without raiding the resources of his barony. But his mind only momentarily flickered away from worrying over his lost son and brother. Though if Spar and Hal had stumbled across this treasure he was amazed that they had ever left it. Surely they should be sitting on top of the treasure, with their faces stupefied by wonder, much as the Chaplain's was now. He frowned at the man. It was unseemly behaviour for a churchman.

'We could finish the new cathedral,' the tonsured priest muttered, rapt.

Branwolf raised an eyebrow at his brother-in-law. 'A church to the one great God built on the proceeds of pagan jewellery. It has a chilling ring to it.'

The Chaplain's blue eyes lifted quickly, suddenly piercing deep into Branwolf's soul . . . but then relaxed. He paced quickly round the heaped metal, plunging his torch close to the treasure to reveal coats of mail twined with silks and satins. The fabrics were studded with sapphires and pearly gems that sparkled like stars on a frosty night. The ancient thread of the cloth was so gossamer-fine that the mere weight of the delicate jewels tore strips in the wispy stitching. Their eyes skimmed over chalices, golden candelabras, brooches of finely wrought silver, torcs fashioned into dragons and snakes, and a silver statue of a unicorn with two perfectly matching sapphire eyes. Sparkling in the firelight the jewels came alive after centuries of incarceration in the blackness of the sun-forsaken world.

'If they had been here, you'd think they might have left a torn bit of cloak or something like it. I can't imagine them seeing this magnificent treasure without climbing all over it . . . But there's nothing.' Father Gwion sighed with disappointment. 'Except!' He plunged his hand into the rattling pile of metal plate and pieces of armour that looked only big enough to protect the torso of a young boy. 'It's fur; bearskin, maybe?'

Branwolf fingered the skin, its tanned hide on one side, the matted dark hairs of the other. 'It's not torn from their clothes, I'm sure. This looks like bear, but black bear, and there are none this far south.' From the north, then, he thought to himself fearfully. And how long had it been down here?

'Come on we're wasting time here,' he said brusquely.

They turned left out of the treasure-filled cave and Branwolf was immediately disheartened as he felt the ground sloping downhill rather than up towards the surface.

The air smelt stale and his hopes were dwindling fast. Father Gwion abruptly burst into a sprint and Branwolf at the same time saw a cool white light glowing in the tunnel ahead. A moonstone! His heart leapt as he pounded down the corridor, his leather soles slapping furiously on the bare rock until he came to a halt level with the Chaplain.

'Oh my dear God,' he murmured helplessly. The moonstone

cast its pure light on maggoty carcasses, half-eaten deer, the rotting flesh of a mangled fox, decomposing ibex and even the torn body of a decayed mountain lion. He looked at the moonstone and then again at the carcass-strewn lair.

His voice came as a harsh whisper as he asked his brother-in-law, 'You did say Hal was carrying a moonstone, didn't you?'

The Chaplain nodded.

Carcasses . . . Blood . . . The moonstone . . . A dead-end . . . He stepped forward, hardly daring to examine the mutilated remains in case he found his son's body amongst the carnage. The floor was slippery with fresh blood, decaying hide and the white translucent membrane of strung out entrails that the carnivore had tossed idly about in his lair. It was the den of some crazed rogue cat, he thought, that kills mercilessly, never bothering to fully eat its prey.

The tonsured priest crunched over the bones and leapt at the moonstone. Branwolf hardly noticed as the man momentarily stared deep into its heart and flicked an anxious glance towards him. With a crestfallen face, Gwion hurriedly fell to the gruesome task of turning over the bodies as together they searched for any human remains.

Oh my God, oh my God, a hand. The Baron closed his eyes for a second, hoping that what he had just seen was nothing more than a trick of the light but it was still there. A human hand. He knelt and lifted it, but the flesh was so rotten that the tendons peeled away and the knuckle joints tore away from the rest of the hand. It couldn't be either, Hal's or Spar's, but . . . Without caring that he bloodied his hands with maggot-ridden flesh, he swept aside the rotted hindquarters of a stag, which lay on top of the body. The Chaplain was at his side.

'What have you found?' he asked with desperate fear in his voice.

Branwolf was too choked to reply. Most of the carcass was eaten except for the gathered embroidery of a peasant's smock and the buckle of a belt crudely fashioned from iron. He gave a great sigh of relief. Not Keridwen, definitely not Keridwen but probably a shepherd taken alone on the upper pastures. 'Nobody we know,' he mumbled.

He was still puzzled by the trail of blood. He couldn't imagine what type of creature lived in this hole but whatever the creature was it was bleeding heavily. Possibly it had cornered Caspar and Hal and was now dragging them away to another lair. The trail of blood . . . The other passage. It's taken them there, he thought frantically, starting out of the horrifying chamber and back down the tunnel towards the large arched cavern.

There his dozen men were already huddled excitedly together by the yellow-stained underground stream. Their backs were hunched over as they examined an object held in their midst.

'Give me a report, one of you,' the Baron ordered, startling them all.

One of them revealed that he clasped a dagger. It was studded with sapphires and emeralds but the metal itself was rusted and fatigued with age.

'It must be a thousand years old, my Lord.' He proffered the weapon to his liege-lord. 'Me and Wilbert, Sir, we followed that tunnel opposite.' He pointed vaguely behind him and poured out his tale, tripping over the words in his haste. 'It led to a shaft, Sir, a shaft and a rope, leading out into blessed daylight. That's where we found the dagger at the foot of the rope. What's it mean, Sir? Will it lead us to Master Hal and Master Spar, Sir? Are they safe?'

The rest of the men chorused the questions, immediately expecting their overlord to have all the answers.

He raised his hand to silence them. 'Did anyone else find anything?'

'Sir,' another broad-faced soldier barked, 'yes, Sir. We followed the trail of blood – stinking foul blood and all. It led us to a wide opening, high up above the cavern ceiling but it were too high up for a man to climb out of. The blood trail ended there, but there weren't no signs of Master Hal and Master Spar.'

Branwolf's brow furrowed into deep lines of concentration. 'Then the blood trail can't be anything to do with them. We found the moonstone that Hal was carrying. It was in a cave full of animal carcasses, which means that some large vicious animal is living down here. The trail of blood must be coming from it or one of its kills. The boys must have dropped everything in their haste to get away from it. The rope and the dagger you found show us they must have gone down *that* tunnel – there's no time to waste. Stay close together and keep alert. Let's go.'

And so at the end of the constricted tunnel the Baron came to the rope which dangled down through a shaft of daylight. The shaft was narrow and its clear welcome light dragged the men's eyes upwards. The Chaplain who was lighter and more lithe than the Baron leapt at the rope and hauled himself up hand over hand. He disappeared over the lip of the shaft and Branwolf impatiently followed after him. He blinked as the daylight stung his eyes. Father Gwion was already crouching down, examining the ground. Branwolf sniffed the air. There was a new scent, strong and pungent, like cattle or horse but gamier.

'Well,' the priest grimaced, 'that rope certainly didn't get there by accident.'

'No,' Branwolf agreed. His voice was heavy and low. 'No. It's the last bit of the puzzle. First we hear a clattering metallic chime, reminiscent of mining? We find a strip of black bear cloth and now a rope.' He fingered the twisted cord. 'Nettle stems, I'd say; a bit primitive for a Torra Altan rope. And that smell . . .' He stepped away from the shaft opening and examined the crushed heather and the broken bracken fronds. 'A broad trail leading north. And – ugh – droppings, no longer steaming but still fresh.'

'Troll? Vaalakan troll?' The Chaplain looked at him with lines of taut nerves twitching his narrow face.

Branwolf nodded and took a deep despairing sigh. 'I'd say they're alive – definitely alive – but captured by a party of enemy spies. Get up here, men,' he bellowed down into the depths. 'Get up here fast.' As he waited for his men to emerge out of the tunnels he slowly stepped round, trying to orientate himself in the mountains. He looked up at the sun that was creeping towards the western horizon, as he tried to find his bearings. A circular crown of jagged peaks thrust towards the setting globe, overshadowing the glassy waters of a tarn cradled in their roots. 'A day's ride west of the castle,' he muttered to himself. 'Mirror Lake Valley.' He recognized the valley from a recent wolf hunt where they had chased a large white beast that had been taking lambs from the upper pastures. Its rare pelt had fetched a high price.

He glared at the trail ahead and grunted in frustration: he would have to delay before tracking the enemy. It would be quicker and more effective in the long run if he returned to Torra Alta before chasing after them. He could never hope to catch the Vaalakans on foot.

The last of the smouldering torches were nearly burnt to their stubs and it would be impossible to retrace their route through the tunnels. They would have to make the hard journey over land.

He didn't wait for his men to climb the rope but shouted down to them to head east back to Torra Alta as fast as they could. He had no doubt that he would make better time than any of the soldiers and he couldn't afford to wait.

With the fading light of day casting his moving shadow ahead of him, the large, dark Baron set off at a purposeful jog. The Chaplain breathed heavily at his heels, sometimes moaning quietly to himself, as they kept up a gruelling pace. Hurtling through the dusk, Branwolf was tricked by tiredness into hearing Gwion's moaning to be pining for the treasure they had left behind in the cave. But soon they had only moonlight to guide them, and they were forced to a scrambling walk. Here, too, the ravines were steeper and the scree slopes more treacherous. The Baron was grateful for Gwion's loyalty and help, as he had been before so many years ago. As the stars were smothered by the lilac glow of morning they eventually stumbled through the higher pastures above Torra Alta, marked out by dry stone walls crumbling through lack of repair. They fell onto a trail leading directly back towards the castle and, encouraged by being so close to home, Branwolf put on a last burst of speed.

When the western tower of Torra Alta lanced above the craggy mountains, Branwolf forced his exhausted legs to stumble over the last rise. At last he could see the magnificence of his castle. The smooth whinstone battlements were shining like a burnished shield over the Pass, caught in the glory of the autumn sunrise. He leapt across hillocks, zigzagging back and forth as he careered down the steeply shelved sides of the canyon. The track beneath his feet hardened from beaten earth to rock as he reached the brink of the sheer canyon walls. Without hesitation he followed the track as it descended into a snaking ledge that cut into the rock-face. It was just wide enough to drive a herd of goats down or for mounted men to ride warily in single file, assuming they held no fear over the precipitous drop.

A stableyard at the base of the Tor harboured spare horses. These were hitched to the front of wagons, providing the greater power needed to get the heavy loads up the treacherously steep road to the castle. These cock-horses were large beasts with muscle-packed rumps, sure-footed and reliable on the mountain tracks. Generations of Torra Altans had dedicated their lives to producing such fine animals. They were mostly young geldings, and expensively maintained since their strength was vital to the welfare of Torra Alta.

Weaving between the waiting wagons, the Baron made haste to the stables. 'Get me a horse!'

'I've got no saddle horses, my Lord,' the groom explained. But even as he spoke, seeing the look in the Baron's eye, he was moving towards a great, sleek horse ready harnessed for hitching to the front of a cart, tacked up in its collar and long driving reins. The Baron took the reins before they were offered, coiled them up and leapt up onto its broad, bare back, jabbing his heels into its side and turning its head towards the road.

'Stand aside,' he yelled to a wagoner whose whip was raised, ready to drive his horses up the first section of the road. 'Stand aside. Let me through.' The heavy horse thundered up the road, nobly making the task of carrying the Baron seem light and easy. Compared to its usual load of the six-wheeled wagons, encumbered with siege supplies, it was.

Half way up the Tor, the cart-horse was blowing hard, but still clattered past mule trains that hurriedly pressed themselves against the side of the rock-face. He gave the animal a long rein so that it could carefully pick its footing over the narrowest parts of the spiralling road. Branwolf glanced below at the precipitous drop that stretched hundreds of feet to the miniature scenes on the valley floor. His heartbeat remained steady. He inched past a last precarious wagon, then spurred the cart-horse on noisily up the steep slope of the Slide to thunder beneath the teeth of the portcullis into Torra Alta's open courtyard.

The courtyard was teeming with activity, as was usual since Morbak moved towards them, and the Baron was relieved to see the Captain through the hubbub of confusion all around him. He came stamping wearily across the cobbles to greet him, coated in a film of grime, like a miner.

'We didn't find them, Sir,' he murmured.

Branwolf nodded. He dismounted and let the Captain take charge of the horse. 'I know. The Vaalakans have them,' he said. 'I'm going after them. Get me my bow and a selection of arrows. I want ones quilled for long range as well as ones for close flight with deep penetration powers. There's a large carnivore prowling about in the mountains. Arrange supplies for me from the kitchens: a good solid pack.'

The Captain saluted and turned to hurry away, barking out further orders to the soldiers around him. He side-stepped to avoid the Chaplain who, short of breath, came charging into the courtyard and slithered off his horse.

Branwolf marched quickly towards the stables, considering whether to take Firecracker, his son's horse, who was by far the fastest in the stables. But the hot-headed animal might be unreliable and too easily spooked in the mountains. How his son managed the beast he could never quite fathom. When the groom hurried out to greet him, the raven-haired Baron ordered instead, 'Get Sandstorm ready for me, and with a good rug under the saddle. I'm going up into the high mountains. Bring him out to the portcullis when you are ready.'

'My Lord,' the groom stammered, 'I'm sorry, I can't. He's missing. Someone took him out last night.' His face was agitated as he nervously brushed straw from his breeches.

Before the groom could say more, Branwolf had thought again. 'Just get me Conqueror then; he's fit and strong.' He returned to the inner courtyard in front of his keep, where Gwion intercepted him.

'I'm coming with you,' he announced determinedly.

The imposing Baron shook his head. 'No, I need you here. I need you to look after the castle. We must prepare for siege and morale will be low with Spar and Hal captives of Morbak. Your job is here, to give us all purpose and guidance.'

'But, Branwolf, you can't go alone.'

'I'll be faster.' He turned to the Captain. 'How's Catrik?'

'Not good, my Lord.'

Branwolf felt his chest tighten. Catrik was his oldest and most faithful friend and had guided him through many troubles since his childhood. 'I must just see him before I go.'

The old retainer was a deathly white beneath his beard. His breathing harsh, uneven as he muttered prayers. He stared vacantly at the ceiling while the castle physician dressed his wounds until Branwolf clasped his old friend's hand.

A trickle of blood bubbled from the corner of his mouth as he tried to speak. 'Did you . . . find them?'

'No, but we will. I have their trail now,' the Baron reassured him gently.

'The moonstone . . .' With great effort Catrik spoke, in the breath of a whisper, but a racking cough overtook him.

'It's all right. You did your best,' Branwolf said to calm him. He nodded towards the physician. 'You will be cared for, and when you can speak you will be heard,' he said clearly, to

Catrik, and marched out of the Keep to ready himself for the long, lonely chase he must take up without delay. The cook waited for him in the shade of the great open doors, with ale and bread, and fresh water, free of sulphur, to soothe the cuts on his hands. In moments he had picked up his weapons and the reins of his sleek black charger. He turned to his brother-in-law.

'You are now my next-of-kin here and I leave you in charge while I'm gone. The Captain will organize the garrison. Make sure you seal that tunnel up again.'

Moments later he rode alone out through the portcullis, his long bow slung over his back alongside two quivers of arrows. His hand fingered the pommel of a broadsword secured to the high-cantled saddle before he checked over his throwing daggers and a hunting knife thrust into his belt.

Chapter 8

The great she-wolf's pale grey eyes remained fixed on her mistress, following her step with devotion. The hooded girl was lame and her face was hideously damaged, yet she had great presence. The unflinching courage in her stance made Caspar hold his breath, shifting his eyes between the misshapen girl and the she-wolf, which kept a protective gaze on her mistress. The girl confronted the big man, who flexed great muscles beneath his tight skin in agitation as he returned her stare with perplexed and guarded eyes.

'Nak! Nak!' Kullak pushed his way in front of his chief and threatened the maimed girl with the point of his crossbow. 'Begone to your devils, witch. Nak!'

The girl's stare did not waver. She spoke in a soft clear Belbidian accent warmed by the musical lilt of the mountain folk. 'Get this sham of a priest out of my way and let me heal your prisoners.'

The Vaalakan leader put his heavy hand on Kullak's shoulder and pulled the protesting man aside to tower directly over the witch. 'If they dies, you dies. If they lives, you lives but you all my prisoners and will comes with me to Lord Morbak,' warned the Vaalakan. 'Is bargain, yes?'

'Agreed,' nodded the girl as she swept her shredded skirts aside and knelt down next to the injured boys. For the moment Caspar did not care who she was, where she came from or why she had given up her freedom to help them. All that mattered was she was here to help; Hal needed help.

She took a cursory look at Caspar's ankle, a glance at the moribund hound and then more seriously at Hal's ashen face.

'You'll have to wait: you'll live for the moment.' She smiled a crooked smile. 'Let's see to your friend first, shall we?' Caspar watched with restored hope as the girl pulled back the fur-skin to examine Hal's chest and stomach. 'You've done well to keep him warm,' she commented as she gently probed Hal's torso. 'I need some herbs to stop the bleeding.'

'But he's not bleeding.' Caspar was confused.

'Inside,' she explained and then turned to face the Vaalakans. 'Give me water – boiling water.' The chief brought the cauldron over to her and then stepped back out of her way. From a leather pouch, which she kept concealed in her skirts, the girl withdrew a handful of long-stemmed hairy leaves and another herb with smooth oval foils. She crushed them in her fingers before stirring them into a ladle full of steaming water. The mixture effervesced for a while and once it had calmed, she poured the frothy medicine drop by drop into Hal's mouth.

'My name is Brid,' she whispered. 'The Goddess gives me the power to heal you, friend. This potion of woundwort and loosestrife will stem the loss of blood within your body.' She enticed a few more droplets into Hal's throat. 'Soon you will feel better. Sleep, friend, sleep and mend.' Once she had administered all of her powdered herb concoction she made a fresh, more concentrated brew. She neatly snapped a twig to form a quill and dipped it into the mixture.

'These are the runes of healing,' Brid began to chant as she drew an angular sigil onto Hal's naked chest with the twig and potion. 'I, Brid, call upon the Mother, merciful giver of life, to help our friend. The runes call you, the runes speak to you. These are the runes of healing: Mother Goddess lend me your power. Brid your daughter calls on your love: I invoke your blessing with the runes of healing.'

She slumped back, resting on her ankles. Her powerful presence faded for a moment as the strength drained out of her, channelling through her finger-tips that rested on Hal's chest. Faintly she murmured the words again, 'These are the runes of healing.' Her whole body quivered with exhaustion and her breathing became laboured. Her one good eye closed and she collapsed into sleep. In the few minutes that she was silent the entire party, the Vaalakans, Caspar, and her grey wolf, were transfixed. They stared at her, spellbound by her witchcraft, all except Kullak whose suppressed hissing continued as he circled the group in agitation.

The girl breathed deeply and regularly, sighing in and out. Caspar became gradually aware of Hal's breathing as it became stronger and more regular. It kept pace and time, inhaling and exhaling with Brid as if she breathed for him or even was breathing life into him. A warmth returned to Hal's lips as the sickening blue colour faded away. Brid slowly opened her eyes.

'He's sleeping now,' she murmured. 'He's come back from the brink of the Otherworld and will sleep now for many hours. In the morning he will wake.'

Caspar's pent-up tears of grief pricked at the corners of his eyes as he was overcome by relief. He dabbed at them with his blood-stained sleeve. The strange bedraggled girl crawled round next to him and lightly pressed her hands each side of his wounded ankle, waking up the excruciating pain in his leg that had been numbed by his fears for Hal. He felt sick as the bolt ground against bones beneath the skin.

'Please.' He tried to sound brave. 'Please, the dog – is there anything you can do? He tried to save me . . .'

'First this,' Brid ordered. 'I can't do anything for you until we deaden the pain.' She delved deep into the leather herb-scrip and retrieved a scroll of wrinkled greyish-brown bark. 'Here, chew this. It'll take a little time to work and I'll see to the dog while we're waiting.'

Anxiously Caspar examined the bark, stroking the ribbed inner surface before tentatively sliding it into his mouth. He grimaced at the bitter taste.

'Is he alive?' Wartooth's survival leapt foremost into Caspar's concern now that Hal was breathing peacefully. The dog had slept at the foot of his cradle when Caspar was a baby and had followed him around the castle ever since . . . and far beyond it, on stag- and boar-hunts. The beloved animal lay unmoving against Caspar's side, still covered by the fur-skin. The boy stretched out his arm to stroke the dog's blood-matted fur. Why didn't you keep out of trouble, Wartooth? Why did you have to be so brave and loyal and devoted? Caspar repeated his question without much hope in his voice.

Brid did not answer. She stretched out the dog's neck, feeling for a pulse in his jugular, and then combed her fingers through the short grey coat to the shattered shoulder blade. 'He'll not hunt again,' she said sadly and Caspar took that as a euphemism for dead and closed his eyes, to squeeze the tears back. He was vaguely aware of the girl continuing to speak but his mind was with his hound. Suddenly he grasped something of what she was saying.

'What?'

'He looks very old so the bones won't heal well, poor fellow, but there's no other damage. The bleeding has stopped.'

'He's going to live then?' Caspar lurched excitedly forward from his prone position only to be cruelly punished by his wound.

'Not forever, but if I can get the bolt out, a few more years perhaps. It's gone in straight.' She started to murmur to herself as if trying to decide what to do.

'What is doings with the animal?' The ginger-bearded chief bent down towards Brid and lifted up her swollen face with a sharp jerk. 'The animal not in bargain. You sees to the Belbidak boyling now, or I cuts the neck of animal with axe, I cuts it, see.' He raised the double-bladed cleaver above his head and Brid responded with a gesture of obeisance. 'You does your work good, or you lose the other eye, witch.'

A drowsy feeling began to distance Caspar from his pain and Brid's gentle words echoed as if she was calling from the other side of the valley. The long stalk-like legs of the wolf crossed the edge of his vision, seeming to stretch up into the sky from where he lay and he could hear a sound like a cat lapping milk. It took him a moment to realize that Brid's wolf was licking Wartooth's wounds clean.

The girl looked at him crookedly and raised her eyebrows as she prodded the wound, testing for his response. 'Good, you're not feeling it so much now. The willow bark I gave you is to be thanked for doing its job.'

Caspar watched as if he was outside the scene looking down on someone who looked like him but was not him. Brid moulded two rounds of mud in her palms and put them aside in readiness, before taking hold of his ankle. Carefully she placed a rock underneath the shaft of the bolt just where it exited the skin.

'Vaalakan,' her distant voice commanded. 'If you want this boy to live more than two days, slice through the shaft of the bolt right here.' She pointed with her finger. The red-bearded chief was true and swift, delivering an accurate blow.

'Ready, friend?' warned Brid as she began to ease the bolt out. Once the cleaved end of the bolt disappeared into the ankle, blood began to seep out of the hole left behind. Brid carefully packed the wound with the mud that soaked up his escaping blood. Caspar was aware of the bolt dragging against his shin bone pulling the sinews and tendons aside in its passage; but he felt no pain. Brid's nimble fingers twisted the bolt to free it from the adhesions already forming around it and at last the shaft slid out, coated in clots of blood. Blood spouted from the round hole and she quickly stemmed it with the mud-pack. She waited as the mud turned red and became sodden, then replaced the mud-pack with another. Gradually the loss of blood eased and Brid caked the entire ankle in the clay, bandaging her work with shreds of cloth torn from her skirts.

'Sleep now,' she whispered and Caspar had no strength to disobey.

When he awoke it was dark; only a soft grey light from behind the eastern peaks hinted at morning. The fire was low and one of the Vaalakan axemen sat hunched with his back to the embers, watching studiously. The others were asleep, except Brid who cradled Hal's head in her lap and was stroking his brow.

'How do you feel?' she whispered to Caspar, seeing he was awake.

'Awful. My ankle's throbbing and I feel sick, but,' he laughed as if to make light of it, 'I don't mean to complain. How's Hal?'

'Asleep. His pulse is strong though.'

'Thank God.'

'No. Thank the Mother,' Brid retorted stiffly.

A shiver of fear prickled along the boy's spine at her words and for a moment he dreaded that this pagan witch was brewing some devilish plans for them. But he looked again at this small ugly creature who had so willingly helped them and his superstitious fears drifted away. He knew nothing about this small girl with her hideous deformities, bulging blind eye and tumorous cheek. But there was something other than her gruesome appearance which was even more disconcerting. Caspar could not quite place what it was that disturbed him. Small and neat, she looked only just a little older than himself. Yet she also seemed ancient, wise. In fact, steeped in wisdom that had been gathered over centuries, with a strong powerful heart and a brave soul – all this incarcerated in her vulnerable, crippled body. And yet, Caspar mused, unlike her face and ankle, her arms and body were strong and wholesome, the skin smooth and tight like a young rose-bud touched with the dew of morning. There was something else incongruous in her voice and clothes: she had both the accent and the muddy attire of a peasant girl but they were contradicted by her erudite speech.

'Who are you? Where are you from? Why are you helping us?' Caspar asked insistently.

'I'm Brid. I'm here because I felt the power of the Eye awaken.' She surreptitiously nodded towards the muscular bulk of the Vaalakan chief who sat hunched with his bearskins heaped over his shoulders, half-concealing a dim ghostly glow. It dawned on the boy that she was referring to the moonstone. 'Someone touched it, someone with the power to speak to it and its song drew me.' She frowned thoughtfully at the freckled youth, for a split second fixing him with her eye, and then lowered her voice to a conspiratorial whisper that made him feel uncomfortably disconcerted. 'But we won't talk of it now.' Her strong fingers combed through the coarse hair on the back of the injured deer-hound as she spoke, then fondly patted Wartooth who lay nested together with the wolf. 'I tracked you with the help of the dog here, who was nose to the ground on your scent. I took the bolt out of his shoulder by the way. It's up to the wolf to help him now. The Vaalakans won't be interested in the dog.'

'What have you done to him?' Caspar could just make out a pale grey patch of shaved skin around the dog's punctured hide, with signs marking the naked flesh. 'More runes of healing?'

'No.' Brid lowered her voice. 'But none here will know the difference. No, they are a message.'

'For whom? How? No one at Torra Alta can read runes.'

'To their shame and possible downfall.' A hint of disgust threaded through Brid's voice. 'No, for the Crone: she'll know what to do.'

'An old woman,' Caspar scoffed.

'Be careful, boy. If it weren't for me, your friend might well be dead because of that stupid Vaalakan with his purging herbs, and you might well be on the way to losing your leg to gangrene.' Brid pulled her lame leg up towards her chest and hugged her knees as if putting a barrier up between herself and the disparaging boy.

'My name's Caspar, not boy. But – forgive me. I have not thanked you properly. I'm sorry I upset you.'

'So you should be. Don't question the wisdom of things you obviously know nothing about,' she snapped.

Are women always so contrary, thought Caspar in despair. They seem to take offence so easily. He tried to remain placatory. 'What is the message? How will it get to this woman?'

'I suppose it's not your fault,' she relented, 'that you know nothing of the old ways, nor that the menfolk of Torra Alta who are meant to protect this land have betrayed their Gods and left us all vulnerable to these butchers.'

'You're right, it's not my fault.' Caspar was beginning to get exasperated by the girl. 'Just tell me: to what do I owe your charity . . . and the moonstone, how do you know about that? Why are you so intent on it?'

Brid laughed, a sound like trickling water sparkling in the sunlight. 'Moonstone indeed. You mean the Druid's Eye. I felt the moonstones awaken. Five of them at first, but they were weak and I knew they were not the One Eye. All the same, it was significant. I felt them descend into the womb of the earth. So I came here. I brought the wolf with me across the valleys until I could see the towers of Torra Alta in the great canyon. Then I could feel the pagan stones alive beneath my feet, their vibrations coming up through the soil.'

'Magic!' breathed Caspar to himself.

'The stones give out a powerful radiation,' Brid said patiently. 'Anyone who is even half alive can feel it.'

'I suppose I did feel it,' agreed Caspar uncomfortably, but thought to himself that none of the others had.

'Then suddenly I felt the surge of energy from the One Eye and I knew someone had reached her; someone with power had found the Eye. I felt the jolt like lightning stabbing up through the earth's crust.' Suddenly her gaze seemed to pierce right through him. 'And it was you, wasn't it, who reached her? That's why I'm here.'

The pagan girl's words were madness, some sort of horrible necromancy. He felt that her mind must be creeping under his flesh, searching for his soul. How did she know about the frosted blue-lipped woman that *he* had seen in the moonstone?

'You reached the thoughts of the Mother.' Brid's words were relentless. 'We need you to reach her. I cannot reach her, nor can the Crone, not without your help. I felt the bones of the earth tremble with emotion. You have to help us. We need her, the whole world needs her, otherwise all will be lost. The balance of life is lost without her.'

Only the hope that this was all some drug-induced fantasy

from the witch-girl's herbs stopped Caspar's horrified disquiet from swelling into panic. The girl was talking about fiendish witchcraft and somehow implying that *he*, the son of a baron, had the power of the devil in him. He was already engulfed in this corruption, his soul threatened. He tried to pray but all he could think of was the Chaplain telling him to drive out the heathen will that festered in his soul . . . and he had always found the Chaplain unconvincing.

'Your nose is broken,' Brid said suddenly, as though she had just noticed.

Caspar touched his face. 'I'd forgotten about that. Hal did it.'

'Figures. Normal destructive behaviour one would expect from boys your age.' Brid was annoyingly condescending again, dismissing Caspar to face the pearly light of dawn that crept softly into the Hart's Leap Valley. Seeing the highlighted contours of her face, a mixture of curiosity, pity and revulsion confused Caspar. He could not help staring at the bulging eye-socket, seamed across its centre by a line of gluey, congealed eyelashes. The left side of her face bulged, pulling the skin sideways and curling her mouth into a distorted sneer. Perhaps it's some canker in her cheek bones, he thought, and then started to shiver, or worse, perhaps it's contagious. In the centre of her forehead a blue mark was painted onto the skin. He wondered if the rune was some kind of warning.

'Don't stare at my face: it's not polite.'

Caspar was embarrassed. 'I'm sorry, I didn't mean to. I hope it gets better,' he stammered realizing he was not saying the right things at all. 'I mean, how did it happen? Oh I'm sorry! I mean . . . I shouldn't have mentioned it.'

'Forget it, I'm not offended and you don't need to worry, it's not infectious.'

Caspar's distrust mounted each time she seemed to read his mind. He pointed out gloomily that now she had saved their lives they were all, of course, prisoners.

'Yes, but that's not quite so final as dead, is it?'

'I'm worth your freedom?'

Brid nodded.

'Tell me again, why?' Caspar was suspicious.

'Because you can reach the woman. The power in the Druid's Eye will show you. You can find her.'

'What woman? Who is she?' Caspar was frightened. A cold ghostly feeling was emptying his soul and he refused to accept anymore that the image in the stone had anything to do with him. 'I won't have anything to do with necromancy and unresting spirits. Just forget it.'

Brid's tone became more cajoling. 'What are you frightened of? She will not hurt you. You need her – Torra Alta needs her just as much as I do.'

'This is all madness. I only saw some sort of spectre or mirage in the stone. An image of a dead woman. She looked dead in the stone.'

Brid suddenly looked weak as if her confidence was sapping away from her. She whispered, 'No, she isn't. I can't believe it.'

'How do you know?'

'I just do,' she said flatly, turning to the wolf and thoughtfully stroking its pricked ears as if to draw comfort from the animal. 'She has to be alive.'

'So you don't know?'

'No, I don't know!' she snapped. 'I can only know for sure when we find her, we have to find her. I've been looking for her all my life and now at last you are here to help me.'

'I don't like this "we".' He tried to deepen his voice to make it authoritative and worthy of his rank but he still sounded weak in comparison to the girl's easy confidence. He did not like the way she took control. 'Why should I trust you?'

'Because I have traded my freedom to save your leg and Hal from that useless Vaalakan and his ideas of healing,' she reasoned.

'Well, unless you start waving your magic wand to get us all back to Torra Alta, I don't want anything to do with your witchcraft.' The boy bristled with displeasure. How did this girl know so much? It wasn't natural. The best solution was to wait for Hal to come round and take charge. And what about Wartooth? She still hadn't explained the message.

'We're not going back to Torra Alta.' She stated it simply and firmly as if *she* was the authority amongst them, and not the brutish Vaalakans. She certainly didn't seem to respect his position as the heir to Torra Alta. Caspar's thoughts were diverted by a low moan from his uncle. Wincing with his own pain, Caspar wriggled on his elbows to be close to his waking kinsman. Brid, too, anxiously stared into the dark youth's face.

Hal's eyelids flickered and slowly he drew them open. 'Spar, is that you? Thank God you're all right.' He rolled his head round to look warily in the direction of the other face peering at him. His mouth dropped open and his eyelids froze for a second as if he was trying to work out what he was looking at. A sort of horrified, throttled scream tried to escape from his mouth but he controlled his fear and clutched at Caspar's hand. 'I think I'm hallucinating: I can see a demon crouching over me.' He laughed nervously.

'That's Brid,' Caspar tried to explain.

'You mean it's real!'

'Don't worry –'

'Are we dead? Are we in Hell?' Hal hurriedly pushed himself up to a sitting position but slumped back clutching his ribs. 'Vaalakans! Nothing's changed then. We're still prisoners.' He turned his head away from the girl, refusing to look at her as if denying her presence. 'What's going on, Spar? God, my ribs hurt.'

'They're not broken,' Brid said tartly, as if the boy was making too big a fuss, before Caspar could explain anything.

Hal gaped in horror at the runes inscribed on his skin. 'You devil, you witch,' he started to scream. 'Get away from me, witch.'

The uproar from the Belbidians alerted the enemy warriors, who circled the prone bodies like vultures. Brid stood up to face them.

'Well, little witch? They sounds very alives to me. You

done well. Now you must keep bargain. Kullak!'

The big Vaalakan waved the crossbowman forward and grunted something at him and the slight man stepped nervously forward holding a length of rope. Hissing anxiously he averted his eyes from Brid's piercing stare. But she did not resist as he wove a tight knot around her wrists. He handed the end of the rope to his chief and scurried to a more comfortable distance, away from the one-eyed girl.

'Will they lives, yes, if they ride on the animal?' The Vaalakan chief indicated the snoring troll that had ignored the call of the dawn light and had not yet stirred from its noisy slumber. Brid nodded which gave the signal for the Vaalakans to break camp.

While the Belbidian captives had wavered on the brink of death Scragg had kept a low profile, but now his status seemed to be restored. He made a show of ordering two of the axemen to collect their bedding and stack the cooking utensils. He paused for a moment to eye the wolf and Wartooth, who still huddled close to Caspar, before kicking the animals with his boot.

'Nak! Nak!' he growled, which brought Wartooth unsteadily to three of his paws, tail clamped between his hind legs and a stiff line of hairs bristling along the length of his spine. The wolf displayed a shocking line of sabre-like fangs that, for a moment, made Scragg hesitate before reaching for the handle of his axe.

'Home, girl,' warned Brid and the wolf backed down, retreating from the circle of men. Wartooth limped precariously, with his fourth leg crooked up beneath his body, as he followed close on the wolf's heels. He paused just a moment to look at his master for reassurance.

'Away, boy.' Caspar gave the dog the familiar command that sent him on ahead in the hunt, and the dog faithfully obeyed. 'I hope he will be all right,' he sighed sadly.

'The wolf will look after him, you can be sure of that.' Brid spoke softly again. Now that she was tied and helpless, much of her authority had dwindled. The daylight was harsh on her disfigured face and bluish streaks of smeared woad made her ugliness so complete it was no wonder Hal had thought her a demon.

A piece of raw rabbit meat enticed the troll to its feet and the two axemen callously stowed the bundles of fur and various cooking pots onto its humped back. With equally rough-handling they loaded the prisoners as well. Hal was white with pain when they lifted him up. He slumped forward against his nephew for support.

'Here.' Brid extended her tied hands up towards them. 'It'll numb the pain and speed the healing.' Caspar reached down and took the willow bark from her strong, hardworking hands.

'I'm not taking anything from the witch.' Hal was defiant.

'I really don't like you very much,' Brid spoke candidly. 'But hopefully when you learn not to be so afraid of me your manners will improve.'

'I'm not asking you to like me, witch, and I'm certainly not afraid. Preposterous!' He laughed derisively but the mirth quickly turned to a stifled cough as it stabbed at his injured ribs.

'Her name is Brid,' Caspar introduced the girl, thinking that some political intervention between the two was needed. Somehow Hal's suspicious, antagonistic attitude towards the girl made Caspar feel protective instead. She might be a heretic, but she is a Belbidian, and in times of war they should stick together regardless of faith. 'Hal, this is Brid: Brid, this is Hal. And we are not going to fight amongst ourselves.'

'Aren't we?' Hal was unrelenting, still rubbing gingerly at his chest to remove the runic markings, even though the skin was tender. 'As far as I'm concerned, she isn't one of us.'

'May the Goddess preserve us!' exclaimed the exasperated girl.

'May God strike you down and send you to Hell,' retorted Hal, but this sent Brid into paroxysms of laughter and the Belbidian youth was taken aback. 'What's so damn funny?'

'You are. You have about as much power to invoke the help of a God as . . . as . . .' she looked about herself for inspiration, 'as the tail on this stinking troll here. You don't even know which God you are calling on.'

'There is only one!' Hal replied triumphantly as if he had scored a winning point in the argument.

'You are a wise and learned old man and you know that,' Brid taunted.

'And you? What proof have you got that your Gods listen to you?'

'You are my proof: you'd be dead if they didn't.' She smiled crookedly at him and Hal looked away in disgust.

The tiresome argument annoyed Caspar and he was angry with himself for being unable to stop it. They paid no heed to his placating suggestions and for the long hard morning Hal and Brid snapped and quarrelled tirelessly, which to Caspar's indignation provided entertainment for the Vaalakan chief. The ginger-bearded man now marched one pace ahead of the troll as he idly swung the moonstone in its lattice leather pouch. Brid watched it incessantly and Caspar found himself desperately trying to see its hypnotic light which hid in the brightness of day. He told himself that escape was all he was intent on but, all the same, the thought of the moonstone preyed on his mind.

'Vaalakan,' Hal arrogantly called ahead. 'Hey you, Red Beard, where are you taking us? Hey, Ruddy-bard, or whatever your name is.'

The big man looked at them coldly. 'To Lord Morbak,' he grunted by way of reply. 'He wipe the smile off boyling's face.'

'And why?'

'For answers to question,' he replied with a smug smile, glancing down towards the swaying orb.

'What question?'

'Morbak ask.'

'And why should we answer him? Do you think we are such weak fools?'

'Ah! Belbidak fools, no one refuse Morbak.' The Vaalakan spoke with surety and it was his candid confidence that struck the cold blade of fear deep into Caspar's heart. Would he really give away secrets – to save Hal, would he? The answer was too painfully true: yes of course he would.

'And the girl?' Caspar demanded. 'She knows nothing. You don't need her.' Even though she was a heretical pagan she did save Hal's life and his leg so he felt honour bound to repay her. The least he could do was to try and beg for her release. He looked down at the hooded figure dragging her useless leg. She looked so helpless and forlorn, nothing like the commanding presence of yesterday. Another voice in his head laughed at him. Don't be so stupid, Spar, she's hideously ugly and a witch at that. What do you care about such an ugly girl? But she saved us, she is brave and loyal and her voice is exquisite.

'Important she is for you? Come forward for helps you, she does. I, no fool, boyling.' The ginger-bearded Vaalakan sniggered. 'And too, Lord Morbak likes sport. He hungers for entertainment, and the girl and a troll make good entertainment, they wills. Good sport for pleases Lord Morbak.'

'You're going to feed her to a troll! You are a revolting people, evil and sick.'

The big man's shoulders shook with laughter. 'He-trolls don't eat girlings, little Belbidak.' The insinuation in the man's words appalled Caspar more than anything he had ever heard.

'I'm sorry, Brid; you didn't need to hear that. I should have kept quiet,' he apologized.

'No,' she replied. 'It is more fearful to face the unknown. Better to be prepared.'

The journey dragged through interminably long days. Drawn-out periods of depressed silence united the three captives, each contemplating the baneful horrors that lay before them. The pain in Caspar's ankle had lessened to an ache, though Hal still refused any comfort from the willow bark. Without the pain Caspar was able to think more clearly. Eventually, the image in the moonstone began fading from his memory like a dream disappearing back to the unconscious mists of the mind.

Harsh scree slopes and sparsely covered rocks gradually gave way to more gently rounded hills softened with tufts of grass and banks of heather. Stunted oaks and smooth-barked beeches grew on the gentler inclines and Caspar realized they were dropping into the more hospitable climes of the northern foothills of the Yellow Mountains. Finally they brimmed a ridge and the horizon dipped away into the plains of the dense deciduous forest, draped in gold, copper and bronze with the early onset of autumn. A narrow band of pasture bordered the hills before being swallowed by the trees of the Boarchase Forest.

No landmark struck Caspar as familiar so he decided they were far to the west of their usual hunting ground. The forest spanned a tract of land many leagues wide and he had explored very little of it.

'The Boarchase,' Hal grunted. It was the first word Hal had spoken for many hours. He had become sullen from Brid's company and the pain of his ribs. 'And look!' Unable to point with his hands because of the trusses, he tossed his head towards the lowlands below. 'There's a nest of these Vaalakan rats already spawning within the borders of Belbidia.'

Caspar could just make out some distant activity half hidden in the crisp foliage of the autumn forest. An advance camp of Vaalakan spies. He could see them like ants crawling around a circular defence of stakes constructed in the depths of the woodland. So the first of the Vaalakans were already encamped on his lands. He struggled frantically but vainly against his bonds until the wound in his ankle throbbed with stabbing pains.

Chapter 9

'Have you sided against me, then?' Hal sat with his back to the stockade wall, glowering at Caspar. The wall of imprisoning stakes had a grid-work of poles closely lashed together to form a ceiling that imprisoned them within the cramped circular pit. Hal lashed out against the unyielding walls in his frustration, then sat rubbing his bruised fist. The stench of a nearby troll seeped into their pen and the constant salivary sound of its gnawing at some bone ground on their nerves. The tedium of their imprisonment was broken occasionally by bursts of activity as messengers and spies slunk to and from the camp. For several days their emotional strength was sapped by their helpless frustration at being held captive while enemy spies freely made sorties into the mountains around Torra Alta.

'It's not like that. Can't you just listen to her, Hal?' pleaded the younger boy, feeling increasingly exasperated by his uncle. He thumped the ground with his fist impatiently.

'She's a witch and an ugly one at that. And she's just a girl. What does she know of man's wars? Nothing. She knows about roots and flowers and twiddly bits of herb for cooking. She could probably thread a needle better than I could but I'll be damned if I'm going to listen to a little snip of a girl about serious matters like the future of Torra Alta.' Hal scuffed at the ground with the back of his heel and stared stubbornly at his nephew.

'Prejudice makes fools of many a wise man,' sighed Brid with deliberate condescension. It was the first time she had spoken for some while and Caspar was afraid she had been deeply wounded by Hal's scornful remarks; but she seemed more bored than upset by the harsh words.

'Don't you get cocky with me, witch,' Hal said bitterly.

'Frightened that I'll put the evil eye on you then?' she laughed, pulling down the lower eyelid of her good eye to show the moist red of the inner tissue. 'Listen, Caspar, we don't need him. If he's going to be that stupid and stubborn he can stay behind and rot here at the mercy of the Vaalakans for all I care.'

'I'm not going without Hal.' The younger boy's eyes flared with a stubbornness that could only be matched by his uncle.

'Oh Mother,' swore Brid, 'back to the beginning – round and round in circles.'

'I don't get this "going" bit.' Hal's bitter sarcasm made his voice like acid. 'It seems to me you're forgetting the small problem of a dozen, maybe more, ox-like men with hungry axes waiting to chop off your dumb heads when you decide to "go" from here. What are you going to do? Fly on your broomstick? How do you expect me to listen to your blasphemous madness – your evil heresy, when you won't even explain how you are going to escape?'

'I've told you. Now listen carefully this time and maybe you'll remember.' Brid's patience was finally exhausted. 'I sent a message with the dog. Morrigwen will have it by now. Two more nights and she'll be prepared, then we'll make our move. We've only got to get to the edge of the encampment.'

'And now, what's this "only" bit?' sneered Hal.

'You'll just have to trust me, because you wouldn't believe me if I explained.' The girl clutched her knees to her chest and stared down at her bare feet. The right ankle was at an impossible angle, sickeningly twisted with the knobbly tarsal bones protruding through the skin, where the ankle should have been smooth and rounded. Caspar could not help gawking at the deformity.

'If I wouldn't believe you, it sounds like a good reason not to trust you, wouldn't you say?' Hal's logic sounded solid and Brid was stumped for a moment for a reply. 'I mean,' continued the older youth, 'Spar's a fool, easily taken in by talk of magic. You can pull the wool over his eyes but you're not making an idiot out of me. I want some facts.'

'All right, all right, I'll show you.' Brid tossed back the overshadowing hood that partly shielded her face from inquisitive eyes to reveal a knotted mat of hair, tangled and twisted, clinging to her skin. It was impossible to tell what shade of brown it might be because of the coating of grime. 'Just one thing though. The rest is too difficult to do twice.'

Caspar was intrigued and wondered whether she was about to produce another root or herb from the lining of her cloak; one that might turn the Vaalakan camp mad or blind, he fancied. But they all fell instantly silent as the plank of wood barricading the entrance to their stockade rattled and groaned as someone drew it open. Brid scooped the hood back over her head and retreated into it. A familiar sneer twisted Scragg's face as it appeared in the opening. He stood with his legs astride and hands on hips, taking in deep satisfied breaths before waving three heavy-weight men forward into the stockade.

'Borog now here. He and Morbak very close. Borog a Vaalak chief. So you is advised to keep arrogant mouth shut. You comes with me, you comes.' Scragg turned his back on the prisoners leaving his subordinates to the rough work of bringing out the Belbidians. No concession to Brid's sex or to Hal's and Caspar's injuries saved them from being manhandled to their feet. With their arms screwed behind their backs they were forced to follow the young Vaalakan. Scragg marched stiffly ahead with his chin proudly tilted upwards as if he were enjoying a new found status amongst the troop of spies. He led them towards a cleared area of pasture, recently stripped of its vegetation and surrounded by a high fence of hurdles cut from forest saplings. Caspar studied the circular clearing, wondering if it was a pound for livestock or trolls, but then he noticed the two sturdy stakes driven into the black soil. He realized with a growing sense of foreboding that they were entering some kind of temporary arena.

'Borog has impatience. We already send message to Master about magic stone. He already knows we have it from you now so Borog saying you is not so important now. He want games now. No wait for Morbak,' Scragg told them, smiling right across his square face. 'We is testing your strongness and braveness. Good sport it is.'

A wooden stand erected at one end of the arena provided a privileged seat for the Vaalakan under-chief who was surrounded by perhaps two dozen warriors. He was surprisingly short for a Northman but made up for it with a more than generous amount of blubber and a lofty head-dress of antlers and eagle feathers that proudly proclaimed his superior status. Kullak was quickly at his side, jealously pushing himself in front of Scragg, to whisper and point excitedly towards Brid. Evidently there was some rivalry between the two Vaalakans. The blubbery man listened and then raised a puffy hand to order the prisoners forward.

The fat lips chewed out a string of Vaalakan words directly at the prisoners and when he had finished he raised an eyebrow anticipating a reply. Kullak put a hand tentatively on the fat man's shoulder and whispered again, which made Borog cough and, staring with annoyance at the Vaalakan shaman, he jerked his head in the direction of the prisoners.

'The Chief has thought you speaks Vaalak, but I, Kullak, is interpreter.' He looked around him to make sure that all Vaalakan eyes were on him. Scragg glowered jealously from behind Borog's shoulder. 'The soldier-chief is kind man with big heart.'

'And an absolutely enormous stomach,' interrupted Hal. Kullak ignored him.

'He gives you choice. One boyling only is defending girl? She is in arena, yes? Bait, like goat tied to stake. Which is defending girling from Vaalak warrior?'

Caspar eyed his uncle whose head was down staring at his foot as it drew circles in the soil. Even if Hal was stronger than him he evidently cared little for the girl's welfare and so Brid stood a better chance if he, Caspar, championed her.

Caspar made a movement as if to step forward but the guard restrained him, so instead he announced with brave dignity, 'I will be her champion.'

His clear voice was drowned out by Hal's simultaneous, but less chivalrous proclamation. 'Damn it, I suppose I'll have to do it.'

Kullak translated to his under-chief while Hal and Caspar argued vehemently with one another. The shaman raised his hand to cut through their protestations. 'It is decided, it is. You Belbidak,' he pointed at Hal, 'you is bigger so it is more sport. We begin.'

Three lounging soldiers stood at these words and raised dented silver horns to their lips. A discordant blast from them brought another dozen troops hurrying into the arena, jostling for the prime places which would provide the best spectacle. Still protesting, Caspar was dragged away by the guards to be held at the foot of Borog's seat. Hal's expression was blank as he prepared himself mentally. The under-chief growled at a warrior beside him who reluctantly handed over his double-bladed axe and his helmet to the youth. Hal hefted the weapon.

'Thank you,' Brid spoke in a low voice.

'Don't,' retorted the grim-faced youth. 'I'm doing this for Spar, not for you because, if I don't fight, that young fool will – and he'd go and get himself hurt.'

Brid was escorted away by a guard who manacled her good leg to one of the stakes, leaving her hands free so that she could struggle entertainingly but with no hope of escape. A small defenceless figure, she backed up against the stake and pulled her hood close about her face. Hal advanced towards her, gripping the unfamiliar weapon and pressed the visorless iron helm onto his raven head. He paced steadily across the open arena until he stood five yards from the girl and then pivoted neatly on his heel to stand full-square in front of her.

The axe was designed for a bigger man and to Caspar's dismay he could see that Hal had difficulty wielding the foreign weapon as he practised a few slicing swings. Distinct pain scarred Hal's face as he raised his arms, putting pressure on his injured ribs, but he nobly persisted in familiarizing himself with the action of the double-bladed axe.

The obese Vaalakan under-chief made a loud unintelligible declaration and Kullak bounced to his feet and translated into halting Belbidian. 'Who claim the girling? Ugly girling but still has body of girling. Who fights the Belbidak for the girling?' Booing and hissing erupted through the crowded troops, who even far from home and their Vaalakan women, scorned the offer of this girl. Caspar felt almost ashamed for her, but was relieved that her hideous face provided better protection than Hal with his cumbersome axe. The jeering was silenced by Scragg who leapt into the arena skilfully brandishing his own gleaming axe. He grinned at the crowd whose mood rapidly altered to appreciation at the prospect of some bloody action. He swaggered across the black soil, bowing to the cheers from left and right before saluting the under-chief and concentrating on his opponent.

'I is forbidden to kill you, I is, but I hurt you bad – bad so I takes the girl, I does,' he warned. 'She is ugly, yes, troll-ugly, but I have girl for proof, for trophy. I show that I Vaalakan has Belbidak women as me please. The Belbidak is too little man. No protects his own girling. Too little and weak like is all Belbidaks.' To cheers of support and delight he repeated his words in Vaalakan for the benefit of the gathered spies. Borog was stirred and rose to his feet, clapping gleefully.

Vainly, Caspar struggled at his bonds. Brid was making her own preparations and, rather than cowering meekly, she gripped a length of the chain between her fists aiming to injure Scragg if he approached her. The Torra Altan youth and the young Vaalakan warrior circled each other almost as if an invisible cord threaded their eyes. Scragg feinted from side to side, testing Hal's response. Caspar could see clearly for himself his uncle's quickness of foot, but more obvious was the weakness in his upper body from his recent injuries.

'You might not be allowed to kill me, but if you want the girl that's just what you'll have to do. I'll show you all that no Belbidian man abandons their womenfolk. From the most beautiful to the most wretched, I fight for the honour of all.' Hal's noble words carried easily across the open ground and Caspar knew that despite his prejudices against Brid, Hal's words were true: his uncle was patriotic to the core. 'I'm going to cut that sneer right out of your face, Vaalakan,' he bravely threatened.

The enemy warriors cheered as Scragg made his move. From a low crouch he burst forward, holding his axe high over his left shoulder, but with a skilful twist of the wrist he swung the axe down and round to the opposite shoulder. Then he sprang. Caspar did not want to watch but it was too awful not to. If Scragg landed the blow Hal would lose an arm or a leg in the blinking of an eye. Hal feinted forward, drawing Scragg's blow but then sprang back to avoid the slicing blade that carved a whistling arc through the air a hair's-breadth from his kneecaps. For a second Caspar could breathe again.

The Vaalakan, however, deftly adapted his misplaced blow, guiding it expertly to the zenith of its stroke where for a split second it hung in mid-air. Then he began a new trajectory targeted directly at Hal's helmeted head. The thin wedge of polished blade split the air and time stood still for Caspar. Scragg was about to cleanly sever the top of Hal's skull. But at the very last moment Scragg deftly twisted the blade so that the flat of it smashed against the steel plate shielding Hal's temple and sent him reeling sideways, sprawling to the ground.

Hal was down but still struggling. He rolled back and forth in the mud to avoid Scragg's bone-splintering attacks, using his axe more as a pike-staff than a cleaver to try and divert the blows. 'Attack!' urged Caspar. 'Get to your feet. Come on, Hal, you can do it.' Unfortunately it was all too obvious that the dexterous Vaalakan was an accomplished fighter as he tormented Hal with his menacing axe, like a cat playing with a mouse before neatly dispatching it with a flash of its claws.

'Hal!' Brid suddenly shouted out to him, 'get back towards me. Get to your feet.'

Still prone on his back, Hal was too occupied by Scragg's

axe to answer her. Ducking and cringing from the tormenting threat of each blow, he kicked his heels into the ground and wriggled backwards away from the slicing cleaver.

'Get to your feet, Hal,' she shouted again. Brid, with her eye anxiously on her reluctant champion, stretched the chain to its full length and limped backwards in a full circle around the stake. She dragged her heel to score a deep line in the soil. 'Get back to me.'

The heavy swing weight of the axe required strength and stamina to wield and Scragg was, at last, visibly tiring with the repeated effort of controlling the cleaver. The pause between each attack became momentarily longer and Hal grabbed his opportunity, kicking his feet underneath him and springing up in one acrobatic movement. Though Scragg gracefully wielded his weapon in long sweeping arcs, the inexperienced Torra Altan found the heavy-headed cleaver too unwieldy. Instead he gripped the axe half way down the shaft and charged his opponent, chopping wildly into the air. The Vaalakan withdrew one pace, momentarily surprised by Hal's speed and ferocity as well as the deafening battle-cry that howled from the youth's lungs. The blades clashed with a flash of sparks but Scragg, practised at hand-to-hand combat, had already regained his balance. With a flick of his wrist to adjust the angle of his blade, he wrenched Hal's weapon from his grasp and sent it spinning through the air.

Anticipation briefly silenced the Northmen as Hal's axe spun through the air, out of reach, and the heavy thud as it dented the soil was easily audible across the hushed arena.

Brid's cry was startlingly loud and all eyes swept across the open soil to fix on her. 'Hal, listen to me.' Her shout was urgent and compelling. 'You have to get into my circle.'

Bereft of his axe and with arms outstretched, Hal kept low, like a cat preparing to pounce. Bravely he faced his opponent, who now took his time, confident of certain victory, relishing in his glory and soaking up the cheers from his fellow men.

Caspar could plainly see Brid's scuffed line encircling her stake. He watched in bewilderment as she drew angular patterns in the earth and persistently urged Hal to retreat to her circle. Her intentions were too esoteric to guess at and Caspar doubted that Hal would heed her call. Apart from his distrust of Brid, surely, thought Caspar, his uncle would never run to the succour of a girl whilst he faced a man in combat.

The loose folds of her cloak rolled off her slender arms as she stretched her hands to the heavens. An inner strength seemed to well up out of her soul and grow inside that small defenceless figure, arming the frail broken body. As when she had first come to their aid, Caspar felt the power of her presence. Instinctively he knew that Hal must obey her.

The foul bloodlust disappeared from the air as Brid captured every eye and ear by raising her voice to sing out, 'These are the runes of protection. Mother, hear your daughter in her moment of peril and unleash the runes of protection.'

Hal's eyes flitted nervously between her, his axe lying several paces out of reach, and Scragg, who was preparing to make another strike. Caspar bit into his lips as he waited for Hal to make a dash for the weapon but to his surprise his uncle answered Brid's call and sprinted back to the stake. Scragg let him run: it seemed to please the arrogant Vaalakan's sense of drama. He laughed scornfully at his opponent's rapid retreat and began a slow elaborate approach, garnishing his marched attack with an impressive display of his ability with the axe. He tossed it high into the air, watching its elliptical spin and stepped forward to catch it behind him. Hand over hand he kept the axe rotating, twirling it as he steadily advanced on his defenceless prey. Again he cast the weapon high into the blue sky and caught the handle without altering his rhythm or pausing in his movements. Absorbed in his moment of glory, Scragg was wallowing in the admiration of his fellow men. It gave Hal and Brid time.

The girl stood at the full stretch of the chain, which manacled her ankle to the stake, and Hal stood a pace in front of her and a pace nearer the stake. He was breathing hard, one hand clutched to his ribs and the other on his knee to support his exhausted body. His eyes looked out from beneath the protection of his open-faced helm and focused acutely on the ceremonial approach of the Vaalakan.

Scragg halted three paces from Brid's circle, still twirling his axe with perfect balance. Up the axe went again in slow twisting circles, the blade whistling as it arced through the air. It hung poised for a split second at the apex of its arc before gravity called it back to earth in the same spiralling pattern. Watch the man, don't look at the axe, Hal, Caspar willed his uncle. But Hal stayed crouched, his eyes flitting between Scragg's feet and legs, waiting for the moment, waiting to see the trigger that fired Scragg's charge. Never once did his eyes follow the distraction of the axe.

The double-bladed cleaver swung up again and Scragg's feet split slightly apart. This time, Hal, be ready, thought Caspar. He's coming at you this time. The axe was twisting back down again towards Scragg's skilful grasp and a barely perceptible flex in his ankles and knees showed the beginnings of a crouch. The axe touched his fingers and already Scragg was in full flight, the weapon poised above his head ready to deal a severing blow the moment he covered the five paces. He made two of them before Hal flinched a muscle. The Belbidian was ready, like a hawk hovering over its kill, but he waited for the precise moment with the patience and self-control of the hunter.

For all Scragg's skill and agility, for all his training with the double-bladed axe, he could not outmatch the simple dexterity of a mountain man from Torra Alta.

'Now,' commanded Hal fiercely, leaping up and back to coincide with Brid's lame sprint forward. The chain whisked beneath Hal's feet just as Scragg leapt at him and it bit into the Vaalakan's shin. He fell, arms outstretched at Hal's feet, the chain entangled around his ankles in an embarrassing spectacle. Brid flung herself into the centre of the circle, tightly wrapping Scragg's thrashing feet and pinioned his legs to the ground, leaving the rest to Hal.

The young Belbidian youth reversed his backward spring and immediately fell forward onto Scragg's shoulder blades, pinning the axe-man to the ground. Scragg kicked out madly like a wild beast snared in a trap. But when Hal managed to land some well placed punches to the brute's kidneys and neck, the Vaalakan's grip weakened on his axe handle and Hal wrenched it free with triumph. He held the weapon like a short hatchet and chopped down at the side of his disarmed opponent, nicking a slice from his ear and releasing a spurt of bright blood. Scragg shrieked.

Not trusting his accuracy with the cumbersome weapon, Hal kept the sharp blade pressed against Scragg's jugular and hunched himself over the weapon, preparing to hammer his weight down on it if the Vaalakan struggled. The Vaalakan's neck was twisted round and the wild eyes squirmed with fear, blinking out the blood that flowed across his cheeks from his earlobe.

'Do you yield, vile Vaalakan?' roared Hal, leaning a little onto the blade. Scragg's teeth were barred like those of a fighting terrier. Anger, rage and humiliation hissed through them but no surrender. 'Do you yield?' Hal asked again.

Jeering broke out amongst the watching Vaalakans, followed by a chant. Even if the barbarians did not understand Hal's speech, his actions were clear in any language and the Northmen were disappointed: they wanted the promised spectacle of violent sport. A cacophony of jeering hoots baying for Scragg's blood chilled the arena, but a blast from a ram's horn silenced the cries and Kullak spoke for all the barbarians.

'Kills him, Belbidak, kills him. He deserves to die, he does.'

The triumph and ferocity in Hal's pose seemed to diminish and his eyes flickered uncertainly between the vanquished warrior, Brid, and the jeering Vaalakans. At last his eyes met those of his kinsman, who strained against his bonds and was pressed up tight against the barrier. So many times during the last interminable minutes Caspar thought he would see his uncle maimed or fatally wounded. Hatred for the Vaalakans consumed his thoughts and, maddened by his fear for Hal and Brid in the arena, he desired Scragg's blood as much as the crowd. 'Kill him, kill him,' he yelled wildly into the arena, but his voice was drowned by the deep-throated snarling Vaalakans. But then, Hal's gaze brought him back to himself and for a moment their eyes searched each other in silent communication and Caspar slowly shook his head. No, it would be wrong to kill Scragg. Not in the arena. It would make them as low as their enemy.

'Yield, man!' Hal demanded again.

'Kill me,' begged Scragg hoarsely. His voice was throttled by the pressure of the blade against his neck and his face was darkening with the lack of oxygen. 'By name of Vaal-Peor, by name of any Gods, I begs.' The degradation before his men crumbled his pride and the young ice-blond man closed his eyes to shut out the humiliation, his body rigidly anticipating the blow. Hal's fierce pressure on the Vaalakan's neck gradually relaxed and he rose slowly to his feet, drawing the great axe up above his head and pausing to take careful aim. The blade impacted with a jarring clang as the forged steel severed the links in Brid's iron chain.

The axe blade trailed in the black earth as Hal dragged it by the handle towards Borog. His head bowed with exhaustion, he never once looked up at the howling sea of encircling faces, but trudged wearily towards the fleshy under-chief, only pausing for breath and to look back at Scragg's prostrate form lying face down in the mud. He ignored Brid, who was now so weak and drained after her efforts that she could barely even limp. She kept dropping to her knees, crawling after him. The awesome presence that she had commanded during her invocation to the Goddess, like a blazing furnace of life within her heart, was extinguished. Brid was once again no more than a broken creature.

Half way across the expanse of stripped earth Hal stumbled to a halt, clutching at his side. He leant on the axe handle for support and looked between the jeering faces surrounding the combat arena and the vanquished Vaalakan warrior. Brid crawled nearer, unable to place any weight on her deformed foot, trailing a snaking length of chain that chinked over the earth. At last Hal looked at her.

His fingertips stretched out towards her. 'I ought to thank you. Your Goddess and your black magic can't be all evil if they so humiliated that Scragg.' She did not reply but a faint smile broke onto her distorted lips as she reached up towards him. Supporting himself on the axe handle and, with his arm around Brid's tiny waist to hold her up, Hal faced Morbak's under-chief.

Borog's blubbery cheeks pushed up into his eye-sockets giving him a sly, slit-eyed appearance and he glowered at them. Caspar thought Borog was perhaps worried about Morbak's view of the spectacle laid on for the entertainment of his spies, now that it had not turned out so well. Morbak would likely take a dim view of one of his skilled warriors prostrate in the mud. A degree of satisfaction boosted his spirits.

'You fights badly,' Kullak stammered as he translated Borog's words, holding up his palm to shield himself from Brid's one-eyed stare. 'You is weak, but your braveness to be good show for Morbak. After questions he desire blood, much blood – and deaths.' Kullak managed a smile at this point though Borog remained inscrutable. 'For now you waits for Morbak, you does, the passing of two moons till he has marched the Dragon Scorch. Next time the boylings fights alone, they does. No witch-girl trickery for help.' Kullak hissed warily at her under his breath as he paused for Borog's last words. 'The witch will face the he-troll. Morbak will like, will like much.'

Two months! They would languish in the stockade while the horrible implications of Morbak's interrogation grew in their minds. Caspar had no faith that the mysterious crone Brid talked about would come to their rescue.

'But it doesn't matter if he does question us,' Caspar suddenly announced as if he had been arguing for some time with himself. 'I don't know anything that would jeopardize the safety of Torra Alta.'

'I'm afraid you do, Spar. Just think about it,' protested Hal with a weary touch of condescension. 'You know that Torra Alta doesn't have enough food to last more than half a year if totally isolated under siege. You also know that Morbak has good spies who will have found the Pass through in the west, the Jaws of the Wolf, but they've never been there in late autumn. They don't know how early the snows come – you do.'

Caspar thought how over the next few months the jagged peaks around the Jaw of the Wolf would become white pointed fangs ready to rake death through his army. If Morbak didn't know that, it was vital they didn't enlighten him. Then thousands of Vaalakans would die in the snowdrifts and avalanches rather than be diverted to making a full attack on Torra Alta.

'We have to escape or die trying, so that the knowledge in our heads is beyond Morbak's reach,' Hal insisted, and Caspar's resolve joined his.

A rattling of the bars on the barricade silenced them instantly and a hand pushed through a pail of water and a stale loaf of unleavened bread. The ginger-bearded Northman poked his ruddy face around the barrier to examine them.

'Only breads and water till Morbak comes,' he grunted but without the malice that swamped every word of many of his kinsmen. 'And you gives no trouble. Scragg is gaoler now, he is. He whetting his axe blade and is angriest with hatred. Give no trouble. You is warned, you is.'

'Good,' muttered Brid to herself.

'What do you mean good? I can't see anything good in this situation at all.' Hal's tolerance of the girl had considerably increased since the fight in the arena and he had allowed her to dress his wounds, but there was still an edge to his voice.

'Scragg is nursing a sorely wounded pride. The only thing that's going to make him feel better is humiliating you: it makes him more susceptible.'

'Susceptible to what?'

'To me, of course. Neither of you two young gallants with your long pompous titles and noble ancestry have come up with any plans. You're going to have to go along with mine.'

'Just hold on a minute; you are not forcing me into anything,' objected Hal.

'Come on, Brid,' pleaded Caspar with a little more persuasion in his voice, 'can't you explain?'

'All right, but I want a promise first.' She pushed herself up off the cold ground. 'I help you so you help me. I need the Druid's Eye and I need Caspar to help me wield its power – to find the Mother. If she is alive, we have to find her.'

'But who is she?'

'She is a high-priestess to the great Goddess, Daughter of the Moon and One of the Three.'

'A witch, you mean.' Caspar felt a revulsion brought on by a lifetime of religious indoctrination against the Old Faith. The heretical women had been hunted out by the devout King Rewik who had sworn to purify his lands of Devil-worshippers. 'I won't help you find a witch. I'd rather rot here.'

'Calm down, Spar, we haven't got time for any of your overheated emotions,' Hal said unexpectedly. 'I for one feel that getting out of here is the most important thing.'

The image of the deathly white woman with the mass of red hair sealed beneath the skin of the moonstone filled Caspar's mind again. He couldn't think clearly. Some devilish trick of this witch must be giving him these strange feelings. He yearned to see that face again; he longed to touch the moonstone, to reach deep into its heart to find the ghostly dead-looking woman.

'Without her, our power is weak and our knowledge limited,' Brid continued with her explanation. 'Without her we can not invoke the power of the Goddess. Without her the magic of the trinity is lost.'

'As a faithful believer in the one true God that seems like a pretty good reason for not helping you to get her back, even if she is alive – or even real.' Hal's clear logic helped Caspar to regain control of his emotions.

'You need her as much as I do.' Brid's voice was high with passion. 'Torra Alta was dedicated to the Great Mother. The castle will not stand without its rightful Goddess to protect it and she will not do that for the men of Torra Alta now that they have abandoned her. All Belbidia is slowly dying, just like Vaalaka died when the Northmen turned away from the Goddess to the cold-hearted Vaal-Peor.'

'Belbidia isn't dying,' the raven-haired youth protested. 'It's the wealthiest of the countries of the Caballan Sea. The wheat from Faronshire, the cheese from Nattarda, the beef from Jotunn – we have so much and the other countries pay handsomely for it.'

'Yes, and the Mother Earth pays bitterly for it. You men of Belbidia with your new God who does nothing to teach you of the balance and cycles of life, you will destroy everything. You are as dangerous as the Vaalakans who would merely strip the ground bare more quickly as they pillaged through the heartlands.'

'That is just heretical nonsense,' Hal sniffed. 'It's just totally illogical.'

'I knew you wouldn't understand,' the deformed girl retorted, her voice girded with condescension. 'But you must believe me that Torra Alta is the castle of the Great Goddess and we must find the Mother to save it from the Vaalakans, or you are lost.'

'You can save Torra Alta?' sneered Hal in disbelief. 'You are a small girl not much older than Spar. Just who do you think you are?'

'Daughter of the Moon and One of the Three. I am a high-priestess too. I thought it was obvious.'

'And you called our titles pompous,' scoffed the dark youth.

'And Morrigwen, the Crone, is the third?' guessed Caspar, ignoring his uncle and piecing the picture together, though he was not all together as impressed as Brid's tone indicated he should have been.

'Of course. The Goddess is represented on earth by the Maiden, the Mother and the old Crone – the three-stages of womanhood.'

'That doesn't say much for the rest of the poor girls if they are represented by you,' Hal blurted out tactlessly.

Brid sniffed at him, tilting her nose into the air disapprovingly. 'If you represent the manners of the men from Torra

Alta, I wouldn't bother with any of you and would welcome the Vaalakans with open arms.' She sniffed again, making Caspar feel mortified by his uncle's ungracious words. Even so, the very un-beautiful pagan priestess seemed undaunted and continued to answer the question. 'But Hal, no, I alone can not save anything or anyone. Without the complete circle our power is weak: help unite us and together we will rid this land of the accursed barbarians and their bloodthirsty god.'

'We can't refuse you, Brid,' Hal reluctantly resigned himself to the girl's control. 'We have to escape and you are the only one with a plan – our only hope. Our last resort,' he added pointedly.

'Do you promise to help me?' she asked seriously.

'Is our promise good enough?'

'The promise of noblemen from Torra Alta? Of course. Even if they are unspeakably rude I know their word is true.' She laughed happily as if all their problems were over.

'Then I give my word,' replied Hal grandly.

Caspar was silent and she raised her eyebrow at him.

'Well, if Hal does I suppose I have to as well,' he conceded.

'Good.' Brid smiled crookedly. 'Then I'll show you how we get out of here.'

Chapter 10

Brid crumbled a handful of dry twigs between her palms, trickling drops of water into the powder to make a muddy, unappetizing paste. Hal plucked at his travel-stained breeches in agitation, mumbling something about women always taking such a long time, whilst his nephew sat calmly propped up against the stockade wall. Caspar felt relieved that at least they were making progress towards their escape – even if he still did not quite understand Brid's plan.

'The hardest part,' she said as she continued to work patiently, 'will be to get you two to the edge of the woods.' She stopped fumbling with the herbs and started to chew on them. When she spoke again her teeth were stained brown and Hal cringed at the sight of her. He screwed up his face in revulsion but relaxed a little when she drank some water to cleanse away the paste.

'What are you trying to do? Turn yourself into a frog?' Hal gently prodded his rib-cage to test his injuries and grunted with satisfaction. He could move more freely and with less pain now.

'No, it's to relax the muscles. Willow bark for the pain, of course. Camomile and the bark of stagbush to prevent muscle spasm. This is going to take some time so try and get some sleep, as I told you.' Brid did not say any more and the two boys shrugged at each other in bewilderment. Hal crept closer to his nephew, leaving Brid to her preparations and, too anxious to sleep, they talked quietly for some while. After discussing the Vaalakan camp, and pondering on Torra Alta, they kept returning to the enigma of Brid.

'I don't like bossy women,' Hal grumbled.

'She'll hear you,' Caspar scolded. 'Anyway she's only like that because she has the plan.'

'But she promised she'd tell us what it was.'

'No, I didn't.' Brid's voice was a little drowsy and slurred. 'I promised I'd show you: there's a difference. And that's just what I'll do. First, I need your help. Both of you come here.'

'Bossy!' repeated Hal as he stiffly rose to his feet.

'My ankle, Hal.' She hitched up her tattered skirts to her grubby knees. 'You have to pull hard, really hard. Caspar hold my knee and pull against him.' The boys did as they were told without questioning her. The days in the stockade had taught them that Brid never gave a straightforward answer so there did not seem any point in arguing. The joint was surprisingly loose and stretched easily. 'Now twist it straight.' Brid gave out a stifled yelp and sighed deeply as her ankle snapped back into place.

'Dislocated!' Caspar exclaimed in disbelief. 'You're not a cripple. You did that to *yourself*. But why?'

'Protection.' Again Brid gave a simple explanation which explained nothing at all to Caspar.

'Now for the rest. Some eyebright I think.'

Caspar furtively stared at the congealed interlocking mat of gluey eyelashes that appeared to stitch her bulging eyelids closed. He wondered what possible good eyebright could do to such a deformity. She mashed the leaves and small white flowers of the herb into a paste with the remains of their bread and some water, and applied it to her swollen eyelid. Finally she rinsed away the sticky resin. Slowly the eye widened to reveal a grey, inhuman tissue underneath. Caspar felt his stomach turn over. Definitely some cancerous growth, he thought, as he turned his eyes away from the bubbly, grey cauliflower-shaped material which Brid had in place of an eye.

'Don't worry, it's only cobweb,' explained Brid as she gently enticed away the gossamer strands which packed out her eyelid. To Caspar's astonishment and disbelief, she peeled away a ball of grey sticky matter to reveal, her eye; clean and bright and a beautiful shade of green. He wondered why he had never noticed the emerald-green of her other eye before and then realized that he had only ever stared at her hideousness. He was drawn again to the vivid colouring of those eyes. No, not emerald, he contradicted himself – they are too vibrant to be likened to a cold gem – more a verdant, summer forest. Or, when she pierced him with those soul-searching eyes and he shrank from the intensity, he felt the colour was alive with power. Dragon-green, he thought to himself. Dragon-green.

'The last bit is so simple.' She spat a walnut onto her palm and the cyst-like deformity on her cheek smoothed away, revealing a perfectly symmetrical, oval face, disarmingly alluring even under the layers of mud.

'But how could you talk with that great thing in your mouth?' demanded Caspar.

'Practice,' she replied laconically. 'And stop staring. Anyone would think you'd never seen a girl before. Now I need the water so you had better take what you want first.'

Caspar could not reply. His jaw was a full two inches lower than it should have been as he continued to stare gormlessly at the transformed girl.

'I just can't believe it,' Hal repeated over and over, as stupefied as his nephew.

'Do you mind?' Brid's reproving tone reminded them of their manners. 'I wish to wash and I'd rather you didn't stare at me.'

Caspar gave an embarrassed cough and averted his eyes only to see Hal continue to stare with a ridiculous expression glued to his face.

'Hal!'

'What? Oh, yes, sorry.' The youth dragged his eyes away reluctantly and the two boys sat facing the far wall of the stockade. Waiting impatiently, they talked in low voices, while Hal periodically threw furtive glances over his shoulder towards the maiden. 'She is the most beautiful girl I've ever seen. Do you think it's real, or just another of her tricks?'

Caspar looked despairingly into Hal's excited eyes. 'I

thought you said she was a horrible witch. You've changed your tune a bit, haven't you?'

'But she's beautiful -'

'And that makes things different, I suppose,' interrupted Caspar tartly.

'Well, doesn't it to you?'

'No, of course not. From the minute I saw her I thought she was special and it's something that comes from within her, nothing to do with her looks.'

'I'm sure,' scoffed Hal sarcastically and snatched another quick glance towards the girl, his lips broadening into a pleasured grin. 'She's lovely.'

'Well, don't go getting any ideas about her,' Caspar snapped a little too vehemently.

'Why? Would that make you jealous?' taunted Hal.

Don't say anything, Caspar warned himself, otherwise he'll only make some arrogant comment along the lines that his chances with Brid would *naturally* be far greater than mine and it'll only encourage him. Nothing like a bet or a challenge to bring out the worst in Hal.

'You may turn around now.' Brid had a manner that made everything she said sound like a command and Caspar looked into her beautiful, perfectly matched eyes and desired nothing but to obey her.

Grumbling, Hal begrudgingly shoved himself to his feet. 'She might be beautiful, but she has no right to talk to me like that. What she needs is a good man to teach her some respect.'

Her hair floated in waves, caressing her shoulders and framing her oval face in ringlets. At last Caspar was able to discern her true colouring now that the plastered-on mud had vanished. There was no special magic in the colour of her hair, a common soft brown streaked with traces of copper, but the depth of the shine drew the eye, as the evening sun highlighted its shimmering touches of red and gold. Rich silky hair for running fingers through, he thought longingly. She was wrapped in Hal's cloak while her dress and hooded robe were hanging to dry on a splinter of wood on the stockade wall.

It was difficult at first to concentrate on what Brid was saying. Caspar realized how deluding and effective her tricks had been in disguising her beauty. He remembered how his eyes had always been ghoulishly drawn to the bulging eye-socket and swollen cheek, filling his brain with thoughts of cysts and canker, and how the deformed ankle had destroyed her grace of movement. But now his eyes freely roamed across her face and body, fascinated by the patch of bronzed skin that showed beneath the cloak. Occasionally when she moved, she exposed a little more shoulder and his eyes widened with delight and longing.

Hal nudged him with his elbow. 'Notice how she's chosen my cloak to wrap her naked body in – and not yours.'

All at once Caspar knew what Brid had meant by her hideous deformities giving her protection. In a camp of soldiers such a lovely creature would have suffered terribly at the hands of the men who were slaves to their desires. She certainly would not have been left in a stockade with them. No, she would have been imprisoned in Borog's quarters, and Scragg would never have left her alone.

'Are you listening to me, Caspar?' Brid's lilting voice demanded. He watched her move her full curving lips and heard the music of her voice but did not absorb the words.

'He might respond better to Spar. Hardly anyone calls him Caspar, except the Chaplain of course,' Hal informed her.

'In that case – Spar, are you listening? Do you know what you've got to do? Spar?'

'Huh? What? Yes, of course I was listening,' Caspar lied. It was so hard to concentrate on her words.

'Hm . . . I'll tell you again. We wait for the moon. It will be full and bright and its light will bless me with the glory of the Goddess. Scragg, our *favourite* Vaalakan, is conveniently on guard.' She nodded towards the barricading door. 'He is going to find out what it is to be a defenceless victim for a change.' Brid gave a wicked little wink; but rather than being pleased with her plan Caspar was horrified.

'You can't. That's, that's . . .' he stammered, feeling quite sick with emotion.

'He's jealous.' Hal volunteered the unnecessary and tactless comment, which provided Caspar with a vent for his pent-up feelings: he punched Hal hard and unexpectedly in the eye. They kicked around on the earthy ground.

'Mother, save me from these children,' sighed Brid, bringing Caspar sulkily back to his senses. His pride was hurt, and he now felt silly in front of this gracious girl. Feeling too ashamed to meet Brid's eyes, he hid his red face by studying the ground, though he could still feel her gaze burning through his skin and searching his soul.

'Now,' continued Brid; her composure unruffled. 'We wait for the moon's blessed light to reach its zenith. She will light our way and protect us as we make it to the forest – aided of course with a little stealth. Now, Hal,' her lilting voice took on an imperious tone, 'empty that water tub and have it ready behind the door. There's nothing more you can do except wait. I have a few more preparations to make.'

'You empty it, Spar. She might be getting us out of here but I'm not being ordered about by a girl,' Hal demanded haughtily.

'I can't believe you're so petty! Anyway, why should *you* go around giving me orders?' Caspar carefully tilted the wooden half-barrel so that the remaining muddy water drained slowly onto the floor. He was careful to tip it gently so the water was soaked up by the earth inside their prison rather than cause a suspicious flood of water, which might alert the enemy. Brid had her leather herb-scrip open in her lap and was sorting through the myriad collection of plants and roots. Finally she picked out a small four-leafed plant much like a four-leafed clover. Amazingly, there was still some dark juice in its stem, which she squeezed into her palm by rolling it between her fingers. With her index finger, Brid used the inky secretion to replace the marking on her forehead. Muttering some secret prayer under her breath, Brid ceremoniously re-drew the sacred sigil. Spread more thinly, the dark plant juice painted a rich blue rune on her skin.

Caspar expected the blue woad to mar her beauty but to his surprise it seemed to complement that mysterious inner quality of grace and sensuousness. She was more than just a girl with red bowed lips, wide intriguing eyes and smooth bronze skin; she had strength and wisdom. She was talented and knowledgeable, which made her far more interesting than all those wilting flowers who picked painstakingly at their tapestries, fearing to leave the shade of the castle walls lest the sun damage their lily-white skin.

'Brid?'

'Yes.'

'Nothing.'

'No, go on. What did you want to ask?'

'No. Nothing. It doesn't matter. I was only thinking that at home, in the castle, the girls . . . I mean, doesn't your mother disapprove of your running across the mountainside alone?'

'I haven't got a mother,' Brid replied, her matter-of-fact tone reducing the boy's bumbling questions to a stammer of apologies.

The girl rose in one dismissive movement to feel whether her clothes were dry.

Now that Brid was so fascinatingly beautiful, Caspar found his attempts to speak to her had turned into blushing stammers and he struggled to find something sensible to say until he remembered her dislocated foot. 'Your ankle, is it better? Does it hurt?'

Brid hitched Hal's long cloak up to her calf and, poised on one foot, she pointed her other toe and made slow elegant circles with it. 'Mm, think so. As long as the muscles stay relaxed nothing tears, and in a few more hours it'll feel normal. I'll have another look at yours before the light fails.'

The Maiden priestess made the youths turn away again so she could change into her fresh blue skirt and white bodice. It laced up tightly around her waist to outline a slim body just beginning to round out into womanly curves. She discarded her old sacking smock top which had been like a tent smothering her smooth lines and with delight she pirouetted to show herself off.

'That's better, isn't it?' she asked teasingly for their approval. She needed no answer since the amazement in the youths' eyes said everything.

'No shoes?' It was the only safe comment Caspar could make.

'No shoes,' Brid affirmed. 'Well, I couldn't carry them, could I? And nothing would fit with my ankle like that.'

'You should ask your Goddess for some,' mocked Hal.

Brid seemed offended and did not reply for some while. She busied herself with Caspar's fast-mending wound, refreshing the poultice and tenderly feeling for scar tissue. She was pensive and silent, before replying curtly, 'It's not like that, you know.'

'Oh?' Hal prompted.

'You can't just dance withershins around a moonbeam three times and say please can I have a pot of gold, three wishes, and a kingdom. You have to strive for what you want and make it possible. The Gods are not easy masters and you can only ask their blessing for something that is possible and pray that they make it probable. And if you are sincere in your request and loyal to your God then you are more likely to be answered. Rather than ask for miracles, it is better to learn about the gifts from the Gods that are freely available, like the herbs.'

Caspar suddenly realized how serious Brid was about her religion and he felt subdued and unable to speak in case he intruded on her thoughts. When Hal had no derisive comment to make about the girl's beliefs she relaxed and returned to Caspar's ankle.

'Good, there's no infection. It might hurt and you shouldn't run on it or move it too much, since it might open up again, but I'm afraid that can't be helped tonight.' She turned to Hal. 'Let's have a look at those ribs.'

Raising his shirt up, Hal gave a lewd wink to his nephew over the top of Brid's head as she placed her cool hands on his naked torso. Caspar turned away, ignoring Hal's coarse behaviour. He felt that Brid was above such comment and should be treated with more respect.

They tried to sleep, but anticipation kept the boys awake. Brid knelt on the floor, gazing up to the sky and bathing her face in the silvery light of the moon. Her lips moved as if in prayer. It seemed an eternity before she sighed and quietly got to her feet to nudge the other two prisoners.

'It's time,' she announced.

'Aren't you going to use some runes or ask for help?' asked Caspar, suddenly anxious that they might fail.

'The Goddess blessed me with all the help I need for this when I was born. I need no witch-craft, only woman-craft.' She tied her cloak about her neck but threw the folds back over her shoulders so that her elegant, girlish figure and alluring shape were clearly visible. 'Ready?'

'As we'll ever be,' Hal confirmed, standing behind the doorway with his back pressed against the stockade wall and holding the heavy water butt in both hands. 'Oh – and good luck.'

'Thanks. Here goes.' Her voice became gentle and pleading, as soft as silk and as inviting as warm honey. 'Scragg,' she called. 'Scragg.'

He's going to ignore her, thought Caspar with a growing sense of pessimism. He thinks she's ugly; he won't open the barricade to her. He's not stupid: he'll know it's a trick.

'Scragg, I have information that you need. Information about Kullak that your Lord Morbak won't like,' Brid improvised. 'Listen to me, Scragg. I know that he is not a real priest and you want him thrown out of favour, don't you?'

'What tricks is this you are playing, ugly witch?'

'I have proof. Open the door so that you can see. Are you afraid? Big man with an axe, are you afraid of a girl and two little boys?' She smiled teasingly at her companions.

'I'll get her for that later,' Hal whispered.

The barricade slowly creaked open and, as it began to move,

Brid put something small into her mouth. She carefully closed her lips but did not swallow. The doors of rough planking, bound by hessian rope, groaned as they opened a little wider and the glow from the campfires fell onto Brid's clean body, sparkling in her eyes, her hair radiant in the firelight. Young, fresh, innocent-looking, she stood still for a moment. Even though Caspar could not see the Vaalakan the other side of the door, he could imagine the man's stunned face as Brid's unexpected beauty struck him. She stepped forward and slowly raised her hands to her bodice, teasing the laces open. From behind the door Scragg's large hand lunged forward and grabbed her by the waist, wrenching her through the opening and out of sight.

A desire to protect the maiden exploded in Caspar and he lurched forward to follow her but Hal pressed him back against the stakes.

'Stick to the plan,' Hal urged through closed teeth. 'It's her plan after all, so she'll be all right.'

Reluctantly Caspar stayed still, waiting, listening, and hating himself for allowing a girl to be in such danger on his account. Five minutes seemed an eternity, but that was how long she said it would take to work. At last there was a rattling sound as the latch was drawn back. The rope hinges creaked open as Hal and Caspar slipped through the gap into the night.

'Is he dead?' Caspar asked hopefully as he examined the prone body of Scragg lying in the shadows, a purplish black stain oozing from his lips.

'No.' Brid's voice was urgent as she rapidly retied her bodice. 'He'll come round in a minute, so you'd better crack him hard with that barrel. I could only use a minimum number of berries in case I swallowed any myself,' she explained, helping to drag the body inside the stockade. 'Yew berries are far too dangerous.'

Scragg's body was much heavier than expected so Hal and Caspar took an arm each and heaved him into the stockade. There was something very satisfying about the vile Vaalakan becoming the victim of Brid's herb-lore. A clot of red blood caked his ear where Hal had removed a portion of the lobe. Once the body was safely inside, Hal stooped for the Northman's axe. For a moment he raised the blade above Scragg's defenceless jugular, but then relaxed and let the axe drop to his side.

'I was thinking that one less Vaalakan would be a good thing but somehow I just can't do it when he's defenceless,' Hal explained regretfully. 'But I'll keep his axe.'

'Hurry up,' Brid urged from her post on watch outside the stockade. 'Quick, before someone comes.' The boys crept out again and secured the door. 'Remember, stick to the shadows and if we get separated, head for the trees.'

On hands and knees, they stealthily crawled around the exterior circumference of the stockade, Hal leading and Caspar bringing up the rear. Ahead of them lay a patch of bare ground with no cover for twenty paces separating them from an array of tents neatly planted in the soil. Hal went first. Stooped over, he scurried across the earth and fell into the shadows of the tents. Brid and finally Caspar followed after. Silence was their only friend as they negotiated the reindeer-hide tents.

'Which tent is it?' Hal breathed in the merest of whispers.

Caspar's hand was a ghostly white in the bright moonlight as he waved it towards the circular tent near the edge of the group.

Hal looked at him in surprise. 'How do you know? I was asking Brid.'

A disconsolate shiver ran through the red-haired youth as he realized that he could clearly sense the throbbing power of the moonstone. It was unnatural. Why should he be able to feel it when Hal couldn't?

The autumn night was still and bright in the light of the moon and the younger boy felt distinctly conspicuous as they crept towards Red Beard's tent. At least the snuffling snores from the sleeping Vaalakans and the restless groans from the chained trolls covered up any noise they made. When they reached the tent a thin white light slipped through the cracks in the taut reindeer hides and Caspar felt as if the light of the moonstone was stretching out fingers to reach him. Brid turned, pressing her finger to her lips, warning them unnecessarily to keep quiet as she waved them down. Caspar pressed his face into the soil as he was startled by the rattle of a troll's chain. His heart thumped against his ribcage and he held his breath, waiting for the noise to disturb the watch. When he looked up again Brid had gone.

'She's in the tent. She just went inside,' Hal hissed. 'She's mad. She'll have all our throats cut.'

Caspar's heart leapt and every muscle tensed. He couldn't just let her go into the tent alone. Hal grabbed his wrist and pulled him down. Only then did the youth realize he had lurched forwards.

'She'll be safer on her own: she moves so quietly, like a shadow.'

Straining his ears, Caspar listened for any noise from Red Beard's tent but he could hear nothing over the rumbling grunts from the trolls. He held his breath and already it seemed that she had been inside for an eternity. He was wondering if she was armed with more of those lethal berries, when suddenly they were alarmed by a deep gruff cry coming from within the tent: Red Beard was awake. There was a gasp, then silence and finally a deep male sigh of pleasure. Brid must be loosening her bodice again, the boy thought, suddenly overwhelmed with a noisome feeling in his stomach.

The light in the tent lurched and swung in an arc. There was a heavy thud followed by a stifled cry and then another heavy thud. Then silence.

'My God, what's happened!' Hal murmured but Caspar was already on his feet, limping hurriedly towards the aperture of the tent. Brid's creamy face smiled at him and he felt a huge sense of relief. She tightened the laces on the bodice, covering up the white cleavage and pushed past the boy, firmly gripping the leather leash of the moonstone, which seemed to sparkle in her grasp. The Vaalakan's muffled cry roused grunts from nearby tents.

'Come on, quick. Let's get out of here.' She was breathless.

Caspar looked deep into the tent and dimly saw the huge bulk of the bare-chested Vaalakan lying slumped over a heap of skins. There was a large gash on his forehead, oozing blood. The youth was stunned. My God, she hit him with the stone – she coshed him. But she's so tiny and only a girl: how could she have done it?

Brid's soft voice was in his ear. 'I took him by surprise,' she whispered as if she had read the boy's thoughts. 'Now come on; let's get out of here.'

She leapt soundlessly on her bare feet through the gaps between the pitched tents, weaving around the ropes that staked out the skins and secured the flimsy structures against the wind. The light of the moonstone was furled within her skirts. Trying to creep noiselessly, Caspar and Hal slunk after her, stalking through the pitch shadows between the tents, and keeping out of the bright light of the moon. Brid was already beyond the camp and running through the heather when Caspar tripped on a rope and fell heavily to the ground with a resounding thud. A troll leapt to its feet. The raucous rattle of its chain running through a hoop distressed the night.

'That's done it now. Just run for it, Spar,' Hal urged. 'Run for your life.'

He made the edge of the camp and the cover of brambles and bracken beyond when the first angry shouts from the Vaalakan spies screeched into the night. Sharp jabs in his ankle forced him to limp severely as he hurried after the other two. The ground was laced with strips of brambles that ensnared his feet and ripped his shins. We're going to make it, he kept telling himself, as he watched the other two leap ahead. The barbarians will be disorientated from sleep. We've got a couple of minutes yet: we'll make the thick shelter of the forest.

A horn blast screamed into the night. It was harsh and fierce enough to shake the cold rocks of the mountainside and stir them from their endless sleep. The hunt was on. A clash of metal meant the men had found their arms and now the camp was wide awake, yelling and calling. Caspar's damaged ankle kept folding under him. With a stiff leg he hopped and dragged himself forward. The cries became louder as they gained on him. Why had he listened to Brid? This was madness. He'd already suffered one crossbow bolt and he didn't want another one separating the vertebrae between his shoulder blades.

The mass of cries became individual shouts as the swifter men hurdled the roots and stumps in a charge through the wet bracken. They're close now, thought Caspar, very close. But he could no longer see either Brid or Hal: they had merged into the shadows of the night. Please, dear God, let them make it. Let them escape. And then thinking of Brid he added in his mind: Mother Goddess help her. He knew it was a heretical thought but he doubted that his own God would reach out to help a pagan priestess. Maybe Hal was right: maybe since he had seen her as beautiful he no longer believed that there could be anything evil about her even if she was a heathen.

A heavy tread thumping the ground just to his rear urged Caspar to one last burst of speed. He did not even look round. He heard the Vaalakan grunt and an iron-hard fist clamped itself to his leg and another one clawed at his clothing, dragging him to the ground. Caspar smashed the booted heel of his good leg into the man's face, feeling it connect with a satisfying crunch. The Vaalakan's grip loosened just enough for Caspar to scrabble away on his hands and knees, lashing out backwards to throw off his attacker. But the man, heavy and strong, was on him again, rolling him over and grappling to hold him down. The smell of his steaming breath poured over Caspar's face. The boy was pinned by his neck to the ground, though he still struck out with every frenzied limb, whipping his head from side to side. In a moment that seemed to last for ever Caspar watched the man draw his arm back, silhouetted, to prepare for a hammering blow to his skull. One instant the head was staring down at him, glowing eyes mad with the bloodlust, promising his death, and the next, in a flash of hooves and metal, the head was spinning away through the air. A fountain of blood spurted up from the severed neck before the body slumped down on top of him.

Grappling with the headless weight of the Vaalakan, Caspar finally managed to throw off the body. Struggling to his knees he saw the flank of a cream horse glowing in the moonlight. It pivoted on its haunches and a silver flash reflecting off a smooth blade caught and parried a moonbeam. The horse was galloping back towards him.

'On your feet, Spar!' Hal yelled above the clamour of the approaching Vaalakans. The reins were knotted, enabling Hal to hold the fearsome weapon in one hand and still have a hand free for Caspar. He galloped straight at his nephew, lowering his arm to catch him and with no time to waste grabbed Caspar's upheld wrists. Hal's fingers dug deep into his kinsman's forearm, but even then the young boy was not convinced that his uncle would be strong enough to hold him. For two strides his feet whipped through the brambles and his body banged against the flank of the charging horse but at last he kicked his leg high enough to find Hal's foot. Using his uncle's boot as a stirrup he swung up behind him onto the smooth back of the galloping horse.

Clamping his arms around Hal's waist, Caspar's spirits rose with the confidence induced by the power and elation of being on horseback. The steed beneath them took long, steady strides thundering through the undergrowth, heedless of briar and gorse, the animal's basic instinct of flight aroused to the full. This was a heavy-boned horse with solid muscle bred for strength and stamina rather than speed. He was a true mountain horse with stocky legs and a broad back, which at least made the bareback ride more comfortable. Caspar's own horse was a hot-blooded animal from the southern plains whose gallop was like lightning, to this one's thunder, whose nimble hooves flashed and danced to the tune of its own god – the god of the wind whom it chased with devotion.

The trees loomed up out of the pitch of the night and Caspar was thankful for Brid's bright moon. They had outdistanced the Vaalakan foot-soldiers, covering the furlongs of open ground in comparative ease; but a gallop through unknown woods in darkness would be more than dangerous. Hal sat tall and reined in the charger from the smooth gallop into a jog, which bounced Caspar along in his less secure position on the horse's lower back. Caspar clenched his teeth together to avoid biting his tongue as his lower jaw rattled up and down to the beat of the animal's trot. A gentle squeeze from Hal's calves urged the steed into the rhythmical, easy movements of a canter. With their heads bowed over they plunged into the shelter of the silver birches, keeping low against the pounding shoulder of the horse to avoid the over-hanging branches that whipped past unnervingly close.

'Where to now? Where's Brid?' Caspar demanded.

'I don't know. She said she'd get help and to head for the heart of the forest,' Hal explained. 'Have we lost them yet?'

Craning his head round, Caspar could only make out the white trunks of silver birch trees that merged to form one pale mass of wood behind them. The uproar of outraged Vaalakans, however, was still plainly audible above the muted thud of the horse's hooves on the leaf-mould. 'No. I can't see them but I can hear them. Keep going!'

As they pressed deeper into the forest, the canopy of branches closed overhead, blotting out the creamy moonlight and only the occasional sheet of thin grey light slipped through onto the forest floor. The darkness forced them to a halting trot for fear of unseen branches overhanging their path. At this pace, they were no longer increasing their distance from the Vaalakans. Caspar could feel the tension prickle down his back as he imagined the Northmen hacking towards them through the undergrowth, hefting their great sharp axes.

'Can't we go any faster?' pleaded Caspar.

'I'm doing my best,' Hal snapped, giving the phantom-white stallion a free rein to pick his own way through the trees and pressed him on to a steady trot. The animal judged the distances well for itself, but made no allowances for the humans on its back. The overhanging branches glanced lightly over its own ears but scraped remorselessly across the bent spines of the two boys. Whenever the creamy stallion curved its body around the barky stem of a tree, it invariably neglected to leave enough room for the boys' bony knees.

'Do you think we're going the right way?' Caspar asked after minutes of silence, his ears finely tuned to the sabre-rattling cries from the pursuing Vaalakans. 'What happens if we can't find Brid? Are you sure she got away?'

'Definitely. She flew off on a horse exactly like this one. Let's hope she's not just abandoned us, hey?' Hal's voice was trimmed with cynicism. 'And where's she going to get help from out here?'

'I think they're gaining on us.'

'We can't go any faster without breaking our necks.' And, as if to emphasize that the forest was no gentle giant that would tolerate this riotous intrusion, a long gnarly branch snagged at Hal's clothing, then whiplashed back into his nephew's face. 'Ow! You can't gallop through a forest without respect for the solid wood.'

'The Vaalakans aren't going to treat us with any more respect either.'

She has the moonstone now, Caspar thought. Maybe she only wanted the moonstone . . . Then a worse thought struck him: the Vaalakans might have caught her.

Hal ignored his persistent questions, focusing only on the clamour at their heels.

'Do you think the horse can see better in the dark than we can?' Caspar winced as another branch scoured across his thigh, the dry lower twigs snapping off. Black shapes loomed in and out of the darkness. Faces stared out of the wart-like knots of trees. Fingers and arms formed by roots and saplings groped out of the earth, like corpses emerging from their graves. 'If the Vaalakans don't get us the forest will. There's a strange feeling in these woods; and I don't like being unable to see.'

Suddenly the stallion skittered to a halt and backed nervously, despite the merciless drumming of the boys' heels into its side. The bright red of two nocturnal, hunting eyes flashed ahead of them, caught in a shard of moonlight, and then vanished into the dark. The horse snorted nervously: out there lurked one of its natural enemies and no encouragement could urge it forward. Then somewhere to the left, another pair of round eyes glared at them. And then another. A muted patter of light paws, nimbly galloping over the leafy carpet of the forest floor, bristled the hairs on the back of Caspar's neck as he sensed beasts all around them. A large shape burst out from the blackness of a shrub and ran across their path to be absorbed into the black of the thickets again.

'Wolves,' whispered Hal. Caspar could sense his uncle's arm muscles tighten as he closed his grip on the handle of the stolen Vaalakan axe. Mountain wolves had a fearsome reputation amongst those born in the Yellow Mountains. Every mountain child had suffered restless nights after hearing eerie tales of these great beasts who stole lambs from the folds and babes from the cradle.

The wolves, however, seemed to have passed them by and were lacing back and forth through the forest behind them in their silent hunt.

'What are they doing?' Caspar breathed.

As he listened to the rustling leaves that the wolves scattered with their padded paws, it gradually dawned on Caspar that their movements formed a pattern. The wolves were moving from all parts of the forest, quickly through the trees towards the Vaalakans.

The unearthly din of the Vaalakans charging behind them in pursuit was silenced by a blood-curdling scream that became many screams. Caspar understood that Brid's help had arrived. The carnivorous pack ran through the stampeded Vaalakans, and a horrible snarling and snapping of teeth, the nightmarish screams of humans mingling with the salivating snarls of the lupine legion, left no doubt that the enemy numbers were being thinned. Abruptly the screaming stopped: there was deathly silence.

Some distance ahead, a pale shape flitted behind the black

tree trunks and the stallion beneath them gave a whicker of recognition, lengthening its stride. The woods came alive again with figures moving purposefully. Wolves were converging on the shadowy figure of a horse as it emerged into the space left by a lightning-struck tree.

Here, through the thick thatch of branches that roofed the forest, the bright moonlight penetrated to touch Brid's hair and stroke her face. The great horse beneath her pranced in the circle of light, the companion to the horse he and Hal rode. And it was easy for Caspar to believe that she really was blessed by the Gods.

She raised an arm in greeting and hailed them forward. 'There's a trail ahead.' With a flick of its long, white tail, her horse galloped off, leaving Hal and Caspar hard pressed to stay on her heels. The sound of running wolves haunted their tracks.

Chapter 11

They galloped westward away from the buff light of dawn, which broke with a whisper hardly disturbing the slumbering forest. A drizzle sifting down from the grey sky teased the dry coppery leaves of the oaks. A phalanx of wolves loped alongside, risking the heavy hind hoof of the stallion which lashed out whenever one of the carnivorous pack ranged too close. Caspar was greatly relieved when the last of the shaggy-maned beasts slipped silently into the shadowy forest.

Brid finally reined in her horse to a less exhausting pace. She jogged along the narrow trail for a few more strides before slipping into the thick of the trees on the right. There a trail soon opened up to cut a wide swathe through the forest, upwards to the crest of a rise where they found themselves above the level of the surrounding trees. The horizon to the south soared into the jagged peaks of the Yellow Mountains and to the north they could just make out the forbidding cliffs of the Dragon Scorch marking the southern boundary of Vaalaka. Cradled between the two opposing ranges, the forest nestled comfortably along the length of the Sylvan Rush Valley. An occasional evergreen pine thrust tall and verdant out of the sea of dry, deciduous trees. The dark grassy line of the trail ran perfectly straight for as far as the eye could see, rising and dipping over the contours.

Brid had vanished into the forest.

They soon found her, waiting patiently, giving her mare a long rein so that the horse could nibble at some choice greenery that sprouted from the roots of a beech.

'There's a clearing through here,' she said simply. 'We'll stop and give the horses a rest.'

She slid down and threaded her way through the trees, allowing the mare to trail behind her. The undergrowth was too thick and the branches too low to remain mounted so Hal and Caspar followed suit. Caspar took care on dismounting to land on his good foot and limped after the others.

'How do you know there's a clearing?' he asked curiously. 'We're a long way from home.'

'From your home, maybe.' As usual, Brid never volunteered any information unless pressed and that was her total, insufficient reply.

'I thought you lived in the mountains . . .'

'I do.'

'Well, what are you talking about then?' Hal demanded fractiously, frustrated by his nephew's ineffectual line of questioning and the girl's laconic replies.

'Home,' she said sombrely to Hal, 'is everywhere west of the Silversalmon. I have friends in the mountains and friends in the forest. And Morrigwen dwells within a day's ride of here. She sent the wolves and the horses for us, of course.'

'Of course,' Hal echoed sarcastically.

'But how do you know there's a clearing through here?' Caspar repeated.

Brid sighed. 'We're following an ancient route. Mother Earth has many lines of power linking her centres of energy: this is one of them and I can feel – sense – the power in the soil. Besides,' she added more pragmatically, 'I saw the silver-firs from the last rise.'

Of course, there was a clearing. But Caspar sensed no special aura or ambience in the place. The firs, with their frosted-green fronds and bursting cones formed a circle, too perfectly symmetrical to be natural. Right in the centre of the glade stood a lone specimen, out-stretching all the others, like a spire reaching for the sky.

'When the light's better, we'll take a look from the top,

but first we'll get some rest and some food,' Brid decided in her imperious manner.

'You're going to climb that?' said Hal incredulously. 'I think you'd better leave such tasks to me and Spar.'

'I don't really care what you think. Spar's not going anywhere with that ankle of his least of all gallivanting up and down trees. And as for you! You won't even begin to know what to look for.'

'What are you looking for then?' demanded Hal, seemingly thrown off-balance by Brid's sharpness.

'Absolutely!' replied the girl, as if Hal had just proved her point. But the two boys continued to stare expectantly at her, until she conceded an explanation. 'All right.' She threw up her hands in surrender and then absent-mindedly wiped back a lock of hair that trailed across her face. 'The trees are planted in a special place. We're on high ground here and the silver-firs grow taller than all the other trees. So, from here I can see many things: which way the wolves are hunting, where the deer are running, if a storm is blowing up. Right now, more to the point, I can see if any Vaalakan spies managed to escape the wolves and whether they have picked up our trail.'

'Aren't we heading the wrong way?' Hal demanded. 'Surely we'd be safer from the enemy if we headed south into the Yellow Mountains and back towards Torra Alta? Besides Branwolf will be mad with worry – well, for Spar here anyway.'

'You promised me you'd help me find the Mother.'

'But you've got the moonstone now: isn't that enough?'

She shook her head and like a beautiful maiden in a story she lowered her eyes. They were dazzling in the light reflected from the white marbled surface of the moonstone, but when she looked down the brightness seemed to go from her eyes to the stone. Carefully she placed her palm on its surface and the creamy white patterns rippled aside to reveal a clear pool that shimmered as if the wind whispered across it. Then the ripples stilled and the hazy patterns drew to a focus. The ancient face of a white-haired woman was suddenly staring at them with blue far-seeing eyes. Hal could see the woman's dry lips move as if she was talking but he heard nothing. Brid silently nodded to her, then withdrew her hand from the orb. The image was swallowed by the white swirling patterns as if a sea-mist had suddenly blown in off the ocean to smother the land.

'Who was that? Is *that* the Mother,' the older youth demanded. 'And what has all this got to do with us?'

'Of course it's not the Mother,' Brid snapped. 'That's the whole point: I can't reach her. She's gone too near the Otherworld. But Spar can. Look!' She snatched Caspar's hand and thrust it onto the moonstone.

A stab of pain snapped the boy's muscles taut. A searing heat, like the tip of a sizzling hot branding iron, scorched through his nerves and burnt with white energy in his brain. The white liquid swirled angrily like a storm over the surface of the moonstone and then cleared to a frosted glaze that veiled the sight of the mysterious, red-haired woman again. Her mouth was stuck open in a frozen scream, showing her blue tongue and bloodless lips. The eyes stared horribly with pain – a deep, all-enveloping pain that tore at her whole being. Her mouth didn't move but Caspar could hear a rushing noise, like the sound of a waterfall in a distant dream, strangely disjointed as if his mind were far from his body. It was a noise he had heard only once before when trying to break his colt. He had been thrown to the ground and the animal's sharp hooves had kicked his unprotected head. The outside world had instantly become blank and soundless until he had come round to that same rushing noise.

'She's dead.' There was an unutterable sadness in Brid's voice. 'She's dead. It's too late: she's slipped across to the other side. All is lost.'

Caspar looked deeper into the woman's fixed eyes that were like cold hard sapphires set in her diamond-hard face. They stared at him, motionless and glazed. The sound of rushing water swelled to a roar that thumped in his ears and the boy's head pounded as if he were being beaten with a hammer. He felt caught inside the dome of a huge bell that was tolling out a death knell. But from somewhere he caught the barest whisper like a breath of fresh air. The eyes – he was sure, yes – the eyes, he could feel them reaching into his soul, reaching towards him as if clinging to him for life, for the warmth of life. He felt those eyes sucking at his soul as a terrible creeping cold dragged the warmth from the marrow of his bones. The image was like a parasite sucking away at his life-blood. Then there it was again: the warm breath of a whisper. Was it someone speaking to him? He couldn't tell. It was like a far distant cry, a plea. *Help me. You are my life. Help me. Help me.* Suddenly the real world outside his head slammed into his brain. Everything was shockingly vivid and compellingly close after the unreality of the dream-like world within the moonstone.

Hal was shouting at him, yelling at him. 'Let go! Let go!'

Caspar looked at his uncle. His freckled face was the picture of a simpleton confused by the complexity of human speech. He looked stupidly at his hands. They were white – a sickly purplish white and spasms ridged the muscles on the back of his hands as his fingers hooked around the orb. His uncle was frantically trying to prise them off. They broke away with a jerk and in disbelief the small youth looked at the ends of his numb fingers. There was no pain but he couldn't move them and they were as white as . . . as snow, he thought helplessly.

'Oh Mother,' Brid breathed. 'Frostbite.'

'She's not dead,' was all Caspar could say. 'She's not dead. I felt her eyes look at me. They looked at me.'

Tears were silently pouring down Brid's cheeks but when Caspar spoke she snatched at his words almost angrily in her desperation. 'What did she say?'

'He's got frostbite, for God's sake,' Hal objected. He stared angrily down at the small girl who finally relented.

Tenderly, she reached out her hands for Caspar's wrists and turned his palms over to look at his fingertips. 'She's so near death, she's having to draw life from you. Hal, light a fire quickly. We need to get him warm and I'll heal the frostbite.'

'Necromancy!' Hal swore in disgust. 'We are touching on

the evil spirits of the Devil. You cannot hold us to our promise. We have to get back to Torra Alta. '

'You can go, but not Spar.'

'I'm not going anywhere without my nephew: he's my responsibility, and I'm certainly not leaving him in the hands of a Devil-worshipper. What has this evil stone got to do with Spar? Why does it have this horrible power over him?'

'Don't you know?' Brid asked. Then she looked at Caspar sorrowfully and shook her head. She took a deep breath as if she was about to say something but then let it out with a decisive sigh. She shrugged and said quite lightly, 'It's the stone from the heart of Torra Alta. It's a gift from the Goddess to the castle, a sign that she gives her protection to the fortress in return for your worship. Spar can feel it because he is the rightful heir. It is his stone and nobody else's.'

'Except Branwolf's of course then,' Hal added logically.

Brid didn't reply but turned to look at the shocked youth who was muttering incoherently through chattering teeth.

'We promised, Hal. We must find this woman.'

'Why?'

Caspar didn't reply. He didn't know the answer.

'Get some firewood now,' the girl ordered. Hal looked at her in disbelief before stonily turning to gather dry brush from the edge of the glade while Brid hurriedly scooped heaps of crisp leaves together and started a fire. Caspar let the girl gently blow on his hands. He bit back the scream rising in his throat, as the pumping red-hot blood pulsed towards the numb tips of his fingers.

The warmth from the fire gradually chased away his shivers, and as she tended his hands, the priestess began once more to question him about the image in the stone.

'I couldn't hear anything,' she explained. 'You must tell me what she said.'

Caspar felt drained, and deeply sorrowful. 'Help me; she said, help me.' He knew from somewhere deep within his soul he could never rest until the woman's desperate plea was answered.

'We must restore the faith in the Great Mother,' Brid said passionately. 'The King with his New Faith is stretching the land to breaking point. With the cathedrals, the palaces, the taxes, he's stripping the country.'

'Belbidia has never done so well. I don't believe any of that, Brid,' Hal sneered.

'I've seen the men logging. Vast tracts already are being carved out.' She became impatient. 'You don't have to believe me about what will happen to all Belbidia but without the Mother we can't do anything to stay the tide of Vaalakans. The heart of Torra Alta is weak without her and vulnerable to attack.'

'Torra Alta's heart is strong!' Hal objected. 'Even now at the foot of the Tor we are building the foundations of a cathedral whose spire will, one day, reach higher than the top towers of Torra Alta.' The dark youth exaggerated.

'You are fools all of you.' Brid turned her flashing green eyes and fixed them on Caspar. 'You will help me?'

He nodded weakly. 'I promised.'

Hal gave a disgruntled snort and sat down with his back against the deeply ridged bark of the silver-fir and pulled his cloak down over his eyes. 'A promise is a promise,' he conceded, 'but I think you're mad.'

'I'm not, you know,' Brid whispered to Caspar. 'We have to find her: Torra Alta needs her. We have to do whatever it takes, however crazy.'

Caspar was suddenly too tired to question Brid further. She looked so innocent and beautiful – a child-woman whose confidence and faith warmed his heart and he believed in her. The warmth from the fire flowed through his body with the pleasure of honeyed mulled wine. He slumped down next to Hal, and he was quickly asleep.

Slowly the image of the agonized woman crept like a prickling hoarfrost through his mind and he felt her feeding like a parasite off his heat. But quite suddenly the image rippled and distorted before focusing again. Blood coursed strongly through the woman's veins bringing a rose-red vibrancy to her cheeks. The eyelids swept closed and then opened again to reveal living liquid eyes. Suddenly the sense that she was sucking away his heat evaporated and he felt the enveloping warmth of blissful security. Her long hair was brushing against his face and she kissed his fingertips. A tingling warmth replaced the numbness of the frostbite. He looked up at her; she seemed enormous like a powerful and all-giving Goddess. She made him feel small without making him feel vulnerable. *Spar, find me. You need me.*

Suddenly the image of a Vaalakan war axe cleaved through the moonstone and hacked into the woman's shoulder. A hand pushed her down as if holding her under water and her mind was crying for pity. *Not you, no not you. I never did you any harm.*

A dark voice possessed with bitter hatred cracked into the dream. *You killed my mother. You killed her so that you could kick me around like a worthless dog.*

No, believe me; I loved you, I loved you. No . . . the woman's mind cried as she struggled violently to the surface before being pushed under again. Bubbles dribbled from her mouth.

When Caspar awoke it was full noon and Brid was prodding a small, smokeless fire with a twig before skewering a skinned and gutted rabbit onto a makeshift spit. He frowned at the Vaalakan axe that rested next to his kinsman's grasp and then at the moonstone lying close to his head. It glowed brightly, the white patterns swirling in a furious maelstrom and Caspar could feel the energy of its pulse. He wondered if its dark magic had been creating his nightmares. Slowly he sat up and stretched out his hands, flexing his fingers. They moved so freely that for a moment he thought that the horror of the frostbite must have all been part of his dream. But then the bandages . . .

Brid silently looked at Caspar's hands. She blinked and, for the first time, Caspar thought she looked surprised. Over the last few days Brid had shown no sign of being fazed by anything, however shocking. 'It's healed!'

Hal looked in disbelief. 'Frostbite takes weeks to heal, if it ever really does. And it scars. It couldn't have been real in the first place. It must be the moonstone's power of suggestion over his fanciful mind,' he announced firmly.

Brid ignored the older youth's comments. 'Well, how do you feel, Spar?'

'Hungry! Absolutely ravenous!'

'We'll have some breakfast in a minute.' She smiled warmly.

Hal shifted uncomfortably, rubbing at a numb leg which he had slept on awkwardly. He nodded towards the sizzling carcass over the fire. 'It'll burn in a second. How did you catch it?'

'I didn't.' The slender girl turned her spit.

'I suppose it just hopped happily up to you and threw itself at your feet, then.'

'Oh yes, of course.' The tart edge had crept back into Brid's voice when she spoke to Hal. 'I'm much too stupid to take the offering of food from my wolf, you know, much too stupid. After all I'm only a girl.' Hal's sarcasm was obviously becoming contagious.

'I didn't see the wolf,' the older boy replied.

In answer Brid pointed to the circumference of the glade where two bright eyes stared out of the shadows. Caspar turned slowly on his good heel and realized that they were completely surrounded by a dozen or more pairs of the same round eyes. One of the pairs inched forward through the undergrowth. A large she-wolf stepped uneasily into the glade, looking anxiously from side to side, obviously distrustful of the open space. Another fat rabbit hung limply from her jaws.

'Good wolf, well done,' encouraged Brid, gently and slowly reaching out her hands while keeping the fingers curled in an unaggressive gesture. The wolf tip-toed up on its elongated legs and crouched beside her, keeping a wary eye on Hal and Caspar who returned the same distrustful looks.

'Hey! You can't use an axe for that: you'll dull the edge,' Hal quickly protested as Brid borrowed the sharp blade to rip open the rabbit's belly, tearing away the skin from the red flesh.

Brid laughed. 'Do you want to eat it with the skin on?' she

asked whilst choosing another straight twig to spit the second rabbit with.

The fresh meat tasted succulent and delicious to the famished boys and gradually their hunger abated allowing them to relax even in the ever-alert presence of the she-wolf.

'Are you sure she's safe?' Hal reached out a hand to test the wolf's response but she immediately laid her ears flat and peeled back her serrated lips. With lightning reflexes he snatched his hand away

'Of course she's not safe: she's a wolf, isn't she?' Brid laughed. 'But she's trustworthy and gentle just so long as you are. She won't snap if you trust her. Give her time. Treat her like a pet hound,' advised Brid as the beast crept up to her, nuzzling her hand as if demanding to be stroked. The young girl happily obliged. 'Now for the tree. We'd better take a look and see if there is any activity. Your hands somehow are fine now but what about your ankle? Do you feel up to the climb, Spar?'

'Much better now.' Caspar forced a smile to his face to disguise his discomfort and twirled his foot to demonstrate the full range of movement in his ankle joint. 'Must have been the sleep and the rest. I'm coming with you.' The memory of the nightmare sealed in the stone was gradually fading. Like the frostbite, it couldn't have been real: it had simply gone – vanished.

Hal jumped to his feet and unclasped his cloak to free himself from its hindrance. 'Never one to be left behind, is Spar.'

The branches close to the trunk were evenly spaced and free from prickly pine-needles, so the climb was relatively straightforward even for Caspar who refused to admit that his ankle was a problem. He was even so impressed by the speed with which his injury had healed. He looked gratefully towards Brid, surprised by her aptitude to climb trees, which he had previously regarded as a strictly male preserve. She swung deftly from branch to branch with a blatant disregard for height that told clearly of her mountain breeding. Caspar, however, was more perturbed by the way she had hitched her skirts into her girdle to stop them snagging on broken branches. Any woman in the castle would have been ashamed to display as much leg and he felt embarrassed for her, despite the fact that she seemed totally uninhibited.

The view was spectacular. All to the north lay the copper and bronze of the forest scattered with the dark lines of trails and patchy circles of evergreen where the firs dominated. To the south rose the golden jagged mountains with their crags, ravines, waterfalls and gorges – wild and forbidding, barren and rugged. The mountains filled Caspar with pride and love: he was looking homeward.

The grey clouds of early morning had evaporated under the bright sun and only in the dark, shadowy hollows of the forest did the few wispy sheets of mist remain to hide the forest's inner secrets. At the southerly edge of the forest a broad swathe-like scar gouged across the woodland, eating into the tall straight firs and Brid sniffed disapprovingly: 'They shouldn't take so many trees.'

Ignoring her comment, Hal breathed a sigh of relief. 'Well, there's no sign of them. Despite events with the witch's moonstone we seem to have outrun the Vaalakans.'

'Mmm.' Brid shaded her eyes from the glare of the sun and, with one arm hooked around the branch of their swaying eyrie, she pointed towards the east. 'Look at that flight of woodcock.'

Caspar squinted against the bright sun and Brid reached over to pull his chin round to point in the right direction. 'There.'

Caspar nodded. 'So? What about them?'

'I'd say that's where our friend Scragg is right now. He hasn't found the trail yet so up until now their going's been rough, but it looks as if they'll stumble on it pretty soon.'

Hal was nodding. From the top of the silver-fir the track was clearly visible as a dark line running straight like a clean sword-cut through the belly of the forest. 'They're not too far off it. What are we doing wasting time? We slept too long.' He slid down from branch to branch and neatly dropped the last dozen feet from the lower boughs of the fir to land cat-like on the forest floor. The others followed.

The two boys made straight to bridle the horses but Brid stopped and knelt by the roots of the tree, diligently scraping runes into the soil by the fir's spreading feet.

'We haven't got time,' Hal snapped. 'What are you messing about there for?'

'I can't leave this sacred grove without giving proper thanks to the spirit of the far-seeing tree.' Nodding apologetically at the fir she broke off a twig from its lower branch and Caspar raised a quizzical eyebrow at her.

'What's that for?'

'A sprig from the far-seeing tree: in the right potion it clears your head to see beyond the obvious into the distance. Then you can understand the whole more clearly.'

'Oh,' was all Caspar could think to say.

'You have a lot to learn, Spar.' She smiled a little condescendingly.

Hal was already astride the snorting stallion which pawed the ground, anxious for the gallop. 'Brid, you'd better ride behind me, so that we'll make better time.'

'Are you trying to tell me that I can't manage the horse myself?' she asked incredulously.

'That had occurred to me,' Hal replied, haughtily but with a hint of teasing in his voice. 'But actually I was thinking of the horses. You're lighter than Spar so it'll even the weight out better between them.'

The raven-haired youth grinned at Caspar smugly.

He always has to compete for everything, Caspar thought disgustedly to himself as he vaulted lightly onto the mare's back, turning her head to follow the stallion's prancing step. They weaved carefully through the trees but once back on the trail they pounded into a gallop. Caspar kicked the mare on, pursuing the stallion's streaming tail and Brid's long flowing hair. Why couldn't she have come with me? That would have evened the weight out even more. The small youth cursed himself for not thinking of that earlier. He doesn't even like her, so why does he have to try and score points like this?

It felt good, though, to hold the reins himself. The mare balked underneath him as she coughed to clear her lungs after the morning's rest, but then put on an extra spurt to catch up with her stallion. They galloped flank to flank until Hal raised his hand and they pulled up to a steady canter. Caspar felt like a wild spirit of the woods racing with the wind as they funnelled through the ancient cursor that cut through the forest. He could feel a grin stretching his face despite the threat of Scragg at their heels. Brid turned her head towards him and her lovely eyes fell on his smiling lips.

'Caspar,' she shouted over the sound of the thudding hooves on the soft earth as she emphasized his full name. 'It suits you. In a tongue from the far south it means horseman.'

The young boy wondered once again just how Brid had managed to gather so much knowledge in her short years. He patted the coarse neck muscles of the broad-backed mare and felt pleased with her words.

Lost in his daydreams, Caspar cantered towards a hollow where a strange, unnatural mist seeped out of the forest and flooded over the track. They had seen pockets of mist from the top of the silver-fir but this seemed thicker than the wispy white shreds that draped the lower paths and dells. Reining in, he sat deep into the dip of his horse's back as the fog clamped down around him. Suddenly he could no longer see beyond the mare's ears, which were now flattened to her skull. The last thing Caspar heard was Brid's clear voice floating through the fog.

'Stay on the trail. Don't come off the trail and you'll be safe.'

The mare was skidding to a halt, her hocks bent deep underneath her, but it was not enough. At first branches whisked by unnervingly close, then they whipped at him from both sides and Caspar realized that he had veered away from the protection of the ancient track.

'Easy now, girl,' he soothed the mare bringing her to a halt. She stood still stamping her hooves and snorting nervously.

Somewhere to his right a chorus of sibilant, high voices echoed back at him. 'Easssy-now-girl.'

'Who's there?'

'Who'sss there, who'sss there, who'sss there,' the myriad of disembodied voices wailed back at him.

'Show yourself,' Caspar shouted, mustering his courage.

'Ssshow yoursssself, ssshow yoursssself, ssshow yoursssself,' the fog echoed.

The eerie mist and ghostly voices were unnerving. Caspar had trouble trying to stop his jittery emotions transferring to the mare.

'Hal! Hal, where are you?'

Somewhere mingled in with the ghostly echoes, Caspar thought he heard a thin cry through the fog. 'Spar, over here. Spar! Spar!'

Turning the mare's head in what he thought was the direction of Hal's voice, Caspar pressed his mount forward, but before she could take one pace the horse was surrounded by long green tendril-like hands. They came out of the fog, twisting around the boy's legs and winding around the mare's neck, as if they meant to drag them into the umber depths of the forest.

'What are you doing in my woods?' a single voice whispered. It was the voice of a woman, soft and sultry but with considerable strength and authority.

The horse panicked, rearing and thrashing out with her forelegs to free herself from the menace of the green hands that snaked about. The disembodied arms had too many joints in their wrists and elbows. The mare reared again and, as she threw up her neck, Caspar was unable to lunge his body forward to keep his balance because of the cold, clammy hands that wove around his waist. They dragged him down onto the crisp, leafy floor of the forest.

'You can't come into my forest without paying the proper respects.'

The sibilant voices wailed in the fog, 'There'sss a toll to be paid for crosssing her foresssst.'

There was nothing Caspar could do to resist the hands. Struggling violently against the unseen enemy, he achieved nothing. His legs were snatched and he was bumped along the soft leaf-mould without a break in the pace. He could not tell how fast he was being dragged. It was not painful, no, it was more like floating. He felt totally out of touch with his surroundings as if the fog had tucked them into a private, hidden world.

Quite suddenly, Caspar found himself rolling on the ground free from the bodiless limbs as they withdrew into the fog. He leapt to his feet, hurriedly brushing himself off to try to purge the unclean feeling that he had been embraced by a nest-full of snakes. He spun round, staring into the white fog, and sunk his body into a low crouch as if he was preparing to wrestle with the fog itself, if no other creature appeared.

'Show yourself,' he demanded haughtily. 'I am weaponless. Are you too much of a coward to show yourself to me, defenceless as I am?'

Something tapped him on his shoulder and he spun round, eyes wide, trying to pierce the fog. Cackles burst out all around him and Caspar had the distinct feeling that he was being toyed with. His other shoulder was nudged, again from behind. Punching out into the fog, his fist connected with nothing but the thin moist air. There was malicious cackling in the foggy air. Caspar abandoned himself to its madness and was shocked when a lone voice demanded, 'Who's Hal?'

The voice was hard but still slurred with a snaky hiss to it.

The fog began to lift. Shafts of sunlight threaded through the trees creating dappled bands of light and dark on the forest floor. He breathed deeply, hoping that the sunlight would chase away the ghostly shadows and reveal a perfectly normal explanation for his experiences – like woodcutters' children playing some practical joke. But as he drew in the musty, forest air all he could smell was the evil of a huge presence that he could sense but not yet see.

A gust of wind swept away the last shreds of ground-hugging cloud and Caspar dropped to his knees at the sight of her. A cold knot gripped his stomach, twisting his intestines into a tight ball. His face froze into a picture of revulsion and horror as he felt the creature grappling for control with his mind.

She reached out one of her six hands towards him and curled a long-nailed finger in a gesture of beckoning.

Caspar tried to resist. 'What do you want with me?'

Her green tongue flicked out and licked her green lips. 'You trespass in my kingdom. Your freedom is forfeit: you will obey me.'

'You will obey,' the voices hissed from behind the trees. 'You will obey her.'

The creature's red eyes burned through his eyeballs and ate into his brain, searching out his inner desires and seeking to corrupt him. He wrenched his head from her probing stare but her will pulled it round again.

'Look at me, boy. I am the great Cailleach. I am all woman, a creature of desires and wants. Be my creature in this forest.' She ran four of her hands down her naked body, rippling over the line of her multiple breasts. She looked like a cross between an insect and a sow in pig rather than a woman, thought Caspar, revolted to the pit of his stomach. Still she pulled him towards her and he found himself shuffling forward on his knees whilst his hands shielded his face from her stare.

'Come and join with me in the forest and we will dance in the woods for ever, you and I.'

'Let me go! Let me go!' he cried out. He had a terror of this creature. The place stank of fear and blood. The silence was uncanny and the boy realized that this part of the forest was devoid of birdsong: it was unnatural – supernatural. The creature's tongue flicked out and in again slowly.

'Don't be frightened of me. Come closer; let me whisper of pleasures in your ear. You'll never want to leave my cosy nest.' She reached out several of her arms and then clutched them towards her as if yearning for his proximity, whilst the remaining pair of arms ran up and down the folds of her body.

Crawling towards her, Caspar felt nauseous but was unable to resist. Finally her hands clutched him all over and sucked him into a tight embrace. Her sweet heavy breath filled his lungs.

'Well, tell me, young male, what drew you into my woods?' She leered at his body. 'Tales of my lustful body, desire for the great Cailleach, or are you just a trespasser?' She hissed long and lingeringly over the word trespasser, daring Caspar to admit to such a crime.

'We – I . . .' he stammered.

'Ah! We. How many is we? Plenty of young healthy boys?'

'No, I'm alone,' Caspar burst out and immediately a burning pain shot through his head and he clasped his hands to his temples.

Cailleach laughed raucously so that her four pairs of breasts heaved up and down, shaking convulsively on her green body. 'Don't even try to deceive me, young male. You're like a baby rabbit whose neck I could snap in my little finger if I wished. So there are three of you: Hal, your brother I perceive . . .'

Caspar was relieved that this huge grotesque female though powerfully strong was still fallible, but the second he let the thought form in his mind he tried to block it.

'Hmm . . . and another. You are confused about the third. I cannot picture – no wait – a small girl. How tedious, how very dull.' She yawned and then snapped one of her thumbs in a flicking motion towards the blackthorn trees which surrounded her bower. 'I want some entertainment.' She yawned again, displaying her cavernous mouth.

A slim nymph slid out from the undergrowth. A skirt of leaves was tied about her waist but otherwise she was naked. She twisted and turned to the wailing sighs coming from the unseen voices. Gradually the sighs moulded into a lamenting song. The slender-bodied nymph, almost boy-like with her shorn hair and narrow angular hips, shook and shuddered as she lunged back and forth to the rhythm of the song. Her head began to swirl in circles as the rhythm became a beat and the song more of a commanding chant. Caspar was gripped with a sudden horror as he saw the knives in both her hands flash back and forth, crossing and recrossing, in sharp slashes through the stale air. Her head fell back and her eyes, upturned and unseeing, flickered in a trance. The knives slashed the air again as her legs buckled and her knees thumped to the ground. Her narrow body shuddered to the beat, her hands held out in supplication to the multi-limbed monster.

The chanting built steadily to a drumming crescendo and Caspar clamped his hands over his ears to block out the noise, though his eyes remained transfixed by the baleful movements of the dancing nymph. The green-skinned ogre kept one arm crooked around the Belbidian youth, keeping him helplessly pinioned to her side, as she slowly stood up from her cross-legged position. To the rhythm of the building chant, she rose to twice the size of a full-grown man. One hand after another she pointed at the entranced nymph. Finally the fifth arm jabbed outward, the talon-like fingernail uncurling as she slid the forked tongue out of her mouth and sighed, 'Now, now, now.'

The young nymph wrenched the knives sharply backwards, as if snapping a whip, and two red slits, like gills, appeared on either side of her neck. For one lucid moment, her eyes beheld the monstrous creature. Just for a second, the trance was gone and nothing but fear and the comprehension of living-hell was written in her clear eyes. Then her muscles sagged under her as the arteries spurted her life-blood onto the earthy forest bed. She slumped heavily forward, gurgling blood from her throat. The knives fell from her hands and her fingers clawed the air as if they clutched at someone, imploring them for help, but finally her tormented body failed and she lay inert, claimed by death.

'Yes! Yes!' Cailleach stood proud, one hand held high in a victorious fist before she sagged her great weight down again into her cross-legged position. Almost purring like a cat she stroked Caspar's head as if he were a pet. 'That's better, my little love. That's better. Now that they no longer worship the Great Mother, they worship me! They worship me!' she shrieked and shuddered with demented laughter.

Caspar choked on the bile that flooded up into his mouth but his mind was numb.

'You cannot escape, so don't even think about it.'

Caspar could not think at all, but gradually he was aware of the multi-limbed demon crooning over him, stroking his body. He convulsed with revulsion. 'You are mine.' Her wet tongue flickered lustfully across his mouth. 'Forever.'

Chapter 12

Dusk was falling when Branwolf finally returned to Mirror Lake Valley and he stared at the dark mouth of the shaft leading out of the underground cave system. It was now too dark for him to track the Vaalakan trail. His drooping eyelids and befuddled brain warned him that he hadn't slept for two days: he had to rest. Reluctantly he slid from his horse and took shelter in the lee of a moss-covered rock for the night.

At first light he examined a line of crushed heather which marked out the Vaalakan trail. The vegetation was already beginning to spring back up but he found the occasional scuffs in the ground from a claw or boot to direct him northwards. An uneasiness crept over the man as he discovered splashes of thick blood clinging to the parched brown bracken. He dismounted to take a closer look. It was the same dark, foul-smelling blood that they had traced in the caves. The injured creature appeared to have escaped the caverns from a different route but was now travelling northwards, covering the same ground as the Vaalakans. He remounted his stallion, not knowing what to make of it.

The trail of congealed blood was at first easy to follow but gradually the red-brown stains smearing the bracken began to lessen. He wondered whether it came from one of the Vaalakan trolls that had somehow been injured and separated from the others and was now limping after them. When the full sun crept up above the peaks, breathing its welcome warmth into the gloomy valleys, Branwolf found it still easier to track the broad trail. He looked gratefully eastwards towards the dawn horizon as the sun blessed the peaks with its brilliant touch and the mountains burst into vivid golden hues.

Conqueror's graceful paces smoothly covered the ground as the Baron spurred him forward. He resisted the urge to kick the black stallion on to a faster pace, knowing that the animal would soon tire. In the long run they would cover more distance if he demanded an easier pace now.

The trail took him past the gleaming waters of Mirror Lake and led him due north towards the Boarchase Forest. He knew these mountains so well, though the range itself stretched for eight days' ride from east to west. As a boy, just like Hal and Spar, he had ridden recklessly through the valleys and struggled to climb the highest peaks. Sometimes he had risked trying to scale the treacherous cliff-faces just to see the magnificent views of crag beyond crag stretching away like rows of teeth into the far horizon. And sometimes simply to prove that he could. Later, of course, there had been more purpose to his explorations. In his search for his wife he had ranged through the thickets of fir trees and birches that clung precariously to the thin wind-swept soil. He had even ridden to the head of the Dragon's Claw valley where he had peered into the crevasses of the grey, rippled glacier. Forever calling her name, he had howled with the pain of his loss, like a wolf baying at the moon, crying for its unreachable beauty.

Branwolf leant back against the cantle and loosened his grip on the reins to give Conqueror his head as they slithered down the far side of the ridge. The horse kept his head up and his hocks well under him to keep in perfect balance. The heather had already been torn away in places where the Vaalakan animals had slithered down the steep slopes and he could see deep score marks from the claws of a large bear-like beast. Trolls, he thought bitterly. Once down into the next valley the ground was softer where the rainwater collected off the steep valley sides and he craned forward over the horse's broad shoulder looking for tracks. He halted his stallion and reined back. Now the long footprint of the troll was easily discernible, the scratch marks of its six nonretractable claws clearly embedded deep into the soft earth . . . and another just ahead, a left foot this time. He frowned at it. Imprinted within the spoor was another footprint. A wolf, or maybe a large hound. It might be a little small for a wolf and the tracking was subtly different.

Trundling in the wake of the troll were the halting tracks of several human footprints. The prints were mostly large, shapeless moulds without soles or heels as if they were made from skins bandaged around the foot. At last he found what he was looking for: smaller footprints with the firm stamp of a riding boot. They must have been made by Hal and Spar; they must have been.

He kicked Conqueror on again, reminding himself not to ask for more than a sensible steady pace as he followed the trail ever northward. The Vaalakan spies had kept to the easier going terrain of the valleys, which at least meant they left more tracks in the softer ground. Drawn by a movement, the dark broad-shouldered man looked up at the northern horizon. A bird of prey, circling high in the heavens against the deep blue of the sky, soared on the rising thermals. The Baron estimated that its stretched wingspan spread more than ten feet across. The eagle continually circled over the same spot, occasionally tipping its wings to spill some of the warm air so that it could drift effortlessly downwards.

Branwolf's heart thumped. A high-pitched scream terrorized the blue heavens, as the king of birds stalked the sky. Even Conqueror laid back his ears. Instinct told the stallion to be wary. The black-crested eagles of the Yellow Mountains were so big that they had even been known to kill a weak foal, lamb or goat kid. The eagle was far ahead, covering the impossible distances between one crag and the next unscalable peak with a single effortless beat of its wings, before gliding on the air currents. It's circling over a kill, the man thought with certainty as he watched it continually soar without once making a stoop for live prey. He decided it must be eyeing some carrion already claimed by a larger predator, waiting for the bear or mountain cat to take its fill and slink away before stealing the pickings.

It was an hour or more before the horse had covered the rugged terrain that distanced them from the prowling bird of prey. As they approached, it circled away to perch on a high crest of rock far to the east. Branwolf looked down into the valley to see the bloody kill. He scowled uncertainly.

The black stallion threw his head up and danced sideways, wary of approaching the carcass. The man gave his steed a firm slap reminding the animal to behave like a war-horse and to concentrate on his commands rather than on his fearful instincts. Obediently the black stallion sidled up to the disembowelled carcass.

A mountain lion, he thought with disbelief. A young male freshly killed. Now what could possibly have killed that? He thought for a moment and decided that the Vaalakans must have shot it and that either wolves or maybe a rogue troll had then savaged the dead lion. There was nothing else out here that preyed on the big cats. He grunted in satisfaction and was about to move off when something else caught his eye. Stamped into the soft earth was a claw-shaped imprint, in shape much like an eagle's with its three toes pointing forward and a spur jutting out behind – only this track was too impossibly huge. It was clearly defined and nearly two feet across. It wasn't possible. But the three toes and their hooked talons digging deep into the earth's crust were vividly distinct. He thought of the deep underground caverns with their treasure-trove and the mass of half-eaten carcasses.

He mounted quickly, spurring his horse away from the place as he vainly tried to outrun his fears. Not after all these hundreds of years, he thought in horror, there can't be any left. No, he couldn't believe it. There would have been evidence before now. Someone would have seen it. But out here in the mountains a day's ride from the barest pastures? What if it spent most of its hours down there in the caves, braving the surface only to forage at night? After all there were many people who had never even seen badgers. But this monster had a footprint spanning two feet, and was evidently strong and fast enough to bring down a mountain lion. He tentatively fingered his bow, wondering which arrows would be best for penetrating the scaly hide.

Something was wrong though. Was it mere coincidence that the monster was taking precisely the same trail as the Vaalakans? Was it hunting them? Perhaps it had a special taste for human flesh or perhaps it was after any stolen treasure. Surely that was just superstitious folk-lore: animals don't covet treasure – well except for magpies, he thought doubtfully. Could the dragon really be hunting the thieves that had stolen some of its treasure? My treasure, he corrected himself. For the first time Branwolf prayed that his boys had been taken by a large and well-armed troop of Vaalakans. The more warriors there were, the better chance they had against a dragon.

He leapt back onto his horse whose shod hooves cut deep crescents into the thin soil of the mountains. He was angry now. How could Spar have been so deliberately disobedient? He couldn't forgive his son for being irresponsible. Hal maybe. Hal had always been foolhardy and Branwolf accepted that as the natural recklessness of youth. But Spar, no. He couldn't afford to be irresponsible. Branwolf had done his best to instil a sense of duty into the boy's head but, he decided, Caspar had obviously inherited too much from his mother.

Both of them full of whims with no sense of reality, he thought in dismay, soaring like hawks on the wings of their dreams. Keridwen had so fiercely fought against Rewik's ideas of progress, recklessly proclaiming that the new Church tax would plunge the peasant folk into poverty. Poverty in Belbidia! The idea was preposterous. He had been young; he had been angered at the outrageous way Keridwen had dared to tell him, a mighty overlord, how to run his Barony. No woman of Belbidia could defy her man; it was unthinkable. He bristled with anger, thumping his heels into the belly of the stallion who laboured up the steeply rising slope. Conqueror thrust his noble head low and forward to help him utilize the power from his hindquarters.

Branwolf reflected how Rewik had ordered the cathedral to be built at the foot of Torra Alta. Of course he had agreed to the King's demand despite his wife's fury and it was only after Keridwen had gone that he realized the terrible price of the construction. Marble from Camaalia, gold from Ophidia, satins and silks from Glain . . . the list was endless. The foundations alone had taken six years to build and now with hindsight Branwolf was forced to concede that perhaps his wife had been right. He had been young and too ashamed to admit that he wanted to please his King and did not have the will to defy him – not then. But Torra Alta had paid the price. His garrison was depleted and vast tracts of majestic hardwood forest had been felled for timber exports to Farona and Caldea. Where the axes had hacked into his forests there were no boar – and he needed the boar. Their tusks fetched a high price abroad. A distant tribe, dwelling far to the south of the deserts of Glain, prized them as a potent symbol of manhood and so paid a ridiculous price for them. The Torra Altans ate the boar meat, of coarse, but the tusks paid for the grain needed to feed the great war-horses. The land of Torra Alta was not fertile enough to support the growth of these fussy eaters. In his mind he could hear Keridwen chiding him. Irritated with himself he drew the horse to a halt, letting the stallion stretch down his neck and suck deep breaths into his lungs.

'I was wrong, Keridwen,' he cried out into the mountains and the horse started and laid its ears flat. 'Can't you forgive me? Won't you come back to me? I was angry with you but I'm sorry.'

He thought of his young boy insistently asking about his mother. The Baron had been furious with Caspar for his persistent questioning. But perhaps he should have told the boy – perhaps he should have told the boy everything? However, the Chaplain had urged him not to and he had trusted his brother-in-law's judgement. It wasn't fair on such a young child.

His thoughts leapt back to the present, churning over the image of Hal and Caspar facing the terrors of the Vaalakans. He must catch up with them. Poor Caspar. Hal at least had had Elizabetta with him through his childhood. The woman had only recently returned to Farona, the home of her family. She had asked Hal to go with her but he didn't want to leave the wilds of Torra Alta for the tameness of Farona's well-bred civilization. Hal must have instinctively known that he wouldn't fit in at the King's court. He didn't dress well enough, didn't understand the fineries of courtly conversation. His insatiable appetite for chasing young girls would certainly be frowned upon, and his sporting activities curtailed. The boy had accepted that it was better to remain here, always to be second to Spar rather than give up the freedom of Torra Alta's wilderness.

The horse was breathing smoothly now as it snatched at a tuft of grass growing in the shelter of a boulder fallen from an overhanging crag that shadowed Dragon's Claw Valley. He had let the animal rest after the steep climb once he'd forded Hart's Leap. 'Come on then, boy,' he muttered. Then he saw the marks of blood, still bright red, which glared at him from a scoop of slush cradled in the hollows at the foot of the valley. Where the blood had seeped into the crystalline structure of the snow it had been preserved by the cold and was still a vivid fresh colour. He looked away from the stained slush up towards the forbidding grey monster of the glacier with its fissures and crevasses that gouged a deep valley into the Yellow Mountains. He had crawled across its surface to look for his wife, returning for three summers at the peak of the melts. But he never discovered a trace of her. He shuddered as he looked up at the river of ice and a chill sense of evil crept into his bones. He smelt the air. It was as fresh and as pure as the mountain air anywhere else in his terrain but his instincts distrusted it. He looked at the blood and the circle of foot-prints around it. A circle . . . he thought; blood . . . snow . . . Somehow it smacked of some devilish sacrificial rite.

'Spar!' he abruptly yelled into the heavens, his voice carrying high into the distant peaks and echoing through the valleys. Suddenly he was fearful that the blood had something to do with his son. The only reply to his desperate cry came from an eagle, its scream like the high-pitched tone of a pipe pealing out a single note to proclaim its territorial rights over all the land below. Mine . . . mine . . . mine . . . it seemed to scream.

He hurried away from the snow-field, slumping back into his saddle as he descended into the next valley. The sun was sinking into a valley far to the west and the peaks of the jagged mountains were snatching bites out of the molten orb of liquid red. He pushed his horse up to the left, climbing out of the valley to get a clearer view of the western horizon. He was amongst the highest mountains of the range and he could see for ten leagues through the clear thin air. Far in the distance the vicious peaks of the Jaws of the Wolf raked the sky. Great points of rock, with sides too sheer for even gorse or heather to cling to the fissured crags, dominated the horizon. Their narrowly chiselled couloirs cut deep gorges between the peaks, which held the winter snows in their shadowed recesses well into the middle months of the year.

Scanning the valley below for a suitable place to spend the night, he finally spotted the shelter of a cave. At least now he only needed to build a fire to keep the mountain predators at bay while he slept. He found a stream, filled his canister and left the horse to suck at the cool surface of the water before building his fire. He stripped the saddle from the horse's back, pulling the bridle over its ears, before replacing the rug over the horse's sleek hide to protect the animal from the cold of the mountain night. He threw down a scoopful of grain and his horse snuffled gratefully at the food, scattering the chaff with the breath from its nostrils as its rough tongue scraped against the rock.

Branwolf woke with a start, his heart thumping in his throat. Instinctively he reached for his bow and slotted a broad-barbed arrow to the catgut. The arrow was designed to pierce even horse armour and bring a charger down in the heat of battle. He felt instantly safer as he strained his ears for the noise that had shaken him from his sleep. The horse was rearing and struggling against the rope collar that tethered it to a rock. Was the wild scream he had heard just the shriek of his horse, or only the howl of a vixen? He rushed to steady the startled stallion in case the powerful war-horse injured itself on the rope. His flesh prickled as he listened for the unnatural scream that had shattered the slumber of the mountains; but he didn't hear it again. Once or twice he fell asleep, briefly, but by dawn he was ready to move on.

In the early morning light he frowned at the tracks in the ground. The troll now made a deeper impression and was obviously carrying a heavier burden. Branwolf shrugged his fears away; it might only mean that they had become too troublesome on foot and were more controllable tied to the troll. He punched his fist into the soil, feeling helpless before remounting and tracking ever northward.

I must not lose hope. If I lose hope, I have lost everything. They rely on me. Belbidia is relying on me to hold Torra Alta. And without me at the head? Well, what is a castle without a leader? The Captain would manage, he thought doubtfully, and his brother-in-law, he would do everything to keep the barbarians from the civilized lands of the south; but he was a churchman not a warrior. But Branwolf greatly admired a man with such physical determination as Gwion had shown in the search for Hal and Caspar. What other man of the cloth could physically work so hard and determinedly as his brother-in-law had done to try and find Hal and Spar? Surely his diligent commitment deserved recognition in the Church. Branwolf recalled the stuffy lowland bishop criticizing Torra Alta for using the old names for the months of the year rather than adopting the new calendar. The Baron had no intention of learning a lot of silly-sounding names that only confused everybody. It was one thing changing gods but quite another to rethink the calendar. He had no doubt that his own outburst had further damaged Gwion's chances of promotion. But even if the modern bishops frowned upon such behaviour amongst their orders, it was only natural in Torra Alta.

Now something else caught his eye and he slid from his horse to examine the tracks more carefully. The imprint of a bare foot left the mark of five small toes in the ground. He stood over the spoor and measured it against his boot. The print had been left by a small child. He crouched to examine the curious pattern of the barefoot trail and frowned at the left footprint that appeared badly twisted. A shepherd's lost child stolen by the barbarians, he wondered. Sacrifice? Virgin sacrifice, he wondered with horror.

By noon he reached the northern foothills of the Yellow Mountains. The tracks he followed were criss-crossed with other footprints in several directions. More trolls he thought in disgust. He picked out the original set of tracks that he had followed right across the Yellow Mountains, easily singling them out by the tiny bare footprints. Below him stretched the wide swathe of the Boarchase Forest and he furrowed his brow, trying to make out the shapes around thin trails of smoke that curled up out of the trees.

A camp right here in my lands, he despaired, growling at the thought of Vaalakan spies lurking in his forests. He didn't have enough men to defend the entire length of his northern frontier and he had to accept that the Boarchase was vulnerable to attack from small raiding parties. His forest reeve had long since warned the woodsmen to take shelter south of the castle where he offered them temporary homes in the lowland foothills. But most of them had stubbornly refused, preferring to hide deep in their native woods. He took comfort in the knowledge that the Northmen would not linger long in the forest. They would hasten to the lowlands of Belbidia, the prize of the great oxen herds and fields of full-eared wheat that lay beyond the Pass. But Vaalakan spies already here, he thought in deep disquiet.

The black stallion backed nervously, pawing the ground like a threatened bull. Branwolf looped the reins over the pommel, swung his bow round and notched an arrow to the string. Something was out there. He sidled around the jagged edge of a boulder that obscured his view and his eyes beheld a huge grey-skinned he-troll with its tusk embedded in the live belly of another beast like itself. This second troll lay feebly moaning as its fellow feasted on its entrails. The disembowelled animal raised its head, pathetically trying to fend off the he-troll, perhaps its mate, with a claw. She was dying, but dying too slowly. A chain attached to the ring on her nose made Branwolf guess that they had both broken free from their Vaalakan owners. A gurgling wail bubbled in the she-troll's throat and her head slumped back to earth. Branwolf raised his bow and with one quick merciful shot buried an arrow between her eyes to pierce the brain and end her suffering.

It was a mistake. The bloodied face of the he-troll flicked round, spraying out shreds of gut from his fangs as it roared at the Baron. For a split second the man took in the flat-nosed face. The troll's nostrils were torn and bleeding, probably where the hog-skinned beast had ripped its ring clean through the gristle of its nose.

Huge and cumbersome, it reared up onto its short back legs, straightening out its hunched spine to threaten the Baron with its long bear-like claws. Branwolf snatched at another quarrel and, with steady fingers, slotted it to his bow just as the beast reared up to tower over rider and horse. He wrenched back the catgut and a target of blood sprang up on the troll's ribcage around the arrow-shaft that pierced it. Undaunted the beast scratched at the embedded quarrel with its claw and the arrow fell away uselessly to the ground. As Branwolf snatched for another arrow the large beast was moving with unexpected speed and was already on him.

One slash of the troll's left claw across the stallion's shoulder sent the great war-horse staggering on to its haunches. As he was flung to the ground Branwolf struggled to regain his aim but the troll had him trapped beneath its claws before he could fire. Helplessly, he suffered its thick breath in his face as it rolled him back and forth, tossing him between its six-toed claws. It lunged, raking the upturned fangs into Branwolf's stomach. He summoned the last of his strength and fought to get a hand to his gutting knife. The blade was sharp enough to joint venison. In a frenzy he stabbed with the knife, slicing through the flesh of the animal towards its heart. It rolled away from him with thick gobs of black blood oozing from the corners of its mouth. Its eyes stared at him. In the flicker of one horrifying moment, Branwolf thought he was looking into the eyes of a human. Mercifully they closed.

With all awareness of time lost, he bitterly struggled to hang onto life. Spar needs me. He felt cold, deathly cold. He wanted only to sleep.

When twilight sucked away the warmth of the sun, Branwolf became vaguely aware again of his surroundings. He wondered when the wolves or the eagles would find his body. The mountain wolves must have smelt the scent of blood by now. The Vaalakans, he thought! The Vaalakans will find me. If they capture me they won't bother with Spar: they will just kill him. I must get off the trail. Dried blood had already congealed into a scab, where the troll-tusk had torn great rents across his stomach, but as he moved the skin split open and liquid pus oozed from the wound. His quivering horse seemed unable to place any weight on its wounded shoulder but he felt for its reins and used them to haul himself up to his knees. He looped his arm through the reins and the stallion hobbled obediently forward as he hauled himself painfully along on his elbows and knees, crawling inch by inch away from the trail. It took most of the night for him to crawl three hundred paces away to the west to the shelter of scrubby birch trees. It was warmer in the trees: they kept the wind off. Next to a spring that bubbled up between the rocks he found a nest of moss to rest on. He listened, for hours. Conqueror was in pain, he could tell. I'm sorry, old boy, he thought.

He woke with a cold sweat pouring off his forehead. His chest was damp and his arms and legs ached. The wound smelt and he realized that fever had bitten into his body. He lay there in the shade of the trees all day, listening to the quiet munching of his horse. As twilight came again he forced his exhausted body to stretch an arm towards the cool, life-giving waters of the stream. He sucked at the trickles of water that ran from his fingers. He breathed heavily for several minutes as the world went in and out of focus, before he managed to drive his heels into the leaf-mould and scrape himself over the mossy ground. At last he could dip his head into the quenching water. Swallowing painfully, he forced himself to gulp down the water, hoping it would cleanse his body of the poisons of the putrefying wound. He found it difficult to suck through his cracked lips but at last he took his fill and dropped back exhausted into the moss.

That night the fever tore at him in his raving dreams. 'Keridwen,' he cried out. 'Keridwen, give me strength to mend so that I may find our son.' He dreamt that demons hovered over him, feasting at his belly while he lay helplessly looking on. He shook himself from the dream. The night was cold and bright and the light from the points of stars threaded through the trees. He must still be dreaming: he could still hear feasting noises. It was like the sound of hogs snuffling through wet swill, only too loud, too deep, and the ground shuddered with the movements of some ponderous animal. He heard the sound of more salivary gnawing and the splintering of bones chilled the night. As he struggled to move the pain in his stomach soared. Gradually losing consciousness, he was aware of a great bulk approaching as the slithering rasp of its movements drew closer.

Dear God, don't let me be eaten alive like that she-troll. Dear Keridwen, save me from the beast . . .

Chapter 13

The monstrous green female cradled Caspar's inert body possessively to her multiple breasts. Suddenly she stiffened.

'Someone's in my forest. Get them!' she cried. The simple order sent unseen feet scurrying through the forest. 'My slaves,' she hissed. 'They live simply to please me, just as you will.'

Murmuring in a strange, sibilant tongue, the ogre reached up into the sky with one hand as if imploring the heavens. The unnatural fog slipped down from the crisp, autumnal trees just as if she had dragged it out of the sky. The thick moist air smothered Caspar in the all too recognizable aroma of death.

'Is it one of your playmates perhaps, my pet?' she hissed gleefully. 'More toys for me, I hope. Ah! but you don't seem pleased. Tut-tut, but you should be pleased to see your friends. Don't you wish to see your brother again? But the girl . . . I have no time for the girl – unless perhaps – yes, unless she dances for me.'

Caspar could feel the creature's pulse quicken with the intensifying emotions in her body. Waiting to see what her slaves would ensnare in the forest, she wailed impatiently. Caspar waited with dread. Please, Hal, don't come. Stay away from this creature from Hell, he willed.

'So you still have the strength to fight me, do you?' The monstrous Cailleach leered at him, sliding her serpent's tongue out between her lips and smearing him with a slow, sensual lick. The curling tongue explored his chin, his mouth, his nose and then circled his eyes. With his arms pinned to his side, Caspar was unable to wipe the slimy saliva from his face and revulsion churned in his gut. 'You will not hold out for-ever, and soon I will have another one to play with.' She laughed mockingly again. 'There is enough of me for both of you. My faithful slaves will bring me the other little buck soon. They will bring him to me out of the fog. I have waited long enough.' She clapped a pair of hands impatiently.

But the forest-coloured wood-nymphs, who managed to remain so completely inconspicuous in the camouflage of veg-etation, did not return. Instead, a needle-point of silver light pierced the fog, growing to form a bright full moon. To either side of the circle of light shone the silver shapes of a waxing and a waning crescent. Cailleach hissed, her grasp on Caspar momentarily relaxing as if she had been taken by surprise, but then the clutch hardened into an iron fist, crushing his bones. Caspar sensed she was smitten with rage.

'What are you doing in my forest, Crone? Get out of here before I destroy you.' The fog thinned despite Cailleach's efforts to drag more out of the sky. 'You have not had such strength for many seasons. The earth has spun her dance a dozen times around the great star since last you were so brave.' Cailleach was puzzled. 'You have been weak, old Crone, so where have you stolen your strength from now?'

'Give me the boy. He is mine,' demanded a quiet voice from the direction of the silvery moons. The voice was thin and wavering with age but still possessed that cut of arrogance which has its seeds in undisputed authority. 'Mutant thing of the underworld, your days in this forest are numbered. The boy is mine, of my domain, and never of yours. Give me the boy and your punishment from the Primal Gods will be lessened.'

'Ha! Old, decaying, dried bag of bones, you do not have the power. Look at me!' She stood to her great statuesque height. 'I have the power now: the wood-nymphs worship me.'

A circle of clear light formed around the figure that dared confront Cailleach. The fog seemed unable to touch her. She was small and delicate and, like the green monster had said, her face was haggard with age. Dragging the memory back from the depths of his terrorized mind Caspar recognized her as the woman whose image Brid had summoned in the moonstone. Thin, crêpey skin hung from prominent cheek-bones. Her eyes were still a fierce azure-blue though the dark sky-blue colouring was flecked with white, like tattered clouds, now shrouding their original purity. Yet the intensity was still there, searching.

The Crone took another step forward. Shimmering, silver hair cascaded to her waist like a waterfall brimming over the back of her craggy head. 'Creature of the underworld, I do not fear you. I already have one foot in the grave reaching towards the Mother's womb. I oversee at the birthing of infants and lead them out when it is their time to shake off the flesh once more. I do not fear your threats of death because I can walk in the Annwyn, I can tread through the Otherworld, and lead souls across to the other side to their birthing again. I have the knowledge of reincarnation: you have the knowledge only of death, which any scullion with a sword or a cudgel can steal from the Primal Gods.'

Unable to comprehend this battle of words, Caspar felt he was trapped between a clash of giants. He feared that any moment a thunderbolt would flash from their palms and he would be blasted into oblivion by their wrath. Never, never, if he even lived to see Torra Alta and his father again, would he disobey an order. All this, all these terrible things had befallen him since he had sneaked down the well in flagrant affront to his father's commands. Please forgive me, Father, he murmured to himself, not sure whether he meant the Baron or the one true God he had been raised to worship. However, faced with these mysterious powers in female form who wielded death and spoke of reincarnation, his faith, already battered, was floundering.

Cailleach flared up, stretching hands out into the trees and dragging forth the slender nymphs that served her. 'Kill that puny Crone!' she screeched. The green waifs were reluctant to obey and withheld from approaching the grey, old woman who stood bent over in her clean circle of air. One wailing wood-nymph tried to resist Cailleach's grasp by fleeing deeper into the forest. The huge mutant creature dragged her back by an ankle and bent the slender waif over her knee until the spine splintered like snapping wood.

The frail, grey-haired lady spoke in a voice as ancient and strong as the Yellow Mountains. 'I am Morrigwen, the first of the Three, and in the name of the Great Mother, by the blessing of the Moon, I command you to cease.'

'You have not the power,' Cailleach countered vehemently. 'You are alone and your magic is worthless – just empty words without the union of the trinity.'

Morrigwen raised her left hand and Brid stepped lightly out of the forest. 'I am not alone,' the Crone's stony voice replied.

'Two is not enough. The Primal Gods will not hear you.' Cailleach was trembling with outrage yet now uncertainty crept into her voice.

'Two is not enough, I concede, but the boy can reach the third.' Her voice altered to an urgent command and the captive boy realized that she was addressing him. 'Caspar, I have the Druid's Eye. Reach out to it with your mind. Reach out and touch the Mother.'

He choked as Cailleach's vice-like grip tightened around his neck and he could no longer speak. No, I cannot call on these heretical powers, he thought in mortal fear. But Brid's gentle voice reached out to woo his ears.

'Think of the love of the Mother. Think of her, adore her and put yourself in her hands. You must believe. You need only think and believe in her love.'

Caspar's thoughts were tormented by the image of writhing snakes coiling up through his veins, staining his blood a putrid green. He fought hard to grasp on to a lucid memory.

He struggled to drive the pure evil of Cailleach from his soul by muttering the good words of the scriptures. He imagined his black-robed Uncle Gwion sermonizing before him and struggled to let the holy words fill his thoughts, but they brought no comfort. They left him feeling cold and guilty. The Chaplain despised him, always talking of sin and Hell and of how he, Caspar, was unworthy of the great love of the one true God.

'Think of the woman's face in the moonstone, Spar,' Brid's voice pleaded again.

Instead Caspar remembered the jarring shock when his naked hands had first touched the magical globe. But then wonder embraced his mind as he felt the woman trapped in the moonstone reach out towards him with a pure and perfect love. Caspar held on possessively to that image, his emotions eagerly grasping at their comfort. I am lost, he despaired. My soul is lost to these women because they will save me. Then a rush of empowering energy surged up through the earth's mantle to mettle his will. Awe-struck by the brilliance of the force channelling through him, the boy quailed at the sense of the power welling up in his heart until, despite himself, he felt strong.

'At last,' Brid breathed.

Morrigwen withdrew a golden sickle from the girdle of her green robes, and with her other hand she lifted from around her neck the carved bone charm of a horse's skull. Holding them both, she raised her hands in invocation. Cailleach gave out a long shriek of pain that drained away into a thin wail of despair.

Morrigwen's voice rose easily above the monster's sad noise. 'I hold the golden sickle that will cut the threads that tie you to this flesh-bound life. I hold the skull of the mare of night who will carry you to the nether reaches of Annwyn, through the underworld. You will never again return to walk the surface of the earth to torment the souls of men whilst we have the strength to oppose you.'

Brid held aloft a sprig of rowan tree. 'I have the spirit of the tree that seeks out evil and chases it from this living world.'

Words entered Caspar's perplexed mind: I have the love of the Mother. Though he did not say them aloud, the words joined Brid's and Morrigwen's and gave their power to the invocation.

Cailleach fell limp and slumped back onto her stony altar, though her powerful arm still crunched his bones in its grip. When Morrigwen moved, it was with the strength and agility of a young woman. She strode forward determinedly and hacked at Cailleach's arm with the golden sickle. The limb severed cleanly from her trunk without any blood. Wearily Cailleach clasped one of her opposite hands over the bloodless wound, swaying with pain, but her voice was too weak to cry out. Morrigwen dragged the boy away from the ogre, her severed hand still fiercely clutching around his throat.

'We've no time to deal with that,' Morrigwen explained urgently. 'We have to get away now.' As the old Crone dragged Caspar away from the blackthorn grove, her fierce power became progressively weaker. She began to stoop from her erect stance more and more with every pace, her stride becoming slow and laboured. Brid rushed to her aid and as they paused for a moment's breath, Caspar turned back to stare at the ogre whose severed arm still throttled him like an iron choker. She was frozen solid. Her arms – only five now – were petrified into an ungainly statue.

By the time they had reached the ancient way that ran through the forest, the small youth was gasping for breath and the world swam before his eyes. The severed hand would not release its garrotting hold and he collapsed onto the sward, the hazy image of Hal's face swirling before him.

Morrigwen's distant voice croaked somewhere in the background. Though Caspar was unable to distinguish the words, he sensed the urgency and uncertainty in her tone.

Brid was closer to his ear. 'We need to find the Mother . . .'

'I can't breathe,' Caspar choked. 'Please help me. I can't breathe.'

Then Hal was there. He grabbed the green hand and tried to wrench it free, grappling with each finger to prise it off his kinsman's skin, but the giant palm squeezed tighter.

'Stop!' Brid shouted. 'He's going blue.'

'Fire,' Morrigwen suddenly ordered. 'We will purify it with

fire, like burning out a tic. Quick, some kindling, and water too.'

Scorching heat at least made Caspar know that he was still alive. The fine hairs on the back of the green hand singed with a sharp acrid smell which tore at his throat.

'Keep him wet. More water,' Morrigwen directed, as Brid applied cold compresses doused in pure water to keep the singeing fire away from the boy's skin. Rapidly she renewed each poultice as it warmed in the flames that the old Crone held onto the severed hand. Caspar closed his eyes tightly against the tear-making fumes as the flesh began to smoulder and the putrid stench lay heavily about them.

At last the grip lessened and Morrigwen was able to prise away the charred hand with her golden sickle. Caspar gasped in a sharp breath, burning his lungs in the hot air.

'Keep dousing him with cold water, Brid. And, Hal, fetch more kindling. This thing needs a large pyre if we are going to destroy it so that it cannot contaminate this world with its evil.'

'It might draw the Vaalakans,' Hal objected.

'Silence, child.' Morrigwen's voice resumed its stony tone. 'We must totally destroy evil, whenever we find it. The Vaalakans can't be helped. Now don't touch that thing.'

'I wouldn't dream of it,' Hal grumbled sulkily after his scolding.

Morrigwen manoeuvred the hand on top of a thatch of brush and twigs with the help of two rowan branches, then plunged the torch into the heart of the bonfire. She placed the rowan on top. 'It must all be burnt,' the Crone emphasized.

The pillar of smoke was dense and black, billowing straight upwards into the still, blue sky.

'We must go,' urged Hal.

'No. We wait.' Morrigwen was unmovable. 'All of it must burn and I must stay to see it through.'

'Don't cross the old woman,' warned Brid quietly.

'I heard that, young girl. Don't be impertinent with me.

How is Spar? How is my boy? No burns I hope, if you have managed to do your job right.'

Caspar answered wearily for himself: 'No. No burns. I feel all right, I think, except very cold, icy cold, just here.' He touched the side of his neck where Cailleach's palm had been pressed against his veins. 'It's numb in fact.' He coughed and spat into his hands and a trickle of green liquid slid through his fingers. He looked at it in bewilderment and shock. 'What has that thing done to me?'

Morrigwen wrapped her bony fingers around his neck, pressing tenderly. Caspar felt some warmth and feeling return. 'We need the Mother,' she sighed sorrowfully. 'How sorely we need her. I can do nothing for you here. The moment that thing is cremated we'll ride for my dwelling. Now, Brid,' she ordered, 'cut another sprig of rowan.'

She handed the young girl her golden sickle and Brid searched through the trees until she found the chosen tree. After first begging permission from the spirit of the tree, she cut off a sprig from a branch and gave it to Caspar.

'Here, hold this and don't let it go,' she warned. 'It will help to ward off the evil spirits.'

Morrigwen diligently raked through the charred, powdery ashes and finally grunted with satisfaction. 'It's done. We can leave now.'

Hal's militaristic bent brought an urgent cry of 'To horse!' from his mouth. 'I can see Vaalakans on the horizon, and moving fast. They're on trolls.'

Looking back along the trail, Caspar made out a movement more than a league away. It was moving fast as Hal had said, but he could not be sure what it was.

'Young man,' Morrigwen admonished. 'You leaping about like a mad hare isn't going to speed anyone on their way. Get down right away and help Spar up first and, for that matter, myself. You can help me on to Brid's horse. I'm a bit old nowadays for such cavorting.'

'Women!' Hal muttered defiantly to himself. 'The enemy's in sight, for goodness' sake.' All the same he slid down from the stallion and ran to give his nephew a leg up. It was then his face became suddenly anxious, seeing Caspar's weakness, but the younger boy managed to smile some reassurance.

Once up on the mare, Morrigwen rode as capably and aggressively as Brid had, her old, knobbly hands taking the reins. With the young girl sitting obediently behind her, she urged the horse onwards and together they rode fast away. The two boys leant forward, Hal onto the stallion's neck, stretching his hands forward to let the horse reach into a full gallop with Caspar slumped onto his back. Caspar clung on to Hal's heavy cloak, wondering how fast a troll could move. He had once seen a brown bear overtake and bring down a stag. The animal might have seemed cumbersome and heavy but it had a surprising turn of speed.

They galloped headlong for as long as the horses could endure. Gradually the easy flowing strides became laboured and halting as sweat foamed around the horses' cream shoulders. The stoical mounts were blowing too hard to maintain a gallop and simultaneously they drew up to a walk. There was nothing their human burdens could do to press them on faster, despite glimpses of the Vaalakans on the horizon.

'Have they seen us?' queried Hal.

'Bound to have,' Morrigwen replied. 'And if not, the trolls will have our scent by now. We will let the horses get their breath before continuing at a steady pace, so that we still have something in hand to make the last stretch home.'

'You mean if the Vaalakans haven't eaten us by then. Come on, we must ride fast.' He made to dig in his heels but the old woman stopped him with a thunderous 'No!'

'Stupid old bat,' Hal growled under his breath, but he did not attempt to disobey the old woman.

'We must have speed in hand for the last furlong,' Morrigwen stated calmly.

Hal sighed and sat straighter, propping up Caspar who slumped listlessly forward onto his back. He allowed the stallion to walk at its own pace and soon the women on the mare had walked some lengths ahead along the forest trail. Some way to their left he could hear the sound of running water filtering through the trees and he guessed they must be following a route parallel with the Sylvan Rush River. The grassy trail was dappled with sunlight but to either side the shade of the woods was impenetrable. At last Brid and the old woman were far enough ahead for the youths to talk together privately.

'Where did she come from?' Caspar asked, referring to the Crone's sudden appearance in the hideous presence of the ogre.

Hal knew what he meant. With a shrug, he said, 'When you vanished into the fog, Brid said we'd have to get Morrigwen to save you. We galloped along this track but the old woman was already hurrying towards us. It may seem weird, but she already knew we needed her.'

'We *need* help,' said Caspar faintly. 'Our God's not helping us right now, is he? There, back in the forest with that monster, Brid said, "We must find the Mother" – and I understood what she meant. I felt her power run through me. It must be because I'm so closely linked to Torra Alta, the castle once dedicated to the Goddess. I felt the power. It destroyed that creature. That power is what will protect us from the Vaalakans. The power of the ancient religion of Torra Alta.' His voice was hopeful but weak. 'I feel cold,' he added.

'Blasphemous rot. These women are softening your brain.' Hal sounded disapproving.

Caspar remembered the power of the old Crone as she vanquished Cailleach's evil and the physical ferocity of the girl's will.

Hal looked worriedly over his shoulder at his silent friend. 'There is no greater help than God's. What's happened to you, Spar?'

Caspar did not answer but rubbed the back of his neck, trying to massage away the cold ache. 'Look! They're getting closer,' Hal shouted.

A group of figures appeared behind them on a distant brow following the line of the cursor, which ran like a furrow through the forest directly towards them. A dozen galloping shapes descended into the same hollow where the fog had sucked Caspar into Cailleach's dense world of trees.

Even so, the heavy grunts of the trolls were clearly audible before Morrigwen allowed her rested mare to surge forward into a canter. The stallion was already battling against the bit, his instincts to lead the herd away from hunting predators goading him on. He bucked once, throwing his heels into the air to show his impatience and then resigned himself to a steady gait.

'How far?' Hal called to Morrigwen.

Brid answered instead, 'Over this crest and the next, then we're there.'

A triumphant yell came from behind them as the Vaalakans found their quarry clearly in striking distance. Caspar twisted round and saw Scragg shockingly close, perched on top of his hog-backed troll, an angry fist raised in attack as he led his men forward. Lowering his arm the blond Vaalakan reached down to his saddle-flaps and unhooked a new axe from its sheath. He whirled it expertly above his head as he perched on the rolling troll.

Morrigwen twisted round to judge for herself the distance that separated them from the enemy and at last signalled the boys forward to a faster pace.

Hal grunted through tensely clenched teeth. 'When is this old Crone going to use her heels on that horse, for God's sake?'

Not until they reached the brow of the hill did Morrigwen order a full-blown gallop. The horses stretched out their necks with the ears flattened to their heads and exerted themselves to the utmost. Brid's blue skirts and the flowing green robes of the old Crone billowed out behind them and their long, unbraided hair mingled to form a streaming silver and copper banner.

'Ride for your life,' Brid shouted. 'We have to cross the gateway at . . .' Her voice was lost in the thunder of hooves and the cries of the Vaalakans, who were hooting with glee at the scent of their prey.

The trees flew by beside them as they covered the ground with long, pounding strides, the stallion's white streaming mane whipping against Hal's windblown face. Brid urged them on with a wave of her hand. Somehow the mare was winning the race to safety, perhaps because of her lighter burden or simply because the old Crone was able to encourage her to a greater speed.

The rough grunts of the trolls were growing louder as their great bodies gobbled up the ground with enormous, untiring strides, exhaling hot, rushing clouds of steamy breath.

'It's just the other side of the rise now,' Brid shouted, barely audible.

The rise, however, was steep and the solidly built mountain horses found the climb more of a strenuous labour than the fiery southern breeds would have done. Give me Firecracker any day, thought Caspar, but immediately felt disloyal – the stallion's great heart was beating its stoical best for them. The trolls were gaining rapidly, ten lengths behind them now and closing.

'Come on, boy, come on. We've got to get one last burst of speed,' Hal pleaded with the stallion but ceased to kick him on since, like any other accomplished rider, he knew when the horse was giving its all.

With thundering strides the leading troll was breathing down their necks, the leading ice-blond Northman hunched over the animal's bristly mane. The blood-curdling sound of Scragg's voice reached them, 'Ah! Belbidaks, I haves you now,' but worse still was the sound of his axe whistling through the air.

Brid and Morrigwen crested the brow of the hill and hot on their heels came the stallion, grunting with the effort. Scragg drew closer, leaning out to the side of the troll to take a swipe at the stallion's rump but the axe sliced impotently through the air.

'Here.' Hal took the reins in one hand and unhitched the stolen axe that he had secured to his belt. 'Do something with this.'

Even in his cold, confused state, Caspar remembered how Hal had struggled with the cumbersome weapon in the Vaalakan arena. At the last second the younger boy decided he might cause more injury to the smooth round rump of their stallion than to Scragg if he tried to brandish the double-bladed cleaver. He kept hold of the axe and, instead, fumbled with the brooch clasping his cloak. He threw the long streaming garment behind them and saw with satisfaction that it wrapped itself about the troll's ugly face, momentarily blinding the animal, then snaring its back legs. The beast stumbled, and Scragg clung to the troll's hog-like mane, off-balanced. The Belbidians momentarily gained a bare half-dozen desperate strides.

'We won't make it. These women are mad!' exclaimed Hal in horror and Caspar felt his stomach disappear into his boots at the sight of what lay ahead. Off the old track that had guided them straight as an arrow through the forest, a second narrower track led away to the right, where a crescent-shaped clearing opened up in the trees. The edge of the clearing was marked out by stakes on which hung a multitude of animal skulls, glaring out with empty eye-sockets at any would-be trespasser. In the middle of the clearing crouched a mud hut, much like an old peasant woman with her brown cloak drawn over her shoulders to protect her from the weather. The problem, which had so dismayed Hal and Caspar, lay between the hut and the stakes where a green swamp swayed and gurgled like simmering porridge.

The mare slowed for a moment, allowing Brid to turn and shout at them. 'Don't hesitate. Stay right behind us, absolutely right behind us, and keep galloping.' Then, seeing the expression on the boys' white distrusting faces, she wrenched the reins from Hal's fists and led the stallion herself. Together the women forced the horses to side-step quickly away from the trail before galloping ferociously into the gurgling quagmire. The stagnant mud squelched and sucked at their hooves, but somehow the horses managed to skim the surface. Each kick of their heels splattered their cream flanks in thick sludge and sprayed the riders' cloaks in slimy duckweed. Two strides from the far bank the horses gathered one last burst of speed to leap for dry land and Caspar thumped heavily into his uncle's back as the stallion pecked awkwardly on landing. But they had crossed the quagmire and were now safe on the marsh-moated island!

More of the magic of the Mother Goddess, thought Caspar gratefully. Brid managed to twist round, giving them a broad grin and chucked back the reins. She was a happy sight, he thought. Mud droplets splattered her smooth cheeks, stained her dress and coated her long tangled hair but, delighting in their victory over the enemy, she was radiant. She pointed behind them and Caspar saw the great troll – and Scragg! – floundering in the quagmire. The blond-haired men were heaving on ropes to drag them out.

Hal snatched up the reins and hauled the stallion into a rear, gleefully hooting and jeering at the enemy. 'Ha! They're stopped. They can't make it.' He whirled the loose ends of the reins triumphantly through the air, accidentally catching Caspar smartly on the cheek.

'Good old Mother Earth,' Brid laughed as they pivoted round to face the Vaalakans and skidded to a halt, the horses blowing hard.

Morrigwen gave her a stern glare. 'Don't be blasphemous, child.'

'How did we manage that?' Hal asked, panting as he followed Morrigwen's example and dismounted.

'Actually there's no magic, only a hidden causeway one cubit beneath the mud's surface. But it's a good leap before the start of the firm footing so you need to enter at a fast pace and another before the end, hence the need for the gallop. Too subtle for blundering trolls: they didn't stand a chance.'

Looking from the safety of the bog-protected island, they could observe the Vaalakans hitching the rope to another troll, struggling to win the battle against the hungry suck of the quagmire. Hal smiled. Scragg appeared to be shouting at them but the distance blurred his words and they could not understand him.

'They want the moonstone,' Caspar said flatly. He felt a lethargic cold dragging away his energy and he struggled to express his worries to his uncle. 'It seems vital to them. Perhaps . . . perhaps Brid is right, about what will save Torra Alta? If it is so important to the enemy . . .' His voice trailed off as he took in his surroundings: they were on a marsh island. Suddenly it occurred to him that they might have leapt into their own trap. 'Are we trapped?' he blurted.

'Do you think I'm such an old fool, my boy?' Morrigwen asked haughtily. 'A mindless filly that runs over the cliff to escape the wolf? Come on, we'll leave the Vaalakans to it and finish this part of our journey, shall we?' The two young boys looked blankly at one another and Caspar wearily shrugged his shoulders. Hal reached out a hand to relieve his nephew of the burdensome axe and together they rode slowly towards the mud hut.

Now that they were closer to the peasant's dwelling, they could see that it was larger than it had appeared from a distance. The entrance, shrouded by a hide-skin curtain which sufficed for a door, was actually big enough to squeeze the horses through. Caspar cringed away from a human skull skewered above the lintel then found himself in the darkness within.

'Why the skull?' Hal asked, staring quizzically at the flesh-picked bones, less upset by the human remains than his nephew.

'When you are as old as I am,' Morrigwen replied, 'death is always very close to you. I put it there as a reminder.' Brid showed her first signs of vulnerability by reaching towards the old woman and squeezing her hand for reassurance. Morrigwen patted it fondly. 'But without death, there can be no rebirth. Reincarnation keeps the wheel of life turning and brings little ones, like my beloved Bridget and my young Spar, to the living world.'

Puzzled and disconcerted by the old Crone's proprietorial

attitude towards him, Caspar waited for his eyes to slowly adjust to the dark. He had expected to find perhaps a cauldron in the centre or at least some skins for bedding, but the room appeared empty except for a number of small animal bones. They lay on the bare earth arranged in careful patterns as if to form some message. The dark reminded him of the black soul of Cailleach and he was again aware of the cold ache in his neck, now that the heat and the excitement of their escape had passed. He rubbed the skin, pinching his knobbly spine to try and regain some feeling.

'Does it hurt?' Brid asked anxiously. She gently helped Caspar down from the stallion.

Listlessly the wan boy replied, 'No, I can't feel it,' at which Morrigwen made a dissatisfied grunt and stooped to examine the bones, readjusting them quickly. Rising, she reached for a brushwood torch that was cradled in a wicker nest by the door. She struck a flint and the torch crackled into life, illuminating a black well in the centre of the hut. The light touched a series of steps. They formed a spiral stairway that curved out of sight. 'This is the way.'

'What are the bones for?' Caspar's quizzical nature was still not fully repressed by the cold discomfort in his neck.

'Just runes,' Morrigwen replied succinctly. Brid had learnt her annoying habit of giving inadequate answers from this old woman, Caspar thought.

'Are those old rabbit bones supposed to be magic then?' scoffed Hal.

'They're hare actually and no,' Brid replied with a tilt to her nose. She was busy brushing the slime and sweat from first one and then the other horse's quivering flanks and mane. 'This is a stronghold against enemies of the Mother: all faithful friends can enter and if they can read the runes they will know which path to take.' She led the horses to the door, removed their bridles and spoke to them softly, 'You know which way to go, now. To the woods with you.' And each with a whinny, the two beasts with the colouring of moonlight burst into the open once more to run fast and free.

Brid joined Morrigwen at the top of the unexpected stairs spiralling down into the earth. It turned out there were several paths they might take. At first the walls were smooth but then the way delved deep into the soil, weaving through great tree roots. A thick tap-root dropped straight through the tunnel in front of them, sprouting hairy filaments that hung like tentacles from the tapered stem. It drilled directly down through the tunnel floor and back into the earth.

'We're beyond the perimeter of the quagmire now,' said Brid, waiting for Caspar, who was beginning to feel the presence of a cold, burdening weight around his neck.

'Is it far?' he asked wearily.

'No, we'll climb soon,' she reassured him.

'This place gives me the creeps,' he admitted. 'It reminds me of being in the labyrinth under Torra Alta. It's like a catacomb stuffed with the ancient, maggoty dead.'

'You're bound to see things in a bad light until we've cleansed you of the touch of Cailleach,' Brid remarked soothingly. She reached out her hand and Caspar grasped it gratefully, feeling her warmth flow through her touch.

'It's just the cold in my neck,' he explained. She led him forward and the well-trodden ground began to rise. A circle of bright sunlight lay ahead where the tunnel bore them up and out into a secluded glade, somewhere unknown and untraceable in the Boarchase Forest beyond the touch of the Vaalakans.

They were welcomed by the clear music of a stream meandering between the roots of the trees, tarrying on its long journey to the sea. The common fir and birch trees, which dominated most of the forest's acreage, were replaced by a wealth of varieties. A glade opened before them circled by great oaks, stout majestic kings, dressed in robes of gold and bronze for their autumnal pageant. In the centre of the glade Caspar, despite his weariness, counted thirteen carefully arranged specimen trees. Intrigued, he noted each variety: birch, rowan, alder, willow, ash, hawthorn, oak, holly, hazel, apple, beech, yew and elder.

'The sacred trees,' Brid sighed, opening up her arms as if to embrace them in welcome. 'There's much magic locked into the sap of trees, each one with a different, secret power if you know how to ask the dryads – the tree-spirits – for their help. You must not steal the magic: you can only ask for it. Intuition and understanding is given by the hazel; the apple helps in making a choice; the yew, the tree of reincarnation, helps give protection to an infant at its birth; all have different qualities.'

Morrigwen led the party forward between the intermingled boughs of the trees to the arboreal circle where a simple mud hut, just like the one in the centre of the quagmire, nestled comfortably in the soft shade.

It appeared to be a simple, peasant's shack with perfectly circular walls and an overhanging conical roof of marsh-reed thatch. Whimsically, Caspar reflected that the squat mud hut under its pale thatch, like the other hut, reminded him of a stooped over woman in a brown sacking smock, shading herself from the sun beneath a wide-brimmed straw bonnet. The arched doorway was curtained by a hanging doe-skin. As they approached, the hide curtain rippled and a familiar nose poked out around the edge of it.

'Wartooth!' Caspar's spirits lifted but his legs felt too leaden to run and greet the old hound. Similarly the tall dog did not rush immediately to greet his master, as the youth had expected, and he was worried that something was wrong. Then, as the dog finally lolloped forward in a very lop-sided bound, he realized what the problem was.

'I'm sorry,' said Morrigwen. 'He won't be much use as a hunting-dog now. I couldn't save the leg. He'll get his balance on just the three soon and be able to move more easily, but at least it doesn't hurt him.' Wartooth limped between Hal and Caspar, wagging his tail furiously with his head lowered and angled to one side in a pathetic, puppy-like gesture of supplication.

The cold weakness was spreading further down Caspar's neck, making him feel too numb to return the dog's welcome as warmly as he wanted. Instead he merely kneaded the scruff of Wartooth's neck and bent his head down to receive a wet lick from the dog's long tongue. Morrigwen hitched the doe-skin aside and invited the two noble-born youths into her humble dwelling. They stooped their shoulders and slipped under the low arch.

Inside it was warm with a bright orange glow from the central fire. A thin wispy coil of smoke lazily climbed to the roof and escaped through a small hole in the thatch. A large iron tripod supported a bulbous cauldron, which dipped its bottom into the licking flames, and a homely aroma filled the hut, of broth mingled with wood-smoke and a sweet-smelling straw which covered the bare beaten-earth floor. Around the fire squatted five or six low three-legged stools, slanting at different angles on the uneven ground, welcoming them all to relax and warm their toes by the hearth.

'What on earth's that?' Hal exclaimed, pointing to a crea-ture that sat with its snout almost in the embers, basking in the warmth of the fire. It was like a large lizard with a spiny webbed ruff around its neck, which it raised and lowered as it pleased. It was surprising enough to see a lizard lording it like a cat over someone's hearth, but what was even more remarkable was its colour. The creature was scarlet from the tip of its nodulous snout to the point of its arrow-head tail.

'A salamander,' Brid replied, which did not enlighten the two boys at all. 'A red dragon, a fire spirit.'

'Oh!' Hal actually sounded impressed for once. 'Does he bite?'

'No, but he's not very keen on Wartooth yet.' Morrigwen was momentarily attending to her abandoned broth, giving it a stir with a giant wooden spoon. 'And mind you don't go upsetting my animal with any curious prods. I'm watching you, young boy,' the crotchety woman warned.

The salamander was also watching intently and its unblink-ing eyes tracked the Crone round the room, following the dim light of the moonstone that hung from her neck. She hobbled to the fire and wearily lifted the orb to place it on a stool, sighing, 'It feels too heavy to hold. The heaviness of its sorrow.'

The salamander stiffened its ruff and its tongue flickered rapidly in and out before it took excited gulps and placed a claw proprietorially on top of the moonstone. It hissed at Wartooth, warning him to keep away. The hound, whose puzzled head had been tilted to one side staring quizzically at the orb, peeled his lips back and snarled at the lizard.

On one side the interior of the hut was simple and homely, much like Morrigwen and Brid, who on first inspection appeared as peasant folk in their unadorned clothing. Rolls of furs were heaped in piles to serve as bedding. The rushes were wisely and carefully swept back from the fire in case any spitting embers chanced to ignite them. The other side of the hut looked as if it belonged to someone else entirely, revealing the esoteric nature of the women's calling. Where the furniture was sparse-to-absent in one half, the other was equipped with an expensively carved oak table of extravagant craftsmanship. The table itself was circular and four tall candles stood in holders round it – marking the points of the compass, Caspar guessed – and casting an even light. Each candle was linked by the arc of a white line chalked on the floor, which in its entirety formed a closed circle. Beneath the table, in the centre of the circle, could be seen a pentagram, a five-pointed star, carved out of the wood and resting on the ground.

The far walls of the hut were lined with cupboards and shelves containing storage jars of all sizes, though the largest were free-standing against the wall. Vessels and chalices; more candles, some blue and some white; bundles of dried herbs hanging from the thatch; rows of apples lined up neatly in trays, stacked on top of each other for storage after the harvest; all squeezed in under the low roof.

Most surprising of all, though, was what rested on the table. It was a long sword with an elaborately designed hilt. Caspar's eyes fell on the weapon and his heartbeat quickened as he was struck with the sheer power of the artefact. The vulcanized white steel of the hilt was fashioned into the image of two battling dragons, their forms trapped forever in the metal as they wrestled over a ruby gem inlaid in its centre. Etched on the pommel of the sword was the same stellate symbol of the pentagram. And the smooth uniform glint on the blade itself showed that it had been forged from a single bar of flawless metal.

Caspar knew far more about bows than swords but he knew enough to be certain that the method used in the forging had been extraordinarily rare. Catrik had told him it was extremely difficult, and so immensely expensive, to find iron of sufficient uniformity and quality to be forged into a single blade. If the iron was anything but perfect the tiniest disparity in strength left a weak spot in the metal, making the blade liable to shatter on impact. It was cheaper by far to take rods of different irons, twist them tightly together and hammer weld them under a white hot heat. This fashioned the rough core of the blade before it was encased in harder grades of iron. Only the finest swordsmiths in the world knew how to forge a sword from a single bar vulcanized to form a white-hard steel. Undoubtedly, this blade, lying in the care of these peasant women, was a princely weapon. He was surprised that such an elaborate sword had no engraving or ornamentation down the central groove of the fuller to match the intricate carvings of the hilt.

Hal's interest had also been snatched by the sword and he took an eager step towards it, his eyes bright and gleaming with fascination. Morrigwen seized his arm.

'Don't meddle! And never enter the circle,' she ordered in a tone so fierce that Hal looked at her with a shocked hurt expression.

'The sword,' he explained. 'I only wanted to take a closer look.'

'I suppose,' the old woman conceded, 'that if I don't show it to you now, you'll only steal a chance in the middle of the night and disturb the elements, doing no end of harm. No warning has ever prevented a young boy's curiosity from enticing him into danger.'

Before entering the circle, she moved between the four candles starting from the one in the east and moving sunwise around them before stepping boldly into the centre. She lifted the sword, reverently balancing it on her upturned palms, and walked back around the circle, blowing out each candle. Stepping out of the consecrated ground, she presented the hilt of the awesome weapon towards Hal. Beaming from ear to ear, he grasped it delightedly, his arms dropping a full six inches with the weight of it when Morrigwen let go.

'The dragons fighting over the heart of Torra Alta,' Morrigwen said. 'This is the sword that protects the heart of the castle but its magic has faded with the decline of the Old Faith. Once there were runes along its blade . . . and now it is smooth. The Mother is dying and the power in the runes is dying with her.' Morrigwen was mumbling in the sorrowful tones of a frail old woman bitter at the loss of times now past. The boys looked at each other and shrugged.

It must be my sword then, Caspar thought vaguely, struggling to collect his sapped thoughts into a logical pattern. If it is the sword of Torra Alta, it must be mine . . .

'Now let me have it back. It has to be kept safe.' Her tone was sharp and impatient where before it had been weak, morose. 'I want to look at Spar now: he doesn't look too healthy.'

'Just how it should be,' said Caspar inexplicably, and moved towards the fire for warmth.

'What are you talking about, Spar?' Hal asked him worriedly as he frowned at his shivering nephew. 'It's not cold. What's the matter?' The auburn-haired boy did not reply so Hal turned to Morrigwen. 'I think he's hallucinating.'

The effort of thinking about the sword was too much for the boy whose mind was slowly being eaten into by the lingering cold creeping up from his neck. 'I was just thinking that this place is right. So homely.'

'Is that a bruise?' Hal suddenly demanded, pulling Caspar's collar away from his neck to prod the skin with the fleshy part of his thumb. 'You feel as cold as a lizard.'

The poultice that Morrigwen applied barely stung when she pressed it against the boy's discoloured skin, though he should have found the steaming-hot cloth scalding. 'It's a compress of hot starch,' she explained. 'It holds the heat well and we've got to try and burn that poison out of you.'

Brid took a pestle and mortar from the shelf and carefully chose some roots and herbs from the dry plants that hung in bundles from the roof. She sat lightly down on one of the stools and began pounding the herbs into a powder.

'Purple foxglove and abscess root, better known as sweat-root. The first is to heat the blood and strengthen the beat of the heart. The second is to open the pores and purge the evil from the body through copious sweating.' She poured some steaming water into a bone cup and stirred in the powder with a spatula carved from a hart's antler. 'Drink it as hot as you can,' she instructed, pressing the goblet into Caspar's cupped hands. She scooped up the remaining unused leaves of fox-glove and the wiry pale roots, tidying them into the leather pouch that hung from her neck.

As the night drew in and the fire was stirred up, Caspar was swaddled in layers of fur, but still the boy's shivers intensified. A deep furrow sank into the skin of Morrigwen's wrinkled brow as she looked down on her patient.

'I need some stronger medicine,' she sighed at last, after sitting hunched over, rocking back and forth in meditation. She pushed herself up from the low stool, bracing her back with one arm whilst reaching for a crook with the other, which she used for support. 'All this rushing about has made my bones ache.' She hobbled over to her young accomplice. 'Go out into the forest, Bridget, my beloved, and find me a young urchin with some pox or plague.'

'What?!' Hal shouted angrily. 'What? You really are mad. You're going to bring us in contact with disease.' He started forward and grabbed at Morrigwen's sleeve in protest. The Crone, however, was still nimble enough to give him a sharp rap over his knuckles with the head of the crook.

'Never meddle in what you don't understand.' Morrigwen's

austere authority, along with her acerbic tone was enough to unsettle the young man's self-assurance and he fell silent, keeping his vigil at Caspar's side. His wan nephew snaked a hand out of his covers to grip his forearm tightly for a second.

'Believe in her, Hal: she is old and wise and has much power. I saw it in the forest.'

When finally Brid returned, she cradled a young toddler in her arms, which screamed so that its face was crimson and distorted. Its anxious mother clucked at the Maiden's side, wringing her hands and whimpering in distress. Tears streaked her ruddy cheeks.

'Simple sweating ague,' Brid announced with satisfaction. 'Don't worry,' she smiled at the terrified woman, 'we'll cure her in no time.' The grieving woman did not seem in the least comforted or reassured by the two witches.

Morrigwen ignored the peasant-woman's wailing protestations. 'Good. Place it by Spar.' She sent Hal out of the hut into the night to wander in the grove whilst she applied poultices to the infant's brow and then placed them directly onto Caspar's body. Brid, meanwhile, prepared a syrup of feverfew and willow bark that she dribbled into the baby's mouth before returning the bundle to its mother.

'By morning she will be well again,' she promised.

'So sad, so sad,' Morrigwen moaned. 'Our own simple people, even the women, have forgotten us and the old ways. So very sad.' She sighed regretfully as the peasant-woman ran shrieking from the hut, bringing Hal's startled face to the doorway.

'What did you do to that woman? She looked terrified.'

'She'll be all right when the baby is rosy pink and smiling tomorrow. She thought we were some kind of Devil-worshippers trying to kill Spar here with ague, but what we really want is for the sweating fever to burn out Cailleach's poison.'

When Caspar awoke he slung off all the furs that cocooned his body. His skin was coated in hot sweat.

'How do you feel?' Brid asked anxiously.

'Absolutely awful,' he moaned.

'Good.'

He drifted back off into a tempestuous sleep where fiery dragons roared their flames of hell at an axe blade carved from ice. It swung like a pendulum back and forth at his neck, with each oscillation biting a little deeper into his flesh. When he awoke again, he had a thick head and was feeling giddy and weak. His chest was covered in small dark red spots, like pinpricks of blood. Brid was grinning at him, holding out a small spoonful of syrup.

'I don't know what you are smiling at,' Caspar growled. 'Leave me alone: I feel awful.'

'Of course you do. But the green mark on your neck is gone and this syrup will cure the fever.'

He did not have the strength to resist and the sickly liquid running down his throat quickly made him drowsy. When at last he awoke for the third time, it was nightfall once more. Brid, Morrigwen and Hal were seated around the fire, supping at a tasty-smelling meal. The old Crone was talking in a soft lullaby voice that she gilded with a hint of mystery to add awe to her story.

The sound of Caspar stirring interrupted their tale and their glowing faces all turned in unison.

'How do you feel, my boy?' asked Morrigwen.

'Much better,' he yawned. 'Much better, thanks.' He wrapped a skin around his shoulders and shuffled over to one of the stools by the fire and pointed towards the broth. 'Do I get to have some? I'm famished.'

'Of course!' Morrigwen dipped the heavy ladle into the cauldron, slopped out a generous portion into a dish and handed it to him. A smile folded up the wrinkles at the corner of her mouth. 'You heal well, my boy. In fact the only thing that hasn't healed right is that nose of yours.'

'I did that,' Hal admitted. His tone was not in the least remorseful but smacked of arrogant pride: the lasting injury had been made by a single Belbidian, not an army of barbarians or a monstrous she-demon.

Caspar laughed. 'And you'll get this in your face too, if you take that attitude.' The broth tasted good. 'Was I missing out on a story?'

Chapter 14

'In the beginning, the Sun smiled out alone in the great black universe and, after an eternity of meditation, its thoughts formed together, manifesting themselves in the great subconscious; and the Annwyn was created. And from the Annwyn have all things been created, from the smallest creatures in the oceans to ourselves. We are all of one and come from one and, in the end, return to the one.

'But first, the great Being of the sky dreamed a dream of a lovely woman. Waking, it proclaimed, "I am he, lord and master of the sky, and this beautiful woman will keep me company as I dance through the aeons." So he decorated the universe with bright stars to create for her a beautiful home, but all along he couldn't decide how his bride should be. He couldn't decide on her character and temperament but kept changing his mind. In the end, when he did at last create our great Mother Earth, he also created a Hand-Maiden for her, the silvery Moon, whose ever-changing tugs and pulls had great sway on Mother Earth's emotions. With every phase and revolution of the Moon, the beautiful woman altered in character so that the Sun would never be bored with his wife.

'However, being a female, and after many aeons waltzing through the galaxy, admiring the pageant of stars, the Mother Earth longed to have children. She begged and begged of her lord and master to grant her this one wish. The Omnipotent Star finally gave into her want and decreed that creatures could be born from the great subconscious so that Mother Earth might care and nurture them on her body. But there was one condition: however much she would rejoice as each creature was born, so would she suffer at the loss when they were taken from her. Where there is life, there must be death. And, as long as she nurtured and nourished her children, the Sun would cast down the light of day or deny the same to give the dark of night, so that the balance of good and evil would keep their equilibrium. The lordly Sun also declared that the pull of the Moon would dictate the children's chances and guide their fate whilst they worked out their earthly lives.

'And so from the Annwyn the seeds of life were planted in the Earth and the little creatures were born. They fed from the Mother, rejoicing in their short lives before returning to the great subconscious, where the souls bided their time waiting for the rebirth and their return to life again.

'The great Lord of the Heavens became more inventive with his woman's children, endowing them with more and more sophistication. He gave fins to the fishes and limbs to the worms as well as creating beings of higher and higher intelligence until, eventually, the first man and woman were born on the Earth. The Great Mother looked at her new-born daughter and smiled. The humans lived happily alongside the beasts, the trees and the flowers, and had many children of their own. And they learnt to grunt and squeak and sigh. So was language born upon their tongues. The envelope of their minds broadened and stretched, reaching out to delve into new concepts. They began to ask questions, querying why? And how?'

'What were their names – the first man and woman?' Caspar interrupted.

'You see! They were just like my young boy here, always full of questions. The young mind of the human continually seeks knowledge, always digging deeper for more information. If I told you her name you would ask me why was she given that name and who named her that. Maybe I'll tell you later what they were called.' Caspar guessed that the old Crone had forgotten their names for the moment.

'Go on,' Hal urged. 'You have to ignore Spar: he always interrupts.'

'Well, Mother Earth looked at all her children and was worried as she saw that knowledge frightened them. She watched them shy away from shadows in their minds as they questioned their existence. They asked, "Why are we here and what happens when we die? What happens to our thoughts and our love when we are gone?" The Mother could not answer her children.

'The tribe of children grew and multiplied. One day a daughter came to her grey-haired mother, holding a baby in her arms – a small girl. "Mother, I have a daughter now and when she grows she will ask me many questions, and what will I tell her? Will there always be a tomorrow for her? Will the sun always rise? Mother, I am frightened for her."

'The old woman looked at her daughter and her granddaughter and feared the unknown for them, just as she had done for herself throughout all her lifetime. The grey-haired crone went from her hut and walked far away from her people into the forest and there she found a cairn of stones and a babbling brook; and the feeling of the force of the Great Mother was strong.

'She prayed to Mother Earth, begging her for the higher knowledge and the answers to her questions, but the Great Master of the skies forbade the Goddess to answer the woman. For a full rotation of the Hand-Maiden's dance about the Earth, the Sun and the Earth and the Moon argued between themselves. The Mother was frustrated to anger, spitting the bile of volcanic lava and thrashing tumultuous waves so that her waters raged. But it was not until the Moon was full and pure and white, making the Earth seductive and gentle in her mood, that the Mother was able to entice a favour from her Great Lord.'

'Excuse me,' Caspar interrupted again. 'But can I have some more broth? It was so good.'

A generous scoop of steaming broth, with plenty of chunks

of mutton and barley grains, was gladly ladled into his empty bowl.

'I'll have some more then, too.' Hal held out his wooden bowl.

'Never to be outdone by your young friend,' laughed Morrigwen, scraping out the cauldron. She clearly understood the friendly rivalry between them. The old woman rocked gently on her stool, staring contemplatively into the fire, and fell silent for a while. Maybe she's fallen asleep, thought Caspar: after all she is old. To him she seemed as old as the mountain ranges or the waters of the Silversalmon that had shaped the canyons around Torra Alta. The battle with Cailleach and the forced gallop must have been taxing on the old woman's strength.

'Now where was I?' Morrigwen started.

'The Earth was being seductive,' Hal prompted.

'What?' The old Crone sounded confused.

Brid began helpfully, 'The Sun had just refused the Earth's wish to . . .'

'Oh yes, oh yes of course. I'm not senile yet, you know. I *can* remember.' She mumbled away to herself as if reciting some ancient poem before breaking back into the flow of her story. 'It was not until the Earth resorted to her gentle, feminine wiles that the Sun granted her wish and the Great Mother was able to speak to her daughter. It was a terrible thunderous voice and the woman covered her ears and trembled with fear.

'The rumbling words rolled out, "Daughter, I have watched you grow, loved you, and cared for you. What is your distress?"

'"Great Mother, I do not ask for myself, but for my children and my children's children," trembled the woman.

'"That is only right," boomed the Earth. "A mother's thoughts are only ever for her children."

'"They are frightened; they fear the great unknown," explained the woman. "They fear death; they fear the reason for life; they do not understand your purpose with us."

'"My children have grown," sighed the Mother with a voice

249

like the wind. "At first they thought only of food, warmth and comfort but now their minds have stretched. They think on yesterday and contemplate tomorrow: will the crops grow, will my baby live, will the flood come? I will give you a gift, my wise woman, the gift of insight so that you can understand the great subconscious and be reassured by the existence of the Annwyn. I will give you the gift of knowledge so that you understand the powers in the herbs, and the trees, and the roots, so that you can ease your children's suffering. I give you the secret of the runes so that you can call on the elements and divine the answers to your questions."

'"Great Mother, I thank you," stammered the crone.

'"These are dangerous gifts and I honour you with them because you ask only for your children. These are perilous gifts only to be used at a time and a place that is right, and at an hour that will be controlled and protected by the maiden Moon. Her mysterious powers are so strong that she sways my oceans back and forth. She controls the emotions of women, who are sensitive to her light, with her mercurial magic. Learn to understand her cycles and she will guide you on the right path when your runes of divination are too weak."

'"Great Mother," the woman dared to speak, "I am truly grateful, but I will not live forever. Who will answer my children's fears when I am gone?"

'"You may choose from the people one girl to whom you may teach your powers. The Moon will bless her with the sight and, once she is grown to womanhood, she in her turn will choose another. And so the line will continue."'

The old Crone stared wistfully into the heart of the fire before raising her flecked blue eyes to examine the expressions of her young audience. 'And that, my children,' she sighed, 'is how the Maiden, the Mother and the Crone, came to be set apart from other women. We are blessed with the sight and, in return for this great gift, we sacrifice our lives to the service of the Great Mother. We must also worship the Moon, who is the source of all magic, and use our gifts to help our people.'

'Do they choose their own daughter each time?' Caspar dreamily asked, intrigued by the fantastical story. The boy's blue eyes flitted secretively towards Brid whose gaze was lost in the dreamland of embers glowing beneath the cauldron.

'At first – so the legend is told – but not now. It became unwise because the families of the three chosen women gained power which interfered with our ability to guide all the people. So now, since the time of the Old Tribes has passed and the customs of civilization have overcome the old ways, only an orphan is chosen to become One of the Three. But once she is chosen she feels like your own – like your own flesh and blood.' Morrigwen drew her hand up to her face and pressed her temple as if to relieve a pain in her head. A tear pricked at the corner of her eye and she tried to smile but the weight of the sorrow was too much to disguise. 'When I was still the Mother, the girl I chose was beautiful beyond measure. She understood the ways of the birds and beasts of the forest, and the language of the trees before I had even taught her the first principles.' Morrigwen smiled wistfully in remembrance. 'But she was never keen to study. Her instinctive powers were strong but her knowledge could have been greater. She was too eager to rush headlong through the forest or hunt in the mountains to pay much attention to the properties of herbs and roots. My Bridget here is very studious, however.' The haggard witch smiled fondly and patted the girl's shoulder.

Brid's deep green eyes looked back up at the old Crone and she smiled a thin smile of reassurance. 'We will find her. We have the Eye now and we can find her. Spar can reach her.' She turned to look pleadingly at Caspar but he shook his head at her.

'No, please. The moonstone's so cold and it hurts. It's like raw energy.' He rubbed at his neck which still ached, remembering also the frostbite he had suffered from the touch of the orb.

'You are right, boy, you are not yet strong enough to look into the Druid's Eye again,' Morrigwen stated protectively. 'We will wait, but not for long. We don't have long. My own

251

personal loss is nothing compared to the terrors that will befall the world if we don't find her. It wouldn't matter if there were twenty Torra Altas guarding the Pass: Morbak is marching on us and there is nothing we can do to stop him because of his overwhelming numbers. I can smell them on the wind. The nomads have betrayed the Great Mother by giving their worship to that dread God of Ice, so now in the north, the Earth's bounty is frozen or withered.'

The Crone suddenly thumped her wooden crutch angrily into the ground. 'But worse, much worse, they know about the Eye, the Druid's Eye. I've seen signs that they have been searching for it in the old haunts – the sacred groves deep in the wood. There is someone in their number who knows its power, knows that it will lead us to the Mother, knows that if we find her, their cause is lost. There is one amongst the enemy with great sight; I can feel his shadow – yes, it is a man.' She picked up the moonstone and cradled it in her crooked fingers, stroking it as if it was the smooth head of a beloved infant. 'I can feel his shadow sniffing for the Druid's Eye. I have it, now . . . but I still can't reach her! I can't feel my beloved child.' A tear dripped from the end of her thin nose and trickled round the moonstone. The swirling patterns rushed to the tear drop and eddied around it in curious possessive whirlwinds. 'I can't feel her!' the Crone howled, throwing her head back in grieving anguish. Brid gently eased the orb out of her clawing grasp.

'Hush now, we will find her.' She looked beseechingly at the two noble youths from Torra Alta. 'They will help us find her.'

Hal was nodding calmly. 'We have to find her. I don't know about all this Earth magic and hocus-pocus; I just know that the enemy is desperate to have the moonstone. They obviously believe it is some kind of key. Whether this woman locked inside the stone has real powers or not, *they* certainly believe she does. Since they believe that she will prevent their victory, they are doomed to failure if we find her.'

Morrigwen turned and laughed at him. 'You think you know

so much. You think you understand . . . well what does it matter what your reasons are? You've brought the Eye out from its hiding place and you've brought Spar . . . But it's important that you know about one thing. They don't want the moonstone to find the Mother, they want it only to destroy it. She is so near the other side now and it's only the stone linking us to her that keeps her alive. They want her dead and they dread that the Eye will bring her back to full life.'

'Why Spar, though?'

'Yes, why me?'

Brid took a deep sigh as if she was about to say something but Morrigwen gripped her arm. 'You are weary, boy, and we must not tire you. You need all your strength. But with you lies the balance, the very last hopes for the world. When the New Faith first came up from the south we were driven steadily northward, even out of the capital, Farona, which was once our sacred city where we held council. Now the Great Mother's last stronghold is here in the fringes of Torra Alta, caught between the two destructive forces of the New Faith and Vaal-Peor. The Barony of Torra Alta is her only remaining territory.'

'The New Faith is not destructive,' Hal snorted.

'You have much to learn.' The Crone shook her head. 'But we have time to right that wrong so long as we can throw off the Vaalakans. But you must see now that with only myself and Brid left, Torra Alta holds only the very last threads of the Old Faith. It is the only place of balance left. Spar is the heir to this Barony and he must lead it back to the right path. He is our future.'

'I always knew you were terribly important,' Hal laughed, but there was a dark look in his eye.

'Come on.' Brid stood up and carefully placed her hand on Caspar's forehead, feeling for his temperature. 'You shouldn't have been up for so long.' At her touch the auburn-haired youth flushed a deep crimson. Ever since Brid had transformed herself into a beautiful maiden, he had felt uncomfortable in close proximity to her.

Hal pulled his nephew to his feet. 'Not bad for a pagan girl, eh? But you don't get to have her as well as Torra Alta, you know. You've got me to reckon with.' For a second Caspar thought the older youth was serious but then he looked at the broad grin and decided that his uncle was only trying to goad him. The raven-haired youth punched him playfully on the knee and leant over to whisper in his ear: 'Would you like to make a bet on which one of us she'd prefer – or is the competition too hot for you?'

'Oh stop it,' snapped the younger boy. 'I wasn't thinking about that at all.'

'Oh yes? And what would you like to swear that by? Yesterday's porridge?'

Brid's dragon-green eyes flashed angrily at them as if she had heard what Hal had whispered.

Hal plunged in with a sincere-sounding apology, moving closer to her and delivering his smooth remorseful words in a quiet chivalrous voice. The youth remained chatting in gentle tones by the fire. Brid laughed, filling the peasant's hut with an elfin music that could steal the heart and tantalize the soul. Caspar felt the jealousy tighten around his stomach.

Morrigwen spoke up authoritatively. 'Tomorrow we must move on before they find a way to reach the Druid's Eye, so you'll all need your sleep. They will be already hunting for us.'

The withered old hag and the Maiden slept at one end of the hut, properly secluded from the two boys who buried themselves in thick piles of furs. Caspar couldn't sleep.

'Why did you have to say that about Brid?' he suddenly challenged the hump of bedding which covered his uncle's back.

'Hey!' Hal sounded affronted. 'I was only teasing. I didn't realize you were really keen on her. I'm sorry.' His apology was so innocent that the fierce storm of Caspar's quarrel was instantly stilled.

'I don't know what I think of her really, except that she's so beautiful and caring. But she's a bit frightening, too,' Caspar admitted. 'She knows too much.'

'Huh! She's only a girl.' Hal was dismissive. 'Don't get taken in by all these stories of Goddesses and Moons giving them power: they're just ancient superstitious fairy tales. They invent stories to make themselves more mysterious and seem more powerful. Remember your scriptures and you won't be bothered by them, specially not –' Hal yawned, wearily turning over '– in the broad-daylight of tomorrow. It's a far cry from understanding herb-lore to claiming you have the blessing of divination from the moon. God created the moon – and the sun and the earth – after all,' he finished emphatically.

'But you weren't there in the forest. You didn't see the creature with six arms. You didn't see Morrigwen and Brid destroy it. You didn't feel the power.'

Hal did not answer. He was peacefully asleep.

It was the sound of a swishing broom that stirred the two boys from their slumber. Brid was busily sweeping the old straw, which carpeted the mud hut, outside before fetching in some new. When she saw that they were awake she danced over, swirling the broom as a partner, and then playfully wafted the bristles over their faces to tickle their noses.

Hal sneezed loudly from the dust and the young girl laughed apologetically. 'I didn't mean to make you sneeze. Come on, wake up and get some fresh air before breakfast. And fetch me some kindling while you're at it.'

'It's not morning yet,' Hal groaned, making a tent out of the fur covers and disappearing under it.

'I'm afraid it is,' Brid replied, threatening them with a pitcher of water. The prospect of being drenched brought Caspar kicking from his bed. He dragged Hal's blankets after him, clutching the furs modestly to his body, so leaving his uncle to scrabble for his breeches.

'Come on,' Caspar demanded. 'Let's find a stream and freshen up.'

'So much energy for someone that's been at death's door for the last two days,' mumbled Hal, ignoring Brid's stifled giggles as he stuffed the ends of his shirt into his waistband.

Still rubbing his eyes, he stumbled after his nephew and started to make for the door, but then stopped and thumped his way back to the sleeping pallet. 'Forgot my boots.'

The forest stream was not as icy cold as the mountain burns but it was refreshing and washed the cobwebs away with a healthy, cool sting. Hal plunged his head into the waters, swishing his raven hair beneath the surface. He pulled himself upright with a gasp, flicking his head back so that his sodden hair sprayed out a bow of water droplets. The droplets arced over the surface of the quiet stream and landed in a studded line of ripples. 'That's better.' He patted his cheeks smartly to make sure he was fully awake. 'Right, what about this kindling?'

'Take only the dead wood.' Morrigwen was unexpectedly standing behind them.

'You nearly made my heart stop,' Caspar gasped.

'Of course we will,' Hal replied. 'It burns much better.'

'More to the point, young man, it doesn't please the Dryads to snap branches from their bodies. And choose some dead wood from under the hazel trees. Perhaps its smoke will infuse some much-needed clear thinking and insight into your minds.'

Caspar was inclined to disagree as he inhaled the fumes: the smoke simply made his eyes smart, though the smell had a homely aroma. He sat on the stool balancing a full platter of oatcakes and coddled eggs on his knee. His uncle's cheeks were already puffed out with food as he ate ravenously.

'Can't we have any of that?' Hal wafted his plate in the direction of the spitted roast that Morrigwen was patiently basting.

'For breakfast? No! Anyway, this is for later. We've got a long journey ahead and considering the amount you two eat, we'll need an extra pony just to carry the food.'

'Where are we going,' Hal demanded. 'You're not just ordering me about like a queen snapping at a scullery boy. My brother is the Baron of Torra Alta – your liege-lord.'

'I'm very impressed,' she said with heavy sarcasm. 'But I'm

too old to bow so you'll have to excuse me. I'll tell you where we're going when I'm ready.'

Hal looked stunned and Caspar was secretly pleased that someone was able to put him in his place. No woman had ever spoken to Hal like that – with the exception, of course, of his mother, Lady Elizabetta – and it obviously came as a shock that any woman could have so much authority. Morrigwen's tone was light and unruffled. 'But eat as many oatcakes as you like. There's some honey over on the side.'

The younger youth didn't stop to consider Hal's pride as he succumbed to the thought of the sweet honey. 'Um. Please.' The honey was thick and pale, almost white in colour, with a triangular slice of honeycomb wedged in the middle. He took a large dollop and then ran his tongue over the spoon, delighting in the sweet taste. 'There's nothing quite like honey.'

'Men are always seduced by the sweet.' Morrigwen smiled as she sought for a large saddlebag amongst the sacks and baskets that were jumbled into a corner. She wrapped some cold meats in cloths and packed on top some apples, hazelnuts and cakes. Finally, when she thought that the boys were not looking, she slipped in the pot of honey. Caspar hid his smile behind his hand, not wanting the woman to see that he had caught her being sentimental and spoiling them. She might have a sharp tongue at times, he thought, but she does have a soft heart.

'What are you all doing sitting around looking as blank as grey clouds on a stuffy day? Go and find the horses: Brid will show you where to look. Go on, get out of my way.' The old Crone was sour once more.

The boys jumped to their feet and Wartooth rose from his crouch at Caspar's side and attempted a three-legged hop to follow them. He had not yet found his balance. 'Wait there, boy.' Caspar rubbed the dog's muzzle and pointed a finger to the floor, commanding the dog to stay. Wartooth gave a pleading whimper but slid his single foreleg forward so that his elbow barely touched the ground. He was obedient but still he trembled with eagerness to follow his master. Caspar waited until Morrigwen had shuffled to the far end of the line of cupboards where she was rummaging for supplies, before sneaking out one of the cakes from the top of a saddlebag. 'Here, boy,' he whispered, surreptitiously bending down and slipping the stolen goods to the dog. The hound's doleful eyes snapped wide for a second and the spoilt pet wolfed the cake down whole, gulping noisily. 'That never touched the sides,' the thief whispered dotingly.

'Hurry up!' Brid's voice demanded from outside, bringing Caspar guiltily to the door.

'Don't you need a halter to catch them with?' Hal was asking the girl.

'No.' She sounded surprised and held up a bundle of white shoots with tiny clover-like petals and black, nodulous roots that looked like shiny beads. 'Alfalfa always does the trick: they love it.'

She was right, Caspar thought, as the horses came pacing towards them, necks outstretched and lips rolled back to reveal the greedy teeth that sought the alfalfa shoots. The cream stallion and matching mare had rejoined a small herd of six horses who found lush grazing in a shady glade downstream of the old Crone's grove.

'The dun's very willing and the roan's strong,' Brid advised. 'But take your pick. Only, leave the dark grey: she's a bit moody.' As if to prove that Brid was always right, the old steel-grey mare lashed her head round and took a sharp nip out of the dun's rump when he came too close. Brid castigated the mare with a smart rap on the nose.

'We'll take your advice,' Hal said, deciding for Caspar as well as himself. 'I fancy the dun.' The promise of more succulent shoots enticed the selected horses to amble happily after the three young people who strode back to the hut. They resigned themselves to a brisk rub-down with handfuls of straw, which removed the worst of the mud clinging to their coats.

'Are you ready with the horses yet?' Morrigwen demanded.

'What's taking you so long? Youngsters nowadays always seem to dawdle. Come inside and help me out with these saddle-bags.' The old Crone had packed four bags, which they neatly fastened to the buckles on the cantle of each saddle.

'I'm glad to see that you actually have such sophisticated equipment as saddles,' Hal mentioned cheekily.

Morrigwen raised her disapproving brow. 'Oh you are, are you?'

Alerted by the aged woman's acerbic tone, Hal must have realized that he was overstepping the mark a little and so softened his comment. 'It's hard work on steep slopes without stirrups and after the last bareback gallop . . .' He changed his tack. 'I didn't mean any harm. Your ways aren't really that primitive and rustic.'

'Your lack of tact is almost comical, Hal, really it is. Now, before we go –' Morrigwen straightened herself up and began to twist her silver tresses into a braid to keep it out of the way for the journey. 'Before we go, I have something to present to you.'

They followed her meekly back into the hut. Wartooth leapt smartly to attention and greeted them excitedly as if they had been gone for days rather than a matter of minutes. The sala-mander tightened the fins on his ruff and hopped nonchalantly onto a stool, looking as proud as a king and as aloof as a bishop. He kept one disdainful eye on the inexplicable antics of the humans, and the other possessively on the moonstone.

'These are sad times,' Morrigwen began slowly and rever-ently. 'These are sad times and the tide of fate is running against us. It takes the power of the Moon to change the waters of the Earth and we must pray hard so that she pulls in our favour and drives this foul, Vaalakan flood from our lands. We are the ones that must do this task and the onus is a heavy one.' She lit the candles surrounding the ceremonial table, in the same ritualistic manner as before and then beckoned them all into the consecrated area.

Caspar immediately felt naked, as if a host of eyes were peeling off each layer of clothing for critical examination before appraising his skin. He felt as if someone was trying to lift off his flesh to study the ebb and flow of his blood beneath the surface. He twisted round and round to see where the eerie feeling came from.

'He can feel the spirits,' Brid remarked to Morrigwen.

'What spirits?' Hal asked.

'Can't you feel them?' The sensitive boy sounded astonished as he wrapped his arms around his body to shield himself.

'No.'

'They are everywhere, asking questions. Who am I? What do I want? Where am I going? Do I intend evil? Hundreds of questions, on and on.' Disconcerted, his vulnerable eyes were growing wide.

'Don't worry, Spar,' Brid reassured him, placing a warm and welcome hand on his arm. 'They can't harm you while you stay within the circle. Lighting the candles beckons them from the spirit world as we summon the power of the four elements. While we stand here in the balance, keeping the equilibrium, we can let the magic flow through our bodies and it can't harm us.'

'Are you sure?'

'Quite.'

Hal still stood calmly, looking quite relaxed though evidently amused by the conversation. 'Nothing seems strange to me at all, except Spar of course, but he always is strange.'

'Now concentrate,' Morrigwen commanded. She reached her hands up towards the thatch. 'Mother Goddess, bless our journey and guide our hands. Show me, lead me with your light.' She opened her fist and let five small bones rattle out onto the oak table. They fell into a distinctive pattern: four together and one standing alone. 'The solitary bone,' the witch divined, 'represents the sword. The four have fallen into the pattern of a rune: ᚻ, the rune of Hagal. It is Hal's rune.'

She reached her hand up to place it on the young man's shoulder and looked earnestly into Hal's eyes, searching for the truth of his answer. 'The Great Mother chooses you to bear her sword: do you accept this honour?'

'Me? You mean the sword is for me?'

'For use in the service of the Mother,' Morrigwen corrected.

'Yes! Yes, of course. The sword is for me: I can't believe it,' Hal exclaimed excitedly, oblivious of Morrigwen's words about the service to a pagan deity.

As Hal was chosen over him to receive the magnificent gift, disappointment tightened in Caspar's throat. He clenched his fists hard to help him control his emotions. Why Hal? He doesn't even believe in this heathen pantheon, why should he be honoured by their gift of such a noble, precious weapon? It's not fair . . . Suddenly he felt the spirits leap out at his emotions, grasping them and tossing them back and forth. 'Are you jealous? Do you hate him? Do you want him out of the way? How powerful, how driving is the jealousy? Do you wish he no longer existed to steal the glory, or steal Torra Alta? Do you hate him?'

'No!' Caspar shrieked out loud, urgently and angrily.

A startled look leapt onto Hal's face, then he looked bewildered and hurt.

'I didn't mean . . . no to you. I'm glad you have the sword, really I am. It's simply . . .' His voice trailed off as he was unable to explain himself.

'It's simply that you would have liked the sword, too, and the spirits asked you lots of painful questions,' Brid concluded, with an understanding that far outstretched her years.

Caspar nodded with a shamed face.

The bones rattled out across the oak board, chattering to rest in the centre of the pentagram. They appeared to fall into a definite design – perhaps patterned by chance, perhaps through the guidance of some unseen Goddess. They formed a circle. Morrigwen drew in a sharp breath as if shocked by the result of the divination.

'I cast the bones for you, Spar, but the gift is not mine to give. You will have to claim it for yourself. It is a terrible gift. More terrible than the great sword.'

'What is it?' asked the boy.

'An egg.'

'I don't understand.' After Hal's gift of the sword this offering of an egg turned his disappointment nearer to humiliation. Was this ancient priestess mocking him?

'I know, my child, but one day the purpose of the Great Goddess will be revealed. For the moment, I'll give you this.' She loosened a chain that hung around her neck and withdrew a pendant that had rested against her skin. It was a simple mandala carved out of wood. 'It's hazel and will bring you guidance on your quest.'

Caspar could not smile.

'Don't be disappointed, Spar. The time is not right, that's all; but this mandala will give you guidance and clear your thoughts: it's from the tree in my sacred grove.'

Like the smoke, thought Caspar, forcing his lips to politely curve upwards. 'Thank you.' The words were difficult and the boy was still deeply hurt. He put on a proud face and smiled brightly to hide his disappointment, hoping that his brimming eyes would not betray him. He blinked several times.

'Now it's time.' Morrigwen used the end of the broom to prod the salamander away from the moonstone. It hissed angrily and its spiny ruff sprang upright in a threatening gesture though it reluctantly obeyed its mistress and backed away, spitting. Morrigwen slid the moonstone out of the pouch and cupped it in her hands, stepping carefully towards the centre of the consecrated circle. 'Spar,' she commanded.

Caspar nervously stepped back, now afraid of the dark magic in the orb which had sucked away his body heat. He felt it was like Cailleach's dead hand freezing his body.

Morrigwen's white spiky eyebrows arched with concern. 'It won't hurt this time. It only hurts because your mind is untrained to reach out across the distances. If you touch it through me and Brid there will be no pain.'

Reluctantly Caspar stepped forward and gingerly placed his hands on top of Morrigwen's knobbly bones. Brid pressed her palm into the surface of the moonstone and with Hal looking over their shoulders the four of them stared expectantly into its heart. The patterns danced gracefully and calmly, as though a soft breeze was sweeping away the early morning mist. Caspar felt he was flying high in the air before stooping hawk-like into a dive and hurtling expertly towards his prey. The bloodless face of the woman screamed suddenly out of the stone. She didn't move but he could hear her scream – a terrible scream filled with heart-rending pain. Morrigwen went rigid with emotion and wrenched her head away from the sight and the horror of the scream.

Caspar was shivering uncontrollably as he felt the woman's glazed eyes reaching towards him. They touched on Morrigwen and Brid but swept out beyond them, seeking his warmth. Their eyes met and immediately he felt a penetrating cold suck at his heart. Her eyes hooked into his soul, a clawing talon clutching at his life.

'Witch,' he screamed, 'leave me alone, witch.' Suddenly the freezing pain eased and he watched in wonder as the dead glaze, coating her eyes, melted. He felt a warmth, a huge protective love, flood towards him. The thrill of the encounter was there for a bare but beautiful second. Then, like in his dream, a giant hand crept into the picture. At first it looked like a flock of crows but their flight formation moulded and shifted until it formed the outline of a giant hand reaching out of a black robe. A sense of evil and hatred filled the room and the hand dragged at the face of the woman, pressing the image back down into the stone. Her fingernails scrabbled frantically at the giant arm as it pressed her deeper and deeper. A muffled cry haunted Caspar's ears and he wrenched his hand away from Morrigwen's wrists, clapping them to his head, trying to block out the scream that went on and on. A rushing wind whirled into the room, bringing with it a cold darkness.

The spirits around him caught the noise and threw it back between them. Still the sense of evil lingered with them. There was a smell of blood and fear and the spirits whispered between themselves: 'Jealousy, jealousy, jealousy . . .'

Brid's bright green eyes flickered with fear. 'The hand's reaching out for the moonstone. I can feel it.' There was disbelief in her voice.

Morrigwen's face was white. 'We should never have done this. It must be the circle that intensifies the power of the Eye. He felt us. He can feel the power of the moonstone when we awaken it. We must move quickly. We must go – now!'

'But which way? Where?' Caspar asked, bewildered and shocked. The only feeling that lingered was the fleeting sense of love that, for the briefest second, had welled out from the moonstone.

'She tried to tell us,' Morrigwen croaked. Grief was making it difficult for her to talk. 'She blew out all but one of the candles.'

Caspar looked around him and realized that the sense of darkness was real. Only one candle flickered while the other three smoked thin wispy trails from their snuffed wicks.

'North,' Brid declared decisively.

The ancient silver-haired priestess paced sunwise around the circle before returning to the solitary flame. She snuffed out the last candle, which expired with a thin trail of black smoke that wafted up towards the thatch. Caspar felt the prying eyes withdraw and close as the flame died. Tension eased out of the air.

They stepped out of the circle and Morrigwen shuffled over to one of her humble-looking cupboards. She opened a drawer and drew out a clinking chain of silver. It was adorned with images of the moon in its three phases: waxing and waning crescents dangling either side of the full circle in the centre. It fastened with a brooch fashioned into a five-pointed star. Brid lowered her head to receive the adornment and then eased a torc in the image of a spiralling dragon up her smooth bronze arm. Finally she twisted a rope of silver thread through her knotted hair.

The old Crone pressed a silver circlet to her brow; even that simple, plain band was enough to bestow her with a regal air. Caspar was astonished at how the jewellery transformed the women, reinforcing and magnifying the authority in their bearing. Satisfied with her appearance, Morrigwen rechecked that the saddlebags were properly secured and supervised as the two boys carefully roped an objecting Wartooth to the back of Caspar's saddle. 'Now we need as much water as we can carry.' She rummaged through a pile of sacking to retrieve leather canisters, a bladder of elderberry wine and several water-ewers. 'These will have to do,' she declared tipping out the wine. 'Go and fill these from the stream; we need as much water as we can carry.'

Caspar looked with dismay at his horse laden down with an assortment of clinking water-carriers. There was barely room for him to sit.

'At last, now we are ready,' the hag croaked. She gazed northwards.

'We ride for the Dragon Scorch and beyond,' Brid cried.

'We ride for the Mother,' Morrigwen corrected.

'We ride for the glory.' Caspar was caught up in the excitement.

'To horse!' Hal lifted the great sword as he ran to the fore and then stopped to sheepishly grin at the others as he realized that he had been totally carried away by the atmosphere.

The fearsome sword, hiding its splendour in a modest leather scabbard at Hal's side, bounced against the dun's flank as the gelding pranced out into the morning light. Hal took the lead – after Brid had pointed out the way for him. He looked alert and proud. Caspar felt he was overplaying things a little.

Drawing the mandala out from beneath his jerkin, the younger boy stroked the fashioned wood, feeling the notches and indentations. He was shocked when, for a moment, he thought he saw Hal through a mist, though he looked different; larger and thicker across the shoulder. He thought he saw the sunlight glinting off the metal of a chain-mail suit beneath a thick, leather gambeson. His uncle seemed to be holding the reins in a studded gauntlet whilst his other hand raised the sword, waving it forward as if to lead a charge. There was a thunder of hooves all around him. Slowly the noises faded to a whirring sound and Hal came back into focus; his beaming expression was as youthful and fresh-faced as ever. Perhaps there is something in this mandala, after all, Caspar thought hopefully.

The blue roan moved easily into a jog, tossing her head and fretting with the bit as Caspar nudged her forward to ride alongside his uncle.

'May I look at the sword?'

For a second, Hal looked at his nephew suspiciously, his olive-green eyes full of possessiveness, but he blinked it away and replied, 'Of course.' He eased the weapon out of the scabbard that made a sigh like the sound of hands smoothing over satin.

The hilt, engraved with the wrestling dragons, was a little large for Caspar's grasp. He knotted the reins and looped them over the pommel so that he could take the weight of the sword in both hands. The feel of the hilt gave him a sensation of authority and leadership. With this in his hand he could command like a king. He ran his forefinger down the length of the fuller, which grooved the centre of the blade, and felt a surge of invulnerability course through his veins. This was a weapon of terrible power. Carefully he traced his finger along the sharp edge to the very point and shuddered at the sickening sense of death. Caspar shivered and handed it back.

'Morrigwen was right,' he said, gladly relinquishing the weapon to its guardian. 'The sword is not for me.'

'I think it's magnificent! There's nothing to beat it in all the world.' Hal looked at the blade adoringly.

'Do you feel less sceptical about Morrigwen and Brid now?' queried the younger boy.

'They seem all right, I suppose. A little peculiar and far too full of themselves, of course. Their knowledge of medicine is very powerful and Morrigwen is kind, in a twisted, strict sort of a way, but Brid . . . Well, Brid is simply the most beautiful girl I have ever seen.' Hal looked wistful.

'But don't you believe in them? Don't believe who they are?' Caspar insisted.

'I'll believe it when I see it.'

'But the sword, can't you feel the power in the sword?'

266

'Well,' Hal faltered. 'Well, yes, it makes me feel like a king, but surely that's nothing to do with them: it's a mighty sword.'

'You've held many swords before now and none has ever made you feel like that,' Caspar pointed out. 'It's only steel and some precious stones, after all. There has to be something else to give it that feel of power, don't you agree?'

Hal's brow knotted into a disconcerted frown. 'I don't see that it matters. Their God, our God, whatever, we must stop the Vaalakans either way.'

'And this woman in the moonstone, you agree that we must find her?'

A pout formed on Hal's lips as he considered the question and reluctantly agreed: 'Yes, I think we must – if she's alive of course and that seems very unlikely. But we must look because we promised Brid and a promise is a promise.'

'And not because her power will help save Torra Alta?' Caspar questioned.

'One woman! Rot! I don't know why she's important to the Vaalakans; but she is and that's good enough for me. I don't believe these women have power: it's just superstition.' The younger whimsical youth looked at his uncle and felt very little reassurance from his cool words of logic. A dread was creeping into his mind that he was actually beginning to believe in this black magic. What terrified him most was that he *wanted* to believe in it. He wished he could share his thoughts with Hal but he couldn't admit to such heretical emotions. He wondered what Hell would be like. But then, since Brid would be condemned to the flaming pit, well . . .

The track widened out as the evergreen trees of the deeper forest gave way to the smooth barks of beech and the dry autumnal foliage allowed more daylight to filter through to the travellers. Morrigwen and Brid trotted forward so that the four of them rode side by side. Caspar felt Wartooth stiffen behind his saddle, as the little salamander popped his head out of the old woman's saddlebag. It took a quick, jerky look around before snatching its head back down into its dark den again.

'He doesn't like journeys much,' Morrigwen explained and then started to point out various trees and plants as they passed them, evidently intent on educating the boy of the New Faith. Caspar tried to listen but his mind was preoccupied with the thought that Brid was riding closely at Hal's side as they talked in hushed voices. He was unable to discern the words. Why couldn't she have come alongside him instead? He answered the question for himself: because she'd rather ride with Hal. Perhaps she found his uncle more interesting. Hal was after all older and taller; his dark hair and olive eyes were, perhaps, more striking to the eye than his own looks. Caspar felt his lip droop into a sulk.

Chapter 15

The sweep of the forest shielded the travellers from the prying eyes of any Vaalakan scouting-parties, though Hal's confidence seemed completely undaunted at the prospect of meeting one of the enemy.

'One swipe – swish,' he hissed, 'and the filthy, blond head rolls to the ground. A quick thrust – agh! – and the sword pierces the plate of armour as if it were parchment. The Vaalakan's eyes bulge as the point stabs his heart. Around the great Belbidian warrior a score of the enemy lie in pieces while he has not one scratch to his person.'

Brid sidled up alongside Caspar and, though she was laughing at the dashing youth brandishing the brilliant sword, she was also disapproving. 'I hope he doesn't really think it's all a game, does he?'

'Hal thinks life's a game.' How had Hal managed to chat away so confidently and casually? *As soon as I get the opportunity to speak alone with the Maiden I behave like a dumb mule.*

Morrigwen led them steadily northward, picking her way through the narrow runs worn through the undergrowth by the boar and deer, to stay well clear of any definite man-made trail. Periodically she drew to an abrupt halt, listening intently, before nudging the cream stallion forward again. 'They've had two days' head start on us and they'll be scouring the forest,' she muttered. 'They're not about to let the Eye slip out of their hands just like that.'

'Their shaman was not a man of strong magic though,' Brid mused. 'I doubt that he'll be able to trace its power that easily.'

'Think, child,' the Crone snapped sternly. 'You can't afford to make such narrow judgements. They may have other shamans. Perhaps that one was more of a warrior and they have a more important warlock in their midst.'

'I didn't sense anyone else with power,' Brid rebelliously muttered.

'Never, *never* underestimate the strength of the enemy, Bridget. I will not live forever and the whole burden of our faith will fall on you. You must be prepared.'

Brid nodded and squared her shoulders as if rising to her responsibility, though she dropped back a few paces from the sharp tongue of the old Crone.

'Does she think the enemy is close then?' Caspar asked.

Brid shrugged. 'She's right: while we were in the hut they've had plenty of time to move ahead of us. They could easily have spread their men out in the hope that one of them will stumble across us; so we must be wary. But,' she smiled confidently, 'they won't be expecting us to go north into the Dragon Scorch – nobody in their right mind would do that at the best of times. So, of course they'll think we're heading southwards.'

'Brid!' Morrigwen snapped again. 'My ears are not so aged that I can't hear you chatting away back there. I've only just told you not to underestimate them. They may know more than you do. They may be anticipating us.'

Brid bit her lip and the healthy glow of her tanned cheeks paled visibly. 'Morrigwen, you are right,' she admitted. 'I was thinking like a child.' She fell to studying the withers of her cream mare, studiously ignoring Hal's comments as he lopped a sprig of beech twig from an overhanging branch with his sword.

'You don't need to worry, fair Maiden: I have the sword. No scurvy Vaalakan will be able to threaten us now.'

'Don't slash at the trees,' she scolded angrily. 'You are *so* arrogant.'

'Of course,' Hal grinned smugly. 'I have good reason to be, don't you think?'

A moment of uncomfortable silence followed. Brid turned her bronzed and silken complexion towards Caspar, ignoring Hal. Rebuffed, the raven-haired youth pressed arrogantly ahead. Brid opened her mouth as if to speak but quickly returned to studying the mare's cream withers.

Snatching the opportunity, Caspar asked, 'No, what were you going to say?'

'Nothing,' she answered quickly and then repeated more tentatively, 'Nothing, only I'm glad, Spar, that you are different.'

'Different from what?'

'From the rest, from Hal. You're not brash or arrogant and you don't pester me for favours like other boys might. You don't demand.'

'I might!' he replied haughtily, not wanting to appear too young or ineffective or, for that matter, too unmanly to approach her.

'Oh don't be silly, Spar. You're not like that at all.'

He was flummoxed. When he gazed at Brid he felt strong and capable like a gallant knight at arms. He imagined himself nobly protecting her from wild dangers with his brave sword. The fact that he didn't have a sword did nothing to daunt his imagination. But when she spoke to him, she made him feel so young. Well, at least she didn't argue with him like she constantly did with Hal. Surely that was a promising sign? He coughed and tilted up his crooked, freckled nose, trying to think of something that would restore his dignity. 'I might, but the laws of chivalry forbid such behaviour.' He bowed in a way that he felt befitted a nobleman, adding a sweep with his fingers since that was how he imagined the heroic knights of old would bow to their ladies.

Brid's face creased into laughter, which was not the reaction he wished. His indignation mellowed though as he realized that her laughter was not mocking him, as Hal's might, but was merely bright and happy. He couldn't fathom why she was laughing though: the Maiden was too mysterious.

At last the narrow broken trail that they had been tracing

through the dense heartwood of the forest opened out onto a cart-rutted track. Morrigwen waved them to a halt as she crept forward to scout out the way ahead. Caspar could hear voices but his pulse steadied as he realized they were speaking Belbidian. With his sword already drawn, Hal instantly barged through on his dun mount, determined not to let the Crone take the fore in any confrontation.

The trees now had room to stretch their branches. Beeches and spreading chestnuts sighed out into the space and relaxed in the sunlight, rustling their yellow and copper leaves in the free-moving air. Caspar made out the shape of a peasant leaning against the long handle of a woodcutter's axe. He was dressed in dun sacking and wiped his forehead with a red kerchief that he pulled from his neck. At their approach, he looked suspiciously towards them and stiffened up awkwardly, as if the work was new to his muscles. A thin woman wrapped in the thick layers of a shawl dropped the heavily laden basket from the crook of her arm. She gaped, horror-struck, at the sight of the intruders. A hard loaf of stale bread rolled onto the ground. The woodcutter raised his axe threateningly and gestured to his woman to shelter behind him. With gritted teeth he growled at the mounted party, 'What is your intent in this part of the forest, strangers?'

Morrigwen tugged at Hal's arm to slow him down and murmured, 'Let me handle this. There have been spies moving in the woods now for several months. Many woodlanders have abandoned their homes on the edge of the glades to take refuge deeper in the heartwoods.' She waved the others back with her fragile hands, dropped her reins and dismounted. The stallion immediately nuzzled the ground with his velvet lips, searching out sorrel and clover beneath the bracken ferns.

As she shuffled towards the simple folk, Morrigwen's stooped form commanded less intimidating authority now that she was no longer mounted.

'Don't fear us, friends,' she said quietly. 'We are the enemies of the blond dogs swarming out of the north. Come here, woman.'

Despite the man's anxious arm extended protectively in front of her, the woman seemed unable to disobey the witch.

'Have you brought food for your man's noonday meal?' Morrigwen asked. The woman nodded meekly. 'Let me add to it, then.' The ancient Crone reached into her saddlebag, withdrew a large apple and unhooked the golden sickle from her girdle. She split the apple laterally. She handed the top half to the man and the lower half to the woman.

'Look at the core,' Morrigwen ordered. 'The pips form the pattern of the five-pointed star, a blessing from the Mother. Eat it and accept the Mother's bounty: in return you can tell us if you've seen anything strange lately at the edge of the forest.'

The peasant woman fell trembling to her knees. 'Oh spare me, the Crone of Death! My ma told tales of one like you, the old woman, the witch! God, He's punishing us with the Vaalakan terror 'cos in our weakness we've let the Old Faith malinger hereabouts in the Chase. It's witches like you what's driven us from our homes.' She flung her apple to the ground as if it were deadly-nightshade.

The woodcutter laughed. 'Don't be ridiculous, wife. Superstitious nonsense. There's naught dangerous about those women in your ma's fairy-tales. They just spend too much time in the moonlight: it touches their minds.' He took a relaxed bite from the apple and looked past Morrigwen to the two Belbidian nobles behind her. 'How can I serve you, young masters? If you mean to use that sword on any Vaalakan neck, I'm humbly at your service.'

Morrigwen snorted in disgust at being snubbed. 'Tell the peasant, Hal, that I wish to know of any news that the dunderhead has of the enemy spies. We need to know where it is safe to slip into the open heath, north of the Boarchase.'

'Excuse the old woman,' Hal apologized for Morrigwen's rudeness, 'but the moon, as you said – you understand. Please oblige me though with any information.'

'I understand, Sir.' The woodcutter gave Hal a man to man nod and raised his eyebrow at the old Crone. 'Strange company for a nobleman though, Sir, if you excuse my forwardness in saying.'

'Strange times,' Hal explained. 'Strange times. But have you any information for me?'

'Night before last we saw a fire in a glade, but we keep in the depths of the forest now. We live alone, trying to make do as charcoal-burners and it don't pay to confront them hellish Northmen. I'm not a coward, mind. Used to be a tusker, slaying boar for the Baron. But now as the boar, specially the big old ones, you see, are a mite thin on the ground, tracking them takes me too far from my family. And I daren't leave them at such times. I have my wife and wee bairn to think of, you see, and them Vaalakans come up on you sudden-like. I've sat in the tree tops and had them walk right beneath me. No feel for the woods those nomads, no feel at all. But they killed Cuthburt, and his wife and little girl. God rest their souls.'

'But here along the northern borders, have you seen many there at the edge of the woods?' Hal prompted after a moment's silence in which the man looked down at the ground, scuffing the leaf-mould with a pensive toe.

'Not long back, as it happens, I did creep right to the edge of the Chase and looked out across the Devil's land of the Dragon Scorch. But I've not seen no sign of an army yet, only scavenging wolves and troll tracks where spies have made it across the wasteland to search out routes through the forest. I keep my eyes out and pray that the good Baron will have the power to drive back these northern dogs before they pour out in their vast numbers into all Belbidia. The reeve told us all to move south, but there ain't work for us. I think we're safe here in the heartwood, though I dread what the Northern hordes will do to the lowlands even if they do let us alone in the Chase.'

Like a glacier flow, thought Caspar, gouging its way through the countryside, death to anything in its path.

'Thank you for your time, good folk,' Hal said politely. Spitting with rage Morrigwen found a tree-stump to serve as a mounting-block and struggled back up into the saddle. Despite the woodcutter's reassurance that he hadn't heard or seen any Vaalakans for several days, Morrigwen quickly crossed the broad track and anxiously pushed back into the cover of the deeper forest. She steadily made her way north-ward winding through the undergrowth.

'We'd be far quicker on the open track,' Hal protested. 'The charcoal-burner seemed certain that there would be no Vaalakans, and besides, I'm not afraid of any Vaalakan.' He swung the sword in an arc and hacked it forward through the air.

'Hey, mind what you're doing with that: you'll be getting one of us soon,' Caspar exclaimed.

As they rode on through the forest, the beech, oak and birch trees gradually yielded their terrain to blackthorn, haw-thorn and prickly long-needled pines. The helpful boar tracks lessened but so did the undergrowth and Caspar could feel the still forest air trapped in the closely packed trees slowly begin to stir.

'Move quietly,' Morrigwen warned. 'We're near the edge of the Chase. If I was a Vaalakan I'd put sentries in the open where they have more chance of seeing us.' When at last they could see the sunlight slanting through the edge of the forest the old Crone drew them to a halt. 'Brid, creep forward and take a look for me. I don't want these boys noisily blundering out in front of the enemy and alerting them.'

Despite Hal's protest, Brid slipped nimbly from the cream mare and lightly ran across the bare soil, weaving through the sunbeams and blending with the shadows. One minute Caspar thought he was looking at her copper-brown hair and green dress and the next he was examining the coppery leaves and lichen coated bark of a slender beech sapling. She had simply vanished. His eyes began to ache with the effort of scanning the shadows but he could see nothing. Hal yawned broadly, showing his impatience at having to wait when suddenly his mouth clapped shut and he sat up straight in his saddle.

'Where did you pop up from?' he exclaimed, looking at

Brid's flushed face suddenly at his side. She pressed her finger across her mouth.

'Shh, they're right on the edge of the wood. I counted ten of them.'

'Are they the same men?' Morrigwen asked anxiously. 'I mean would they instantly recognize us?'

She shook her head. 'No, these men look thin and spare. I think they've only just marched across the Dragon Scorch to be posted here. It means, of course, that there are probably more men posted all along the edge of the forest.'

'Well, it's obvious then, isn't it?' Hal declared decisively before remembering to lower his voice a little. 'We need to skirt along the edge of the forest a little way so that we're out of sight, and then slip across into the Dragon Scorch.'

The Maiden frowned at him and shook her head. 'No, the ground is flat and there's no cover. We could crawl across but we wouldn't get the horses by unnoticed. There's at least half a mile of open ground before we reach the first outcrops of bare rock that would at least provide some cover. Even if they didn't see us, by the look of them they'd attack the horses just for the food.'

'So we just sit here and wait do we?' Hal sneered. 'Come on, we've got to do something.'

'Well, of course we have to do something.' Brid's eyes momentarily narrowed with a withering look of disdain aimed in Hal's direction. Caspar didn't miss her expression. 'I think we need a distraction. If we could lure them into the forest, it would leave the way open for us.'

'And just how are we going to lure them into the forest?'

'Huh!' Morrigwen broke in. 'One so high and mighty as yourself does not have the answer, indeed! And you condescend to ask a witch touched in her mind by too much moonlight.'

'He didn't mean it,' Caspar apologized for his uncle. 'But do you think it's possible to entice the enemy away from their posts?'

'Everything, well nearly everything, is possible,' Morrigwen corrected. 'But it won't be easy. I need to make a plan. If you all wait back there by the holly bush, for protection, I can think in peace.'

'What difference is the holly going to make?' Hal sniffed.

'Its dryads give us strength to protect ourselves. It's a tree for you, Hal, like your sword, an entity of male character – and I don't necessarily mean that as a compliment, just a fact.'

Nevertheless Hal's chest puffed with pride.

The girl shrugged.

Finally Morrigwen returned. 'We need a diversion.'

'Like the wolves,' the young girl suggested.

'No, something they'd chase. Something that'd distract them.'

Caspar was hoping that these wild women with their shocking customs weren't about to suggest that Brid did something outrageous and he was relieved when she suddenly exclaimed, 'The boar, of course. I kept saying they were starving.'

'Of course.' The hag was enlightened. 'The name of a place always leads to its hidden powers. We will sacrifice the boar.'

'What, a ritual slaughter?!' Caspar was horrified. 'You're going to make a pagan killing!'

The Crone and the Maiden looked at him in amazement for several seconds before simultaneously bursting into laughter. 'What can you think of us? I didn't mean a ritual sacrifice, young boy,' Morrigwen cackled. 'I merely referred to them as a sacrifice because they were Belbidian boar and must die for their homeland. The Vaalakans will do the killing. We merely provide the boar as a distraction. Now we have to find a herd and that's not so easy as it used to be. There are fewer large boar around nowadays because their tusks are so highly prized. I find that trade incredible. There's absolutely no magic in boar tusks, but there again, men have very little instinct for magic.'

They dismounted and Caspar loosened the ties that secured Wartooth in place behind the saddle. He pulled the hound down by his shoulders so that he could stretch his three legs. Brid was already sitting cross-legged on a hollow log, her leather pouch in her lap, searching through her supply of herbs. She picked out the sprig of the silver-fir, the far-seeing tree.

'What are you doing that for now?' Caspar asked as he prepared his horse for a hunt by lightening the load of saddle-bags and checking that the girth was properly secure. He had hunted boar since he was eight, which felt like a very long time ago. His only misgivings now were that, with Wartooth injured, they had no hounds to distract the great tusked beasts if something went wrong, and no spear to defend themselves with. Nor were these horses trained for hunting. He shrugged. Between them he and Hal had a lifetime of hunting experience; they didn't need boar-hounds. Since they were only going to drive the pigs and not kill them he doubted they would have much trouble. He looked back at Brid, anticipating an answer but she remained silent. He repeated his question. 'What are you doing with that twig?'

'To find the boar.' She raised the greenery towards Caspar as if it were a toast, but he was still not enlightened by her explanation. She placed the cutting in her mouth, rolling back her lips in disgust at the bitter taste but chewed on nobly. After a few minutes, her head lolled back, her mouth sagged open and her glazed, unblinking eyes stared heavenward. Caspar continued to stare at her, half intrigued and half revolted by her pose but attracted by her sense of power and mystery.

Finally, Brid's head slumped forwards and she put her hand to her forehead, groaning as if in pain. Caspar made a movement to help her but she pushed him away. She jumped suddenly to her feet with her hand cupped over her mouth and made a dash for the deeper cover of the trees, where she doubled over and retched.

'Oh yuk!' Hal was disgusted.

A little ashen, Brid returned and sat down wearily, drawing deep clean breaths to clear her head. She vaguely waved her arm westward. 'There's a large sounder of boar four or five furlongs that way. Twenty or thirty of them. We need to retrace a little way beyond the woodcutter, head due west and then we'll be behind them.'

'Not we,' the old Crone objected. 'They. It's about time these two scullions made themselves useful. My bones don't feel up to a crashing gallop through the trees.'

With responsibility sitting heavily on their shoulders, Hal and Caspar set out purposefully back down the trail, following Brid's instructions diligently. The woodcutter and his wife sat huddled together over their lunch and looked perplexed as the noblemen galloped past with mud flying from the horses' hooves. In their excitement at finally being given a man's task, the two youths spurred their steeds into the thick of the forest. At a hair-raising speed they leapt over logs fallen across their path and ducked overhanging branches without a moment's care for their safety.

The horses became caught up in the thrill of the chase, pulling hard at the bit and jumping unnecessarily high over the logs in their exuberance. They crashed through a bramble bush only to be suddenly faced by the huge circumference of a fallen beech. The hollowed-out trunk must have crashed from its height in the forest, crushing saplings in its fall. From almost a standstill Hal's dun reared onto its haunches and bravely launched its heavy body at the fallen tree, scrabbling over the apex. On landing it stumbled on its forehand and, as it pecked the ground, Hal was pitched onto the gelding's neck. With his chin buried in its mane, he fought to regain his seat.

Caspar was better prepared, holding the reins firmly as the blue roan landed, and pulling her head up to keep the horse in balance before kicking her straight on back into her stride. Confidently composed, he urged the roan to deftly side-step the broad trunk of a chestnut and they skimmed past its deeply grooved bark without a break in the reckless pace.

Crashing through a thicket of hawthorn, they hurled themselves into the midst of a herd of tusked and hairy forest boar. A high-pitched squeal pierced the air as the horses crashed through the branches of the undergrowth, sending piglets sprawling for safety. Taken by surprise, the hogs ran hither and thither, their back legs sliding from under them as they darted in undirected confusion.

One massive boar stood his ground, head lowered so that the great tusks, yellowed with age, curled up towards the roan's galloping chest. He pawed the ground with his cloven hoof, snorting like a demon. In the split second before the great-headed boar charged, Caspar clung to a branch that was whipping past his head, hoping that it would snap. The branch bent and kept on bending like a soft green sapling but suddenly it gave way with a jarring crack and Caspar held a sharp pike in his right hand. It was a very meagre defence against an outraged and threatened boar.

The stout-legged pig with its vast, dish-shaped face and hunched body made its charge from the rear of the herd, trampling piglets underfoot. The young boy with no time to think, did the only thing he could and met the boar like a jousting knight with his sapling lance lowered at the pig's skull. From this height it was impossible to get a good aim at the brute's chest, which, Caspar knew, was the only effective place to stick him. A metal-tipped pikestaff would have been a more appropriate weapon but he was already fully committed to meet his challenger with nothing more than his sharp stick.

The branch scuffed the flat surface of the boar's broad snout, ripping out a slice of hide before digging in to bite against the solid bone of the skull. Caspar felt the impact jar into his shoulder before the branch snapped like a dry twig. The bleeding boar was unstopped in his stride, his gouging tusks still aimed at the horse's chest. The boy dug his right heel into the roan's ribs, loosening his grip on the left rein, so that rather than wheeling left, the horse leapt bodily sideways. The pig roared past, skimming the mare's hocks.

This time, Caspar wheeled the roan on her forehand, ready to face the great forest pig again, though he did not know how he was going to stop its charge. The hog's momentum rammed it into the trunk of a tree, where it bowled over and flipped upright again with its hindlegs spurting out in its efforts to turn. It shrieked hellish squeals, like the savage howls from the dog pits long-since outlawed by the boy's father. It paused for a brief moment to orientate itself and charged again. Caspar swallowed hard, despairing of any hope until a movement caught the corner of his eye.

Hal's dun leapt forward into a full charge, the broadsword held like a dagger in the youth's hand as he lunged downwards, thrusting it between the shoulder blades of the hog. The blade crunched through the vertebrae and penetrated down into the heart. The squealing howl of the boar announced its death, though the trotters still drove its body on. The stumbling animal cannoned into Caspar's roan, hotly followed by the dun, which Hal was unable to halt in sufficient time.

The shock of the impact sent Caspar's big roan reeling backwards, collapsing onto her haunches before falling heavily sideways. The dun stayed on its feet but Hal was launched over its ears to land face down in the leaf-mould. Thrown clear, Caspar was quickly back on his feet, desperately trying to pull the reins free from his horse's thrashing hooves.

'Easy, girl. Steady. It's all right now.'

The roan pushed her nose forward to counter-balance her weight and heaved herself up. The saddle-flaps hung beneath her belly where the girth had slipped and the stirrups jangled around her knees. The horse trembled with shock and the young boy deftly loosed the girth in fear that she might bolt with those treacherous stirrups hanging loose. The saddle thumped to the ground.

'I know, I know, horses can't stand pigs at the best of times,' Caspar continued in his soothing voice, crooning meaningless words to the mare.

Nursing his head, Hal carefully stalked his own mount. The dun gelding was dancing with wild eyes and flaring nostrils at the edge of the clearing, distrustful of any human that would drive him into a scene of such carnage. The hog still writhed in the aftermath of death throes. The rest of the herd was gone.

'Damn fool!' Hal muttered to himself, having eventually caught the dun gelding with the promise of some sorrel.

'Who, me?' demanded Caspar, resaddling the roan and hitching up the girth.

'Yes, you. You and me. How many times have we hunted boar? At least a dozen times in every season I can remember. And hunting boar on unfamiliar horses? Ridiculous! We should have been killed, charging in like that.'

'We nearly were.'

'Damn fools!' Hal was furious with himself. He handed his nephew the dun's reins to hold while he retrieved his sword. He braced one foot against the boar's blood-soaked back and heaved at the hilt until finally, with a grating noise, the sword scraped over the bones. It eased out and eventually yielded to his tug in a wet slurping gush as fresh blood spurted from the enlarged wound. Hal staggered backwards.

'We'll have scattered the herd across the whole breadth of the forest and it'll take from now till kingdom-come to round them up,' Caspar sighed, handing Hal his reins and vaulting back into the saddle. 'What do we do now?'

'Morrigwen will kill us and Brid will think we're incompetent children.'

'I didn't think you cared what they thought,' Caspar taunted.

'I don't,' Hal snarled, but he was not convincing. 'Anyway they are not going to find out. We head back into the forest and circle round behind the scattered herd and, this time, we make a more sensible approach.'

Hal's taken charge again, thought Caspar as he cantered away from the boar's carcass. Weaving through the tree-trunks he made a large and difficult circle, swinging round to where they guessed the sounder of boar would be. Caspar, himself, had failed to add anything practical to the plan to regroup the hogs and it had not occurred to him how easy it would be to get lost and separated in the woods. Hal had planned everything: circle away at a collected canter; count the paces; wheel round still counting and then make a slow zigzagging path back towards the dead boar, driving the piglets forward; then wait for each other. Hal was good at plans.

The unfamiliar trees and constant weaving made it very difficult for Caspar to keep his bearings: he lost count. Was that seventy or eighty paces and how many paces have I made since? Don't know, he thought. I'm an idiot. Hal will count carefully, retrace his steps to the boar and where will I be? Lost in the forest. Instinctively he reached for his hazelwood pendant and continued in his wide sweep through the trees. Now, he thought, I'll stop circling and start the drive back when I see some kind of sign.

The sign, when it came, was startlingly obvious: he glimpsed the hindleg of a piglet as it disappeared under the cover of a bracken frond, squealing loudly. Caspar clicked his tongue and paced the jittery roan back and forth, gradually working northward again towards the dead boar. He was glad of the bright sunlight filtering through the trees to the left of him as it kept his bearings true and slowly he wended his way back towards the allotted meeting-point. The growing intensity of noise from the little grunts and snuffles in the undergrowth gave Caspar confidence that he was getting a sizeable herd together as did the roan's increasing unease.

'Steady there, girl. They're not going to hurt you,' Caspar soothed.

Just short of the clearing the boy reined in and waited for Hal. He did not have to wait long. The dark youth reappeared at a jog, standing high in his stirrups and looking anxiously about him. Caspar saw no piglets running ahead.

'Not one,' Hal exclaimed. 'I haven't found one.'

'They probably went ahead then. Anyway I've got more than a dozen.'

'Good. Well done.' Hal relaxed. 'This time, we'll take it nice and slowly. Ready?'

Of course, I'm ready, Caspar thought irritably; but only nodded.

With slow easy strides and on a loose rein they marched forwards, clicking their tongues and swishing branches to keep the drove of pigs moving forward. The horses finally relaxed, now resigned to the proximity of the hogs. Whenever they heard the deeper snorts of a fully grown animal they stopped dead, talking in louder voices until the animal snuffled along through the undergrowth in front of them.

'Can't we spare that one?' Caspar asked, hearing the squeal and suck of a young litter and the attentive grunts of a sow suckling her young.

'I suppose so,' Hal agreed reluctantly.

They curved away and resumed the slow drive, leaving the sow behind them. The still air of the forest became fresher and the leaves began to stir into a rustle as the trees thinned out. They reached the boundaries of the forest and paused.

'Well, what do we do now?' Caspar asked, looking blankly around him and seeing no sign of the women. 'This is the right place, isn't it?'

'Yeah, I'm sure it is, but . . .'

'Were you looking for me?' a soft voice queried from the slender boughs of a willow, whose feminine branches curved in an arch above their heads. Caspar jerked his body in surprise, startling his horse.

'Where did you spring from?' he asked as Brid swung daintily out of the tree and landed lightly at their feet.

'Nowhere. I've been waiting for you. You've been ages: what happened?'

'Nothing,' Hal lied, his tone sharp as a result. 'We just took our time so as not to startle the hogs. And we didn't do too badly either.'

Brid had to admit that the boys had managed to muster an appreciable herd, now rooting about beneath the silver birches just within the limits of the forest. 'You were still a long time though.'

'Where's Morrigwen then?' Hal changed the subject.

'I'm right here of course.' The old Crone stirred from her crouched position in the crook of the willow roots and rose to look at them sternly.

'I didn't see you.' Caspar felt he needed to apologize.

'No? That's because you didn't look.' She turned her cold eyes on Hal. 'So, you've had your first kill.'

'No, I –' he stammered. 'How do you know?'

'The sword of course. It sings after a kill, which means you cannot hope to lie to me. The boar gave you trouble then?'

'Yes,' Hal admitted defensively. 'When we accidentally surprised him.'

'We can't afford accidents. Any shaman or warlock will have felt the sword's power shudder through the forest. We need to get moving quickly now. But at least you actually succeeded. Now we'll take a look at the enemy, and try, if you are at all capable, not to make so much noise,' she warned them irritably.

'Sorry,' Caspar whispered as he accidentally stepped on a dry twig.

The weeping birches lowered their skirts to brush over the tall grasses at the border of the forest. The four Belbidians peered out from behind their cover to spy on the enemy troop standing vigil on the tract of flat heath that separated the Boarchase from the crust of the Dragon Scorch. Seed-tipped rushes feathered the edge of the trees, giving the Belbidians cover as they lay flat on their bellies and stared at the Vaalakans no more than a furlong away. Most of the Northmen lounged idly on the ground while one or two stood watch. Many moaned as they clutched at bloated bellies. Either they'd eaten rotten meat carried with them on their long march across the Dragon Scorch or they'd unwittingly scavenged poisonous berries from the forest in their efforts to placate their hunger. Ill-shod, their heads bowed, many leaning wearily on pitchforks, Caspar counted nine men in all. Weapons were scarce. Most bore only pikes and pitchforks. Caspar almost felt pity at the sight of these pathetic Vaalakan warriors.

Hal was evidently thinking on much the same line. 'In the tunnels below Torra Alta we must have fallen prey to their crack troops. This lot don't seem to have an axe or a crossbow between them.'

'We've been watching them for a while,' Morrigwen began.

'They're not particularly fit but it only takes one of them to run for help and reach the next troop of spies and then we'll have more of them breathing down our necks.'

'Pretty well starving, I'd say,' Hal remarked. 'Scragg and his band must have killed a lot of Belbidian meat since they crossed the Dragon Scorch.'

'You're learning to use your brain at last, young boy. Very meagre supplies indeed, so a bit of roast hog is going to go down very well. We just need to call their attention to the hogs. When they realize supper is on the hoof just within reach they'll leave their posts. While they are preoccupied we can sneak out of the forest.'

Caspar thought it all through carefully. There was something about the plan that made him uncomfortable. 'Who or what is the bait, to draw their attention?'

'I am,' Brid announced firmly.

'No!' Hal and Caspar were both adamant.

'If they see or hear the voice of a boy they're just going to raise the alarm and hurl pitchforks at you. We have to draw the Vaalakans towards the boar somehow and this is by far the most effective way. How else are we going to do it? And anyway, since when did you two start giving me orders?'

'From right now!' Caspar stormed. 'Right now. You're a girl: you can't just march out in front of those men.'

'That's the whole point, Spar. They're going to be a lot more interested in me. Me, they'd follow: you, they'd either ignore or probably just shoot with a crossbow. Remember what that was like? They're bound to have one hidden under their rags.'

'I can't see any crossbows and I still forbid you to go.'

Brid laughed. 'I suppose I'm meant to be impressed, oh great heir to the Barony.' Brid's nose tilted skyward. 'To me you are just a boy.'

A purple stain rose up Caspar's neck and flooded his enraged face, clashing with his auburn hair. 'Get yourself killed or . . . or worse, see if I care. You're a stubborn, stupid witch.'

The bony fingers of Morrigwen's hand pinched his arm and

pulled him round to look into her understanding eyes. 'Listen, Spar, if you can think of a better way, we'll do it; but if you can't we'll have to let Brid go. Women are not so weak and frail as you've been brought up to believe. Brid is doing this for the Mother and so for the safety of the whole Barony. You must put the good of your people before your feelings for Brid.'

Caspar snorted disgruntledly and pulled away from her to sulk in the deeper cover of the birch trees. Wartooth hopped along behind him and sat patiently by his master, undemanding and unquestioning, simply content to bring company. Caspar scratched the dog behind his grey ears.

'You're a good old boy, aren't you? I'd send you out there instead of Brid only they'd catch you and eat you with your three legs and I couldn't let that happen. I know you'd go if I ordered you to, you're such a faithful old thing.' The dog looked at him with devotion but without a glimmer of understanding. Caspar sighed and drew a deep breath. 'I can't think of another plan, can you, Wartooth?' Naturally, the dog did not answer and the boy had to resign himself to swallowing his pride and letting Brid go ahead with her plan.

'Get ready then,' Morrigwen ordered. 'And, Spar, get that dog organized. Lash him on tight: it's going to be a bumpy ride.'

The dog whined as Caspar lifted him up and strapped him to the cantle of his saddle with broad bands of leather round his loins and shoulder. Morrigwen checked the saddle-bags to make sure they were secure and they all mounted, except for Brid. Caspar held the cream mare's reins for her.

'We'll be here waiting for you,' he said coldly, feeling distant from the Maiden and unable to put any caring in his voice. He found it difficult to understand a girl with so much independence and he still felt indignant and slighted. Though Caspar fervently wished her all the luck in the world, he kept his thoughts sulkily to himself.

Hal, of course, said the words that he could not bring himself to pronounce. 'Good luck, Brid.'

After unclasping her cloak and handing it to Morrigwen for

safe keeping, Brid untwisted her thick braid of hair. Running her fingers through the strands so that the silken locks fanned out like a dove-tail, she took a deep breath in preparation. Carefully ushering the hogs out to the edge of the forest, she slipped into the shadows of the silver birch trees. Snorting greedily, the rotund animals with their humped backs were unsuspecting of the girl's designs. They moved grunting into the long grasses where she had scattered fistfuls of acorns and hazelnuts to keep the pigs busily in place. Caspar followed Morrigwen and Hal as they withdrew deeper into the forest, out of sight.

Once Brid had emptied her pockets of the last of the nuts, she strode bravely out across the plain, the long grasses clinging to her green skirts. She began to sway her arms and body to the movements of a dance, spinning round and round with her hair swirling out. Her clear lilting voice lifted on the breeze in an alluring lament that drew all eyes and ears towards her.

The Vaalakan men stared at her aghast. Brid continued her teasing dance, drawing the Northmen's gaze back towards the hogs as she swirled like the eddies in the Silversalmon as the river danced towards the sea. At first the men remained perfectly frozen as if they'd seen a ghost but not for long.

'They're heading for her,' Hal choked.

The hidden Belbidians watched with bated breath as three scouts trotted out tentatively towards Brid.

'They're not sure. They might think she's a forest sprite,' Caspar innocently suggested.

'Unfortunately, I don't think they have any such tales,' Morrigwen remarked.

I hope that girl can run fast, Caspar thought to himself unaware that he had already wheeled round the roan, ready to gallop out to the Maiden's rescue if need be.

Brid enticed the scouts forward, making her spinning dance curl towards the boar which still grovelled in the grasses for the scattered treasure of nuts. Suddenly, she ducked down, vanishing into the grass. Caspar could make out the ripple of reeds as she changed course and headed directly back into the forest, striking off at a tangent to her previous route and perplexing the scouts. The Vaalakans faltered in their stride and gazed around them looking bemused.

'Come on, come on, see the hogs,' Hal hissed.

The blond, bare-breasted men looked around them in bewilderment, shrugging their shoulders. They looked like they were about to return to their posts as if the girl had merely been a dream but then, at last, one pointed an excited arm. Two trotted forward, crouching low into a stalk whilst the remaining scout sprinted back to the rest of the troop with the tidings that they had found supper.

With her skirts hitched up above her knees, Brid came sprinting along the edge of the forest and without bothering to place a foot in the stirrup, vaulted up into the saddle. She was quivering slightly but soon steadied herself as they all listened with bated breath to the sound of the mustering Vaalakans preparing to hunt the boar. Within minutes the pigs had scattered into the forest and the Vaalakans were blundering after them with hoots and yells.

'I wish we'd left that great boar alive,' Hal muttered. 'He'd have seen to a few of them.'

When the way was clear they marched out of the forest to cross through the fringe of reeds before cantering over the heath and into the Dragon Scorch. A shudder ran down Caspar's spine. They had crossed the border and were now in the desolate region of southern Vaalaka. He had never stepped one foot off Belbidian soil before in his life.

The wolfish cries from the hungry men drew Caspar's worried eyes. The squeal of a piglet screaming for its mother announced the first Belbidian sacrifice.

'We want to get out of sight as quickly as possible and beyond into those bare hills,' Morrigwen decided. 'At the gallop. Ready?'

Crouching low to the blue roan's mane Caspar spurred on his steed. He held the reins in one hand and stretched behind with the other to steady Wartooth's collar. *I hope they get* away, thought Caspar. Good Belbidian boar going to the Vaa-lakans – awful. Another terrified squeal tore at his heartstrings. He had hunted boar many times but never once felt any qualms at their slaughter, but this was different. He felt that it was going to be a long time before he could eat suckling pig, let alone wild boar again.

The cream mare stumbled as she caught her foreleg in a chance burrow and Brid fell forward onto the long mane, losing the reins in her scrambling efforts to regain her seat. Hal viciously kicked his horse on and leant forward to grab the flapping reins before the cream mare put a hoof through the loop but Caspar was already there. An old goat track, remaining from the years when the melting ice-caps brought life to the wasteland, sliced through the boulders and Caspar guided the roan's nose towards the path. He threw Brid her reins.

'Here. Will you be all right now?'

She did not reply, instead concentrating on the rocky climb that lay ahead. Caspar took one glance back towards the forest and his last sight of the Barony of Torra Alta.

Chapter 16

As in a dream, voices came to Branwolf.

'Is it one of them, Pip?'

'Shh, I think he's dead anyhow; but the dagger must be worth a few boar tusk.'

'Don't go near him, Pip. Wait for Pa.'

'I'm not afraid. Look at him, May; he's cut to pieces. And the smell!'

Dimly a small grubby face with dark brown eyes came into focus. Something nudged Branwolf in the ribs and his reflexes sent his arm up to grab his attacker. The child squealed in shock.

'Don't hurt me, Mister. I didn't mean no harm.'

Through slitted eyes Branwolf tried to glare at the boy but he was too weak and exhausted to struggle. He released his grip.

'Get help, boy,' he breathed through cracked lips. 'Get your father. Get help now.'

'May, come quick. Look, he ain't one of them Northmen. We've gotta find Pa.'

It seemed like hours, perhaps it was hours, before he heard their welcome voices again. He knew his wounds stank. The troll's claws must have been full of infection. Branwolf balanced on the thin edge between consciousness and oblivion with scenes from the last few nightmarish nights haunting his mind. In the dark, long before the children had arrived, he had heard an animal munching and splintering bones, the deep heavy breathing very close. At first he had thought it was the troll returned to eat the remains of its mate, but then he heard it move, foraging – and the ground shook with each step. Even in his delirium, he had known the creature was too big to be a troll. He tried to quieten his own breathing, and he prayed Conqueror would not whinny in fright and attract the beast closer. But at last the first grey light of dawn threaded the trees and the beast retreated.

Later, as the fever toyed with him and consciousness kept slipping from him, he wondered if he had not dreamed the monster. Perhaps, too, he had dreamed the voices of the children but at last he heard them again.

'Over here, Pa.'

At last! The children had returned.

A man's voice scolded, 'I've told you not to come up here. You were not to leave the shack in the forest, and now I find you've been larking about up here in the open. And taken your sister with you. She might be older than you but she's still a girl. The place is covered in troll tracks. We don't know that the Vaalakan spies won't be back just because they've abandoned the camp.'

'But he's hurt, Pa, and he's a Belbidian.'

The deep voice of the man sighed. 'Well, I'll be telling your ma about this, I will. She'll have a few words to say on the matter.'

Branwolf could hear the snapping of twigs as the peasants approached, then a broad, weathered face with stubble sprouting from his chin suddenly loomed before his eyes.

'Hello there, Mister. Are you still with us?'

Branwolf groaned.

The voice dropped to a whisper. He was talking to his children. 'He's carrying a fair few weapons – too many weapons, all a bit fine and fancy. What would someone with wealth be doing out here alone? I never once saw no noble without a trail of men behind him. There's something awry about this. Most like he's a bandit or a thief. Stay back, children.'

'Have you got a name, man?' the stubbly face asked suspiciously. 'What you doing out here in the far north alone?'

'What are you asking him that for, Pa?' the young girl queried in a timorous voice. 'You can see he's too injured to cause harm. We must get him home and help him.'

'Always such a pretty mind you have, my sweet May-blossom. But what if he's a spy from the other side? You can't go round being so trusting, lambkin, not a girl as pretty as you.' His voice then hardened again. 'Listen, man, can you hear me? What's your name? Where did you get the weapons and the horse? That's a war-horse if ever I saw one. You tell me your name, man, or I'll not help you.'

It hurt Branwolf to draw breath. His mouth was dry and his lips felt like rusted iron bars.

'Torra . . .' he began feebly.

'You from the castle?'

Branwolf tried to nod his head. Suddenly it occurred to him that this suspicious peasant would find it impossible to believe he had stumbled on his feudal lord lying half-dead in his own woods; it was just so . . . so unlikely. If he claimed to be the Baron, they would think him a madman and leave him here to be devoured by wolves.

'Bran,' he spoke again. 'Bran – from castle garrison. Troll – attacked me. Please, water . . .'

'Just help him, Pa,' the girl wailed.

At last the man's resolve crumbled. He knelt down and cradled Branwolf's head under one hand while he dipped his other hand into the stream so that he could trickle scoopfuls of water into his raw mouth.

'I can't do nought for you here, Bran,' he sighed regretfully. 'The wound smells bad to me. Have you got the strength to hold on if I lift you up onto your horse? Here, Pip, get your shoulders down here. We've gotta get him up.'

Branwolf's vision swam as they hauled him upright. They had him on his feet and he felt himself fall against the horse's black flank. Conqueror, he thought feebly, you never left me, old friend.

'How are we going to get him up, Pa? He's a big man.' Pip asked.

'May, you'll have to help us, lambkin. Can you do it?'

Branwolf felt an extra pair of arms grab his legs as they dragged him painfully across the horse's back so that his body was slumped across the saddle. The pain tore into his stomach and he cried out, dimly aware that his cry sounded distant and faint as if echoing through far away hills.

It must have been a while before he came round because the next thing he heard was the muffled thump of the horse's hooves on soft leaf-mould. He sensed the soft subdued light of the sun filtering through the thick canopy of trees and was also aware that he was still groaning with the pain.

'Nearly there, Bran,' whispered a lilting voice that, though high, was reassuring and he realized that the little girl was clutching onto his hands, trying to comfort him. This tiny little girl is trying to help me, he thought, soothed.

'May,' he murmured. 'I won't ever forget you.'

'Ma'll know what to do for you.' She lightly patted his hand.

Conqueror's swaying stride was wrong. Branwolf recalled the troll's violent swing of its claw – these Vaalakan trolls were brutally powerful – it had sent his sturdy horse reeling onto his haunches. Perhaps those great troll claws could hook onto cliffs or could crawl up his battlements? Bears after all could climb trees.

At last they halted. May's father yelled orders, summoning his wife and friends to his aid. There was a scurry of activity and Branwolf felt many hands lifting him from Conqueror's back and carrying him towards a makeshift shelter built between the trunks of four tall oaks.

'My horse,' he murmured. 'See to my horse.'

'Don't fret now,' a cool female voice whispered. Branwolf was reminded of his wife. 'We'll look after the horse. Lay him down by the fire, lads. May, there's water boiling over the fire, will you fetch it? And then some broth – he's been out there for days by the look of him.' Gentle fingers touched him. The woman sighed and Branwolf opened his eyes to see a small red-haired woman with soft cornflower blue eyes staring anxiously down at him. 'Keridwen? Keridwen? Is that . . .'

Branwolf for a moment believed he was looking at his wife, but reality returned to his struggling mind.

'No, Bran, I'm Elaine. Here, we've got to cut this shirt off you.' With delicate fingers the woman peeled away fragments of torn wool that had dried onto his wounds. She took a damp cloth and soaked away the patches of cloth that were too tightly sealed to his skin.

'Yuk!' Pip blurted out. His dark brown mop of hair poked beneath his mother's elbow as he wormed his way forward to take a ghoulish look at the wounds.

'It's full of poison,' she said matter-of-factly to her husband. 'Wystan, go and fetch the old woman. I don't know if I can heal this.'

'The old woman: are you sure? We haven't had any dealings with her for years. What would the curate say?'

'Hang him, Wystan, hang him if he won't let me save this good man here.' Again Branwolf was reminded of his long-lost wife. He'd never heard another woman in Belbidia speak out with such passion. 'Go and fetch the old woman while I do what I can for him. I'm sure this man here would rather live by the hands of the old woman than die because of our new found faith.'

'Find the woman,' Branwolf moaned. 'I don't care who she is. I've got to find my boy.' Suddenly his fears for Caspar came flooding back. He struggled to sit up. 'They've taken him!'

Elaine firmly pushed him back and started to bathe his wounds in water. 'You won't make it more than a couple of paces. Now just relax. May, have you got that broth? Here now try this.'

Elaine's tender-hearted daughter helped her mother raise Branwolf up before they tried to trickle small mouthfuls of broth into the Baron's throat with a bone spoon. He coughed and spluttered, distressing his wounds, but on the third spoonful he became used to the hot watery stock and swallowing became easier.

'That's better now, Bran, isn't it? The best thing for you is food and sleep until the old woman arrives. She'll know what's best. Now you just lie back and we'll get you cleaned up.'

What does she mean by that, thought the Baron as he slumped back against the straw pillows and allowed the two females to ease off his boots and slide his breeches from his legs.

'Just close your eyes, May, while you help me,' the red-haired mother instructed. 'Now let's find some more rugs to keep him warm.'

Branwolf didn't have the strength to object as Elaine mopped him with a wet cloth to take away the accumulated mud of the last few days. She dried him and then wrapped him like a baby in blankets, taking care to bandage his wounds on his chest with fresh cloth. 'You're covered in wounds and bruises,' she complained.

'Troll,' he remarked.

'Troll,' she echoed with deep feeling. 'Them Vaalakans built a camp here. There were a dozen or more and they brought their stinking trolls with them. The Northmen cleared out about two days ago now . . . but some trolls escaped. They killed my goats last night. Now sleep.' Despite her instructions she continued to chatter softly. 'I don't know why the Baron doesn't send men to rout these spies from the forest, I don't. We are his subjects and just as the shepherd must protect his flock so should the Baron protect his people. Why doesn't he come out of his precious castle, ride down here and drive them back?' She sighed deeply.

Because, thought Branwolf, I don't have enough men to patrol my whole northern border. The spies will always be able to creep through any gaps left in the line just as the King's troops can penetrate deep into the Dragon Scorch unde-tected by the Northmen. He could defend the Pass – at least up to a point. In the past the largest army to assail the fortress had been the Ceolothian army three hundred years ago. They had marched through Vaalaka unopposed and attacked with a force twelve thousand strong. Torra Alta had withstood the siege for ten months and then the old ballistas eventually ate into the enemy numbers. A few had tried to skirt round through the Yellow Mountains, but the terrain had spread them out and the King's troops had easily picked them off as they dribbled through, disorganized, onto the plain.

Branwolf sighed as he contemplated the statistics. Twelve thousand men had successfully laid siege to a garrison three thousand strong for ten months. He had one thousand men who would shortly be facing maybe ten times that Ceolothian number. The odds were poor and Ceolothians had not used trolls. Dear lady, he thought, I can not defend you out here in the woods. I can provide shelter in the southern reaches of my Barony beyond the castle defences; but that is all.

The broth made him feel more comfortable though he ached with fever. The blankets felt heavy and damp, pressing him into the makeshift settle. He heard the woman pacing. 'They should have been back by now,' she broke out.

Eventually, Pip was the first one to come excitedly into the shelter. 'She's gone. The old woman has gone.'

'We went right to the inner hut, Elaine, and it's empty.' Wystan tramped in after his son. 'Her cauldron is quite cold and the ash in the hearth is cool. The outer hut beyond the quagmire is covered with tracks. Troll tracks, plenty of them all over the place, right down deep into the mud. She's gone.'

'Hm, just like that Vaalakan camp on the edge of the Chase. Seems odd,' Elaine added with a sigh and then stared thoughtfully down at Branwolf. 'Do you trust me, Bran?'

Blurry-eyed he stared up at her face but he was unable to keep the image steady. Sometimes he thought he was looking at Elaine and sometimes he thought he saw Keridwen.

'Bran, I have to tell you that those wounds will eat deeper and deeper into your flesh and I cannot cure them painlessly for you. The old woman knows many healing plants that would ease your pain. I can only draw the poisons with salt and liquor and it will hurt as though I was slicing through your skin with a blunt knife. But you'll have to bear it. The infection will spread and keep on spreading otherwise.'

Thinking only of his lost son, Branwolf grimly nodded.

'May, get as much water down him as you can. The more he drinks, the more poison we can wash through him. Then keep building up the fire, there's a good lass. We'll try and get him sweating. Wystan, fetch the salt barrel.'

'He'll pass out, El. Do you know what you're doing?'

'No, of course I don't. I'm a woodcutter's wife not a wise woman,' she snapped. 'Only the old woman understands the ways of nature now, only her and her young lass.'

As May struggled to raise Branwolf's head so that she could pour more water into his throat, he spluttered and choked but managed to swallow several mouthfuls. Over the brim of his cup he watched as Elaine approached with a wooden bowl cupped in her hands. She stirred it with a spoon before nodding to May to lay the wounded man back down flat onto the hard settle. Branwolf felt cool hands peel back the bandages from his chest.

'Wystan,' Elaine murmured softly, 'hold his arms for me.'

'Yuk – ugh – putrid!' Pip exclaimed in disgust as the bandages were sloughed away. Branwolf smelt the foul decaying flesh.

'Pip, if you're going to be sick, get out of here.'

'No, Ma, no.' The child swallowed hard.

'Now, Bran, this is just a paste of salt. It'll draw out the poison in the wound, but it'll hurt. You haven't got too much whole skin there. Are you ready?'

'Do it, woman.' The Baron took a deep breath and tried to focus his mind on the only thing that mattered: getting strong enough to rescue his boys. For a second he felt nothing as Elaine smeared the paste across his wounded ribcage, then suddenly he felt as if swarming bees were embedding their stings deep in his raw flesh.

'Here, Pip, May, quick,' Wystan shouted anxiously between gritted teeth. 'Help me pin down his arms. He's a strong man. Here's me a woodcutter, wielded an axe all my life and I can't hold him, wounded though he is.'

Branwolf imagined that the Devil was pouring molten metal over him while stabbing his chest with a red hot trident. I'll die. A voice of regret swam up from his subconscious. The pain will kill me.

'Hold on,' a little voice whispered pitifully in his ear. 'Hold on, Bran. It doesn't hurt forever. I cut my finger last week and the salt burnt and burnt and I cried but then it felt better. It won't hurt forever. Please don't scream any more, Bran,' May's frightened little voice implored.

Lost to delirium, Branwolf now saw his wife stooping over his stomach, dragging at his chest with her long curving nails. She clawed out shards of shredded entrails and feasted hungrily like some hobgoblin at his flesh. She was digging greedily for his heart. Dripping hunks of muscles slid from her mouth as her teeth began to sharpen into points like a wolf's. 'Keridwen, forgive me, forgive me. I didn't mean to hurt you. Forgive me, Keridwen.'

His hallucination vanished as violently as it came. 'Hush, Bran, hush. Keridwen isn't here.'

Slowly Wystan placed Branwolf's arms back down by his side. 'Has he made it, El? He's gone limp and I can't see no breathing.'

Branwolf tried to reassure the woodcutter but he didn't have the strength. Elaine raised up his eyelids and peered into his pupils. 'He's still with us.' She smiled warmly. 'He's a strong man. If he's made it this far he'll make it all the way. He must have the determination of steel to survive so long out in the open and then bear that pain. He must have a lot to live for. Them trolls are cruel beasts.'

When Branwolf awoke all his joints ached but he at last felt cool. Dappled sunlight filtered directly down through the makeshift thatch over the shelter. Elaine stood over him bathed in a pool of light, as she examined the lacerations across his chest. Noon, he thought, but of which day? His head at last was clear though his muscles didn't want to respond to his will. He managed to raise an eyelid and focused on Elaine, thinking how beautiful she was. He guiltily chased away the thought. Pip sat on the corner of a knocked-together table, swinging his legs. He was barefoot with breeches that stopped just below his knees and a fringe that flopped down to swish across his nose. Branwolf smiled inwardly; the boy reminded him of Hal when he was younger. Pip was slightly sulky with a definite air of rebellion lingering in his dark brown eyes.

Pip was toying with something in his hands. It flashed in the sunlight.

'Put that down,' Elaine snapped angrily. 'If your father caught you playing with that there'd be a few harsh words. Why aren't you out helping him?'

'I'm looking after them for Bran,' he retorted cheekily, which definitely reminded Branwolf of his half-brother.

'Ow!' Pip suddenly exclaimed.

'Have you cut yourself?' Elaine demanded furiously without any hint of sympathy. 'I knew you would. Now get out of here.'

'I haven't!' Pip denied, squeezing his finger tightly and keeping it out of view. 'But Bran needs me when he wakes up. He'll want someone to talk to, so I can't go.'

'He doesn't need no talking for quite some while, young scamp,' growled Elaine. 'Now get, before I thrash you with the broom.'

'Just you wait, Ma. Another couple of years and I'll be bigger than you!' A large grin framed the boy's toothy mouth.

'Well then, I'll have to knock all the sense I can into you now before it's too late, won't I?' Elaine chased him round the table and he giggled impishly and fled from the shelter. Elaine sighed.

Branwolf drifted back to sleep and when he awoke this time it was dark and the smell of wholesome cooking filled his nostrils.

Pip's excited voice squeaked in his ears. 'Ma, he's awake. I saw him move.'

'Shh,' May's voice was soft though equally high. 'Don't talk so loudly: loud noise hurts when you're ill, didn't you know that? Pa always tells us to be very quiet when he's ill.'

Branwolf's head swam as they eased him upright but after

a few moments the dizzy sickness began to clear. When he'd taken a few sips of cooling water, he found himself saying, 'God, I'm hungry.' Momentarily he grinned to himself as the words reminded him of his two boys, but then he immediately began to fret. The Vaalakans could be torturing them for information about Torra Alta. He tried to kick the blankets that were swaddling his legs but his muscles responded weakly.

'My boy. I've got to find him before the Vaalakans kill him,' he explained to the puzzled-looking peasants gathered around.

'Listen, Bran,' Wystan's steady voice reasoned. 'I understand how you feel. There's nothing more important to me than Pip and May. But, you're not going nowhere on those legs. It'll take you a little while to gather your strength.'

May and her mother each brought two wooden bowls half-filled with broth across to where Branwolf lay on the settle then Elaine returned to the fire.

'El, come now, bring some for yourself,' the wood-cutter commanded. 'It's little enough to keep you from starving.'

He frowned and sipped without pleasure from his spoonful of the thin soup.

'Look at my little May there,' he said presently to the Baron. 'Now, I've got to give my childer good food. But the deer have vanished of late, carried off by them trolls and I can only get boar. It's good meat. However,' he paused significantly, and glanced at the Baron's fine weapons propped up against the edge of the settle. 'We're forbidden from killing the hogs now of course. The Baron himself put out some edict saying all boar must go to him – for the tusks, I believe.'

'I'm sure the Baron wouldn't begrudge one boar going to feed May.' Branwolf smiled weakly, feeling inadequate to the task of comforting this poor man. He would be sure to send messengers rescinding that unfortunate law about boars as soon as he regained Torra Alta. If he ever did. The broth tasted delicious to his parched mouth, and with relief he understood that he was now convalescent, his fever quite gone.

'I'm sorry it's so tasteless,' Elaine apologized for her cooking, 'but we've no salt now.'

'Can't get none either,' Pip chipped in, ''till the Baron's chased away the Vaalakans.'

Branwolf raised his bowl at them by way of salute. 'My Lady, the broth is exquisite and I'm sorry you've used all your salt on me, but one day, I promise, I'll make it up to you.'

'How do you know the Baron wouldn't mind May having boar meat?' Pip suddenly demanded, his child's mind flipping back to the Baron's comment. 'Do you know him then? Ma says that when she were a girl they ate boar every week since there was so many of them. But when the old Baron died the new Baron wanted all the boar for himself. Is that true?'

Branwolf frowned. 'I don't think it's quite like that, Pip. You see, it was just a coincidence that when old Baron Brungard died, King Rewik became more enthusiastic to build cathedrals across the land. He demanded higher taxes from all the Baronies to pay for the cathedrals. No Barony was exempt. Well, for Faronshire, the King's own Barony, that's not so hard. They produce an excess of wheat and can export it at a good price. They have lots of money to pay for the lavish buildings. Jotunn is the same. They have lots of cattle, and Nattarda produces gallons of cream, butter and cheese all of which can be sold. Now we in Torra Alta are a mountain people with little excess of anything. It's a harder, tougher life and we do not live off the fat of the land. We can sell timber, boar tusks and horses but not much else. Before the great winters ravaged the far north, Vaalaka was a peaceful nation and Torra Alta made good money from holding the Pass open for the trade routes; but those days have long since gone. The Baron needs the boar to pay the new taxes and it's not because he loves his people any less than his father did.' Branwolf felt deeply saddened that he should be so misunderstood by his people. As he talked and tried to explain the situation he realized how Keridwen's prophesy was coming true. He had stripped his Barony bare and the people were now paying the price.

'We come from further east, nearer to the head of the Pass,' Wystan explained. 'But with the amount of tree felling, there was nowhere left to hide when the Vaalakans started turning up. So we had to leave our home to come to this here shack in the heartwoods. They've passed by pretty close, a few times this last month, usually in bands no more than half a dozen or so but they don't come this far into the woods.'

'I've seen the castle,' Pip declared, abruptly changing the subject, 'though only in the very distance. In early spring this year we took some logs to the valley where the carters gather, and I saw the castle! That was before we moved out here. We were told that the Baron would give us shelter south of the Pass but Pa didn't want us to go. He said it made us look as if we were scared and he'd never get on with people that weren't woodsfolk so we took ourselves off here instead. The castle was like a spiky crown sitting high up on this needle of rock. I couldn't believe it was real. I couldn't see how they'd managed to build it up there in the first place. The carters didn't like taking the road up. They said the height was terrifying and when you got to the top you could see the whole world from there. And sometimes you could even look down on the eagles and merlins flying through the valley beneath you. When you look down from the castle they say people below look like ants and wagons look like beetles.'

'Is that what they say?' Branwolf smiled.

'And,' continued Pip in one breathless sentence, 'they say all the soldiers carry bows all the time and they can kill a man at four hundred yards and when I'm grown up I'm going to be a soldier. I want to be one of the Baron's archers and wear a tunic with his blue and gold crest on it. If you're a soldier at the garrison, Bran, could you get me a place there when I'm bigger?' He looked at Branwolf with innocent pleading eyes.

The Baron smiled and made an effort to change the subject. 'My own lad has told me a hundred times that when he grows up he wants to be an eagle so that he can fly into the heavens to study the moon; but I have faith that he'll develop some sense before too long. He takes after his mother.' Branwolf sighed and let May take away his empty bowl. Elaine came over to peel off his bandages and inspected his wounds. Branwolf at last dared to take a look at the extent of the damage. He was striped with ugly red ridges that had healed into thick crusty scabs.

'I look like a ploughed field,' he laughed, though he didn't really find much humour in the situation.

'We didn't need the old woman's magic after all, despite her fussing,' said Wystan with satisfaction. 'El still hankers after the old ways. You gave me a hard fight, though, you did. You know I'm a woodcutter and that's hard tough work swinging an axe all day long and it gives you big fat muscles. But I thought I was wrestling with an ox when I was trying to hold you down.'

Branwolf smiled. 'People don't realize how much strength it takes to draw a long bow. It broadens the chest and hardens the muscles.'

'You an archer and not a swordsman then?' Wystan asked with a suspicious frown, jerking his head towards the array of weapons. They had brought in the sword and quivers from the horse's saddle for safekeeping and placed them alongside the throwing daggers. 'You look more like a mercenary to me. And the horse, that's not an archer's horse. I'm no fool, Bran, there's more to your story than you've told us.'

'My horse, has he recovered?' Branwolf asked anxiously, at the same time dodging the man's perceptive questions. 'How's his shoulder? He took a blow from that troll.'

'He's mending. I took him out for a bit of exercise to loosen him up but he was too much of a handful so I brought him in quite smartish. He don't handle the same as the animals we use for dragging logs.'

'No, I dare say he doesn't,' Branwolf replied thoughtfully.

'Well, now that you've taken my hospitality, Bran, are you going to repay us by telling us who you really are and what happened to let this boy of yours be captured.'

'A group of those Vaalakan bastards took my son and because he lives in the castle I'm afraid they'll torture him for questioning.'

'You're another one, then, that wishes that the Baron would send men to get rid of the Vaalakans wandering freely in the Chase.'

Branwolf shook his head. 'No, I'm another father who wishes his son was more obedient and didn't go places I'd forbidden him to go when it's dangerous.'

Wystan nodded with understanding as he looked at his own son. 'The young lads are drawn to danger. They thirst for it, but then they wouldn't be lads if they didn't.'

'Here, look at this!' Pip exclaimed excitedly, pointing to the hilt of Branwolf's sword. 'Pa, look at this – wow!'

Elaine spoke up angrily, 'Young boy, now leave Bran alone: he needs some rest,' and Pip was dragged away by his mother while he still pointed at the weapons with his mouth moving up and down in speechless excitement.

Branwolf pretended to fall asleep. He knew he was weak, but he didn't need legs, not now that Conqueror was sound. He needed only the strength to mount the charger. He didn't have the strength to argue with Elaine but he was strong enough to move on – he had to be. He would have to sneak out in the middle of the night if he wanted to avoid arguing with her. He knew it seemed ungrateful but she would say he was still far too weak to travel. Even so, the boys' trail would already be cold. He could only leave at once in the hope it would not be far too cold to follow.

Once the sounds of ponderous breathing and ruffled snores filled the shelter, Branwolf eased his aching legs out from under the blankets. He reached for his clothes, which thankfully Elaine had washed, dried and folded neatly next to him, and braced himself with one arm against the settle as he pushed himself up onto his feet. He fought against his weakness and with stiff fingers hitched up his breeches and fumbled with the buckle of his belt. He eased himself back onto the couch to heave up his boots but had to pause several times to draw breath. His heart began to pound furiously against his chest, but at least the wound wasn't too sore.

He slid his throwing knives into his belt, picked up his sword and eased the two full quivers under his arms. He was forced to lay one of the quivers back down; it was just too heavy for him to carry all in one go. He shuffled across the straw-covered floor, grabbing hold of the table and falling towards the rickety door. He steadied himself against the doorpost, and the bark he felt beneath his fingers told him the doorpost was actually the trunk of a tree. He rested, leaning on the tree, to listen to the night, apprehensive of monsters and trolls, and Vaalakans. But he heard only the slumbering breaths of Conqueror nearby.

By the time he reached the knocked-together shed where his horse was tethered he had broken out into a profuse sweat and was shaking. Stumbling about in the dark, he found his saddle cloth and saddle. It took several attempts but eventually he was able to sling the weight of the saddle onto Conqueror's back. He eased the bit into the stallion's mouth and pulled the bridle over his black ears before fastening on the saddle-bags and sliding his sword into the scabbard. He was exhausted.

He rested against the tree, drawing deep breaths before going quietly back into the shelter to retrieve the second quiver of arrows. Seeing Wystan and his family still soundly asleep, Branwolf wished with all his heart he could thank them before he left. He was proud to be a Torra Altan and proud of his people.

He searched through his saddlebags and found a small rusted iron dagger with jewels embedded in the hilt. It was the dagger left behind in the tunnels, the one that must have come from the hoard of ancient treasure. It would be worth a small fortune. He wrapped it in a cloth and looked at the stub of the candle still smouldering on the table. The wax was still hot. He pressed some of the warm wax into the cloth, slid his ring round on his finger and imprinted his crest into the wax. 'Thank you, Wystan, thank you, Elaine,' he murmured as he placed the dagger on the table and went out into the night.

He led Conqueror a few paces away from the shelter until he stumbled across a tree stump in the moonlight. He needed some form of mounting block to climb up onto his heavily built destrier. Conqueror seemed to sense that his master was having difficulties and stood calmly four-square as Branwolf struggled into the saddle. He rested his arms against the pommel to support his exhausted body as he guided the horse with his legs, nudging him westwards in the direction where Wystan had indicated the old woman's hut was. If that was where the troll tracks were, that was where the Vaalakans had gone. He'd find it in the morning light but for the moment he had to put in a little distance just to get him started on his journey.

'Now that I'm finally up here,' he informed Conqueror as they rustled through the undergrowth, 'I'm going to sleep and eat up here and I'm never going to get down. I don't think I'd ever have the strength to remount.'

The night was still, disturbed only by the hoot of an owl and the bright red eyes of a fox staring out from the cover of the undergrowth. Occasionally he was aware of the champing sound of deer grazing through the night in the forest glades but otherwise he rode through a deserted world. Except . . .

Yes, he was sure. There it was again, something brushed through the bushes. He tensed as the rustle in the undergrowth drew closer.

Chapter 17

The pale limestone plateau of the Dragon Scorch rose up before them, pitted with age and covered in grey pumice ash where the ground had been singed by volcanic gases. The Vaalakan bluff soared almost vertically above the northerly plain of the Boarchase Forest, scowling down on them like the haggard face of an old man. Sundered by the constant freeze–thaw, ravines scored the time-shattered rocks like tired wrinkles. A gaping cave formed his toothless mouth whiskered about with tufts of gorse. Splintering rock featured the old face, and a tiny thicket of red birch that clung to the shelter of a hollow gave it one good eye and the appearance of an old man winking.

Hal led the way up the first steep traverse. In centuries past, the close-set hooves of goats trampling single-file across the ancient craggy face had worn a narrow and disjointed pathway. Gradually the track became no more than a narrow ledge broken by outcrops into steps and ledges. Where the horses slithered on loose scree the Belbidians quickly dismounted, cautiously leading their animals up the rockier climbs until the footing became more secure again. Hal soothed his horse's neck and muttered a few reassuring words as they were forced to the giddy brim of the precipice by a protrusion of raw rock. The track ahead clung to the overhangs with its finger-nails.

They made steady, careful progress until the gradient of the goat-track was abruptly broken by a giant upward step, before resuming again on a new higher level. The goats must have leapt five feet straight up the blank wall of rock to the pathway above which ran level with the travellers' dismayed eyes.

'All right for a goat,' Hal sighed, 'but for a fully laden mountain horse . . .'

'Impossible,' finished Brid.

Challenging, thought Caspar.

Even Morrigwen was silent and for the first time looked perplexed. For once Caspar realized that all the others had run out of ideas and unless *he* thought of something they would have to abandon the horses. They faced the prospect of a long, gruelling march and he looked anxiously at Morrigwen: she certainly wouldn't manage. And the horses would have an uncertain chance crossing back into the Boarchase. The Vaalakans would find their flesh more appealing than boar meat: the horses were bigger.

'Right,' Caspar was decisive. 'We unload and lug the gear up that ridge ourselves.'

'And the horses?' Brid demanded. 'We can't possibly cross the Dragon Scorch without them.'

'Without the packs, they'll make the jump,' Caspar explained.

Brid looked anxiously between the leap ahead and the precipitous drop below and shook her head. 'It's too dangerous. I couldn't do it.'

'I'm not asking you to.' Caspar smiled confidently, pleased that at last he was making a positive contribution to solving a difficult situation. 'I'm going to do it.'

'No!' Brid objected violently.

'And who's giving orders now?'

'They're my horses,' she argued obstinately. 'You can break your own stupid neck, but I won't have you killing them.'

Hal raised his hand to quiet her. 'If he says he can do it, he can do it. If anyone can, Spar can: he has a certain understanding with these dumb animals.'

'Always look for the secret in the name,' Morrigwen repeated as if reminding herself of an ancient and almost forgotten lesson. 'Are you sure, Caspar, Caspar the horseman?' She emphasized the first syllable of his name. 'We've been calling you Spar all along and I had forgotten that was what your name meant.'

'I can do it,' Caspar nodded with a brave face, sliding down carefully so as not to step out too far towards the edge. 'Unload your packs and back the horses up. I'll take them over one at a time.'

Brid's face was pale and she wouldn't look him in the eye as she passed the saddle-bag forward. Her fingers momentarily feathered the back of Caspar's hand and he felt the confusion and fear pass through the touch.

'I'll be all right, honestly,' he reassured her. 'Firecracker and I used to do this sort of thing five times before breakfast.' He tried to joke but thought to himself that Cracker was the only horse he'd trust for such a crazy feat.

'I don't care about you: I'm worried for the horses,' the girl snapped.

The long, lean fingers of Hal's hand gripped the top of the ledge as he vaulted up to receive the saddle-bags that Caspar heaved up to him. Wartooth was a little more difficult, being a tall, lanky hound and proving to weigh as much as Brid. With stiff legs and a quivering tail he whimpered at being lifted high into the air.

'You got him?'

'Almost,' Hal grunted. 'Well, his collar anyway.'

Wartooth's dew-claw scratched Caspar's cheek as the hound scrabbled to reach the safety of the solid rock. Brid was easier to lift up, though Caspar was embarrassed as he gripped her round the waist to help her jump up onto the ledge.

'I think you are a stubborn idiot,' the girl scolded sharply. 'You're only doing this foolhardy thing to prove yourself. It's too long a drop to trifle with.'

Thankfully Morrigwen was even lighter but her delicate old bones needed careful handling and she complained bitterly as Hal hoisted her up. The youth was pleased to escape from her tongue as he dropped back down onto the lower level of the goat-track to help his nephew with the horses.

'Right, all set? I'll give you my hunting knife when we get back for this.' Hal's white teeth grinned at his young companion. Then he said more quietly, 'I'm not being a coward, you know, backing out of this; it's just you'll do the job a lot better.'

'I know,' Caspar reassured him.

The subdued nature of the mountain breed meant that even on that windswept ledge the horses backed up and waited quietly without fussing. The roan mare, which Caspar had been riding, was at the front of the four. The boy was relieved since he was already accustomed to her stride and temperament.

'Ready, girl?' he asked, squeezing the reins to feel the bit and capture the blue roan's attention. She tossed her head, eager to move off and Caspar spurred her forward. He sat deep into the saddle, gathering her up underneath him as he felt her collect her stride. He could almost feel the rock wall grazing against his left side as he kept the animal as far away from the edge of the precipice as possible. Normally he would have thought it reckless to ask for anything more than a careful walk on the narrow ledge but speed was imperative if he were going to clear the five-foot jump. Three paces before the wall of rock he spurred her on, releasing the pent-up energy in the mare's hocks. On the take off stride he pushed his body forward, sliding his hands up her neck to allow her to curve her spine as she made the leap. He sat back on landing. They had made it.

'Whoa! Whoa!' he soothed her to a halt, loosening the reins so that she could snort and shake out the exertion, stamping a hind hoof in her agitation. The boy slipped from her back and handed the reins to a grim-faced Brid, who led the mare forward out of the way.

The stallion was bigger and already strained to follow the roan mare the moment Caspar was mounted. Although the animal rushed at the obstacle, Caspar sufficiently contained the pace to keep the stallion suitably back from the wall of rock. He made the jump with a comfortable number of inches to spare. The landing, however, had Brid clasping a hand to her mouth to stifle a yelp of dismay as one hindleg slithered sideways on the rocks towards the edge of the precipice.

From the lower ledge of the traverse, Hal nodded up at his nephew. 'Well done, Spar. You're doing a great job, but just watch out for the edge next time, eh?' He grinned. 'I won't be able to cope with these two women on my own so don't go and chuck yourself over.'

'I wouldn't dream of it.' Caspar returned the grin. 'I wouldn't trust you to look after Brid properly!' He had to calm his heartbeat otherwise the cream mare would sense his agitation. He needed to feel confident.

As he settled into his saddle, Caspar sensed that the cream mare was going to be difficult. There was a sluggish response as he gathered her up and he knew his willpower would have to lift her over. He focused hard on the landing, filling his thoughts with confidence and reassuring the mare that she could make it. Three strides before the take-off he relaxed the pressure on the reins. 'Go on, go on,' he urged, kicking her firmly with each stride and rising out of the saddle as her forelegs reached for the lip above. The mare jumped flat and low but Caspar was able to bring her head up to stop her pecking too heavily at the ground. He handed the reins over with a sigh of relief and turned to swing himself down the drop for a fourth time.

'Just one more,' he told Hal unnecessarily.

'Just the dun,' Hal agreed. He handed his nephew the reins with an uncertain smile, obviously a little shaken by watching his kinsman play such a dangerous game. Leaving Caspar to mount, he scrambled up the five-foot ledge and joined the women. Morrigwen's lips were moving in prayer. Brid looked glumly at the horseman below and finally managed a faint smile of encouragement.

'All right, old fellow.' Caspar rubbed the dun's velvety muzzle as it blew out warm air in a rush over his face. 'You've seen the others do it. Let's go to work.' He put a foot in the stirrup and the horse was already prancing forward. Like any herd animal it was agitated at being left behind. 'Steady there, boy. Stand!' Caspar commanded but before he had found his other stirrup the dun took off at a flat and determined pace towards the wall of rock. The boy tried to gather the horse in and get its hocks beneath its body, but the gelding was not listening. With ears laid back, its head was up wildly fighting at the bit. There was nothing for it but to go forward with the animal.

He knew that the striding was wrong but it was already too late to pull up. The dun launched into the air half a stride early. Caspar reached up and forward, trying desperately to give the animal every possible help, but knowing it was not going to be enough. There was a sickening thud and a shriek as the dun's hindquarters smashed into the rock, but at least the gelding had gained the upper level with its scrambling forelegs. Caspar hurtled forward over the horse's ears and somersaulted, landing face down just on the track with one arm twisted through the reins.

Panic-stricken and in pain the dun thrashed out wildly as it scrabbled for firm ground. As he fought to untwist his arm from the ensnaring reins, Caspar was suddenly captured by the same mad fear, terrified that if the gelding went over the edge, it would drag him with it. He rolled fully onto his stomach, digging his toes into a crack in the rock to give himself purchase. Pulling fiercely at the reins he fought to stop the dun toppling sideways towards the edge while at the same time desperately trying to free himself.

Hal was alongside in an instant. With one hand grabbing the bridle he used the other to deliver a deft stroke from his sword, slashing through the leather reins as if they were gossamer. Immediately the younger boy was on his feet, grappling for a purchase on the dun's bridle to help pull up the gelding.

Somehow the dun managed to buck its hindquarters up over the lip of the rock and toppled forward, trembling. Foamy sweat dripped as a thick white froth from its shoulders and dark blood seeped from gashes across its stifle and thighs where the horse had crashed into the rock-face. Its eyes rolled in terror.

A fierce arm gripped Caspar's shoulder and jerked him round and Hal's anxious face shook at him.

'Don't ever, ever do anything like that again.'

Caspar was speechless. He could not think for the blood pumping in his ears and jerked Hal's hand off angrily. He knew his uncle was only concerned but right at this minute the last thing he could face was a scolding. He pushed moodily past to see what could be done for the gelding's injuries.

'Not here,' Hal snapped. 'We'll walk them on to that scrub where the track widens out. It'll be safer.'

They led the agitated horses forward so that they were no longer hovering over the ledge. The dun limped behind on a stiff hind-leg. No broken bones anyway, thought Caspar, but they're nasty cuts and the horse is very shaken. When they halted Morrigwen nudged him out of the way, stooping to take a close look at the wounds. Feeling deflated and unappreciated, Caspar sloped back to retrieve the saddlebags, rubbing his grazed elbow and discovering yet another bruise on his shoulder as he went.

Heavily laden down with water containers and saddlebags he struggled back and forth over the ledge. I'm the one that's risked my neck and all they want to do is tell me I shouldn't have done it, he thought sulkily, dropping the saddlebags and returning for the next load. He at least remembered to be more gentle when lowering the last sacks to the ground as he heard a croak come from the salamander inside.

Wartooth laid his ears flat and snarled at the saddlebag. He then looked guiltily as Caspar snapped his fingers at him in scolding. Finally the young boy returned for the severed strip of rein that lay like a dried dead snake on the ledge.

'We'll have to walk them for a bit,' Hal informed his nephew. 'The dun's very shaky.'

'Yes, actually I know.' Caspar was still irritated at the way everyone had treated him. 'Of course he's shaky, he just smashed into a rock-face.'

'Hey! What are you getting so short about?' Hal looked hurt and yanked the strip of leather out of Caspar's hand.

'You, that's what! I'm the one that got those horses up here and all you do is tell me off. It wasn't all a big laugh, you know.'

'Look, I know it wasn't. I thought that damn horse was going to kick himself over the cliff and drag you with him. I was worried for you,' Hal admitted.

'Well, you have a funny way of showing it, shouting at me like that. Bad enough with Brid and Morrigwen looking down their noses, without you doing it too.'

Hal looked down at the ground and nudged a pebble with the scuffed toe of his boot. He looked sideways at Caspar. 'All right, you did a good job, but you just frightened the life out of me, that's all. I couldn't – no one could have got those horses over that jump – no one but you.'

Caspar grinned and clutched at his uncle's hand offered in truce. 'I was scared witless,' he admitted with a sheepish grin. 'Absolutely witless! And thanks for cutting those reins.'

Hal laughed, thumping the boy in the middle of the back and returned to the task of knotting the dun's reins together.

The boy was just beginning to feel a little better when he was deflated by Brid's icy stare as she reached for the saddlebag.

'You were lucky Hal was there,' she snapped. 'If it weren't for him you'd be down there at the bottom of the cliff brightening up the scree with your blood.'

She spun round so that her loose hair sprayed out and swished across Caspar's face, filling his nostrils with the sweet smell of lavender oil.

Hiding her thin-lipped smile behind the thick-jointed knuckles of her crooked hands, Morrigwen winked at the boy in encouragement. 'You were superb. I'm proud of you. Don't let Brid get to you: she doesn't mean it.'

'I do!' the young girl flared.

Morrigwen laughed.

The occasional flint worked loose under the horses' hooves,

bouncing from ledge to lip and triggering a small rock-fall that rumbled down to the scree below. The dun limped painfully, though Brid's herb-lore had at least stemmed the loss of blood. She had reassured the others as much as herself that there was no damage to either bone or tendon and the flesh would heal well. The goat-track led them into the shadow of a ravine that sheltered a thicket of gorse. They pulled their sleeves down over their hands to protect them from thorns as they pushed past, making slow and difficult progress. Wartooth's expression was one of misery, strapped to the back of the blue roan who rolled her shoulders in slow awkward strides, heaving herself up from one foothold to the next.

'Poor dog,' Caspar comforted him. 'But I can tell you it's not as sickening as being strapped to a foul-breathed troll.'

The dank shadows at least afforded them cover from the eyes of the enemy below, whom they had briefly forgotten in the trauma of their struggling climb. From the top of the escarpment they looked back down towards the strip of heath hemming the northern sweep of the Boarchase Forest. Casper could just make out the dark dots of a few ant-sized men crawling out from the trees, dragging small brown shapes whose squeals and shrieks pierced the heights of the escarpment. A wisp of smoke curled up from the valley.

'Well,' Brid declared. 'They're far too preoccupied to notice us. That's the first of the piglets being roasted.'

'It's a shame,' Hal sighed, which surprised Caspar: he had never known his uncle to be sentimental over game.

'Sometimes we have to make a sacrifice,' Morrigwen agreed. 'Poor little piglets.'

'I don't care about the hogs,' Hal snorted. 'I meant it's a shame we had to provide that plague of Vaalakans with supper. Otherwise, maybe a few more would have died of starvation tonight.' This at least restored Caspar's faith in his knowledge of Hal's personality.

The ravine narrowed to a slit and the weary horses were reluctant to climb it. Hal risked being kicked as he put a shoulder behind their hocks and shoved from behind, whilst

Caspar wove his fingers through the bridle straps to haul them forward. One by one they cajoled the horses safely up onto the top of the escarpment high above the spy-infested Boarchase Forest.

'We'll have to call a halt,' Brid warned. 'The old dun's bleeding again.' She gave Caspar a scathing look as if it were his fault.

They trudged forward seeking out the relief of flatter ground amongst the boulders. Behind them at the edge of the bluff straggled a few spare hawthorns. Their leaves were long-since stripped by the crisp autumn wind and they stood like the last frail remnants of a retreating army, spare and exhausted after a long campaign. A thatch of twigs clogged their boughs and when the Belbidians passed beneath them a clamouring cloud of rooks took to the air. Ahead to the north lay only bare ground except for one last solitary tree. When Morrigwen spotted the bright red berries of the lone mountain rowan she insisted that they took shelter under its protective boughs. The others rested whilst Brid immediately set to work again on the old gelding's hocks, tutting loudly as she pressed a poultice of herbs and mud deep into the wound.

'A bit of pie would go down nicely after that effort,' Hal sighed, resting against the smooth bark of the rowan tree. 'It must be supper time soon and hours since we breakfasted. And what happened to lunch?' he added, feeling rather hard done by.

'You've got to go easy: the rations have to see us through the Dragon Scorch. Don't you boys think of anything else but your stomachs?' Morrigwen asked, scooping open the flap of her saddlebag.

'We're still growing,' Caspar quickly explained. With a smile, he accepted the wedge of rabbit pie when Morrigwen turned to offer it to him. 'Is that all you're going to eat?' he asked Brid as she took a crisp bite out of an apple. 'No wonder you're so small.'

'Too much food dulls the mind,' she retorted, turning her back on him and staring out at the landscape ahead. The grey coloured ground was unnaturally dull where the light was sucked down into the pitted rock. The plateau stretched ahead for miles and miles broken only by grim boulders and shadowy ravines. After the deep colours of the Boarchase, the lustreless grey of the Dragon Scorch was oppressively stark. There was no sign of water. Anxiously, Caspar counted their water canisters and wondered how far it was across the barren land and whether there would be water along the way.

The Maiden was carefully surveying the grim landscape as she absent-mindedly chewed at the core of her apple before tossing it into the dirt. With her back to him like that, Caspar decided that she looked too unapproachable and he couldn't yet bring himself to apologize and mend their quarrel. He decided it was best to leave her alone for the time being.

Hal, of course, readily stepped forward towards the girl to busily point out things of interest. He even spotted a grey fox sloping through the shadows, hunting out the lizards and insect life that sustained it in this waterless terrain. Foxes seemed to be able to live anywhere. His keen eye spotted the tiny speck of a golden-breasted eagle circling above a distant golden peak of the Yellow Mountains. Brid responded with an animated expression, eyes dancing, her long hair floating around her shoulders as she tossed her head.

Biting his lip, Caspar hunched up next to Wartooth, who was sitting lopsidedly in the shade, looking mournful after his journey. The dog worried at his stump where the healed skin was obviously beginning to itch.

'I just don't seem to get it right,' he sighed to the understanding hound who listened patiently without interrupting. 'Why can't people be more like dogs?'

Wartooth wagged his tail, enjoying the attention.

Suddenly Brid's expression changed. Without speaking she pointed southeast down into the Boarchase valley but away from the group of spies feasting on Belbidian boar. A squawking covey of partridges rose into the air, beaten out of the cover of the reedy grasses by fast moving trolls. They were lolloping awkwardly but at a thundering pace towards the other Vaalakans.

'We've got to get moving,' Brid said unnecessarily as they all rose, hurriedly restuffing the packs with the remains of their meal.

'They'll pick up our tracks, soon,' Hal added, his expression now stern and businesslike.

'They'll have difficulty though. The heath is bone dry and the bare rock will leave no imprint. Fortunately the boar and the Vaalakan spies with all their dashing about will have scrubbed over any tracks we will have left at the edge of the forest. But all the same, if they do eventually find a hoofprint they'll be fast on our heels. They've got trolls which'll be far more at home on this terrain than our horses, especially now the dun's injured.'

Brid cast her eyes northwards over the plateau. 'It's so flat and stark we're going to stick out like an oak tree in a field of wheat.'

'We need to pick up one of the old rivers that'll drop us beneath the level of the plateau,' Hal said decisively.

Morrigwen raised one side of her mouth in a half smile. 'Getting smarter, aren't we, Hal? We'll head northeast and then we're bound to cut into one. Let's go.'

The salamander's red head popped up from beneath the flap of the Crone's saddlebag, jerked its head round and snapped back inside its cosy nest as if disgusted with the humans. Wartooth snarled.

To save the dun's wound from opening up again, Brid sat behind Morrigwen on the stallion and Hal took her cream mare. He left his nephew to lead the injured dun, which continued to slow their progress as they trudged steadily deeper into Vaalaka. Over to their right they finally made out a dark line running through the rock where the evening shadows crept out of a dip in the ground. The line contoured the dried out bed of a stream that quickly led them to the wider hollow of a flat riverbed. Caspar presumed that the Vaalakans had different names for each of the rivers channelling through the

Dragon Scorch but the Belbidians only knew the seasonal rivers as the Summer Melts. He had never seen a dried-out riverbed before.

Where the bare rock gave way to soil, the plateau bordering the old river bank was contoured by dips and hollows that marked out rough field patterns and basic enclosures. Without running water these had long since been abandoned. The riverbed itself was wide and shallow where the water had meandered through the plateau, seeking a route that would eventually lead it to the Sylvan Rush River. The ground was smoothly undulating where the waters had moulded the mud into soft curving shapes that had dried into sculpted mounds. It was an unnatural landscape of curving spits, lances and tongues of dried deposits forming curious overhangs that cut steps into the riverbed.

'I always assumed a riverbed would be smooth.' Hal frowned at the terrain. 'Smooth and flat, not all curls and twists.'

Morrigwen shrugged. 'It does at least provide us with shelter from the wind and cover from prying eyes.' She slid from the stallion's back and bent down to examine the riverbed. 'It looks as dry as my grandmother's bones and the pebbles aren't as harsh as the flints up here.'

Unexpectedly Brid kicked the cream stallion forward and guided the animal towards the river bank, plunging down the first few feet of the sheer drop of the eroded bank and sliding down the last few strides that shelved towards the old riverbed. 'Well,' she said with satisfaction from the shadowy incline in the plateau, 'we'll be out of sight down here, but then again we won't be able to see anybody coming either.'

'That's true,' Hal said thoughtfully. 'I think we'd be better staying out in the open. Get back up here, Brid.'

'We'll get away from the wind,' Morrigwen argued.

The youth shrugged as if he didn't have the energy to argue with her.

Caspar dismounted and with Hal's help lowered the old Crone down the steep embankment. She refused to let Brid come back up for her, complaining that her old bones were too brittle to attempt to leap about on a horse down so sheer a drop. She groused at the two boys for handling her so roughly as they passed her between them.

'You're pinching my skin,' she growled at Hal as he reached for her arm and supported her down the shelving bank. 'Don't you have any respect for your elders?'

'An old woman like you shouldn't be out in the wilds like this,' Hal retorted. 'You insisted on coming so it's not my fault if you suffer a few discomforts.'

'Don't you speak to me like that, young man.' Her thin lips mashed angrily together. 'You won't get anywhere without me. You might have a young fit body with strong muscles but you've no sense in your head. We're in Vaalaka now.'

They trudged on for barely a mile before they were stumbling in the dark and Morrigwen decided it was time to stop for the night. Caspar nestled close to his uncle. Both of them pressed their backs against the outside edge of the riverbed where the overhang offered them better protection from the elements. Wartooth's nose nuzzled against Caspar's thigh and he was grateful for the dog's warm breath. He pulled the cloak Morrigwen had given him tightly around his body and watched as the horses snuffled at the grain Morrigwen had scooped out of the saddlebags. They pressed their flanks closely for shelter. It's colder already, he thought. It's colder even than in the mountains and the wind, the irksome wind: it moans pitifully.

By morning the wind had dropped and their spirits rose. Caspar crept up above the banks of the dried-out Summer Melts and declared that there was still no sign of enemy movement. A cold but welcome breakfast of salted venison and oatcakes chased away many of their worries over the pursuing Vaalakans and they felt protectively cradled in the friendly banks of the riverbed.

Hal began to whistle, slightly breathily and a little flat but the melody was merry, reflecting their new sense of freedom. Brid picked up the tune, adding her own magical tones that soared up into the bright azure sky. As they wound their way upstream through the interlocking spurs of rock, where the water had once curled left and right with purposeless indecision, they found gravelly shallows that crunched beneath the horses' hooves. Beyond the gravel beds lay hollows that still cupped perhaps an inch of water in the very pit. They let the horses suck at the surface before moving on and squelching through the muddy river bottom. At last they found firmer footing where the ground had been baked hard more by the drying action of the wind than any sun so far north.

The sides of the river bank towered high above them as the channel narrowed into a ravine. Caspar tried to imagine the fast flowing river and decided that the water would be bubbling over the top of his head if the river had been in full flow. Here in the deep ravine the Summer Melts still trapped appreciable puddles surrounded by spongy mosses that sucked thirstily at the precious water. The boggy, water-logged ground dragged at the horses' hooves.

From the fore, which Hal had claimed as his rightful and natural place in the order of the group, the tall youth twisted round to check on the progress of his fellow travellers. His body swayed from side to side, rolling with the mare's laboured movements as she dragged each heavy hoof from the sucking mud before sinking up to her fetlocks in the soft mossy plants again.

'We'd make better time on the plateau,' he observed. 'But I don't want to contradict Morrigwen: she always knows best. And come on, Spar, stop dawdling,' the raven-haired youth called to his fairer relative, eager for some company on the long trek northwards.

Finding it difficult to encourage the injured dun to a faster pace as the gelding struggled through the sodden ground, Caspar waved a dismissive hand in reply. As he did so, his mouth dropped open to utter a warning but nothing came out. Dismayed, he watched Hal lurch forward as the cream mare disappeared up to her shoulders in rich black bog.

'Stop kicking!' Caspar recovered his voice and found himself instantly at the edge of the bog, trying to control Hal's panicky movements. 'Keep still: you're just upsetting her more.'

'For God's sake, Spar, do something. I'm sinking.' Hal's face was white and he flapped frantically at the reins. The mare lurched helplessly back and forth, trying to break the suction that was clawing her into the bog.

'I am.' Caspar spoke quietly, trying to calm his stricken uncle. 'You've got to keep still. Stop flapping, Hal,' he ordered confidently. But as his uncle continued in his frenzied efforts, Caspar's control also snapped and he screamed at the top of his voice, 'Keep still, you idiot!'

The ashen youth flashed an anxious glance at his screaming nephew and stiffened up like a statue to refrain from kicking the floundering mare.

'That's better.' Caspar was teetering on the edge of the bog, trying to get a fingertip towards the mare's bridle, but she was just out of reach, slowly and inexorably sinking into the dark sludge.

'Now, give her some rein,' the young boy urged, trying to keep the panic out of his voice, 'and don't flap at her. She'll get out on her own.'

With wide eyes, Hal obeyed his nephew. He slackened his white-knuckled grip on the reins, allowing the mare to thrust her neck forward to give her the momentum she needed to pull her thick-set quarters up underneath her. Instantly her shoulders sank deeper but as she kicked her hindlegs into the mud she reared up, dragging out tentacles of mud that clung to her breast and shoulders. At last she managed to pull one foreleg onto firm ground. Caspar snatched at the bridle, throwing his weight backwards to try to counter-balance her mass. Hal leapt nimbly down, swinging under the horse's neck and getting a toe to the edge of the bog. Once down, he grabbed hold of the other side of the bridle and together the two youths helped the mare kick her way out.

Gasping and exhausted, the boys fell back against the bank where the ground was firmer underfoot. Sweat from the exertion and fright poured down their brows, sticking the curls of their fringes to their foreheads. They gave one sheepish look at each other and burst out laughing. The mare shook herself like a dog, sending mud splattering over the hysterical boys and dislodging the saddlebag so it swung round beneath her black and soggy belly.

Taking a dim view of the boys' levity, Morrigwen's sharp tongue lashed out with unexpected ferocity, bringing them rapidly to their feet to rearrange the mare's load. The now half cream and half black mare stood with surprising calmness after the excitement, her velvety lips already curling around the tufts of moss congregating around the pool.

'Just stay behind me and keep your star-gazing eyes focused on the ground, child,' Morrigwen snarled in her crackling voice.

'Oh dear!' Hal said under his breath. 'I think we've really blown it this time.' He lowered his head to conceal a grin, still unable to repress the light-headedness after the unexpected drama. 'Anyone would think I did it deliberately. I mean who would expect a quagmire in the middle of a dried-out riverbed?'

Caspar swallowed hard on a snorting laugh that he felt was about to burst out and offend the old Crone. 'I've never seen you in such a dither, Hal.'

'I know! I felt such a *fool*. There was nothing I could do. But how did you know she'd get out on her own?'

Caspar looked at Hal and lowered his voice as if telling a secret. 'Because I've done it myself. Not in a riverbed like this of course, but in a peat bog in the high pastures.'

'When? You never told me.'

'You know if you follow the Silversalmon north and cut up into the mountains by the shepherd's hut – not the deer track but the other one leading to the summer pastures?'

Hal nodded.

'Well, I took Cracker up there last year – following an ibex – and I just didn't see the bog. There was an over-hanging branch and I pulled myself clear and once I'd stopped kicking him on, Cracker just bucked himself out.'

'Why didn't you tell me?' asked Hal.

''Cos I thought you'd laugh at me!'

A snort of giggles spurted out uncontrollably from both boys. It was some moments before they were sensible again and Caspar added, 'Besides, I don't have to tell you everything.'

A shadow drew Hal's attention. 'Look! Buzzard! Up there!' He pointed to the outstretched wings that glided in a lazy spiral as the bird trapped a soaring thermal of air beneath its fan of feathers. 'I'm amazed they find enough to eat in this wasteland. Lizards I guess.'

Caspar thought, and I won't tell you how I feel about Brid, either. Surely Brid would never be smitten by Hal, the innocent boy tried to reassure himself. They're so different. She'd find him too brash and too cock-sure. But underneath it all, Caspar knew that Hal's cheeky confidence was all part of his charm.

After crunching over the shallows and negotiating the boulders rolled downstream by the once fast-running water, Hal approached the next puddle-lined hollow with more caution. They paused, allowing the horses to suck thirstily at the surface of the muddy pools. Caspar encouraged them to wade in up to their feathered fetlocks so that the cool mud would take the heat out of the horses' stressed tendons after the hard march. He swung his leg over the back of the saddle, and carelessly splashed into the muddy ground. The puddles nearly brimmed to the top of his mended boots and he could feel the water seeping in through Brid's makeshift stitches. He released the hound to stretch his legs and then waded round to the back of the dun to check on the wound.

'It's caked dry,' he answered Brid's questioning expression. 'No swelling, but there's a lot of heat in the leg.'

'We'll rest here for a while then, and give the old dun a chance,' Morrigwen ordered. 'And, Hal, you can get some of that mud off your mare, whilst we're resting.' The old Crone's tone was overbearing.

'Oh! I can, can I?' he replied tartly, not yet prepared to take such a direct order from a woman.

Morrigwen fixed him sternly. 'In fact you will, boy.'

They had finally reached the show-down: Caspar had wondered how long it would take to get to this point. He doubted whether Hal would tolerate being spoken to like that and his heart raced in anticipation of a row that he wanted no part in. Please, Hal, he prayed to himself, please, Hal, back down: somehow he knew that Morrigwen would not.

The Crone's face was fixed into cold, hard stone, creviced and ancient.

With an arrogant toss of his hand Hal let his reins fall onto the horse's neck, kicked his foot over the front of the saddle and jumped into the muddy riverbed. 'In fact,' he echoed with equal ferocity and the ardour of youth trying to assert a position, 'in fact I will not. Moreover, I'll have nothing more to do with you.' He started to stride purposefully away with tense angry shoulders, then stopped dead in his tracks. With nostrils flaring, he swung round and stabbed the air in front of Caspar. 'And you, lad, you can get your priorities sorted out'. Stay with these witches and I'll never speak to you again. You'd better start deciding who your friends are.'

'Hal –' Caspar started to implore. 'Look, just calm down and think about all this.'

Hal's face was red with anger and his clenched fist shook with rage. 'No one and particularly not a woman and especially not an old witch, tells me what to do. Ask me, beg me, implore me, perhaps. But tell me? Never. And you should stop being pushed around by an old hag and a little girl.'

'Can't you forget about your pride for just one minute?' Caspar pleaded.

'If a man gives up his pride, he gives up everything.'

'Oh, don't be ridiculous. It takes more of a man to back down than to strut around like some puffed-up peacock,' Caspar reasoned tactlessly.

Morrigwen showed neither signs of temper, nor any desire for reconciliation. She sat proudly on the moonlight stallion, her dignified expression of placid serenity mirrored in the smooth complexion of her young protégée. She made no attempt to persuade or argue with Hal but just stared down at him with unfathomable eyes. Brid would not even look at the boy but studied the back of Morrigwen's silver hair.

Stabbing his eyes first at the women and then at his nephew, Hal opened his mouth as if to make a retort but then snapped it shut, pressing his lips together sullenly. Being thwarted by Caspar had evidently taken him by surprise. He held his gaze for a long second of combat – then Hal splashed back to the cream mare, reached over her back and unhitched the scabbard with the prize of the long, cold steel of the broadsword.

'That's not yours to take!' Brid was unable to contain herself.

Morrigwen patted the girl's hand soothingly. 'Leave it alone and don't dishonour yourself by arguing with such a spoilt child. The sword will look after itself.'

Leaving the horse, leaving Caspar, Hal marched southward without a backward glance, the sheathed sword slung across his shoulder. Caspar shouted, 'Hal! Hal!' but his voice carried as much power as the gentle breeze and had no effect on his uncle's sulkily rounded back.

Wartooth whimpered.

'We don't need him.' Morrigwen spoke smoothly and calmly.

Brid's dazzling green eyes pierced the dark youth between his shoulder blades as he strode defiantly south towards Belbidia.

Chapter 18

I, Hal, son of Brungard, brother to the great Baron Branwolf of Torra Alta, I have never been spoken to like that by a woman. A peasant woman at that, by God! And in front of a maiden as well. Intolerable. How could Spar just go along with them? He kicked angrily at a loose pebble that clattered over the gravelly riverbed, echoing between the enclosing banks. Still grumbling bitterly to himself he was itching to see the expression on their faces but he was too proud to turn around. Why weren't they begging him to come back, he wondered? They can't expect to go deep into enemy territory without me to help them.

He squeezed the hilt of the sword a little tighter. If they think I'm just going to meekly turn around and help them without so much as a humble apology from that decrepit witch they've got another think coming. The ground underfoot was wet and slurped at his boots. He looked ahead to see the churned mud where he had ridden straight into the quagmire. In all this arid wilderness, he thought bitterly, I managed to ride into the only pool of sludge. He was smarting about what Brid must be thinking, acidly, of him. She might be a witch, a pagan witch . . . but perhaps she was even more alluring simply because she was strictly forbidden to him. She was certainly the most beautiful girl he'd ever seen and for that he might be able to forgive her unseemly arrogance and imperious manner. Well, that was nothing his influence and a spell in the castle wouldn't improve, he thought confidently. When she saw him as he really was and saw the respect that the garrison gave him, she wouldn't treat him in the same way.

He snatched a very quick glance over his shoulder to check that they were all staring after him in complete dismay.

They were still huddled together and Brid appeared to be grooming the horse. Well, perhaps they were only trying to appear casual to save face. But as soon as they realized that he wasn't just going to humbly turn around, they would start feeling a little more disconcerted.

The boggy ground was difficult to march through and Hal suddenly felt claustrophobic, trapped down in the deep channel. He wondered what the world around him looked like and he decided that Morrigwen was being unnecessarily cautious. She was just a foolish old woman; of course she was afraid. They'll come galloping after me in a minute to apologize but in the meantime I'm not walking down here like some crawling lizard. I'm a man and I'll walk on the land not in the riverbed. He sheathed the sword into its plain sheepskin-lined scabbard and clambered up the bank, slipping onto his knees before he reached the top. Perhaps I should have left the sword behind, he thought guiltily to himself. They've got no protection at all now and I should have left the sword with Caspar. He shrugged. It didn't matter; Spar would come running after him any minute now. Hal was fully aware that Caspar looked up to him as an older brother.

The view from the banks above the Summer Melts was dismal. The high windswept plateau stretched endlessly to either side with grey-brown rocks and only the whisper of gorse to break the monotony. Devoid of birdsong, the empty silence was mournfully eerie. The only sign of 'life' was the wind-dried carcass of a rodent lying unpicked in the dust. Southern Vaalaka was bleak. Hal felt terribly alone. Signs of past life haunted this empty world: crumbling field enclosures and cairns of sharp-edged stones showed where people had lived along the bank of the river. Once this place must have borne life and prospered when the summer floods nourished the soil, but now this was a dead, lifeless land stripped bare of any goodness. The wind continually lifted the dry soil, sending dust spirits swirling in eddies about his feet.

The water canister thumping heavily about Hal's chest reminded him that he already felt thirsty. He thought better of taking a drink so soon though, since he judged that he had at least a day's walk until he reached the Boarchase. With no food, the water canister was all he had to sustain him. He thought of the oatcakes, salted beef and strips of venison that he saw Morrigwen pack into the saddlebags and kicked at a stone again. It toppled over the brim of the bank and bounced the half dozen feet down into the old riverbed.

He glanced round again and realized that he had marched much further than he thought. The others were now well out of sight.

He stopped short in his tracks, wondering what to do.

Should he go back and pretend that nothing had happened? After all he couldn't really leave Spar to traipse into Vaalaka alone. And it would be most unchivalrous to leave the fair and beautiful Brid. Think what would happen to her if they were captured by Vaalakans. He wasn't even that happy about leaving her alone with Caspar. His nephew might wheedle his way into her affections now that he was out of the way and he was no longer there for comparison. And she couldn't be more than a year older than Caspar . . .

He slumped down on the ground and decided to think about it all. I'll give Spar ten minutes. He'll catch up with me more quickly if I wait here. That bitter old hag can then apologize and I'll condescend to help them because they will definitely need me.

The minutes dragged by. Hal wasn't at all sure how long he had been sitting there, staring northward, waiting for his red-haired nephew to come bobbing along on one of the horses, but it seemed like forever. He hadn't bargained for this. Perhaps ten minutes wasn't long enough. Perhaps those women were having too much influence over Spar. I can't let a peasant-woman speak to me as if I were her servant.

Of course the moonstone was terribly important – he knew that; he wasn't stupid. The Vaalakans after all were a simple heathen people. If they felt the moonstone had the essence of some powerful Goddess in it then whole armies could probably be turned back by threatening them with her magic. Pagans were so primitive. If they could find this woman, Morbak could be reduced into supplication, terrified by her reputation. If Spar could find this woman, he reminded himself, remembering Morrigwen's words – and remembering Spar's distress at the prospect.

It seemed preposterous to believe in all these deities. No, this was serious. It seemed *wrong*. But so long as he didn't worship these heretical Gods he didn't think his soul would be contaminated. He'd ask Gwion when they got back. At any rate the priest would be able to absolve him. Father Gwion had an endless list of penances designed to save their souls from eternal damnation, though Hal thought he was a little over zealous most of the time.

Suddenly, he snapped to his feet. I'll have to follow them. I can't let them get into any trouble but all the same that old Crone is going to have to learn, so she can fret for a while. I'll just follow discreetly behind them.

He had a twinge of conscience thinking what Branwolf would have to say about all this. Hal sighed. He would certainly be failing in his duty if he stormed off home and abandoned his nephew in Vaalaka, but surely Branwolf would understand if he kept a watch on them.

Having made a decision, Hal retraced his steps at a trot, the great broadsword thumping against his back, but there was still no sign that he was catching up with the others before he was gasping for breath – and very hungry. He slowed to a walk to draw breath.

'What a godforsaken world,' he murmured out loud as he startled a stunted, mangy fox from the cover of a rock. He didn't know why it was called the Dragon Scorch. It was an old wives' tale that thousands of years ago the dragons had burnt the ground with their acid fire, stripping all life and vegetation from the soil. Catrik, though, had said that was nonsense, declaring that a swollen mountain had erupted like a boil on the earth's crust, spuming molten rock and lava into the atmosphere and scorching the land. Hal liked to think that Catrik was right: he preferred the logical scientific explanation. Caspar, though, had remained unconvinced. His fanciful imagination had no problem conjuring a plague of winged dragons so dense that they formed an impenetrable black cloud and completely blocked out the sun. Hal had reasoned that the dense smoke from a volcano would also block out the sun but Caspar had argued that the earth would have recovered from a volcano by now but that the fire from a dragon's belly could poison the land forever.

Hal watched his shadow lengthening to his right. It dipped away into the dried out riverbed below him, which was being gradually swallowed in the afternoon shade. He realized hungrily how long it was since he last ate. He halted to take a swig at his canister, cursing his nephew not only for failing to come back for him but also for not even having the decency to wait for him. Caspar was always the first one to back down in an argument. Hal turned to look yearningly southward to see if he could still glimpse the Yellow Mountains. At first he wasn't sure if he was looking at clouds or mountains but at last he discerned the rugged golden peaks of his homeland. His heart warmed with joy at the sight. It was truly a beautiful sight, especially compared to the haggard and barren wasteland he walked through. He turned back to face the northern horizon. The bleak monotony of the forbidding plateau was only relieved by a littering of fragmented rocks – and in the far distance he could just make out what he thought must be the black peaks of the three Black Devils, which he had learnt about in tutorials. They were the three dormant volcanoes that Hal believed were responsible for the devastation of the plateau around him.

He took a deep breath ready to start his journey again when something caught his eye: just for a second a glint of metal flashed in the sunlight but then was gone. He scanned the near horizon for several minutes but he saw no further sign and he decided it must just have been the sunlight catching the quartz in some rock. He jogged on again with his head bent low, hoping that the dun's injury would still be holding the others up, but a niggling feeling between his shoulder blades kept him continually glancing behind him. He marched on until his thigh muscles began to ache and the weight of the sword dragged on his shoulders where the baldric dug into his skin. He pushed his thumbs under the leather straps to relieve some of the load as he staunchly marched up a slight rise. When he reached the top his breathing was laboured and he turned to get a good view of his surroundings from the higher vantage point.

Ahead lay the limitless expanse of dour grey-brown soil, oppressively uniform, with sinister reminders of death along the banks of the river. Dead trees, withered carcasses, and the signs of old human habitation lay half-buried in the wind-blown dust. Irrigation channels ridged the ground. Once they drained water away from the Summer Melts to feed the pastures but now they were permanently arid.

Hal swung round to survey the land to the south. At first he was greeted by nothing except the unrelenting bleakness of the terrain but then suddenly he saw it again: a bright dazzling flash. This time it was closer, much closer. And there again, directly behind him, following his tracks.

Instinctively he dropped to his knees, suddenly aware that he was silhouetted on the skyline. He waited, watching carefully. The occasional flash of light burst out from the dull soil and Hal decided it could easily be glinting off a weapon. It was a few more moments, however, before his eyes caught on to the waving movement of something wending its way through the rocky ground. Gradually it drew into focus and Hal made out the dark leathery hide of a troll ridden by a tall, blond warrior. It was a moment longer before he could make out the spear carried in the man's right hand. But the glinting came from a sword unsheathed and buckled to the saddle. A Vaalakan with a sword. He raised his eyebrows in surprise though his heart was racing fast. He calmly collected his thoughts, planning a strategy. He felt as if he were hunting a great wolf. There was that sense of great danger.

The Vaalakan might have picked up the tracks of Caspar and the two witches rather than his own trail. Where the ground was waterlogged and the horses left deep imprints they would be easy to follow. Morrigwen was wrong: they would have been harder to trace in the open where the ground was firmer. But if the Vaalakan was following the others, the Northman wouldn't necessarily anticipate that he was waiting for him. Think quickly Hal, he told himself.

Since the blond warrior was riding a troll, he was rapidly gaining on him and it would be impossible to outrun him. Therefore he must lie in ambush and attack him. I am not a coward, Hal said to himself.

He looked quickly ahead for some suitable cover. His eyes fell on the ruin of a mud hut where the pile of dust created a dark shadow in the dull earth. He slunk across the ground and crept down the far side of the rise before skirting the circular mound of earth. He was thankful that his black hair wouldn't draw any attention. After a moment's thought he scooped up a fistful of earth and rubbed it vigorously against his cheeks and forehead, hoping that some of the camouflaging grime would stick to his face. Carefully he slid the sword from its sheath and dragged his bearskin cloak around his shoulders, hunching his back so that his shape blended into the earthy mound. He nudged aside a clod of earth that shielded his line of sight and waited.

For what seemed like ages there was absolutely no sign of the approaching Vaalakan. Hal strained his ears for the characteristic grunts and discontented snorts of the troll. His neck and shoulders were stiff from cranking his head round at such an acute angle and he gently shifted his position, hoping that the troll-borne warrior wouldn't emerge over the brow at that precise moment. He shifted his weight and noticed a broken cooking pot lying amidst the ruins. To his surprise he felt sorry for these people. He could understand fighting men, warrior facing warrior, but the idea of all these women and children suffering from lack of food out here in the bleak wilderness . . . Perhaps it had once been green and lush when the Summer Melts gushed out of the north but what a dreadful place to live. He inched his head round to maintain his vigil on the brow of the horizon.

Still there was no sign of the Vaalakan. Hal worried that his stalker had crept around him, dropped down into the river, and was already past and gaining on Spar – and Brid. Gradually he began to feel sweat prickling on his back as, unblinking, he stared at the close horizon. A cough began to rise in his throat and he swallowed hard. Any animal would hear a cough: it was such an obviously human sound. At last he saw the tip of the spear lance the horizon. He adjusted his grip on his sword and shuffled his feet underneath him to make sure he was prepared to spring up off his best foot with maximum ferocity. Then he kept perfectly still.

The Vaalakan was moving agonizingly slowly. As the cap of the troll's wrinkled skull emerged into view, Hal could hear its feet dragging, each paw slopping lazily forward so that the claws raked the dry earth. The beast halted. Then at last the troll shuffled forward again onto the rise and the tall warrior was framed by the sky. As master of his terrain he towered above the landscape. Tall and thin, he was a daunting sight with his blond hair knotted into war plaits and with short bones twisted through the ends of the braids. The bones rattled as he threw his head from side to side, anxiously surveying the land in front of him. The troll had his nose to the ground and was eagerly snuffling at the dust, scraping with his claw and licking at the soil with its short tongue, tasting for scent. Hal's blood ran cold. *The ugly brute can smell me. So much for my ambush.* He pressed his shoulders deep against the mound of earth and tried to take slow even breaths.

The Vaalakan was a big man. He was undoubtedly less well nourished than Kullak and Red Beard who must have been hiding in the Boarchase and feeding off boar for some while. But he was tall. The youth suddenly felt more like the hunted than the hunter.

He wore sacking leggings with rolls of reindeer hide bandaged to his calves and moulded to his feet to provide warm footwear. A criss-cross pattern of cloth laced his boots up to his knees. His chest however was bare, declaring to the world and his fellow Vaalakans how tough the man was, how unafraid of the harsh cold that must be a Northman's most feared predator. Over his shoulder, however, was the skin of a black bear whose front claws scratched against the ridged bars of his spare ribcage. There wasn't an ounce of spare flesh on the warrior and his deeply contoured muscles and ridged tendons were so vivid that they almost gave the impression that he had been skinned alive.

The troll raised its snub nose, peeled back its fleshy lips to reveal its curved yellow teeth and stared directly at the mound of earth. Its nostrils flared wide as it raked the ground and then reared up on to its hindlegs, revealing its bloated protruding belly, and it roared like a man in pain. The warrior remained settled in his seat, seemingly unperturbed by the troll's awkward behaviour. As the animal lurched upright he merely clutched a knot of stiff bristles that sprouted from the troll's short neck.

When the troll thumped heavily back onto the ground, Hal stared straight into the Vaalakan's pale blue eyes. They were almost colourless, and unfeeling, as if all emotion had been sucked out by the bitter winds that swept through the northern tundra. They reminded Hal of the pale eyes of a wolf as they narrowed in readiness for attack. The warrior couldn't have seen him: Hal knew he was well camouflaged but the Vaalakan definitely sensed he was there. His position was given away by the troll, which excitedly pawed the ground and chomped its curved jaws together so that trails of saliva dripped from its sabre-like tusks.

The blond warrior abruptly jerked his spear arm backwards and hurled it at the earthy mound. Hal flinched backwards as the barb penetrated the soil near him and showered him with dirt. Its aim was all too close for comfort. He hoped the Vaalakan was merely probing the soil and wasn't yet certain that he was there. He couldn't rush the man from this distance. He wanted him to move forward so that he could leap at his back rather than confront him face to face.

The Vaalakan drew his short sword. It was crudely forged and plain, designed for the cut and thrust of close combat, but its short reach was compensated by the long stretch of the warrior's limbs.

'Belbidak! I can't see you but I smells your lily-fresh skin.' The warrior's voice was cool and infinitely confident.

Hal's heart thumped. He couldn't decide whether to rush the man now or to bide his time and wait for a suitable opportunity.

'You is coward rabbit grovelling down there in dirt. I smells your fear.'

Hal's temper gorged his thoughts. 'Never!' he yelled, leaping to his feet and stepping on top of the mound of earth as if it were a platform. 'You are a lying Vaalakan. You cannot smell any fear on me. I am Hal, master of the dragon sword, and I fear no man.'

Much to his dismay the Vaalakan threw back his head and laughed. It was a hollow bitter laugh but all the same it had the deep untroubled ring of hard-edged confidence.

'I am Guth-kak, son of Morbak, and father of many. I fear no one because the world fears me. So you is the little weasel leading Rudbardak so merry dance. He not so smart as me, Belbidak, he still search the boar forest. But I find your tracks. You and your friends marching so bold into Vaalaka. Crawling straight into the mouth of lion-troll.' He laughed again, then spat on the ground. 'Where is the white stone, Belbidak?' he demanded in an icy voice. 'The white stone. The Master must be having white stone and I is one giving it to him. I am Guth-kak.'

'I don't have it,' Hal replied simply, bracing himself between his widespread legs and tightening his double-handed grip on the sword. He was not an accomplished swordsman, he knew that. Torra Altans relied on the bow since hand to hand fighting was presumed to be less useful in the tight confines of the Pass. Expert archers could rain down a storm of arrows from the heights of the castle so inflicting maximum damage without loss to their own numbers. Hal, of course, knew how to handle a sword, but he also knew that the King's troops were all better swordsman than the garrison at Torra Alta. Still the sword he held was magnificent, and a surge of invincibility coursed through his forearms.

'Then the other Belbidaks has white stone. A poor scout you mades for them. First I kill you then I finds the others. Then I kills them and takes stone to Master. If we has stone we walks straight through gates of Torrak Altak and castle crumbles at our feets.'

Hal looked up at this big confident man who had the distinct advantage of being mounted and tried to imagine his small nephew swinging an oversized axe ineffectively at this man. Spar wouldn't stand a chance, he thought. Spar was undoubtedly brave but he was still light and small for his fourteen years and a war-axe had never been part of his training. This Vaalakan would hack him to pieces.

'Get off your troll, Vaalakan dog, and fight me like a man face to face,' Hal bellowed in a voice that he hoped resembled his brother's. 'Are you too afraid to fight me face to face?' the youth sneered again.

Nonchalantly, the blond warrior crooked his leg over the front of the saddle and looked down his thin nose at the dark youth.

'You is very proud for little man, Belbidak. You thinks you is clever to bring me down from troll, but I show you I is more than man. I son of Morbak, son of God.' He unhooked the round shield from his saddle and jumped lightly to the ground, the dried bones decorating his hair jangling as he landed. 'I fights you face to face. I not dishonour my rank by cutting you down from back of my troll. This way I sees your eyes bulge as I slices your neck from shoulders. I later rides through Torrak Altak with your head on end of spear and I uses your entrails for lace up my boots.'

'*Torra Alta*,' Hal roared back at the man. He couldn't bear to hear the name of his beloved home being mutilated by the barbaric tongue.

'Torra Alta now, but soon Torrak Altak,' he shrugged. 'My great father, who is son of God Vaal-Peor, will rule all the world and never one single Vaalak-childling will be hungry again. Vaal-Peor is king of Gods.' He smiled down at the boy. With one quick movement he flicked his bearskin cloak off his shoulder, braced his shield arm protectively across his body and playfully thrust the short sword at Hal's chest, laughing hoarsely. 'You looks like boyling whose steals father's sword.'

Hal charged forward with the broadsword above his head, aiming directly for the Vaalakan's skull and intending to split the man's brains asunder. Guth-kak neatly stepped aside, and as Hal charged futilely past, he turned to thump the boy in the back with the hilt of his sword. The Torra Altan sprawled forward onto the ground, quickly drawing his knees up so that he rolled like a ball and flipped himself nimbly up onto his feet. His breath came in short rasps after being knocked from his lungs.

Guth-kak sneered. 'So, little Belbidak, no one teached you to fight with sword. Perhaps you learns a few tricks in the few minutes left of your life. Patience is what give a man victory. Choosing, waiting, preparing for right moment for strike. Lion never attack openly. He stalk his prey until he close enough and having victim right where he want – and then!' Guth-kak flashed his arm forward, momentarily re-exposing his ribs as the sword arm thrust forward. The tip of the weapon nicked Hal under his chin before the Vaalakan skipped lightly back beyond Hal's reach. 'Lion pounce just when moment is perfect for him. And you sees, you misses your moment. You was to strike as I moved my shield and you misses it.'

Again the red fog of anger blurred Hal's vision. This Vaalakan dog was taunting him and what galled him most was that he knew the barbarian was right. The Captain had told him over and over again that his temper would be his downfall and that it made him behave like an irrational, wild animal. God had given man brains and not strength with which to fight. If he chose to forget his brains in favour of his devilish temper, he would be a danger to himself as well as others.

But knowing that he was wrong only made Hal more angry. In a wild fit he spun at the Vaalakan, spitting like a rabid dog, concentrating only on the cutting edge of his sword and the man's torso. He forgot the shield. He believed in his sword.

Again the Vaalakan neatly stepped aside, thudding the shield into Hal's shoulder to throw the boy off balance, and neatly thrust forward with the short sharp jab of the sword. Hal felt it punch against his ribs as the metal stabbed between his bones. He jerked aside with a yelp, rolling beyond the Vaalakan's reach and clamped his hand to his ribcage. I'm all right, he told himself firmly; it's just a flesh wound and nowhere near my heart. The Vaalakan stalked him, creeping from one soft-soled boot to the other.

'I bored with you, Belbidak. If I toys with you too long, I tires my troll when he have to catch up with your friends. Well, Belbidak, I is sorry, you not much sport after all.'

Guth-kak neatly placed his feet ready to make his strike. He feinted one way, then lunged towards the other as Hal belatedly tried to guard his body with his sword. But still the Vaalakan was toying with him, waiting to get that ideal moment to make a clean kill.

Chapter 19

Abandoning the horses to suck at the muddy puddles, Caspar started after his uncle. Brid's small hand caught his sleeve and her forest-green eyes gleamed at him, imploring him to stay.

'Let him go,' she said persuasively. 'Let him go and cool off. You can't keep running after Hal all your life. Leave him be so that *he* has to come back to *you* for a change.'

'But what if he doesn't?' Caspar asked despairingly. 'I can't let him go, really I can't.'

Brid took hold of him with both hands, tugging him round to face her irresistible eyes. 'Give him ten minutes and he'll come back grinning and cracking some smart remark.'

The boy sighed. 'All right, I'll give him ten minutes,' he compromised, still looking anxiously down the valley to where Hal's back had just slipped from view behind a spur in the curving river bank.

'You gave your word,' Morrigwen interrupted coldly and without any of the cajoling tone of her young apprentice. 'You promised to help us find the Mother, and I'm not releasing you from your oath. Torra Alta depends on her.'

There was nothing more to be said: Caspar could see that. He had given his word and it would be a dishonour beyond measure to go back on an oath. He fretfully resigned himself to letting Hal storm off, but his conscience still nagged at him. How much less dishonourable was it to turn his back on his uncle? But Hal had made his own decision. Resentfully Caspar had to acquiesce to the old woman's demand and, with bad grace, he snapped at the old hag.

'Why did you have to go round dishing out orders like you were his father?'

'You have no respect. That's the trouble with all of you at Torra Alta. It's no wonder the Great Mother has abandoned you to the mercy of Vaal-Peor. I would have expected better from you. And what about the Mother and her suffering? We must find her and release her in order to save your Torra Alta. Isn't that more important than Hal's temper?'

Caspar nodded in agreement: it was indeed. He curbed his resentment and made a lopsided smile by way of apology for shouting at the venerable old woman. 'We'd better get going again then. The horses will have cooled off by now.'

With a fistful of heather, which had managed to sprout from the sheltered crack in the rocky river bank, Brid was now busily rubbing the cream mare's thick coat. She teased out the caked on mud from the long hairs that swept together under the horse's belly to prevent the girth from chafing. The mare had a comical look, though, with a cream upper half and black legs and belly, looking a little like one of those hybrid heraldic beasts. They mounted, Brid taking Hal's abandoned mare and prepared to ride off, with Caspar still fretting that the women might be wrong about Hal returning. 'Ten minutes,' he sighed to himself. 'They said ten minutes.'

With subdued spirits Caspar slouched over the blue roan's withers as he tugged with irritation at the lead-rein pulled taut by the lagging dun gelding. Each time he twisted round he could only see his kinsman's hunched shoulders beneath his dun cloak, marching stiffly into the distance.

Caspar felt like a traitor. He didn't really see it was his fault that Hal had stormed off and left them but all the same he felt responsible. Morrigwen was wrong when she said he didn't have any sense of responsibility. He certainly did: he felt the weight of it dragging down on his shoulders. It was his fault after all that they had been captured because he was the one that had gone down the well and landed them in the lap of the Vaalakans in the first place. It was his fault that his father must now be in anguish wondering about his safety. The freckles on his face visibly paled at the thought. But then if he hadn't gone down the well, they wouldn't be searching for the Mother. And wasn't that the most important thing after all? They had to find her. He remembered the lure of the moonstones, their pulsing energy as they were released from the dark captivity of the ancient oak chest. They had lured him down the well, he was sure of it. Was it really not his own free choice that had taken him down the well, but the urgent call of the moonstones? Perhaps he wasn't so responsible for this after all, though he couldn't imagine explaining it like that to his father.

But he imagined the Baron's grim face and the torture he must be suffering because of his disappearance. It was no use; he still felt qualms of conscience. He looked at Morrigwen's back and sniffed. He thought, she has no right to judge me.

Morrigwen turned round and stared him fiercely in the face. 'You're sulking because you think I'm wrong. But the truth of it is that you confuse responsibility with guilt. You feel guilty that your actions have caused harm. That is a sentiment of hindsight. Responsibility means that you have foresight where you think about your actions in advance rather than regret them later.'

This is all Hal's fault, Caspar thought bitterly. Hal always wants to be in charge and loses his temper when he doesn't get his own way. He resented his uncle's stronger will.

He strained round and squinted into the distance but there was no sign of his kinsman. If *someone* had said they were sorry, Hal would have come back. It must have been well over ten minutes by now. He decided that he could take the waiting no longer and pulled the roan's head round.

Brid rode back and put a pleading hand on his arm.

'Don't, Spar. Don't go back for him. He'll cool off on his own. If you always run after him he'll always be able to tell you what to do. Sometimes you just have to grit your teeth and do what is right. Hal's got broad enough shoulders to cope.'

'I can't leave him.'

'You can. He won't leave you. He just wants you to think he has in order to make you feel bad, because he thinks you've sided with Morrigwen against him.'

'You don't know how stubborn he is,' Caspar objected. 'Hal never gives in. And don't forget we're on horseback and he's on foot. It might take him hours to catch up.'

Brid shrugged. 'He should have thought of that before he stormed off. And the reason you think he never gives in is because you always give in first.'

'You're hard, Brid,' Caspar laughed, suddenly enjoying her company and drawing comfort from her confidence. So he rode on more resolutely, following in the wake of Morrigwen's determination, ever northward along the course of the dried out Summer Melts. He pulled his cloak up and buried his mouth and nose into the soft folds to filter out the choking particles of dust spinning off the ruined landscape. The wind moaned and howled in his ears and he felt its loneliness.

They marched on until the sun began to fall back down towards the earth. Caspar was worried that the riverbed was leading them away from the direct course north, but Brid assured him that it would soon turn northwards again. She explained that the Summer Melts all sprang from the northern tundra and so each Melt would eventually lead them back to the source: the Vaalakan ice-cap.

'Was the Dragon Scorch always arid?' Caspar asked. 'I mean, why does it have no rainfall of its own?'

'Oh it does,' Morrigwen laughed, 'but it seeps instantly away. Without vegetation there are no roots to trap the moisture and the surface is dried by the wind. Without the life-giving floods the Scorch is a dry, barren place.'

Caspar felt the evening chill fall from the sky as Morrigwen raised her hand to order a halt. The evenings came early here in the north, Caspar thought, shivering. It was colder than it should be.

Wearily they dropped from their mounts and Caspar lowered Wartooth from his saddle. The hound appeared to be getting used to his position up on the horse and yawned contentedly as if he had been dozing peacefully for several hours. He woke up quickly however when Morrigwen offered him an oat biscuit and splashed some of their water into a flat pan for him.

'We shouldn't have brought him,' Caspar remarked, staring southward for any sign of Hal as he chewed miserably on a tough strip of dried venison: Hal didn't have any food with him.

'We couldn't leave him. There was no one to look after him and with three legs he wouldn't have been able to hunt for food,' Morrigwen corrected him.

Caspar scaled up the side of the bank to get a better view and cast his eyes southward over the barren range. Pillars of swirling dust were sucked upwards by the wind but nothing else broke the unyielding starkness of the Dragon Scorch. His shadow was long and thin on the ground. He still couldn't see Hal.

'I'm going back for him.'

'You can't,' Morrigwen growled emphatically. 'We need you.'

'I'm only going to fetch him and then we'll catch up with you, I promise.'

'No!'

'I know I sound like Hal, but you can't tell me what to do.' The freckle-faced boy was reddening but still managed to keep his dignity.

'You'll have to tell him, Morrigwen.' Brid looked at the old Crone reasonably. 'I think he has a right to know.'

'A right to know what?' Caspar demanded.

Morrigwen shook her head. 'No, he's still too young and he's been indoctrinated all his life. It might be too much of a shock.'

'You tell me, and tell me now.' The youth's jaw set hard.

The Crone stared back at him, unruffled, but then suddenly her expression changed and Caspar realized that she was no longer looking at him but past him. He turned very slowly, dreading what he might see, expecting a troll or a weapon-bearing warrior, but all that was visible were two grey pointed ears.

Slowly the wolf rose from her crouch. As she stretched herself up onto all fours from her stone-like pose, it seemed that she was being born out of the earth. Wartooth hopped anxiously forward to greet her and Caspar felt an uncomfortable pain in his chest. Suddenly, unaccountably, he felt afraid. The new tide of emotions washed away all his frustration over the old Crone and he immediately forgot her enigmatic statements. At first he thought that he was instinctively afraid of the wolf but gradually he realized that the hazel mandala about his chest was becoming heavy and cold, trying to warn him of danger.

Morrigwen and Brid had the same expression of apprehension on their faces. Quietly Brid stepped forward towards the wolf, but as she did so the animal turned and trotted a few paces away before stopping to look anxiously round at her. Brid approached more carefully and the wolf still moved on ahead.

'What's happening?' Caspar whispered to the old hag who stood frozen at his side.

'I don't know. The wolf's been prowling about; perhaps she's warning us of something.' Morrigwen crouched to the ground, her old knees creaking as she bent over. She placed her palms flat on the ground and closed her eyes as if listening.

'Can you feel that?' she murmured.

Caspar copied her and after a moment he felt a tremble run through the earth's crust. He put his ear to the ground and could hear a rumbling drone. It sounded much like a cascading river or a herd of Jotunn oxen.

'What is it?' he whispered.

'The enemy.'

Quietly they trotted after Brid and her wolf, following the river as it curved away from the north towards the eastern horizon. Caspar realized that they were approaching a larger valley from which their riverbed diverged. The Maiden in her once green but now dusty dun robes, followed the wolf, which

346

crept low on her belly, as they clambered out of the riverbed to get a better view. Caspar gave the old Crone a helping hand and together they crept around a spur of rock that supported the broken remains of an ancient summer refuge.

Caspar squinted between the cracks in the rocks to focus his eyes on a trail of dust that rose high into the sky. 'My God,' he murmured, 'my God, save us.'

The wider valley was bordered on the west by a range of spiny peaks that rose and fell out of the plain like a line of fins on a sea-serpent. The head of the long valley was guarded by three black isolated peaks, the Three Black Devils. Though still far in the hazy distance their very presence threatened the plains. The line of the river curled out from the far side of the most easterly of the three mountains, winding through the flat plain inexorably towards them. The grumbling roar came not from the dormant volcanoes but from the column of dust that stretched back for miles along the banks of the Summer Melts.

'Oh my God,' Caspar moaned again. 'Like millions of ants.' He stared in horrified disbelief up the wide valley at the Three Black Devils, but it wasn't the ominous shape of the volcanoes that unnerved him. Morbak's army stretched, like an endless snake, for as far as he could see along the line of the Summer Melts, broken into columns and legions, all marching obdurately south towards Torra Alta. A constant grumbling came up from the earth, like a distant tremor, under the pressure of so many feet. The wheels of huge towering engines moiled over the hard ground, towed by teams of thirty or forty trolls. Bare-breasted Vaalakan peasants hauled on ropes to keep the siege-engines straight as they rolled across the uneven ground.

A trail of these towering contraptions stretched back out of view, swallowed by the dust trail thrown up by the leading teams. The volcanoes brooded on the horizon, maybe half a dozen leagues from where Caspar hid. Yet the trail of dust marking Morbak's army stretched right to their very roots and snaked out of sight.

He remembered what the messenger had told Branwolf

about the size of Morbak's infantry travelling west of the Dragon Scorch. 'This is Morbak's second army,' he murmured through his dry throat. He tried to calculate how many men marched in the shadow of the Three Devils. Thousands and thousands, I wouldn't even be able to guess the number.

Moving at the pace of a crawl, a section of the first column veered more closely towards them, and when they neared Caspar could see the men were flagging and needed urging on by warriors on trolls. Many leaned against pitchforks for support as they trudged through the arid wilderness. One man fell – and didn't rise. That was when Caspar noticed the pack of trolls lumbering along on the fringes of the column. The snarling pack was on top of the man in no time, greedily feeding. Deaf to their countryman's screams, not one Vaalakan turned to look, as they continued to march on southwards towards Torra Alta.

Where will they get the water for this many men? Their numbers will be halved, he thought, by the time they reach the head of the Silversalmon. Halved, but that left a colossal number. Torra Alta will be smothered, crushed under the sheer weight of their feet.

'Belbidia cannot turn away such a formidable number with only her small garrison.' Morrigwen spoke ominously. 'We need the power of the Goddess. We do not even have the knowledge of the runes that could sustain us through the terrible devastation to come.'

Remembering the power of the runes of healing that Brid had painted onto Hal's chest, the youth cried bitterly, 'You know all about runes, though. Can't you cast some now?' He would even clutch at the heretical magic of these women if it would do anything to turn away this massive army from his homeland.

She shook her head. 'In the coming of the New Faith much was lost, much power and knowledge taken from us. We fled from the sacred city of Farona out to the wilds of Torra Alta and we could take only what knowledge was in our heads. I had never cast the runes needed to plead for divine help in times of war. Belbidia has been at peace for hundreds of years. There will be a terrible battle, a devastation. Without the Mother I cannot call upon the Great Goddess for protection and because of the zealous ways of the King and his Inquisitors we have lost the runes of war.'

There was a silence as they stared gloomily down at Morbak's second army.

At last Morrigwen sighed, 'We'll have to go back a little. We can't risk getting too close to the column. We'll climb away from the riverbed out of the valley and take a route across that ridge of hills whose spine points to the west of the three volcanoes. We'll move northward and swerve away from the Vaalakan lines at the same time.'

'That'll take ages and Hal won't be able to find us,' Caspar protested.

'We've still got to turn back a short way,' Morrigwen reasoned, 'otherwise with four horses we'll be spotted moving here in the valley. Perhaps we'll meet him on the way.' Her voice drifted away and the lines on her drawn face crinkled up into a sudden look of dismay. She lowered her head in concentration and touched her crooked hand to her ear as if she was listening intently.

'Tell me!' Caspar ordered. 'What is it Brid thinks I should know?' he asked a little more uncertainly as he frowned at the two women. Brid's face was also taut with anxiety.

'Shut up, Spar,' she snapped fiercely. 'It's the sword.'

'What do you mean?' he demanded though he lowered his voice to an awed whisper, not wanting to intrude on their concentration.

'It's singing, ringing out across the plain, its great war-song challenging the world.' Brid fixed Caspar fiercely with her startling green eyes. 'Hal is in mortal combat.'

'The fool,' Morrigwen sighed. 'He'll draw them to us. Every pagan priest in Vaalaka will hear that cry.'

In one bound Caspar leapt down the bank and snatched up the reins of his roan. Wartooth's ears pricked up expectantly and the long-legged hound hopped eagerly towards him.

'Stay, Wartooth,' he commanded. 'I'm going straight back for Hal.'

Brid grabbed the bridle to stop him from turning the roan's head. 'No, we'll stay together. You'll only get yourself into trouble too, if you charge off alone.'

'I have to help Hal.'

'I'm sure he's all right, Spar. The sword is singing its song of victory.' Brid almost sounded reassuring.

'Yes, but what if some bastard Vaalakan has used it on Hal?'

'Then it's too late,' she said simply. 'I can hear its song of death. But we've got to head back to a safe distance from the Vaalakan column. Maybe we'll meet him coming towards us. Then we can find a safer route to take all of us north again.' She smiled encouragingly. 'We'll stay together. You can't leave us, Spar, we need you.'

How could he refuse those imploring eyes? Hurriedly Caspar caught the horses, coaxed Wartooth away from the wolf and lifted the reluctant hound back across the rear of his saddle. They set off at a steady jog with the dun still limping behind and dragging on the lead-rein. Caspar felt a deepening fear.

Even after nightfall and they were stumbling through the dark, Morrigwen insisted they should put a greater distance between themselves and the Vaalakan column. Caspar could think of nothing but his uncle's safety. Hal should have caught them up by now, assuming that he hadn't really abandoned him and slouched all the way back to Belbidia. When the horses began to stumble in the dark, Morrigwen drew out the moonstone from within her saddle pack. There was a hiss from the salamander and she struggled with the leash for a few seconds before the reptile released its possessive grip on the tresses. The orb gave them a dim light to creep back along the riverbed until they reached the place where it swung due south again.

'We'll stop here,' the hag announced. 'We have to rest for the night and Hal can find us here.'

'I'm going to keep looking. He may be hurt,' Caspar fretted.

'Your horse is stumbling and you could easily miss him in

the dark. You have to sleep,' Brid argued. 'We'll look again at first light.'

The bend in the river formed an overhang that provided shelter against the cold night. Brid searched for some while in vain for firewood but returned empty-handed. Rather miserable, they tucked their cloaks around them and pulled out the fur pelts stowed in the packs.

The glowing moonstone sat in their midst and Caspar felt it calling him. The mandala around his neck pulsed with a warm welcoming energy as if it too yearned for the touch of the stone. He felt torn by his emotions. On one hand he was fearful of the strength of its pagan magic. He murmured prayers to the one true God, begging him for mercy and to save his soul from these witches who drew him deeper and deeper towards the ways of the Devil. But still he felt uncontrollably seduced by the moonstone. He wanted to embrace it, be one with it, to let his soul dance among the images . . . the evil magic of the Devil.

Morrigwen was studying the orb thoughtfully as she slid it from the lattice pouch and soothed the round surface as if it were the head of a child sitting at her knee.

'We must look into it again,' she murmured softly.

'It's too dangerous,' Brid warned her. 'We're too close to the enemy. Anyone with the sight will feel it. We don't know how far Kullak is behind us. He might know nothing about herbs but he senses the power. He was wary of me the minute he saw me. And he lusts after the power of the Eye.'

'But still we have to look. She told us to go north. She showed us with the candle; but north is not enough. We need to know more. We have to find her, Brid, and the moonstone is the only way.'

'But Kullak may have picked up our trail by now.'

Caspar could hear them arguing but his concentration was focused on the moonstone. A woman's voice was calling him. He turned out his palm and let the light caress him. It was a cold lifeless light that seeped through him, mingling with his body, searching deeper and deeper as if to find his inner soul.

The ghostly light seemed to bring with it soft and pleading words. *Spar, the winter is coming, getting closer. Reach out to me.*

His thoughts were barely penetrated by the hag's harsh words castigating the defiant Brid. 'You have spent too much time of late gazing at that rude and arrogant youth,' Morrigwen scolded, 'now it seems you have been influenced by him. We have to use the stone.'

But Caspar found his eyes dragged away from Brid. His eyes were searching for the heart of the crystal. The light was mesmerizing in its beauty, a ghostly white, but it seemed alive; the surface danced with energy. The liquid rock swirled and melted from one pattern to the next, almost as if it were about to reveal its inner secrets but at the last moment swirling clouds cloaked them from view.

'How much do you know?' breathed the boy. 'Tell me what's in your heart. Your secrets.'

Touch me, it whispered in his mind.

'We'll wait for the moonrise then,' Morrigwen compromised. 'The magic of the Hand-Maiden will bring us greater protection.'

The orb seemed to be growing and its light was pouring out towards the Baron's son as if trying to envelop him in its world.

Caspar reeled back, shouting inside his head: No! He tried to block his mind from the voice calling him from within the stone.

I need you, it whispered with its compelling energy that promised magic and power. *I need you and you need me. We are part of one hope, Spar. Join with me.*

He felt his hand being drawn towards the stone.

Morrigwen was still reassuring her young disciple. 'We will create a circle to confine the force of the magic,' she suggested.

Caspar's hand shimmered over the surface of the stone. Seduced by its power he reached into the liquid rock to let his mind touch its secrets.

Vaguely he heard Brid's shout, 'Spar, leave it!' and then the old woman's scratchy voice, 'No, child, we're not ready!'

But it was too late. The young boy already held the orb between the palms of his hands. A bolt of lightning flashed up his forearms and spangled his eyes, his muscles seizing into spasm with the shock. Caspar felt the jolt of energy burst through his skin and stab towards his brain, drowning out all awareness of the outside world. All he could hear was a whirring noise, a flat buzz like pestering wasps. His eyes were dazzled by the bright burning light.

When the light faded he was gripped by a sense of panic. All he could see was Brid and Morrigwen's faces as if through a grey haze and he could not breathe. A freezing pain gripped his lungs and his hands and feet were numb with cold. A crushing pressure all around his body prevented any movement. Finally he could no longer move his eyes: they stared dead ahead through the solid, frozen mist. Helpless, his mind in a frenzy of panic, he could do nothing to free himself from the great pressure of cold around him. Ice crystals seemed to be forming and expanding in his blood, rupturing the vessels, a myriad fangs tearing at his muscles and tissues.

Someone was laughing at him. A man with thick red hair and bright azure eyes that leered at him was standing over him. *I have the power now. You cannot mock me any more. You took my Mother away from me and now you will suffer.* The man stepped with heeled boots directly over his face. Caspar thought the boots would crush him but they could not reach through the skin of the crystal.

For what seemed like an eternity Caspar stared at the boots but could only feel an intense agonizing cold. Even his bones felt frozen and brittle. Nothing would move. He thought miserably, I'm dying here, crushed to death by the freezing cold.

His own name went round and round his head. *Spar, you have to find me or the castle will fall. We will lose everything to the cruel Ice-God and all Belbidia will become a tundra. Find me, Spar.*

I can't, I'm trying. He tried to shout but his mouth was frozen solid with his tongue sticking out like a spitted hog.

I'm trying to find you but it's . . . so . . . cold . . .

The voice in his head whispered sorrowfully. *You have been so long in coming. I have cried for you, Spar. He will kill you. You must find me so that I can save you.*

Why am I thinking these things to myself, Caspar thought, completely confused by the sense of being suspended in time as well as space.

You're here with me, that's why, Spar, the voice replied.

Caspar still didn't understand. The voice was coming from within his head and yet he knew it wasn't part of him.

He felt himself slipping deeper and deeper into the oblivion of frozen pain. At last the image of the boot stepping onto his face faded and, through the skin of the crystal, he could see a warm light. At first he could only make out dark shapes and then, at last, he could just see Brid who looked as if she were screaming in panic. Caspar prayed: dear God let her save me. But the Maiden looked down in helpless despair. Somewhere from deep within his soul, another prayer formed and Caspar wove his screaming mind about the hope: dear Mother, help me, help them to help me.

In his trance-like state Caspar imagined he saw the ghostly image of Hal appear in Brid's stead. Through the blurring translucent layer that separated him from his uncle, he could make out Hal raising up his great sword like a sacrificial dagger. He's going to sacrifice me as a punishment for praying to the pagan Goddess, thought Caspar, horror-struck, his mind thrown into confusion by his terror. Hal, do you hate me so much? I think of you as my brother. Are you really so bitter that you would murder me like this. In the instant that the sword plunged at his heart, the haze shattered before his eyes and the image of the white broadsword vanished. Instead, he could see Brid's white fingertip resting on the mandala that covered his heart.

Normal sound returned with a scream and it took him a moment to realize that it was his own. He was lying on his back. Brid was squeezing his hand, imploring him to hear her.

He let the scream fade to a wail as the terror of the unknown passed away. His mouth closed and he slumped back, feeling faint and exhausted.

'At least he's breathing now.' Morrigwen's voice was made quiet by the strain on her emotions. 'I told you to wait, my fool-child.' Her words were harsh and scolding but she pressed his other hand with anxious tenderness.

'Just keep breathing steadily now,' Brid's reassuring voice soothed in his ear.

But it took several minutes before the boy was calm enough to recount what had happened in his mind. He began to speak in fits and starts, gradually calming as he became aware of the caring support from the priestesses around him.

'I was frozen in ice, looking up at Brid, and Hal, who was about to stab me with the great sword.' Remembering the evil presence of the man lurking over him, he shuddered with dread. He was filled with a sense of such threatening evil that he couldn't bring himself to mention the man for fear the words would bring him to life.

'You got caught up in the nightmare trapped in the inner crystals of the moonstone.' Morrigwen hurriedly swept the orb back into the saddlebags. 'Vaal-Peor's hand is strong in this. It wasn't real though, child. You were in a trance, staring wildly with unblinking eyes. You stopped breathing.'

'I know. I was frozen, even my eyeballs were frozen.' Caspar shuddered again at the memory. 'What does it mean, though? How is this stone going to help us find the woman? I didn't even see her this time. There's nothing but an evil nightmare locked up inside it.' He looked fearfully to the old Crone for an answer.

'I don't know,' she sighed wearily. 'You might not have seen her but I fear you were caught up in her nightmare. May the Great Mother have mercy on her; her thoughts are trapped in the stone and you were caught up in her mind.'

'I stopped breathing,' said Caspar in despair. 'Does that mean she's dead?' The horror of the woman's last moments were too awful to contemplate.

When the fear subsided, Caspar sat up suddenly realizing

that his surroundings had changed. The silvery light of the moon, now low on the horizon, highlighted new rocks and boulders that hadn't been there before. They were nestled in the crook of two split rocks high up above the valley floor. He was tightly wrapped in blankets and the dying embers of a fire smouldered in a circle of stones.

'How long . . . ?' he began.

'Half the night,' Brid whispered softly in his ear. 'You were reckless, Spar. We had to take you higher into the hills where they'll find it harder to trace us and where they wouldn't see the light from the fire. We needed the fire to break the spell. It took us ages to find any firewood in this barren land.'

Caspar was gripped by a sense of panic. 'Now we've really lost Hal and we still don't know where the woman is.' He tried to raise his hands again but they felt like they'd been skinned. They were covered in white blisters and Brid was decorating them with runes painted in woad.

'You've got frostbite again. But it's not real. It's an enchantment and we can only hope that the runes will break the spell. Kano's rune: the rune of fire,' she murmured, daubing the rune onto the skin of his hands. 'Let its energy heat your bones and restore life to your fingers.'

'We must go and look for Hal,' Caspar persisted. He couldn't bear to be left alone with the terrors of these pagan rituals. They seemed to drag out nightmarish spirits from the depths of the earth.

'You can't go anywhere in the middle of the night, Spar, and certainly not until we've got some warmth back in you,' Brid informed him. 'I'll go. I'll go and see if he's coming.'

'No!' Morrigwen ordered. 'Besides, you'd never find anything in the dark except a broken neck.'

Caspar sank back in defeat, aware that he was too weak with cold to protest further.

Chapter 20

Hal fixed his eyes firmly on Guth-kak's face, trying to read his movements. Nonchalantly the big warrior unloosed a war-axe from his saddle, threw down his shield and faced the brave Torra Altan with two deadly weapons twitching in his fierce, ice-hard grip. The black-haired youth watched how those pale blue eyes swept across his body and stabbed at the left side of his face. Hal was ready. He didn't know which weapon Morbak's son would use in his attack but he knew where he would aim. He braced himself for the assault, trying to ignore the dance of the sword which the Vaalakan was using to draw away his attention. He knew Guth-kak's intent; now he merely had to stand solid and parry the assault.

The Vaalakan feinted in on his right side and then twisted to strike with the speed of a cobra. One step onto his right foot altered his balance and the warrior swung with the axe aimed at the left side of Hal's skull. Already prepared, Hal tightened the grip on his sword and raised the blade to shield his head from the skull-crushing blow of his enemy's cleaver.

The sword, despite its length and weight, was as responsive as a short knife. Hal was able to twist his weapon round to block Guth-kak's axe, bracing himself for the impact. The hammer blow of Guth-kak's heavy weapon clashed against the Belbidian blade.

Hal staggered backwards, his mouth dropping with disbelief as he watched the Vaalakan war-cleaver crack and then shatter like glass as it jarred against the enchanted sword. Incredibly the massive metal of the axe-blade disintegrated into a myriad shards and Guth-kak was left holding a stump of wood. A terrible scream of metal screeched out across the stark wilderness as the ancient sword of white steel pealed out like a giant broken bell. The shock of the impact sent Hal to his knees.

The Vaalakan's lupine eyes bulged in his head and he stared stupefied at his crumbled weapon. A powdery grey dust drifted in the wind while the great Belbidian sword still reverberated, singing out its victory song across the vast wastelands of southern Vaalaka.

Hal felt a powerful surge of triumph possess his mind. He felt like a king, more, he was a king, a demi-god, a terrible warrior to be dreaded across all the world. He was a slayer. He felt the blood-lust throb through his veins. He was eaten up with a desire to maim and kill as if he were one with the destructive power of the sword. A cruel and fearsome weapon, he thought with delight; I could devastate entire armies.

Guth-kak was on his knees grovelling, sifting the dust of the axe blade through his fingers as if he couldn't believe what had happened. Hal looked down at his bare exposed neck and a wide sadistic smile spread across his face. Kill him, kill him, the sword seemed to compel him. He raised his blade to take a clean swipe sideways to sever his enemy's neck. He was too engrossed with his own sense of power to notice the quick flick of Guth-kak's wrist and the flash of cold grey steel as the Vaalakan short sword stabbed at his undefended side. The youth leapt back just as the sword nicked his flesh and the sharp cutting pain brought him smartly back to his senses.

The smug over-confident grin turned into the gritted snarl of determination. The long blade of the enchanted sword was perfectly balanced by the weight of the intricately carved hilt and the jewel-studded pommel that fitted so comfortably into his grip. Deftly he twisted the sword in his hand to take a sideways thrust at Guth-kak's sword-arm. It cut through the forearm as if the flesh and bone were nothing but lard, revealing the spongy marrow and severed arteries before a jet of blood burst forth and spurted across the parched earth. The dry ground sucked it up greedily. Without pausing, Hal turned the blade and swung it back towards Guth-kak's screaming throat. The Vaalakan writhed and shrieked on the ground, twisting away from Hal's stabbing blow, but not twisting far enough. The keen weapon sank into the Vaalakan's belly.

Guth-kak ceased to struggle and looked at the great sword with dismay and disbelief where it lanced him through his entrails, pinning him to the ground. His pale wolf-like eyes began to glaze as they trailed the edge of the blade up from his stomach to the hilt grasped in Hal's fist. He traced the youth's arms to his shoulder, and finally connected with those olive Belbidian eyes. Hal felt as if he touched on the man's soul as their eyes joined in comprehension.

'Belbidak, I am great warrior. Tell me your name, for I must know it for greeting my God.'

'I am Hal, son of Brungard, who is the father of the present Baron of Torra Alta,' the dark youth declared, feeling now nothing but sorrow as he beheld the bravery of his enemy.

'Your father was Baron of Torrak Altak?' Guth-kak choked over the words. 'Then I am slain by the son of a dragon. I am honoured, Belbidak: I die a hero.' His voice trailed away to a frail whisper and then in one last burst of anger his eyes glared at his vanquisher. 'But, I am to be avenged, son of dragon. The scouts be on my trail. They ride fast and hard . . . tomorrow you dies. Now finish me. No leave me here for carrion. Finish me quickly.'

Hal shook his head. 'No, Vaalakan, I will leave you to your countrymen. I do not need to kill you. You are harmless now.'

'Belbidak, Hal of Brungard of Torrak Altak, kill me now for shame of my defeat. Kill me.' Guth-kak's pleading eyes reached up and begged at Hal's soul.

The sword's power over him had passed. Hal could not bring himself to coldly murder this helpless man. 'No, your friends will come for you.'

'If I tells you there are men in Torrak Altak who plot against their Lord Branwolf the Dragon?'

'Liar! Liar! The men of Torra Alta are the truest in all the countries of the Caballan Sea.'

'No, there is traitors. I tells you if you promises to finish me quick. Traitors, I tells you.'

'You lying Vaalakan dog!' the youth roared with rage. The sword seemed to waken to new life in response. With a vicious snarl Hal hefted the great blade, which dragged through the Vaalakan's entrails, and plunged it through his ribcage. He felt the bones splinter beneath its point then drove it cleanly through the man's heart. The blue eyes remained stuck open.

Hal felt a quivering energy tremble through the sword. He had a haunting feeling that it was wailing in a powerful lament, relishing its victory, rejoicing in the bravery of the heart it pierced. Hal shuddered. It's the Devil's work, he thought fearfully. I cannot hear anything, yet I know it's singing. He placed his boot on the dead man's chest and heaved at the hilt of the sword until it yielded with a rush. The white blade was smeared with thick dark blood. Half of Hal's mind delighted in the glorious death; the other half was repelled by the evil cruelty and the barbaric, senseless desire to kill. Still the Vaalakan had tried to besmear the noble reputation of the garrison of Torra Alta; he deserved to die.

Quickly he wiped the blood on Guth-kak's bearskin cloak before hurriedly sliding it into the scabbard. He felt safer when the raw metal was hidden from view, though he was still transfixed by the magnificence of the hilt. The effigy of the two sparring dragons quarrelling over the ruby drew his eyes and he felt sure that the gem pulsed with energy. He pulled away his eyes and focused his mind on the immediate problem.

Spar and the women were in danger, that much was obvious. Scragg and Kullak were seasoned warriors, riding fast-moving trolls whereas Morrigwen, an old woman, was leading the Torra Altans, at an impossibly slow pace.

He stared at the ugly flat-nosed face of the troll. Its small, beaded eyes stared back at him, knowingly, and then it slid its fat tongue out between the yellow tusks and spat at him.

He needed the troll. Much as Caspar spoke to horses, Hal

raised his voice and crooned at it. 'Now there's a good boy. We just want to go for a little ride back into your homeland. You'd like that.'

The troll steadily backed off, dragging the loop of chain that dangled from the ring piercing its nose. With a forced smile covering his gritted teeth, Hal continued to keep the same sweet cajoling tone though his temper forced him to use bitter words.

'You foul stinking brute, no one's going to hurt you. Come to Hal, or I'll split your rotten skull with my sword.' He nearly managed to stamp his foot onto the end of the loop of chain but the troll jerked its head up and leapt backwards just a moment too soon. 'Nice little troll, let's see what I've got in my pocket,' the youth added, desperately searching for anything that might tempt the dumb brute. He found a few crumbs of oat biscuits which he held out on a tentative palm. The troll's nostrils quivered as it sniffed the air. It took one encouraging step forward before snorting in disgust and pulling away.

'Old-fashioned oatcake not good enough for you, eh, you disgusting hog-eyed brute?' Hal dropped his hand in despair. Scragg of course would find Guth-kak's slain body and seek revenge. Caspar and the women would be murdered and the moonstone captured by the enemy. Torra Alta would fall, just because he couldn't catch one stupid brute of a troll.

He stepped back and paused for thought. His eyes fell on the severed forearm that lay in the blood-soaked dust, the fingers curling up, already a sickly grey where the blood had drained from the sliced veins.

'You sick animal,' he crooned at the troll, as he stooped to pick up the dead hand. The warmth from the dead flesh churned his stomach as he proffered it to the troll.

The animal's pupils dilated. It stretched forward greedily with its neck. Hal waited until the hairless animal dragged one of its great claws a pace forward then enticed it little by little towards him. The animal's lips drooled for the severed hand. In one quick movement Hal snatched up the troll's chain and dropped the hand, quickly wiping his own hand on his breeches in an effort to remove the sense of contamination. The troll lunged for the hand, crunching it contentedly between its jaws. Long shards of blood-engorged saliva dripped from its yellow tusks.

'God could never have created a creature like you,' he told the brute in complete disgust. 'You are an abomination. The work of the Devil.'

Now, how do I get up, he thought, looking at the saddle perched on top of the brute's roached back. He certainly couldn't reach a leg up to the stirrups.

Firstly he arranged the chain so that it looped either side of the troll's neck to produce reins. The large ring piercing its nostril could be dragged one way or the other to turn the troll's head. It was crude but effective. Hal gripped a fistful of the hog-like bristles, which sprouted around the troll's back, dug his heels into the wrinkly hide around its knees and hauled himself up until he could reach the stirrup. With great difficulty he swung himself up and tried to seat himself on the saddle. Whereas a horse's back dips conveniently into a cup shape to cradle its rider, the troll's back arched upwards. Hal found himself precariously perched on the hump.

He picked up the loop of chain, pointed the troll's head northward to follow the course of the dried out Summer Melts, and jabbed the troll smartly in its sides with his heels.

The brute refused to move but continued to splinter the bones in its massively powerful jaws before sauntering towards the body of the Vaalakan. Hal could hear it licking its lips as it stretched its neck out towards Guth-kak's opened belly.

Savagely Hal wrenched on the chains, bringing the troll's head smartly up with a shriek of pain.

'Serves you right,' Hal warned the beast, yanking its head back round to point north. Vainly he stabbed his heels into its springy ribcage. When that failed he drew his sword and beat the animal hard across the rump with the flat of the blade. Still it refused to budge. Driven by frustration Hal's temper forced him to twist the blade and he stabbed the animal in the shoulder with the tip. At last the troll submitted to his will and lumbered forward.

Now that the youth had asserted his authority firmly over the beast it became more compliant, rolling forward in its awkward gait at surprising speed across the uneven terrain. Feeling faintly sick, Hal swayed from side to side on the loping troll. From the high ground above the riverbed, where the going was firmer, Hal followed the tracks of the two witches and Caspar which were visible below him. Where the riverbed was hard and gravelly the Torra Altan mountain horses had left no tracks but in the occasional puddles of mud there were clear hoofprints. That stubborn old woman should have listened to me he thought bitterly. They've left tracks that the Vaalakans will be able to follow for days, particularly since they left horse tracks which couldn't be confused with any troll-borne Vaalakan.

The sense of being possessed by the sword's power came back to him suddenly and he began to pray fervently for protection against its pagan magic. He looked at it with loathing, but still some small part of him worshipped and gloried in its power. He caressed the hilt and felt the tremor of confident energy.

'You have made me a man,' he whispered. If only Spar had seen the terrible might of the blow as I vanquished the Vaalakan warrior, a son of Morbak, he thought with pride. I have done a man's deed and slain one of the mighty amongst the enemy. He wondered how many sons Morbak had. The Vaalakans had ungodly customs, marrying several wives, and he might not have been a very important son, but all the same he had been no ordinary Vaalakan.

I shouldn't have killed him, though. He taunted me with those lies deliberately; he knew my fury would make me kill him.

The troll was wayward. With extreme difficulty and a great deal of cruel abuse with the sword, Hal managed to keep its head pointing roughly northward. However, it now refused to move at more than a lumbering walk as if it resented and defied the authority of its new owner.

'So I don't know anything about trolls; I admit it freely. But, dear Lord, don't punish me like this,' Hal raged out loud. He kicked furiously at the thick leathery hide as the brute slowed to a halt, throwing its head about wildly. Suddenly it lurched onto its hindlegs and the frustrated youth found himself tumbling backwards. He grappled for the coarse hairs but he was already too far off balance. Losing one stirrup, he fell with his other leg still trapped in the stirrup iron. He dangled there upside down, straining to free his foot, his head a bare six inches from the ground. For a moment the troll just snorted, then it bucked and reared so that Hal's helpless body was bounced against its flanks, whipped up and down like a lifeless scarecrow. The animal crashed back onto all four legs and bolted.

Whereas the slower gait of the beast had a curious rocking stride its bolt was flat and furious, faster than a horse's gallop. Hal could feel the ground hurtling past a few bare inches from his head. The baldric strapping the great broadsword to his chest slipped round and he could hear the scabbard jarring against the ground. He struggled to get a hand to it but upside down, flailing helplessly, he could barely control his arms. The leather on the baldric snapped and the sword slipped from his shoulder to clatter onto rocks. Within seconds it was far behind them. The saddle slipped. He felt it lurch round and he jerked his head up to protect his skull as his shoulders bounced along the ground. He felt the punch of the solid earth knock the wind from his lungs and then again the relentless bruising as he was pummelled with each stride. At last the stirrup leather snapped and he crashed to the ground, rolling over and over with the impact. He brought his legs up in a tight ball, tucked his head into his chest and covered his skull with his arms as he bounced and rolled across the bare rocky ground.

When finally he came to a rest he couldn't breathe. His clothes were shredded, the skin on the back of his hands was raw and bleeding and he hurt all over. For a moment he hugged his knees to his chest, rocking himself gently backwards and forwards and gritting his teeth against the pain. Then with brave determination he pushed himself up onto his shaky legs.

Immediately he sat straight down again and took a few more uneven breaths. His muscles were still too shaken to bear his weight. He felt as if he had been pulverized. Wincing, he stretched out his hands to inspect the damage.

Seen worse, he told himself firmly as he watched the beads of blood well up along the tenderized skin. I come from a frontier garrison; I can take a few knocks. His shoulders felt worse though. He reached backwards and felt his shredded clothing, but didn't dare investigate further. His head was spinning but it was only a moment before he remembered the sword. Urgently he scrambled to his feet and staggered southwards in an uncertain line, stumbling frequently.

The movement eased the pain a little. After a hundred wincing paces his head began to clear and he strode out more purposefully. The sword, he thought in panic. At the pace that troll was moving it could be miles behind me. He felt lonely and vulnerable without the weapon. The shadows grew steadily longer and the hollows in the bare ground became deeply defined with sunless black as he marched southwards away from his friends. Every line in the earth appeared like the sword and Hal ran expectantly from one to the other, hoping he had found the precious weapon. Gradually, as his head cleared he realized his heart was thumping with fear. Guth-kak had said that Scragg was on their tail and now he was marching straight towards him. He wondered how far behind the Vaalakan scouting party might be.

Just as the sun dipped behind the western horizon, Hal caught a flash of red over to his left. I could have marched straight past it, he thought with dismay, as he ran eagerly towards the brilliant red jewel embedded in the hilt of the sword. The last rays of the sun danced upon the blood-red ruby. He put his hand to the sword and felt a great surge of relief. The loneliness vanished and at last he felt safe again. He looked lovingly at the pattern of the two dragons fighting in mortal combat for the prize of the ruby. It was beautiful. He eased the blade from the scabbard. It slid out with a whisper as it brushed against the inner sheepskin lining, which protected and oiled the shaft, and he ran his finger down the blade. As sharp as a razor, he thought with relief, though the scabbard looked torn and battered from its pounding against the rocky soil.

He pressed his palm face down on the ground preparing to push himself up and stopped short. A tremor ran through his hand, the rhythmical thump, thump of something solid and heavy pounding across the ground. He froze solid, his ears intently alert. At first he thought it must be a troll. His heart leapt into his mouth as he decided that Scragg must be gaining on him already. He clutched the sword as he strained his ears to detect where the heavy pulsing vibrations came from. He could *hear* nothing. The rhythmical pounding that shook the earth could be moving at him from any direction. The only thing Hal was certain of was that it was moving closer.

As he once more pressed his palm to the ground to help push himself up, he was struck with the knowledge that the steady pounding vibrations were too heavy to be a troll. He rose slowly and now he could feel the tremor rising up through his feet, slow and laborious. At last he could tell where the vibrations were coming from as he heard deep laboured breathing and the sound of something large and scaly scraping over the bare rocks.

For a moment his mind was thrown into confusion as he fought to determine what possible type of animal was approaching. Maybe the Vaalakans possessed other extraordinary animals besides trolls. He could see a greyish white hump approaching in the dim twilight. It had a series of pyramidal points sprouting from its spine and he could hear its claws scraping along the ground. It blushed all over in the deep scarlet of the sunset. The barbed tail held aloft and swaying like a banner made it quite clear that it was the dragon from beneath the bowels of Torra Alta.

'I thought you were dead,' Hal breathed, not daring to move. 'I saw you being shot.'

Then he remembered the double beat of its two heavy hearts. Further, he knew the monster was blind but had an excellent sense of smell, using its tongue like a snake's to taste the air. He presumed that its sense of hearing was equally acute to make up for the lack of sight. If he moved would it hear him? The monster was drawing level with him now. The earth shook. Hal wondered whether he was shaking too. All that time, he thought, it must have been on our tracks.

It took the youth no time at all to realize what the monster was doing out here away from the safety of its lair. It was on the trail of the moonstone.

The dragon passed without raising its head from the scent on the dried up riverbed. Hal still didn't move. Although big and cumbersome, the creature moved with remarkable speed. Above its shoulders the stubby points of its atrophied wings flapped in frustration as if it wished to fly. Thank God it can't, thought the youth as he began to inch backwards away from the riverbed. He didn't know if he could overtake it, or even keep up with it, but whatever he did he would have to take a parallel route out of harm's way. He turned west and began a steady jog, counting out a thousand paces.

Pausing only long enough to give his parched throat a little water, he turned due north, hoping his internal sense of direction would be good enough. The stars told him nothing useful, he had never studied astronomy.

'Dear God, keep Spar moving northward,' he prayed. 'Don't let him turn round and look for me otherwise he'll come face to face with that monster.' He cursed the troll for the pains that stabbed through his shoulders as he ran. Then cursed himself for his own stupidity.

Branwolf will never forgive me if anything happens to Spar.

Chapter 21

The moonstone glowed, almost comfortingly. If I don't actually touch the orb it seems harmless if not benevolent, Caspar thought, inspecting his rapidly healing fingers.

Brid gripped his wrist and turned his palm over with a perplexed frown crimping her brow. 'It seems to be all in the mind. The cold and the pain is all imagined and so suggests these symptoms to you.' She shuddered. 'Vaal-Peor's influence is strong.'

She turned as if she was going to move further away and catch a few moments of sleep before the wan light of dawn spread across Vaalaka.

'Don't leave me,' Caspar whispered. 'Please don't, not out here in the dark.'

'Are you afraid?' she whispered half as a tease and half with sympathetic understanding.

'Of course I'm not afraid.' The youth bristled with indignation. 'I just wanted to know what you were going to tell me just before we saw the Vaalakan army.'

'I wasn't going to tell you anything,' she retorted stiffly.

'Yes, you were. You said I had a right to know about something.'

'Oh that,' she laughed casually. 'That was just to distract you. I thought if I hinted at something your curiosity would keep you from going back needlessly after Hal. After all we must be so close to our goal now: we can't go much further north. We can find Hal on the way back.'

'It didn't sound like you were making things up.'

'No? Well, that just goes to show how clever I am,' she teased. 'Can I leave now?'

'Please don't.'

'I'm only going to be over there, next to Morrigwen.'

'All right then, I admit it, I feel thoroughly spooked. I'm worried about Hal . . . and there's something terrifying about the woman in the moonstone. The cold she makes me feel, and the way she calls to me – specifically to *me* – as if trying to creep into my soul. I've never really been afraid before and I can't understand why I am now. All the fears are surely just in my mind, like the frostbite I got from the moonstone.'

'I can think of lots of good reasons why you are afraid,' Brid answered sympathetically. 'Most obvious of which is that massive army crawling towards our homeland. You've seen how barbaric they are. It's one thing to dream or read about war and another to realize the horrible consequences of it. Now you've seen the numbers for yourself, you know Torra Alta will be in trouble.'

'It's more than just that. Those things I know and can understand. We may have been at peace for three hundred years but the reason for Torra Alta's existence is to anticipate attack from the north and to defend Belbidia. Of course I'm afraid of the Vaalakans – but this isn't the same. I can fight Vaalakans, but I can't fight the fear inside me,' Caspar tried to explain. He looked nervously towards the cold light of the moonstone that seemed to be crying out to possess his soul.

The young Maiden smiled reassuringly. 'The image in the Druid's Eye isn't always real. Sometimes it searches your soul; sometimes it searches the past; rarely does it give a clear look into the present.'

'There was something malevolent in it that certainly felt real,' he argued. 'Someone or something that was after me.'

'It's more likely it was after the Mother and you felt the emotion through her. When you can look it in the face you won't be afraid of it anymore. However evil it is you will merely do what you have to do.'

'You know, you talk just like Morrigwen sometimes. You look so young and beautiful and yet you sound so old.' The words just sprang rashly from Caspar's tongue and the boy blushed with embarrassment. 'I'm sorry, I didn't mean it to sound like that. I didn't mean to offend. I mean –'

'Don't worry. I know what you mean. It's no wonder I talk like Morrigwen – all my life she's taught me to try and understand what is happening around me. She always wants me to learn more.' Brid fell silent for a moment and smiled towards the old Crone before whispering to the boy. 'She says that the understanding of life comes from the suffering of it, so sometimes her lessons can be a bit hard. Real knowledge and true understanding cannot be taught: they come only from suffering the cruel blows of fortune. That way you learn.'

'But you haven't lived long enough to suffer.' The boy's eyes were wide with indignant naïveté.

'Some people can live to a hundred and never taste one drop of life. They hug the safe waters of the shoreline, avoiding all the rocks and shallows, all the storms and dangers of being becalmed and never taste the sea on which they sail. They have no salt in their lives. Others are shipwrecked on tearing rocks but rebuild their vessels so that they can push out to become drenched in the briny waters again, tasting life to the full. You see, it's not the extent but the intensity of life that matters. Do you understand?'

Caspar looked deep into those forest-green eyes, falling into the fathomless pools of her wide pupils. Though unable to reach the mind of this mysterious creature, he empathized with her words. 'Yes, I do understand,' he said quietly and simply. 'I'm a hundred years older now than I was when I climbed down the well. I've experienced a lifetime of fear and excitement, so, yes, I do understand. But you seem to know so much, yet you don't seem as though you've *suffered*,' the young boy argued.

'If it showed, then I wouldn't have pushed my boat back into the sea: I'd have stayed shipwrecked. No, the thing that woke me up, slapped me in the face and said, here, feel this, was my mother's death.' She spoke in a flat voice as if keeping her emotions at bay.

'I know, you said before . . . I'm sorry,' Caspar murmured.

She shrugged. 'It wasn't just that she died – everyone dies – but it was how and why she died. You see she was a faithful wise woman, devoted to the Great Mother and generous with her knowledge of healing.'

'A priestess?' the boy queried.

'No. A simple wise woman, but very devout.' Brid's voice became low and trembled slightly. 'It was when the new religion finally came to the far north of Torra Alta. The priests became fanatical about converting not just the nobility but all the simple folk as well – the ones closest to the Earth, closest to the Great Mother.'

'That was a long time ago, though,' Caspar objected. 'How can you remember so far back? It was about the time my mother disappeared. I know because my Uncle Gwion told me that was when he decided to take up the cloth and shepherd the pagan people of my father's Barony towards the way of enlightenment. You couldn't remember so far back: you're too young.'

'Just because I'm shorter than you doesn't mean I'm younger. I was about four at the time but I remember it vividly.' She untwisted her braid and shook out her hair so that it floated over her shoulders. It seemed that the distraction soothed her nerves. 'But yes, it would have been about the same time.' Brid fell silent, contemplating the ends of her hair.

'Go on.'

'A rash of new priests descended on the village with the King's soldiers from the south. I remember them so clearly, tall thin men, with black tabards and the yellow and red crest of the wheatsheaf of Faronshire depicted on the front. They had round helmets and long staffs and it sounds stupid but I particularly remember their feet. They only had sandals on and it seemed so ridiculous out in the stony mountains.' Brid took a deep breath to control the tremble on her lips. She continued in a distant voice as if she was looking over the far horizon into another world. 'It's strange how such unimportant details stick in your mind, isn't it?'

'Yes, it is,' Caspar replied, just because it seemed the right thing to say.

Brid paused, then reluctantly continued. 'They were searching the huts and they found my mother, called her a witch, an evil black-magic witch, and a Devil-worshipper.' She looked up at the boy as if asking for mercy. 'But we don't even believe in the Devil. They dragged her out by her hair, tied her to a stake and burnt her. Burnt her alive. I remember the choking smoke . . .'

'Oh, Brid!'

Brid waved the boy's sympathy aside. 'She was so strong, so resolved. She didn't scream once. I cannot let her down now by running away and hiding. I can't pretend that nothing ever happened. I have to stand up and be counted as one who strove to protect what she stood for.' The campaigning confidence that had risen in Brid's voice faltered and she looked sadly to the ground. 'She was so brave . . .'

'Go to sleep, children,' Morrigwen groaned. 'It will be a tough ride tomorrow away from the riverbed. We must look into the stone properly tomorrow.'

'I'm not a child,' Caspar muttered.

'When you are as old as I am, men of forty seem like children. Now go to sleep.'

Caspar, despite his fears and his distress over Hal, slept comfortably. He felt the healing pulse of the moonstone, but the moment he awoke his dismay returned with abrupt rudeness as Brid's startled eyes looked into his face.

With her finger in front of her lips for silence, she said, 'Just get ready quietly. Something's following us.'

The small figure of Morrigwen was standing with her back to the moon. The crescent of light cupped her body as she stood against the craggy skyline and stared southwards. Caspar followed her gaze but could see nothing. The glow from the moonstone was gone, only gossamer shreds of light escaped from the woman's cloak as she furled the orb protectively in her garments.

'Is it Scragg and Kullak?'

'They won't be far behind,' Brid whispered. 'Not since Hal used the sword and you looked into the moonstone but there's something else.'

'What?'

'I don't know, but I can feel it through the bones of Mother Earth and it's coming straight for us. Quick, get ready.'

It took the youth a moment to gather his thoughts. At first he thought the witches must be imagining things but as he unconsciously put his hand to his chest he could feel the cold heavy weight of the hazel mandala. His heart began to thump.

Within minutes they were mounted and at first they had to pick their way through the rocky terrain using only the light of the waxing moon. To be sure of their footing, the horses kept their sensitive muzzles snuffling over the ground as, nose to tail, they walked in careful single file. The three companions pressed ever northward, winding along the disused ibex tracks that led up into the hills.

'We should have left a sign for Hal to show him which way we had gone,' Caspar pointed out.

'I know,' Brid replied regretfully. 'But he's very resourceful: you said so yourself,' she added more cheerfully, as if she were trying to keep their spirits up. The moon set before the thin light of dawn broke across the eastern horizon and in the utter blackness of the small hours of night, Morrigwen called a halt. 'We are in evil country here,' she whispered. 'The Mother is stripped bare of flesh and lies naked and exposed beneath our feet. Now even the blessed light of the Hand-Maiden is withdrawn from us. This is a godforsaken time and we should rest up and wait until the Great Day Star blesses the heavens with his omnipotent light. The creatures of evil have much sway at this time.'

She edged her horse on a little further until they found a boulder resting against the side of the mountain. It provided at least some shelter from the abrasive wind and prying eyes. Caspar lowered Wartooth from the saddle and they all crept behind the shoulders of the rock.

'I feel like a lizard,' Caspar complained, 'hiding like this under a rock. How long do we have to wait?'

'It'll be about two hours before dawn but if we try and move in the pitch of night we'll only injure ourselves. For now we must rest.'

They sat in silence for what seemed like an hour and Caspar's lids had just begun to press heavily on his eyes, nearly drawing him to sleep, when he sat up with a start. Somewhere below him he could hear a tumble of rocks, as if something had dislodged a boulder on the bare mountainside.

In the silence of the wasteland any noise seemed startlingly loud but there was no mistaking the heavy clumsy movements that had disturbed the ground. In this deserted world it was far too much of a coincidence for any creature to just happen to be following the same track as them. It had to be stalking them.

'We'll lead the horses,' Morrigwen decided. 'We'll just have to pick our way through the dark. We can't wait here to be discovered.'

They set off at a painfully slow pace, feeling their way, and all the time hoping that they weren't walking straight towards some unseen cliff or a troop of Vaalakans that might have split from the main column. Now more adept on his three legs, Wartooth hopped at Caspar's side. The boy was vaguely aware of the wolf following a little distance behind, sometimes vanishing silently to prowl the night, protecting her mistresses' backs as they stumbled on. The track led continually upwards which gave Caspar comfort. The higher he was, the safer he felt. Gradually he realized Morrigwen's reason for leading them this way: the higher they climbed up the west face of the valley, the quicker they would catch the light of dawn.

The din of another rockslide clattered out across the valley. This time it was no longer behind them but far below, near the valley floor.

'Whatever it is, it's having trouble climbing on these sharp rocks,' Caspar pointed out.

Morrigwen was beginning to wheeze and her pace was slowing. At last she turned east and stretched her arms out towards the dawn. The pearly light highlighted her features and combed through her long silvery hair, bringing colour to her flecked blue eyes. She stared down into the valley, trying to make out what was following them but the sun had not yet stretched out to bless the lower lying land. Caspar could hear it, though, scrabbling to climb the rocks that broke away under its weight. Here, the high ground above the valleys was deeply fractured as if the bones of the Mother had been lifted up and shattered in some great quaking upheaval.

The three Belbidians turned to weave through the pinnacles and crags, picking their way higher and higher to escape the creature stalking them. The horses found it increasingly difficult to traverse the splintered ground and they pecked the earth, frequently stumbling to their knees.

Caspar dragged on the reins of the dun who, with its ears laid flat back, struggled to find a secure footing. He could see a thin trickle of blood ooze from its hindleg and thought with dismay that the wound was opening up again. Wartooth, more agile than the ponies even minus one leg, was already perched on a rock ahead of them, as though impersonating an ibex. His hackles ruffled the back of his neck and he peeled back his lips to snarl down into the valley. Caspar followed his gaze and now, in the grey light, he could make out a large humped shape.

'In the name of the Mother,' Morrigwen breathed, 'what is it?'

Caspar felt his heart rising up into his throat. 'I thought the Vaalakans killed it,' he croaked.

Caspar's words were drowned by a roar like thunder that shook the ground and reverberated back and forth between the valley walls. The youth's legs were shaking.

'It wants the moonstone.' His voice was shrill and wavery. 'It was down in the caverns beneath Torra Alta with a hoard of treasure and when I took the moonstone it tried to steal it back. But the Vaalakans shot it with a crossbow. I thought it was dead!'

'I thought they were all dead,' Morrigwen whispered. 'Of all the Mother's creatures they are the most cruel.'

'A dragon,' Brid murmured. 'A real dragon. Spar, why didn't you tell us?'

'After the Vaalakans, I forgot about it.'

Too shocked to move, the three companions stared down at the monstrous creature. 'The Book of Names says that they can fly,' Brid murmured pessimistically.

'It doesn't have wings and it's blind,' Caspar whispered, 'but it's still got jaws and claws and a hound's sense of smell.'

The dragon appeared to recoil as sunlight stroked its back, glistening on the grey-white scales and glinting off the barbed spines that armoured its back. The monster shrunk down into a crevasse that dissected the rocky terrain, slithering away to protect its albino skin from the burning rays of even the northern sun.

Caspar found he could breathe at last.

'It seems,' Morrigwen spoke calmly, 'that we are safe up here on the ridge as long as it is daylight. Safe from the dragon, that is. But now after its roar everyone will know, shaman or not, where to find us. We can't go back to look for Hal now, not with the dragon behind us; we must go on and find the Mother as fast as we can before Kullak catches up with us. If we travel by day and find high ground like this at night, it won't be able to reach us.' She carefully unfurled the moonstone. 'It can't do any more harm to look at it now. We have to find where we are going without delay. This time, Spar, don't touch it before we are all ready.'

Caspar pulled the collar of his cloak up to shield him from the wind, tied the horses together and joined the two pagan priestesses.

Moistening his lips, which were dry with anticipation, he found that his palms were the opposite and sticky with sweat. He was so eager and yet still frightened to stir up the emotions trapped within the magic globe. Brid began the ceremony, creating a circle around them using pebbles and flints to form a barrier against evil forces. Reverently Morrigwen placed the moonstone and its attendant guardian into the centre of the circle – there was still no way of enticing the salamander away from the orb. The little creature's eyes burnt with a fiery white glow and it remained fixed in its crouched guard, occasionally stiffening the erect ruff around its neck.

'Won't that animal upset the magic?' Caspar enquired, suddenly very tense lest something should go wrong.

His words broke the concentration of the intent old woman and she waved him down irritably. 'Don't interfere. It's beyond your understanding.' She started her long chant.

Brid tried to soothe the boy. 'The salamander has only love for the fire. It knows no hate so it cannot twist the spell.'

At last the consecrated circle was prepared and Morrigwen straightened up to invoke the Goddess. Placed centrally in the circle, Caspar found the draw of the moonstone irresistible. His fingers itched to touch the white glow. Something, somewhere deep inside it was calling to him with intense yearning and inexorably he moved forward responding to the call.

But now more fearful of the esoteric nightmare trapped within the moonstone, Caspar listened to the Crone and resisted the unconscious pull of the orb on his mind.

'Brid, a circle of runes. Invoke the runes of protection. Use my sickle.' The Crone's withered fingers snagged at her cloak as she drew out her leather pouch of sacraments and fumbled for the golden tool. 'An enemy shaman may be able to sense the power of the moonstone but at least we can try and shield ourselves by containing the magic within a consecrated circle. Now, my boy,' she turned on Caspar, 'stay clear out of the way and try not to contaminate the spell in any way. At least your scathing friend isn't around.'

Caspar didn't retort or try to defend Hal. Age, he had always been taught, commanded respect; though he still wasn't entirely sure why. He watched as the two women scratched at the earth, scarring angular writing onto the bare rock while muttering strange words of prayer. When they had marked out a circle four feet across, they invited him to step into the consecrated shape.

Three pairs of hands simultaneously touched the incandescent moonstone and released its latent energy. This time Caspar felt only a shiver of the moonstone's former power and, to his relief, there was no pain, nor did he lose control over his mind. Instead, a sharp, itching tingle ran up his forearms and a bright light glowed in his mind.

'I can see the charred soil of the Dragon Scorch,' Brid whispered, not wishing to disturb the magic. 'The sleeping volcanoes and then beyond . . .'

'Into the tundra,' added Morrigwen with a shiver.

At first Caspar searched through a hazy mist and then his mind flew like a hawk towards the pleading cry he could hear across the bleak wilderness. For a second he was at Torra Alta before swooping along the banks of the Silversalmon and soaring up again over the canyon. He was climbing higher and becoming colder. He flew over the mountain peaks then swooped down the other side gliding effortlessly across the Boarchase and then over the Dragon Scorch. The spoilt ground raced past beneath him and his incredibly sharpened eyes caught specks of movement. Vaalakans! More than a score with their vile trolls. The beasts' noses skimmed the ground, snuffling in the dust for scent. Then ahead . . . His heart beat quicker for a second. There was Hal, trotting on foot urgently northwards just ahead of the Vaalakans. Hal, he was alive! Caspar's relief was overwhelming. Then his piercing eyes fell on the dragon. He swallowed hard. Hal was caught between two enemies.

The image of Hal was over in a flash. Again he was skimming over the ground before soaring upwards, high into the wind-tossed sky where the scudding clouds dragged at his wing tips. He swooped over the deeply fissured rocks of the most westerly volcano, looking deep into its dull lifeless crater with its crevasses and shafts that dived down into the bones of the earth. Over to the east beyond the volcanoes a distant column of ragged Vaalakans trudged in an endless snake. Mile upon mile of the enemy wormed through the desolate land on their way to gorge on the riches of Belbidia. Only the fortress of Torra Alta stood in their way.

The volcanoes were behind him now and he was climbing upwards into the thin air. The stark dun of the Dragon Scorch blended into the green of the steppes. On the northern fringes of the grassland, tongues of white ice ate hungrily southwards. He was following the line of the Summer Melts which at first were bare riverbeds but now merged into the forked tongue of white ice. It was cold and the air seemed too thin as if it could no longer support the feather-weight of his wings. The frozen Summer Melts led him northwards and upwards towards the deep tundra. The grey-blue bulge of a glacier protruded from the ice-cap to invade the steppes. Standing on the bare rocks that cradled the monstrous river of ice an insignificant cairn dared to look down on the domain of Vaal-Peor.

His wing tips felt leaden. He beat them furiously though the cold was like an ache deep in his bones. His muscles began to stiffen. The glacier beckoned him, called for him in lonely desperation, but he could go no further. A mist began to fall from the sky and it dragged at his wings so that he struggled for speed until he was crawling through the fog. Suddenly the image vanished.

The three Belbidians all looked at each other blankly, breathing hard after the exertion, whilst the salamander stared on with undaunted ardour into the heart of the moon-stone.

'I saw only a glacier cradled between black rocks,' Brid shrugged despondently. 'I had no sense of direction, though.'

'I saw the glacier too,' agreed Caspar, 'but I also traced the route past the volcanoes.' In incoherent bursts he detailed the rest of his vision.

Brid shook her head. 'I didn't see any of the Dragon Scorch, only sheets and sheets of grey ice, the surface all rippled and waved like the sea.'

Tears brimmed over the lower rim of Morrigwen's eyelids and flooded into the delta of wrinkles that fanned out from them. She had difficulty speaking as she choked on her words. 'I only saw her face.' It was some while before the bent old woman was calm enough to talk coherently through her sobs. 'She was calling for help.'

Caspar reached out a supportive hand to grip the woman's swollen knuckles. 'I saw where we must go. We'll go and find her now. We must head due north past the most westerly volcano and head straight towards the tundra.'

Through the long thirsty march, Caspar could think of very little but the image of the glacier and Hal. His uncle was alone in the northern desert, struggling to catch up with them, caught between the two terrors of Kullak and the dragon. They marched from dawn till dusk picking their way through the splintered scree or scraping across the sweeps of pumice whose moulded undulating shapes had no natural valley or track to ease their progress.

When the sun deepened to the blushed apricot of sunset they climbed higher into the mountains, seeking out an inaccessible cave where they could shelter beyond the reach of the nocturnal dragon. But the ankle twisting boulders lying one on top of the other made it impossible for the hoofed beasts to climb any higher. The safety of the black-mouthed cave lay beyond their reach.

Caspar yanked the dun's bridle. 'Come on, boy. You can do it.' The animal stood quivering with its head high and its eyes rolling as it struggled against the reins.

Nothing he said or did could persuade the limping horse to risk another step across the unstable scree and at last he dropped the reins in resignation. Brid and Morrigwen had fared little better with the other horses.

'We'll catch them easily enough tomorrow.' There was an edge of annoyance to the old Crone's voice as if the taste of defeat were sour on her tongue. 'Take their packs off, Spar, and give them a handful of grain and some water in the pans. They'll come straight to us tomorrow for some more.'

Reluctantly, Caspar slipped the bridle off the dun's ears. They stored most of their luggage and the horses' tack in a small crevice sheltered by a rock. Brid and Caspar divided the food and water between them, taking the provisions higher up into the safety of the cave above the scree. Though they had heavy burdens to carry the two young Torra Altans made the cave long before Morrigwen, who clutched at the moonstone. The salamander's warty head could just be seen poking out from one of her sleeves. Brid skipped down the scree slope, leaping from one pointed boulder to the next before she reached the old woman and offered her hand.

'My old bones,' the hag complained between wheezing breaths. By the time she reached the cave where the auburnhaired youth was resting alongside the deer-hound, she was grumpily snapping at both her young companions.

'Didn't you think to light a fire, boy?' she growled. 'Or are you above such things, being an issue of one of the great Barons of Belbidia.'

'I – There's – No, I don't think that!' He looked at her with hurt stinging his eyes. 'I don't think I'm above anything. It was only fate that made me the son of a nobleman. There's no wood, so I couldn't make a fire.'

He pressed his back against the cold hard stone of the cave and looked resentfully at the hunched shape of the old woman. Of course his father had power, authority, wealth; but Branwolf told him that these things should only be used for the good of the Barony and its people – never for personal gain. Caspar fervently believed in his father's principles and he was angered that other people might see him as greedy and idle. Even Hal was jealous of his power.

But Morrigwen didn't really mean what she said, he was sure. She was just being crotchety because of her anxiety, he decided. She was breathing heavily, squatted down on a rock with her head slumped forward. Wisps of silver-white hair caressed her cheeks but when she looked up her eyes were dark and sunken with black stains shading the crêpey skin beneath the lower lids. Her sky-blue eyes flecked with white stared at him in that uncomfortable way that seemed to creep under his skin and prod his inner soul.

Irritably flicking back his auburn fringe, which was now dulled by the wind-blown dust off the plains, he returned her gaze and his irritation was instantly swept aside as he felt her deep pain. 'We will find her.' The words from the small youth, though full of sincere determination, sounded hollow in the vast emptiness of the Dragon Scorch.

He didn't remember falling asleep but he woke up with a start, instantly alert, his heart pounding against his ribcage. A thin bony hand clamped over his mouth and the old Crone's voice crackled in his ear in the barest of whispers. 'Don't make a sound. Keep perfectly still.'

At first he could hear only the drop of a pebble and then the tinkle of shards of rock sliding over the large boulders of scree. His heart felt as if it were beating in his throat and he swallowed hard. The northern desert was almost completely devoid of animal life and any unnatural noises out there could only be a warning of danger. Worse, Caspar could feel the tremor as some great monster heaved its massive weight across the ground. A crash of rocks splintering on the scree slopes below reverberated across the valley as the great beast climbed higher and even its laboured breathing seemed to fill the cave. Great claws rasped against the rocks, trying to gain a purchase. Caspar's heartbeat raced with hope: he could hear the crashing rocks dragging the beast downwards. It was scrambling for a foothold but the rocks were falling away as fast as the beast climbed.

Finally a great roar drowned the sigh of the wind, like rolling thunder hammering against the crags. The note finished with a fluttering scream as the air-bladder beneath the beast's throat deflated. For a moment there was silence, then clapping against Caspar's ears came the hammering thunder of falling boulders as the scree slope gave way beneath the monster's weight and avalanched towards the valley bottom. A cloud of dust blew into the cave and the boy buried his face in his cloak to avoid choking.

They sat in stunned silence for several minutes. It was too dark for the youth to see his companions but he felt their proximity. Their steady rhythmical breathing was his only comfort throughout the long hours as they waited for dawn. When the sun finally rose it slid reluctantly over the eastern horizon and crept lethargically across the smooth-worn bedrock of the cave and tentatively felt for their skin.

Brid had her back to him. Looking out across the valley she greeted the sunrise with upheld arms. Her hair was loose and fell in waves about her shoulders. She looked at peace, totally confident and natural, greeting the sun like she had done every morning of her life. Caspar frowned for a moment. How had she coped with the harshness of the wilderness and sleeping rough in the cold bare cave? He thought of the young serving girls in the castle and how they would have panicked out here. It was completely impossible to imagine any noblewoman even getting here but, if they had, they would have been utterly distraught. Brid was a pagan and a peasant but she out-shone every high-born heiress in the realm because of the nobility of her soul. She turned and Caspar blushed. Her smile was more warming than the sun.

'Look at this,' she exclaimed, turning to point down to the scree below.

The landscape was different from the evening before. Smooth, exposed rock rather than broken scree now led up to the cave where the rubble had sloughed off the mountain. All the loose debris now lay heaped up, forming angular shapes at the foot of the slope.

'It raked all the scree away,' Caspar pointed out, fully aware that he was stating the obvious. 'We were only just high enough by the looks of things.' The thought made him shudder.

'Come on. We'd better get going. We need to find the horses and choose a better spot for tomorrow night, where it won't be able to reach us.' There was no use panicking over what *might* have happened and Morrigwen's calm voice reflected this view.

The recontoured descent was hard because there was very little purchase to be gained on the smooth rocks now that the scree had tumbled to the bottom. Caspar gripped Morrigwen's arm, carefully lowering her from one sure foothold to the next. Stubbornly she refused to thank him, but the youth didn't mind her mannerisms anymore. He was, however, shocked at her lightness. She can have no more flesh on her than a half-starved child, he thought, almost in fear that she would wither away completely and crumble under the pressure of his grip.

Out of breath, they reached the large boulder that hid their luggage. Caspar froze for a second as he saw the deep scour marks where the dragon had raked at the ground, digging for their belongings. It had obviously become tired of the pots, platters and harnesses, finding neither the prized orb or anything edible, and had been distracted by the promise of a greater prey.

The two cream horses, with their backs to the wind and their manes and tails streaming forward, stood out clearly against the fawn background. After several moments searching the shadows and darker shapes of the rocks, Caspar finally focused on the blue-grey colouring of the smaller mare but the dun was still nowhere to be seen. He hoped it was still camouflaged against the dull brown background. With Brid at his side and a fistful of grain he advanced at a casual pace. The three horses shied away, jittering and dancing with wild rolling eyes, like young fiery fillies and not at all in keeping with the normal sedate nature of a mountain breed.

'I don't like this.' Caspar spoke softly to the girl, pointing to the next hillock beyond. 'There's something over there.'

They buckled the bridles onto the three horses, tethering them to the narrow point of a boulder before pacing anxiously towards the suspicious brown curve that had caught Caspar's eye.

They scrambled over a small hillock and looked down on the dun horse. The ground around it was scoured with the marks of a scuffle but it couldn't have lasted long. There was nothing that they could do for the wretched animal: it was indeed dead.

Caspar walked back towards Morrigwen, leaving Brid to pay her last respects. He had tugged at her arm, pleading her to come away and stop torturing herself with the sight, but her eyes had stared at him with ice-cold determination. He had backed off without arguing.

The little old woman took the news with sombre dignity. 'May the Mother take him back into the womb of Annwyn,' she prayed. When Brid finally rejoined them her cheeks were flushed and she was dabbing at her eyes. After a moment she breathed deeply.

'I learnt to ride on that old dun.' She cleared her throat again pretending not to cry.

Morrigwen was characteristically sharp and shook the girl by her shoulders so that her long brown hair tossed in ripples. 'It's the way of nature, girl. Death is part of the cycle: life, death and rebirth. Face up and stop weeping.'

Bravely the young girl straightened her face and forced a thin apologetic smile at her companions. 'Part of the cycle,' she murmured, as if reassuring herself.

'We have more important things to worry about,' the old Crone reminded them. Ahead of them now, the ridge of hills began to slope steeply down towards the three volcanoes. After dividing the dun's pack between the three remaining horses they headed for the most westerly volcanic peak. Caspar kept casting looks over his shoulder.

'Where does it go during the day?'

'I should think it finds a ravine or cave big enough and hides from the sun. It must be good at hiding; after all, it's remained completely unnoticed, buried in the roots of the Yellow Mountains all this time and surely it must have come out into the open from time to time to forage for food.'

'Do you mean that there could be more of the monsters in the Torra Altan caverns?' Caspar asked in dismay.

Morrigwen pondered for a while, twisting a length of silver

hair that had worked free from the braid. 'It's unlikely that there'd be just the one.'

Brid raised an eyebrow as if prompting the old Crone to explain her reasoning.

'The Book of Names maintains that a dragon can live for three hundred years, so there must have been at least four generations of them living down there for one still to be alive today.'

'Is the Book of Names always right?' Caspar asked.

'Always!' The reply was emphatic and Morrigwen's thunderous face reminded the youth of his older uncle, the chaplain. Once as a small innocent, ever-questioning child, he had asked how, if no one had ever seen the one true God, did they know that the omnipotent deity – the words meant nothing to the child – lived on a cloudy throne in the heavens? The chaplain had been appalled. There had been no reply, only punishment.

'Well, if you're right,' Caspar sighed, oblivious to the old woman's indignation, 'then there is probably a whole tribe of white lizards, toothed and hungry, still waiting to reclaim Torra Alta.' Miles from home and virtually in the clutches of Morbak's troops he found the thought deeply distressing.

They rode on in silence. Caspar looked bleakly at the black earth ahead, punctuated only by storms of dust that whisked across the surface. His cheeks smarted with windburn and he wished he had a beard to protect his skin.

Far to the east he could see a cloud rising up from the ground, churned up by the passage of thousands of Vaalakan feet marching on Belbidia. They had no shelter now between here and the volcanoes, though at least the enemy column trudged past to the east of the Black Devils while they aimed to pass to the west.

'Water the horses,' Morrigwen ordered, stiffly nodding at the half-empty canisters that weighed down the packs. 'We must ride fast to cross this plain before sundown and stay ahead of the dragon. At least the enemy is making enough dust to hide us from their own eyes.'

Chapter 22

The edge of the quagmire was riddled with troll tracks. Branwolf looked at the network of spoors in dismay. It was clear from the tracks plunging into the water that they had tried and failed to reach the ramshackle hut on the marsh island, turning west and east to find a way round. He slid painfully from Conqueror's back. The night had given him no rest. His wounds leaked a clear liquid and one gash on his side had split open again seeping watery blood, but it was the sense of something trailing him that had kept him alert all night.

He stooped down to examine the tracks. It was some while before he found the crescent cut of a horse's hoofprint in the sodden ground. Troll tracks had nearly obliterated any other markings. The horses had clearly galloped straight into the quagmire whereas the trolls had been stopped. He tried to suppress the superstitious feeling that something magical had happened.

It was a long time since he had explored so deep into the Boarchase and he would never forget this particular hut and the quagmire. He had been here before, looking for Keridwen. Now, he prayed he would not be met with the same heart-breaking disappointment. Surely if his son and half-brother had made it to the safety of the old woman's hut he would shortly find them. The confusion of old pagan pathways through the forest would protect his son from the enemy. He didn't care if the hand of the Devil played a part in saving Caspar: he only hoped that shortly he would find him safely hiding on the other side of the stagnant bog. He stumbled towards the trees and sought a staff-length branch amongst the undergrowth. He knew there was a way to cross that treacherous bog curling around the hut. It was part of an ox-bow that led off the Sylvan Rush River, now stagnant and hungry to swallow any intruder into its gurgling depths.

He winced as he plunged the staff into the fathomless mire. The effort made him cough. Blood-specked spittle ran from his mouth.

'Dear Lord, give me strength,' he prayed.

Somehow he knew that his son must be riding one of the horses that had crossed the mud. He estimated that at least eight troll tracks led into the mire and the Vaalakans would not have bothered to pursue mere woodsfolk. They had to be hunting Spar and Hal.

His bones jarred as he struck solid rock beneath the surface of the mud.

'Found it,' he declared to his horse. 'Now it's a bit of a leap until we reach the causeway but you can do it, old fellow.'

He backed the horse up and leaned heavily against Conqueror's flanks, breathing hard before he struggled up into the saddle. He was glad now that he hadn't taken Firecracker, thinking that his son's colt wouldn't have trusted him enough to take the leap of faith into the bog. Conqueror was so well schooled that he would do anything his master asked of him. It took years to train a horse to such a level. If an animal had to charge into the midst of a roaring battle with the smell of blood and the squeal of dying horses thick in the air, it had to learn to trust its master beyond its own instincts.

Branwolf had marked with his staff the spot where he had struck solid rock and now spurred on his black destrier. The horse threw his head high in nervous alarm but plunged in faithfully. The mud splattered high up around his flanks, coating his master's cloak in a thick brown sludge. With one last effort Branwolf kicked him on harder and they leapt for the solid bank on the far side.

He looked at the hut disconsolately. There was no sign of life and no answer to his call. Had the old woman, as Elaine had called her, really found the boys and taken them to safety, even though they were brought up to lead their country into the worship of the New Faith?

He dismounted awkwardly, trying to put as little strain as possible on his wounds, and tethered his horse. When his eyes first explored the interior of the simple hut he was disappointed. It was deserted, apart from some bones. But soon he discovered the dark steps leading down into the pit beneath the earth. Hurriedly, he improvised a torch with some twigs, which he lit after several attempts with a flint. Then in some trepidation he led Conqueror into the hut. Faced with the uneven steps plunging downwards into darkness, the destrier halted abruptly, snorting his displeasure, but Branwolf tugged the reins firmly, coaxing the horse down. Fortunately the steps were broad and shallow and progress at last was made to the last one, after which their descent levelled to a smooth slope.

When the ground levelled off, Branwolf raised his torch and found himself faced with five separate tunnels. He struggled with rising doubts of ever finding his way until he discovered that the ground in one tunnel was firmer and more compacted, as if trodden with far greater regularity than the others. With satisfaction, he found a charred fragment of brushwood that must have fallen from a burning torch. Allowing himself a brief smile of self-congratulation on his tracking skills, he pursued his course. Despite his firm belief in the new God and his promise to the King that he would uphold the New Faith, he still had a nagging suspicion that the old woman really did possess some power. How else could she have managed to outwit the Vaalakans? The thought comforted him since it meant she could protect Hal and Caspar and lead them to safety.

Torra Alta was once dedicated to the Goddess of the Old Faith, he knew, and he recalled there was a belief that the castle would fall if Belbidians abandoned her. Of course, as Gwion had said, it was the Devil that made him fear such superstitious nonsense. He shook himself.

His solemn thoughts were abruptly curtailed by a soft shuffling coming from the dark of the tunnel behind him. But soon he and his horse emerged from the tunnel into the seclusion of another grove, where a second hut stood. Surely if they had made it to the hut, his boys would have found safety from the Vaalakans.

With hopes swelling rapidly inside him, Branwolf flung the hide curtain of the hut aside and ducked under the low mantle. He knew the hut would be empty, because Wystan had said that the old woman had gone, but surely somewhere she should have left a message or be hiding close by. He turned slowly, letting his eyes sweep around the room. The cauldron was cold but there was still some broth in the bottom. The ashes were dull and cool and a heap of rugs lay crumpled in one corner as if someone had thrown them off after a night's sleep. The dwelling gave the impression that its occupants had only meant to slip out for a few minutes to fetch kindling or water but for some reason hadn't returned.

He looked deeper into the hut and shuddered as he realized he was looking at the sacraments of paganism and Devil-worship. He murmured a prayer of protection for his soul as he stepped beyond the cauldron to where the circle and the oak table carved with the pentagram declared this place sacred to the Old Faith. His frustration grew when he could see nothing amongst the chalice and candles that could tell him where the old woman had gone. Where would she go to hide from the Vaalakans? Surely to the castle, if she could, but perhaps that hadn't been possible because of the Vaalakan warriors in pursuit. He drummed his fingers on the table, letting his eyes search for anything that would tell him what to do. The movement rattled a pattern of short divining bones that lay in a disorderly pattern and he looked at them in disgust. He hoped they hadn't once been part of some horrific sacrificial rite. As he examined the table more carefully he saw just the slightest dusting of yellow powder. He dabbed his fingertips in it. Sulphur. It must have been carried in Hal and Spar's clothing. They must have been here. He looked again at the bones, wondering vainly if they formed some sort of message. The bones bounced into the air and clattered back down again as he beat his fist onto the oak board in his frustration.

'God damn you, old woman, where have you taken them?'

He had the creepy feeling that he was blaspheming against a powerful presence who now was frowning at his words. His own disconcertion made him certain that the two boys would not have stayed in that pagan sanctuary a moment longer than they had to. He could almost feel the spirits of the Old Faith wishing him ill, berating him for allowing the construction of the new cathedral and for permitting Rewik's Inquisitors into his lands. Nevertheless, Gwion had rightly taught the boys to fear the old ways and they would have fled the hut as soon as they could.

He strode out of the dwelling towards the grove of thirteen trees to examine the ground. Four sets of hoofprints tracked due north. This had to be Hal and Spar's trail! Why had they gone north? He couldn't believe it. They must still be running from the Vaalakans, unable to turn back towards Torra Alta, unless . . . unless the old witch meant to harm his son in revenge for his own actions in allowing Torra Alta to be converted to the New Faith. Branwolf sighed. He had been young when the King had ordered his Inquisitors into Torra Alta and he had not realized how far Rewik's fanaticism would go. He thought that the task of the holy soldiers was to convert not coerce. He had forbidden the brutal methods of the Inquisitors to be used again in his Barony though much damage had already been done. While other barons allowed the black knights to patrol their lands he had forbidden the burnings. Instead he encouraged men like Dunnock to preach the word of the New Faith to the outlying regions of his Barony where some of the simple folk still clung to the faith of the Mother Goddess. Dunnock was such an ineffective little man, so dull and unnoticeable like the plain brown bird he had been named after. At least he wouldn't demand burnings when he came across sites of pagan worship as he preached through the Boarchase.

He looked at the tracks leading northwards and decided

that he would at least eat the broth left in the cauldron before setting out. The food was cold but wholesome and seemed to give him extra strength. He was still wondering whether it was laced with fortifying herbs when he rode beyond the grove and into a bed of crisp leaves that muffled his horse's footfall. The forest was quiet except for the song of a greenfinch and the rattle of a woodpecker drilling through the bark of a sweet chestnut. He even saw the little known gold crest, a minute bird smaller by a finger-width than even the wren. The world of nature seemed so peacefully oblivious of the turbulent strife of human beings. How could they sing so lightly when he had so many heartbreaking worries?

He rode anxiously on for half a league, the frown on his lined forehead deepening as the hoofprints and the trail in the leaves continued due north. The snap of a dry twig directly behind him made him stiffen. He flicked his head round but could see nothing. He screwed up his eyes trying to pierce the shadows and was about to relax when he again heard the crack of a splintering twig. Carefully he raised his bow. He cursed himself for his lack of caution. He had been so busily worrying about his son that he had forgotten to take any precautions against any Vaalakan spies following him. Conqueror's ears pricked up as if he had seen something. Branwolf followed the horse's gaze to where a flicker of movement was caught in a beam of sunlight – and the cuff of a sleeve was just visible through the tangled stems of a bramble.

'Show yourself or die where you stand,' Branwolf snarled along the length of the arrow-shaft that was aimed directly at the swaying shape lurking in the shadows.

There was a dismayed yelp. 'Oh please, Sir, I didn't mean any harm.' Pip's excited face appeared in the light. 'I saw the crest on the hilt of your sword.' The young boy dropped extravagantly to his knees. 'My Lord, only the Baron himself would carry such a sword and I had to follow you.'

Looking at the young boy who was supplicating himself before him, Branwolf didn't know whether to laugh or cry.

'Oh get up, Pip. What are you doing here?'

'Sir, I followed you.'

'That, my boy, is obvious, but why?' He sighed in frustration at being encumbered with the young boy. 'Pip, just go home.'

'But, Sir . . .' he wailed. 'I don't know the way and I followed to help you. I can't go home. You're not well enough to be riding alone, Sir.'

'I can't look after you, child,' the Baron tried to explain gently, not knowing what to do with the boy. 'Now, you must go home.'

The boy looked tired and was stumbling on his bare feet. 'I'm lost and, my Lord, you need help.'

Yes, I need help but not from you, thought Branwolf as he looked despairingly at the boy. There was nothing else to do but pick up the child and put him behind his saddle. He couldn't possibly leave him to wander alone in the forest.

'As soon as we come across somewhere you recognize, young lad, you're taking yourself off home. How could you have followed me like that? Your parents will be worried sick.'

A flash of guilt swept across the boy's grubby face but it was quickly replaced by the intense excitement of riding on a war-horse behind the great Baron himself. He clung on tightly and Branwolf had a stab of sorrow as this Pip reminded him of Hal and Spar in their younger days. Impressionable, reckless youths all three of them.

'Where are we going?' Pip asked, delightedly gripping on to the Baron's cloak.

'*We* are not going anywhere. You are coming along only until we cross a forest trail. *I'm* looking for my son.'

Despite his frustration with the young boy, Branwolf was actually glad of the company and since the boy was so small, he hardly slowed them down at all. The child chattered on without the slightest hint of self-consciousness, asking after the castle and the soldiers.

'How many Vaalakans can a castle archer kill in a day?' he asked for the third time.

'Not enough,' Branwolf sighed, 'not nearly enough.'

'Can I really come to the castle and train as an archer?'

'Yes,' Branwolf said abstractedly as he followed the snaking trail that curled continually northward. They can't go much further north he thought. We must nearly be at the edge of the Boarchase now. They had been travelling through the woods for almost an hour and Branwolf was wondering if they would ever cross a trail so that he could send the woodcutter's son home. Suddenly he stiffened as a cry startled the forest.

'Pip!' The cry was long, low and distant. 'Pip, answer us. Where are you?'

'Pip! Pip!' Another higher voice joined in the clamour.

Branwolf reined in. 'Well, lad, at least that's one worry less. Over here!' He raised his voice so that the deep mellow tones boomed through the forest. 'He's over here.'

Wystan and a fellow woodsman, still younger than Hal by the look of him, crashed breathlessly forward through the trees on heavy draught horses. The men slapped the ends of their reins back and forth across the sweating necks of their mounts as they laboured to maintain a decent pace.

'Pip, in heaven's name! What has got into you, boy?' Wystan was too dumbfounded however to scold his child harshly. He looked up uncertainly at Branwolf on the heavy destrier. 'I, we found the jewelled dagger wrapped in a cloth with the Baron's seal stamped on it.' There was still a hint of suspicion in his voice though now it was tinged with awe.

Branwolf took a deep breath ready to explain himself but he was cut short.

'But, Pa, he is the Baron. He's Baron Branwolf himself. I saw the crest on his sword.'

'Pip, that's enough,' Wystan ordered, reddening.

'My Lord,' he turned to Branwolf, 'I am your humble servant. Pray, why did you not tell us who you were?'

'In the helpless state you found me, ragged and wounded, I doubted that you would believe me. I feared you would leave me as a madman to die in the woods.'

The thick-set woodsman nodded. 'I would leave no man to die, but I see what you mean, my Lord.' Wystan looked straight into the Baron's eyes with level understanding. 'And I know that no wounds can stop no man looking for his lost child. We can't waste no more time. You ain't well, my Lord, and if Elaine knew I'd abandoned you to your task alone she'd never let me back in the home, such as it is. I'll come along as your servant. Pip, you get on back home to your Ma now. Go with young Hubert.' He turned to the younger man. 'You'll explain what's happened. I must go with the Baron. We're at war and it's every Belbidian's duty to stand by their lord.'

Branwolf was too exhausted to argue. Pip slid reluctantly down from the saddle, sulkily scrabbling up behind the mousy-haired youth. Wystan gave him a fatherly slap on his back and turned his draught horse to follow behind Conqueror's swishing tail.

'I was so worried for Pip out there in the forest alone,' he said. 'You must be worried sick about your own son, Sir.'

Branwolf nodded. Originally he hadn't wanted to take any of his men with him out into the Yellow Mountains, feeling that they would slow him up, but now he was grateful to have Wystan. His injuries had slowed him down considerably and he still found it hard to draw a bow. He had to admit that he might need the man's help.

At last the trail led them to the northern edge of the forest. 'I thought we would have found them by now.' Branwolf's voice was heavy with disappointment. As they rode through the woods, he tried to fit the pieces of the puzzle together. Talking through the events helped him clarify the picture in his own mind so he explained as much as he could to Wystan. 'The old woman would have taken them to safety, surely?'

'Unless, as you say, she's trying to get her revenge on you as the Baron who has encouraged the New Faith, but I don't think so, my Lord. Sure she's a witch and, as Curate Dunnock says, a witch is spawned from the Devil; but I don't think she's one for doing harm. Now El, she's all goodness in her heart but she still hankers after the old ways. She said they used to light fires when she was a little girl and dance in the moonlight. She says they were times of great happiness but now the old country customs have been lost to us all. She even called May by one of the old names.'

'But May isn't an old name,' Branwolf objected.

'No, no, I'm not explaining myself right. El called her Merrymoon when she was first born, after the month in the old calendar. She said it was the most pretty month in the year. But the curate now, that funny little man though he is, he's taught me much about doing what's right by my neighbour and fearing the word of the Lord. He says we ought to be lifting ourselves up above the base animals unlike the pagan ways where they dance naked by the fire which is full of sinful lusts.'

Branwolf had a momentary flash of Elaine dancing naked before the fire and coughed to try to rid himself of such a sinful thought.

'Well, Curate Dunnock said we must call her May, since Merrymoon is a pagan name.'

Branwolf laughed. Mountain people were slow to change and even he himself preferred the names he had been brought up with.

'El objected at first but I said it was only right that we should do what the old man of God said. But I think to be honest Merrymoon was such a mouthful to say that in the end she gave in and said we'd just call her May for short. May,' he sighed. 'Apart from Elaine of course, she's the most wonderful thing that ever happened to me. Pip's my son and he's a grand though rather wayward lad, but he'll be a man one day and able to look after himself, but May . . . She's so small and caring and my heart bursts with pride for her. You just want to hold her and protect her from every tiny thing.'

The woods were beginning to thin now and both men had their eyes keenly fixed on the ground looking out for tracks.

'That's a lot of boar and – oh blessed saints, not again. Look, Sir. Troll,' Wystan exclaimed, halting in front of the claw marks that raked the ground.

Branwolf's heart plummeted. 'They've found them again,' he said flatly.

'Not necessarily,' the solid woodsman tried to sound reassuring. 'They might have found the tracks but that don't mean they've caught up with them.'

'No, you are right.' Branwolf smiled weakly. He drew strength from the woodsman's solid approach to life. There was something reassuring about the way he no longer called him sir or my lord all the time. Instantly that made him more of a companion rather than a subordinate. A Baron's position was one of lonely isolation and he had always been glad that Caspar would have Hal there for support when he eventually became Baron. Then, of course, Branwolf would no longer be there to guide his son, but at least his half-brother would be a companion.

'Look at this. There's a great heap of bones. Boar by the look of it, every bit of them gnawed.'

'Keep looking for the hoofprints,' Branwolf instructed. 'Whatever happened here has virtually covered Spar's tracks. We've got to watch out for when they turn left or right because they can't keep going north.'

'They do,' Wystan said quite firmly as he peeled himself off the broad bare back of his draught horse and hunched over to carefully examine the tracks. 'The hooves are still pointing due north.' He raised his eyes at the bare cliff that gloomily overshadowed the Boarchase valley. 'Why would they be going into the Dragon Scorch and that evil land of Vaalaka?'

Branwolf didn't have any answers. 'We won't know till we've caught up with them.'

'We haven't got any food or water though,' the woodsman despaired. 'We won't survive in the Scorch without water. They say it's like the dragons had breathed their fire across the land and it's naught but burnt black rock.'

'Volcanoes,' Branwolf corrected. 'There's three volcanoes, the Three Black Devils, that have poisoned the land and it's nothing to do with dragons.' He was already wheeling Conqueror back into the forest. 'We'd better get some food and water before we go.'

It was dusk and the deer had moved into the glades for

their evening feeds. The sun slanted through the trees making patterns on the ground where it wove through the network of interlocking branches. Branwolf had edged downwind of the glade and gestured to Wystan to keep quietly behind him. The speckled fawns were almost invisible in the dappled light. It was only when they moved forward to nip the tops off a sapling growing at the roots of a hawthorn that their outline became clearly visible. Branwolf selected a hunting arrow, slotted it to the bow and kept his eye clearly focused on the chest of a young buck. The animal hit the ground with a heavy thud before the rest of the herd had any notion that there was a predator so close. Their heads and ears pricked up for an instant of alarm before turning as one and fleeing for the cover of the forest.

Drawing the bow had opened up a gash under his left arm and Branwolf felt dizzy from the exertion. He wasted no time in arguing when Wystan ordered him to rest by an oak while he gutted the buck. Cutting through the hide of a big animal like that was exhausting work and he knew that he wouldn't have the strength to do it.

'When you get to the bladder cut it out carefully. It's the best water container we'll get. We can do something with the hide as well but the bladder will be more water-tight.'

It took Branwolf several attempts to split the bone with one of his knives but at last he managed to shave off a sliver thin enough to form a needle. On his third attempt he punctured a slit in a suitable place for an eye and helped Wystan shred sections of gut to form thread. They charred hunks of meat over the crackling fire while Wystan worked nobly through the night with his coarse hands shaking as he tried to thread the needle.

'How do the women do this so easily,' he muttered.

'Here, let me have a go,' Branwolf offered, stirring from his sleep.

'No, you rest. You need as much rest as you can get.'

'I've been watching you try to thread that and it's your twelfth attempt. Now give it to me.' Branwolf fared little better but his hands were not as tough and calloused as the woodsman's.

When Branwolf awoke he found Wystan asleep with several bladder-shaped skins stitched together from the buck's hide lying beside him. A heap of nettle leaves lay on the ground from where they had been stripped off their stems. Wystan had plaited the stems and used the ropes to couple pairs of shaped skins together so that they could easily be slung over the back of the horses.

They breakfasted well on venison, somewhat crisped in the fire, but the sleep and the food bolstered Branwolf considerably. He looked thankfully at Wystan. He had managed to kill the deer but he would never have been able to skin it and make all those containers. The full bladder of water bumped against his thigh as they cantered across the heath dividing the Boarchase from Vaalaka. He shuddered as they crossed the border beyond the safety of his lands.

The horse tracks had vanished. The ground was hard and dry and any marks there might have been were scrubbed away by the dragged claws of troll. They scouted the foot of the Dragon Scorch bluff-line for half a mile in either direction but there was not one scratch from a hard hoof. At last they picked up a decisive troll trail that led them east for a short distance before turning north again. They followed a ravine cut by a waterfall that must have once cascaded off the Summer Melts and plunged towards the Sylvan Rush River.

'They must be following Spar's trail,' Branwolf exclaimed in utter frustration. 'Or at least looking for it. It's the best lead we've got.' He bit his lower lip, trying to contain the surge of worry that rose up from the pit of his stomach.

Wystan nodded at him. 'Looks like it, aye.' There was something reassuring about the way the woodsman steadily contemplated everything and it helped Branwolf to calm his fraught nerves. He turned Conqueror's head northwards, cutting through the sparse gorse bushes as they began the steep ascent. Wystan's draught horse, which had spent its days dragging felled trees through the forest, leant stoically forward and with its powerful hindlegs heaved itself up the narrow gorge. The reins were long driving reins that had been cut short and he only had a cloth of coarse sacking strapped to its back. On the steep climb Wystan gradually slid back down the horse's spine and clung determinedly to a twist of mane, though he looked decidedly unbalanced.

Branwolf's chest hurt and his muscles were sore and stiff from the aftermath of fever. He was grateful for the enforced rests while he waited for the woodsman to reach the brow. With their eyes continually skimming the ground for any clues they trotted northward away from Belbidia, following the troll tracks. The broad-chested Baron hung low over his saddle with one arm wrapped around his stomach to ease the pain as he vainly searched for any sign of his son. The tracks spread out and converged with confusing frequency and they could only deduce that the Vaalakans had not yet picked up the Torra Altans' trail. 'At least that means that Hal and Spar must still be ahead of them,' the Baron said before coughing painfully.

The high plateau, with its relentless winds stirring the dust around the bare pavement of broken flint, still gave no sign of hoofprints and the troll tracks were being rapidly obscured by the drifting earth.

'What do they survive on out here?' Wystan asked. 'There's nothing.'

'Like us, they can only eat what they carry with them. If we go much deeper into the Scorch we'll come near to Morbak's second army. My scouts tell me they are marching through the centre on a direct line towards the head of the Silversalmon.'

'It's fair peculiar that your boys would be running this way.'

'I know. Far too strange. It's odd that they've joined up with the old woman from the Boarchase too.'

'The last place I'd ever go voluntarily was here into the Dragon Scorch,' Wystan shuddered.

Branwolf raised his tired eyes and noticed for the first time that the man was not so warmly dressed as himself. The forest was far milder than the slopes of the Yellow Mountains and any man from the garrison was always heavily dressed with layers of wool shirts, jerkins and fur-lined cloaks. He loosened a rug from his pack and slung it at his companion. 'Here, you'll look like a Vaalakan but if you tie that round your shoulders it'll keep out the wind.'

Unlike his son, Wystan was not a man to endlessly chatter and he rode behind the Baron in silence. By evening the ground was too deeply in shadow to follow the tracks and they had to draw to a halt. Branwolf looked at the bleak landscape searching for somewhere to shelter for the night. Splintered boulders littered the ground; an occasional scrubby bush, its leafless branches withered and gnarled by the cold, trembled in the battering wind.

They spent a miserable night huddled in the lee of the horses and as soon as dawn spread across from the east Branwolf was eager to move. The aches in his body wore down his stamina and gradually he found his head slumping to his chest. Several times he jerked himself awake. With relief he realized that Wystan had quietly taken the lead and Conqueror followed dutifully after the steady sway of the draught horse's quarters. He relinquished control to the woodsman, letting him follow the tracks while getting as much rest as he could to allow his body time to recover.

He bumped his head on his chest and shook himself upright, realizing that he must have succumbed to the sleep of exhaustion once more. Wystan had suddenly stopped.

His heavy overhanging brows shrouded his broad generous face. 'They've taken a sudden turn left.'

Branwolf was instantly wide awake and his blurry eyes cleared to focus on the ground. 'Any sign of horses yet.'

The woodsman shook his head. 'No, Sir, but it looks like they've picked up something, 'cos the change in direction is so sudden and decisive.'

The trail led directly to a dried-out riverbed that had once spread like a network of blood-vessels through the arid wastelands. Now the land was like the wind-dried carcass of a sacrificed bull, drained dry of its blood. Branwolf looked down the shelving bank of caked-dry alluvium ridging the edge of the old Melts, to the bed of gravel below. The pebbles left no trace of tracks but within another half a mile the ground softened and became squelchy where a pool of deeper water had once slumbered. One hoofprint was still visible beneath the maze of claw marks, but it wasn't that which brought an amazed exclamation from Wystan's wind-burned lips.

'By the holy saints and their blessed relics!' He visibly paled.

A cloud of doom pressed heavily down on Branwolf's shoulders as he stared at the splayed imprint of the three-toed claw.

'But that's . . . My God, that's two foot across.' Wystan's jaw was gaping open and he looked at his liege-lord for an answer.

'We can't rest.' Branwolf stiffened in the saddle. 'We can't stop now.'

They rode on until the long shadows cast angular shapes across the parched soil. Wystan's pained expression declared that he couldn't swallow this fantastical tale of a leviathan monster. With a contorted brow he seemed to puzzle through the more likely reasons for the footprint but apparently came up with no other explanation. He seemed to shrug away the impossibilities, riding on dutifully and without question. The horses were flagging but Branwolf urged them on at a relentless canter until the jarring ground hammered through their pasterns and turned their rolling canter to a halting beat. He eased up and the two men took it in turn to sleep while the other guided the horses.

Once it was too dark to ride they slept in the crook of a bend in the river. The venison was now hard and dry but at least it sustained them and gradually restored some of Branwolf's wasted reserves. While they solemnly gnawed at the dark meat, Wystan told of how he had met Elaine and worked every hour of God-given daylight to earn enough money to get married. His deep gentle voice lulled Branwolf's distraught fears and a feeling of companionship helped them to snatch some miserable hours of sleep in the grim cold of the Scorch.

The morning sun shone wan and pale through the dust-storms that smothered the eastern horizon and Wystan cheered their spirits by continuing with his rambling tale.

'It was the most wonderful thing, you know, when my two youngsters were born. Elaine was radiant with joy though it meant two more mouths to feed. I was doing all right until this year though. We had so much work because of all the demands for Torra Alta's cathedral. We couldn't cut enough logs though I'm not sure that it was right by the forest, mind. But now with the Vaalakans we have to scrape a living in the heartwood and it's not easy. But the dagger you left for us, Sir. We can't accept it. We only gave you food and shelter and a little helping hand.'

'You can and you will accept it,' Branwolf replied.

'But . . .'

'Well, if you won't accept it for yourself, you'll have to accept it for the sake of your children, for Pip and May.'

'Ah well now, that's different.' Wystan smiled gratefully. 'I'd do anything for them.'

'Go to the ends of the earth,' Branwolf amplified, thinking about what he would do for his own son. Without Keridwen, Caspar was his whole life – even if he didn't manage to show it. He was tough on his son but then he didn't want to spoil the boy. But considering Caspar's whimsical nature Branwolf wasn't sure that he'd made quite a good enough job of bringing up his son. Not for the first time he wondered why Hal had to be the one that showed all the promise, though perhaps he lacked the moral judgement of a true leader. All the same Branwolf was sure his own priorities had also been wrong at that age. It was only the responsibility of having a wife, a young son and inheriting the Barony that had helped him to put things in perspective. He had grown old very fast when Keridwen vanished.

His skin was raw and chapped across his face but at least the coarse stubble covering his chin gave him some protection. Wystan was obviously saddle-sore and twisted himself awkwardly to try and prevent further chapping on the inside of his thighs, though he never murmured a word of complaint. Labouring through the soulless wastelands, they continued to pass the hours by exchanging homely tales. Towards evening the riverbed swept them eastwards and spat them out into a wider valley. They drew to an abrupt halt.

The sight of Morbak's army with its tall siege-engines grinding across the bleak soil silenced them. In the dusky shadows they surveyed with dread the endless marching column stretching to the violet sky-line. Rather than a column made of forty thousand separate men it was like one monstrous snake coiling out from beneath the eastern roots of the Three Black Devils.

'It's like entrails,' Wystan murmured graphically. 'If you string them out they are always so much longer than you could possibly imagine.'

'Spar, where are you?' the Baron futilely implored of the wind. 'We have to find you and get you safely home before this monster strikes at Torra Alta. Gwion will never cope.' Torra Alta will never cope, he added to himself but was not prepared to voice his deepest fears out loud. 'My scouts reckon this army numbers forty thousand men and there are twice that number working their way around the west coast.'

The cold in Branwolf's legs kept him awake that night and he rose to check the horses were safe. Their tendons were hot and swollen from the long arduous ride on the bone-hard ground but there was nothing he could do about that. He had to drive them on at all costs. But they were restless as if they sensed a storm brewing. The slit crescent of the moon cut like a sickle towards the decapitated peaks of the three volcanoes whose black shoulders were just discernible against the midnight blue of the night sky. He wondered whether the animals had an instinctive distrust of these treacherous mountains, though as far as he knew they had been dormant for generations.

The air shuddered as the first clap of thunder rumbled across the plains and he thought he had been right about the horses: they must have been sensitive to the changing atmosphere.

He drew his cloak up close around his neck. Wystan, a

shorter but stockier man, was standing at his shoulder. 'That's not thunder.'

Branwolf listened again to the distant roar, heard its deep throated echo – and then a shrill scream that shrieked from a cavernous belly. 'No,' he echoed. 'That's not thunder.'

Chapter 23

Hal eyed the lizard.

His mouth tasted of tanned leather, his lips were chapped and peeling – and he couldn't remember when he had last eaten. He dropped quickly to crouch behind the boulder beside him.

The ugly green creature basked motionless on the flat of a rock with one leg raised to catch the warmth of the sun on its underbelly. The bulging eyes rolled once in their sockets to glare at where Hal had been before returning to their glassy stillness. The lizard was hideously ugly, the heavy scales of its green hide spotted with nodules and spines. It didn't look appetizing.

The youth stalked it uncertainly at first but the ache in his stomach drove him on. He crept through the shadows on his hands and knees, inching forward with painstaking care. He had caught lizards as a young boy. They scurried through the cracks in the dry stone walls that marked the outer perimeter of Torra Alta's summer pastures. It took patience.

He was within one pace. Very low to the ground, he spat on his hands to help them grip and tensed, ready to pounce. He dived forward flattening his belly on the rock and clapped his hands tight around the neck of the lizard. Muscles more powerful than he could believe squirmed beneath his fingers and the reptile was gone. The tip of a green tail slithered away into the dark crack between two boulders.

Wearily he pushed himself up and contented himself with a single swig of water from his container. He swirled the skin and listened to the liquid splashing inside. It was less than half full. It tasted thick and stale but at least it kept him alive. He looked behind him at the sun skimming the western horizon and turned to trudge forward with his long shadow slanting out before him. Was this God's punishment for his stubborn pride and childish arrogance? Not only did he feel ill with hunger and exhaustion but Caspar was out there alone with a leviathan in pursuit across the Scorch. How could he have been so stupid as to leave him?

His conscience gnawed at his insides more fiercely than his hunger. But strangely the intense pangs of starvation had begun to lessen even though he hadn't eaten. At first he had felt a bellyaching desperation for food. He swallowed continually. Thoughts of roast boar, salmon and suet puddings had tormented his waking dreams, but now the sharpness of his hunger had dulled to an empty sickness and his head was light. The acute sensation of hunger had at least made him feel alert and alive, but now he had a growing sense of hopeless doom as if his body were already resigned to an inevitable fate. He had a numbing impression of disorientation and only his fear for Caspar drove him on.

He had no idea how far it was across the Scorch or indeed whether Morrigwen was leading Caspar and Brid to the other side of it. Only Morrigwen knew. He began to lose all sense of purpose. But, however much the youth resented it, however unfair it was that Caspar would become his overlord and order him around for the rest of his days, Branwolf had succeeded in instilling in Hal a sense of duty to protect Caspar. No one would ever forgive him if something happened to Caspar, but worse, Hal would never forgive himself.

He trudged on, pausing only very occasionally to take a gulp of water. He found that his eyes adjusted to the dark and he could even keep moving at night when the naked moon threw off its cloak of clouds. It was the wind that hurt him more than anything else. It sucked away the heat from his body and the skin around his mouth was chapped and sore where the airborne grit scrubbed at his face. He kept his smarting eyes cast down except when he had to squint into the coarse flying dust to keep his path. The only thing that kept his exhausted body moving through the long cold hours was the thought of the dragon on Caspar's trail.

He didn't care what power possessed the animal to drive it out across this desolate land in pursuit of an incandescent stone. His mind was too tormented by the thought of his small freckle-faced nephew vainly attempting to defend himself and the two women against the strength of the dragon's primeval claws. However annoying the boy could be, however embarrassingly fey, soft-headed and whimsical, he was still his closest companion. He was apt to talk about moons or wonder what it would be like to fly like an eagle just when a pretty girl was in earshot – generally ruining any chances of a successful conquest. However unfair it was that Caspar would become his overlord to order him about for the rest of his days, the elfin-faced boy meant everything to him. They had laughed and cried together through all the days of their childhood and he couldn't imagine life without Spar there on his heels asking what they should do next.

He saw no trace of the others. Any tracks the horses might have left would have been swept away by the fierce whipping of the dust which kept up through the endless day. At least that meant the enemy would have trouble hunting them down. But Hal didn't need to find hoofprints. He followed in the wake of the dragon, a trail carved through stone.

The sight of the Vaalakan column piercing the heart of the Dragon Scorch stopped him in his tracks. He stood helplessly staring at their countless number swarming out from beneath the foot of the most easterly of the three great black volcanoes. It was near dark and he slumped down against a boulder, feeling that all was lost. For a moment he imagined that the Vaalakan army would turn as one and spot him through the plume of dust rising from their shuffling feet, but gradually some logic returned to his befuddled mind.

'We'll never hold out against such numbers. God, give us strength,' he prayed.

He was starving. He no longer knew how much further he

could walk, or even crawl. If he died he would never be able to save Caspar and this made his own survival paramount. There was no food in the Scorch, not even the bones of a dead fox to gnaw at. He looked at the endless enemy line and thought that it must be no more than two miles to the east. They must have food. Reluctantly he turned away from the trail of the dragon and staggered toward the second army of Vaalaka.

The breath of thousands of sleeping men composed a droning sound in his ears. Wriggling on his belly through the dust on the valley bottom he had waited until night to make his move.

He would avoid the wagons. Any food in the wagons would be heavily guarded against plunder, not only by enemies. He might find some rations belonging to a lone barbarian sleeping on the edge of the camp, someone he could silently surprise. He steered well away from where the trolls were chained to a siege-engine.

The Vaalakans couldn't light camp fires since there was nothing to burn in the Dragon Scorch but he could see a nest of men huddled together to protect themselves from the driving wind. With only the soft light of the moon he could barely see into the deep shadows. He wriggled closer until his ears were humming with the sound of heavy snoring. But even if they were exhausted they were restless, probably from hunger and cold.

A thin bleat over to his left distracted his attention. A herd of ibex was roped together a little apart from the column. The moonlight fell on a single man on watch who marched slowly back and forth guarding the animals. Any soldier that stole an animal was bound to be discovered. The herd, therefore, required less protection than the wagons. There were no wolves in the wilderness either so the ibex were barely guarded. Just one man alone.

Hal picked up a flint pebble in one hand and a weighty rock in the other before creeping forward. Waiting soundlessly until the man was no more than three paces away Hal tossed the flint so that it tinkled on the ground behind the Vaalakan. The shepherd swung round and Hal smashed the rock into the back of the barbarian's head.

The sound of water sloshing in a skin as the man fell sent Hal rifling through his victim's fur rags until his hand reached the bladder of water tied beneath them. He ripped it off, making sure the man was fully unconscious before turning to the herd of ibex. If he startled the animals he would alert the camp. Perhaps he could lead one away and kill it further from the camp? He wasn't really sure; he no longer really cared; he just knew he must have food and water.

At first he thought that the kid lying at the edge of the herd was asleep: that would be the safest choice. But as he inched closer he decided that it was lying too still: it was already dead. The long march with little water or food would obviously have taken its toll on the weaker animals. He paused for a second, worrying if it had died of disease . . . still it would be safer to steal the carcass than kill a live animal. He dragged it by a hindleg and slunk back the way he had come.

Not until he had reached the foot of the ridge did he stop to turn around. It was cold but he was sweating heavily with fear and his jaw was aching from where he had clapped his mouth tight in anxiety. He hadn't realized until now how terrified he had been. But he had made it; that was all that mattered.

He had no alternative but to eat the ibex raw. He didn't worry that the meat was utterly tasteless and hardly bothered to chew at the mouthfuls that he managed to wrench away, tearing with sideways bites at the flesh. All he cared was that at last he had food. He allowed himself a couple of hours' rest after eating as much as he could and swilled it down with the Vaalakan's water. He put his hands on his stomach and let his eyelids shut out the nightmare of the barren world around him.

He awoke with his heart pounding in his ears and a cold sweat trickling down the small of his back. A thunderous roar echoed through the valley. For a moment he was unable to locate the bellowing cry in the dark but at last he detected that it was booming out from the most westerly peak of the three volcanoes. Without hesitation he started to run.

It was near dawn before he reached the foot of the Black Devils. Pocked and blistered by their own noxious gases, the three cratered mountains thrust up out of the plain. The left-hand volcano was like an ugly black boil with fractured sides where the earth's crust had split to release spuming gases and molten magma. He looked for a route that would lead him upwards to the dragon's roar. Inexplicably, two horses stood in the lee of a ridge of lava and he wondered if he was hallucinating. Surely that black stallion was Conqueror.

The roar rattled through his brain, wrenching his mind back to Caspar. The dragon's deafening shriek instilled terror into his soul: it was a scream of attack, Hal was convinced.

Chapter 24

Caspar wasn't sure whether Brid was crying or not; he wasn't even sure whether she could cry. She seemed so distant, aloof, like the face of the moon or an eagle rising on the thermals, unreachable, remote and beyond comprehension. Yet her very distance, her very aloofness, made her so desirable. He wanted to reach out and stroke her glossy hair, which sprayed out in the wind, but he didn't dare. She was a high-priestess, her whole bearing, her whole manner declared her status to the world. Yet somehow he felt that, despite her upright stature and dry eyes, she was weeping somewhere deep within her soul.

Perhaps she cried because of the enveloping sense of desolation in the Dragon Scorch, or because she mourned the futility of their crusade. Perhaps she cried for the old dun.

Wartooth, limped alongside, now quite agile on his three legs, and the wolf sloping in and out of the shadows was never far from their sides. Caspar sighed. He was crying inside too. For Hal, for his anguished father, and for Torra Alta and Belbidia in the face of Morbak's army. But most of all, quite inexplicably, the image of the pain scored into the face of the woman in the moonstone had forced itself upon him, and was the reason Caspar was crying. The woman in the moonstone was reaching deep into his heart. Morrigwen said that the moonstone came from the very heart of the castle and so perhaps it was intrinsically linked with him and his future as heir to Torra Alta.

Morrigwen drew to a halt and shielded her eyes from the deep red ball of the setting sun. They had climbed down from the ridge and in front of them the three black volcanoes lanced up into the sky. Beyond them, the narrow stretch of green steppe fringing the tundra. The Vaalakan column was a thin line way to the east, crawling through the shadows of the Three Devils. Caspar shuddered. Three guardians he thought, three headless ogres guarding the straits to the kingdom of Vaal-Peor. There was no trace of smoke, no angry rumble from a torn mantle, yet the sensitive youth felt they were alive. At first with their dour foreboding faces he thought they were glowering at him, like the lowlanders said that Torra Alta glowered, but then he thought what a mere speck of dust in the vast landscape he was, passing by the ageless mountains in a single pulse of time. They weren't glowering, they were laughing at him.

'We'd better hurry,' Brid warned. 'We'll have to make the steeper slopes by sundown.'

Caspar felt a shudder creep up his spine and he clutched at his chest, feeling for the hazelwood mandala. It was cold, dull and cold. He looked at the black, lifeless volcanoes. This was the last place on earth he would want to take refuge.

As they reached the lower slopes, the thud of hooves on the dust turned to a raw grind as they scraped and scratched across the rough pumice. Steadily they began to climb, winding back and forth to ease the strain on the horses.

Without taking her eyes from the sheer cliffs rising out of the plain, Brid murmured, 'We shouldn't be here. These mountains are like unhealed wounds out of the very body of the Mother. We should take our chances on the flat and ride on through the night.'

'There are no chances to be taken with a dragon,' Morrigwen snapped. 'I don't like this black volcano any more than you do but that great lizard will soon catch us up overnight and we'll fare no better than the old dun. These are only rocks, all part of the Mother and the cliffs above will provide good shelter.' They raised their heads to search the pumice slopes of the Black Devil, and the Crone flicked her hand towards a narrow ledge high above their heads. It snaked the westerly aspect of the nearest volcano before climbing steeply towards a fissure. 'We'll be safe up there.'

After scaling the black slopes, they traversed one last gully to reach a thin ledge. The two cream horses stood out against the black rocks like opal studs set in ebony. Without the least concern Caspar scanned the plains below. Brid stared down with equal interest though he noticed that Morrigwen was happier fixing her eyes on the back of the stallion's mane. She hadn't climbed as many trees or scaled as many peaks as her apprentice. The ledge led them to a fissure that vertically split the black rock. The crack opened into a cavern that offered protection against the reach of the dragon's voracious jaws.

'There's an inner cave through there.' Brid pointed to where stray scarlet tones of sunlight delved into the fissure.

They left the horses in the outer chamber, taking only the bearskins and the saddlebag holding the moonstone and its possessive salamander into the sheltered cave. Wartooth crept close to his master, keeping Caspar warm through the night. They had come a long way north and now high up in the slopes of the volcano the air was icy cold. He drew his feet up to his chest and with his eyes still fixed on Brid, who lay so tantalizingly close, he fell into a shallow sleep.

At first he thought he was back at home in Torra Alta and could hear rats pattering along the servants' corridors. His nostrils twitched and he coughed, muttering to himself that the cook must have burnt breakfast, and he was cold, very cold. He reached drowsily for his blankets. The noise of the rats bothered him; it was getting louder and louder. He coughed to clear his lungs of the choking smell just as he was jolted firmly awake by a heavy clattering of rocks hitting the ground.

'My God!' he swore, instinctively turning to the deity of his childhood. He was instantly awake and on his feet, stumbling through the dark to the back of the cave where the two women had laid down for the night. 'My God, it's found us.'

Morrigwen shouted, 'Get back out of here. It's found

another way up and it's breaking through the back of the cave. Get out of here!'

Caspar reached out his hand to pull the old woman out of the cave and as he did his eyes fell on the rock behind the two priestesses. It was beginning to bulge and heave. Morrigwen ran. Just as Caspar pivoted to follow, all thought was drowned as the wall gave way beneath the pressure of the giant lizard. In a tumult of smashing rock, its broad flaring nostrils poked through the crack, emitting a roar of triumph.

'The Druid's Eye,' Morrigwen shrieked. 'The Eye!'

It still lay against the cavern wall. A claw poked out between the torn fissure while splinters of rock peeled from the surrounding cavern wall. The light from the moonstone dulled as its incandescent surface became coated in rubble and dust. But it now lay no more than an arm's length from the scrabbling grasp of the huge curving claw. They stared open mouthed, watching helplessly as huge chunks of rock fell away.

'Leave it,' Morrigwen suddenly yelled. 'Leave it and get out of here.'

'No! Never! No!' Brid shrieked and dived at the orb. Her hand touched the white stone just as the claw crashed through the wall and pinned her shoulder to the ground. In the white light of the moonstone her wide staring eyes were like the startled eyes of a fawn caught in the iron jaws of a wolf-trap. Her trembling arm inched towards the moonstone and in one last desperate effort she grasped its leather leash and flung it towards the old Crone. 'Get out of here. Save the Mother,' she begged, just as the claw pierced the flesh of her shoulder, drawing a bright flow of blood. Before Caspar could reach Brid, the claw dragged her through the wall.

The wolf moved faster than Caspar. Like a wildcat spitting and yowling she crashed through the gap, snarls and growls now mixing with Brid's screams. She wasn't crying out for herself but was urging her companions to escape. A deep thunderous roar shook the core of the mountain and with a cry of agony the wolf was punched back through the wall, her lacerated chest oozing fresh blood. Her lips peeled back in a ferocious snarl as she lay on her side, breathing shallowly. She crawled pathetically forward, still trying to save her mistress. Caspar gripped his axe in both hands and charged into the dark after Brid. The mere flick of the dragon's claw sent him sprawling to the ground.

Behind him the Crone's face was bathed in the white glow of the moonstone, highlighting the contours of her features. Her eyes were as black as the sockets of a skull. This is a place for the dead, thought Caspar.

'Oh! Mother, help us,' Brid's voice wailed. The light of the moonstone fell through the fissure and Caspar caught a brief glimpse of Brid clutched tight in the giant claw of the dragon against its translucent underbelly. Brid's face was as white as the dragon's ashen grey scales.

Raising the axe above his head, Caspar brought it down with all his strength as the dragon reached into the cave with its other claw, scrambling for the moonstone held tightly in Morrigwen's grip. It glanced off the claw as if he'd struck at a blacksmith's anvil. Teeth the length of Caspar's forearm jutted into the cave as the wart-ridden snout pushed forwards. Cavernous nostrils flared and air was sucked away as the dragon inhaled volumes of the dank atmosphere to swell the bladder of skin beneath its throat. The bladder bloated until it was transparent and turgid, looking as if it would burst. The monster exhaled a vast stench of rotting flesh but no flame.

Caspar raised the axe again. Surely the soft tissue of the closed-over eyes would be vulnerable? Surely he could pulp the jelly-like tissue with the axe? In desperation he brought the axe down to hack through a leathery eyelid. Purple blood and gelatinous spongy tissue sprayed out and splattered Brid. She shrieked as the thick liquid spat into her wound.

The dragon roared and a shower of rocks tumbled from the surrounding wall. A forked tongue lashed forwards, whipping across Caspar's face and burning his skin like acid. The injury had done nothing to hinder the dragon. Caspar wriggled backwards and brandished the axe, an utterly pointless gesture since the dragon was blind. One eye rolled beneath the veil of greyish skin, the other a ruptured wet ball of sponge that no longer moved.

With great relief Caspar watched as the white-faced monster withdrew its snout from the tunnel. But the relief was short-lived as a massive claw groped towards him in its place. A tumble of rocks gave way under the pressure of the dragon's weight as it pressed its armoured shoulder into the narrow entrance, straining to reach him. A giant claw raked through the shattered rock. The boy was knocked aside like a feather as it groped from side to side for Morrigwen and the moonstone.

Morrigwen reached inside her shredded cloak and snatched out her golden sickle. She lunged and the point snagged in the dragon's armour and dragged through the flesh. A rush of purplish blood smothered the blade. The monster gave out an earth-shaking roar of pain and retracted its claw, the sickle still embedded in its flesh. Caspar leapt at the sickle handle, hoping his weight would increase the dragon's injuries but he was dragged into the black opening that was filled with Brid's screams. Morrigwen grabbed his arm and jerked the sickle upwards, breaking its tooth-hold on the dragon's claw.

Enraged with pain, the beast smashed into the tunnel walls with such strength and fury that rocks crashed from the ceiling, splintering into rubble on the floor. Caspar hacked at the dragon, aiming at the crevice between two talons. Stepping backwards, the young nobleman wrenched out the cleaver and a jet of blood spurted from the wound, a fountain of thick burning-hot liquid. The claw retracted and Brid's cries became suddenly faint as the monster carried her back into the passage through the volcano.

Caspar stared through the hole created by the dragon's claws. He stared into blackness. Twisting his neck round he looked back at Morrigwen.

'Get my Brid back. Don't let it take her.'

The dragon had turned round where the crevice widened out, its grey-white bulk appearing like a ghostly fog in the dark. The arrow-head tail lashed back and forth and Caspar hacked at it with the axe only to find that the unwieldy blade slid off the scales as if they were sheet steel. The tail whipped sideways, catching Caspar across the temple and sending him hurtling against the side of the cavern before slumping to the ground. He shook his head to regather his senses but by the time he was on his feet the dragon was gone. Brid's distant cries echoed down through the cracks in the rocks from somewhere far above his head while Wartooth yowled and snarled helplessly into the chimney that rose up above them. Morrigwen stooped over the youth, her hand trembling on his shoulder. The pale light of the moonstone left her sunken eyes in darkness while giving only her face a lifeless shade like a ghostly skull. She had always been, like Brid, so in control of herself but now as she begged Caspar for his help, the auburn-haired youth felt even more helpless and inadequate. If Morrigwen could do nothing what could he do?

He cursed their foolishness. It wasn't the height of the caves in the ridge of hills that had saved them before, but the loose scree slopes that were unable to support the weight of the dragon. Beneath its bulk they had become a treacherous landslide. But here the sides of the volcano were firm and the dragon clambered from gritty pumice ledge to pumice ledge without difficulty.

'Why didn't we think it could have found another way up?' Morrigwen despaired. 'My Brid, my Brid,' she wept.

Caspar was on his knees, leaning in despair against the Vaalakan axe handle. He didn't know what to do. Hal would know what to do. Morrigwen held the moonstone aloft and looked up into the chimney through the rock. Stars shone overhead. The walls were impossibly sheer though ridged at intervals just within reach of the dragon's vast frame. He stared at the night sky. It took him a moment to understand what to do.

'Back onto the ledge,' he cried, 'and out through the cave. We'll climb up from the outside.'

The wind had dropped and the clouds had cleared to reveal a star-studded sky. The lower horn of a bright crescent moon hooked the upper rim of the volcano's crater.

'It'll be dawn soon,' the Crone muttered, 'and the dragon will disappear into the crater and crawl deep within the volcano's core to hide from the sun, dragging Brid, my beloved Bridget, with him.' She cradled the moonstone in her hand, persistently brushing off the salamander, which hooked its claws into her flowing sleeves, hissing and flickering its tongue as it tried to reach the moonstone. She grasped the orb by its leash and swung it in a large circle so that flashes of white light arced through the sky, leaving a trail like a comet. 'It can sense the power in the stone. Maybe it can even see the light through that hooded eye but at least its attraction may keep the dragon out in the open.'

In the dark Caspar was unable to pick out a clear upward route. Only the huge white bulk of the dragon washed in moonlight was clearly visible against the ebony-black of the volcano. It roared like a clap of thunder. Caspar had no thought of what to do beyond climbing upwards towards the monster. If he could get closer then, just maybe, he might find some way to help the Maiden.

Terrible though her screams were, he was thankful for the noise because at least it proved she was still alive. He couldn't see the dragon now. An overhang above his head blocked the line of sight. He ran along the sides of the volcano, stumbling in the dark, desperately seeking a way upwards that would draw him level with the dragon. How could they have been so stupid? They should have trusted their instincts and stayed away from the volcano, which now proved to be riddled with tunnels and vents. This black boil on the earth's crust was ideal terrain for the leviathan lizard, a denizen of the deep caverns below the Yellow Mountains.

Despite her desperation Morrigwen was unable to keep up with the boy who, alone, groped through the dark, trying to climb up to the ridge above. The rock was vertical but the moistureless pumice offered a firm grip. He kicked his toes into the rock, feeling for a foothold while scrambling with his fingertips for a firm purchase so that he could swing himself up. In the dark Caspar was struggling. Clinging on with one hand he could find no other protruding rock or crevice to grip hold of. He reached over his shoulder for the axe strapped to his back, unhooked it and gripped it firmly by the handle. It gave him an extra three-foot reach. He prayed it would be enough. Yelling out with the effort, he swung the axe forward, grappling for the upper ledge. It grated across the rough pumice and finally bit in.

Dawn broke across the far horizon as he swung up by the axe handle. The ledge above forked in two directions. In the dim light the youth moved to the right and sprinted round the curve of the mountain. Daylight, he thought in despair. The monster will go to ground and eat Brid at its leisure in the sunless world. Why hadn't he brought the moonstone? At least it would have provided something to barter with. Maybe it was the only thing it could see, he didn't know, but why hadn't it just killed Brid? Was it keeping her hostage against this precious stone of white light? He could see the dragon now, right beneath the very lip of the crater, which hung outwards like a lolling tongue. The overhang shaded the milky beast from the direct rays of the sun.

Brid was standing against the mountain wall, no longer held in the dragon's giant clasp. He wondered why she didn't try to escape since the dragon had his back to her. Her dusty green gown trailed in shreds from one shoulder, exposing her left breast and a raw red gash in the shoulder above. Perhaps she was too injured or too frightened to move? No, Brid would never be too frightened. Then he realized. The slightest hint of movement brought the dragon's barbed tail lashing toward her, thumping either side, and dislodging boulders to crash around her.

She remained still, waiting as the dragon teetered forward on the ledge and flicked its tongue out, tasting the air as if it were searching. A thousand years before, the beast would have spread its wings to circle effortlessly in the sky above the mountain, picking them off one by one. It would have swooped to snatch the moonstone. But now it could only roar and wait for them to bring the orb to him. The thin flap of skin beneath its neck swelled to a taut bladder that vibrated with the rush of air, producing a deep, haunting howl. The unearthly sound would undoubtedly carry to the horizon.

Caspar froze to the spot.

'Get back!' Brid pleaded. Her words were cut short as the barbed tail smashed down a hand's breadth from her feet, the aftershock bringing boulders down from the overhang above.

He had to distract the animal, draw it away from Brid. Then she could escape, running backwards to wherever the ledge would take her. He raised the axe and beat the flat of it against the rock-face, hoping the noise would distract the sickly-white dragon. It jerked its head round for a moment, snaking its long neck out towards him, its tail twitched like an expectant cat. But then, just as suddenly, it jerked away, craning over the overhang to taste the air for Morrigwen and the moonstone.

'Morrigwen,' Caspar yelled down over the overhang, choosing not to argue with Brid but deciding to make his own plans. 'Bring up the moonstone. We'll make an exchange.'

The hag's abrasive voice rasped up from the ledge below, 'Fool boy, we're not bartering with a spice merchant. That's a dragon. If we give it the Eye then it has everything it wants and will probably kill us all.' The Crone's voice was hoarse with anguish. 'I can't get up to you. Do something to rescue my Brid.'

'Bring up the moonstone,' Caspar shrieked. 'We've got to save Brid.'

'No, I can't make the climb. I can only try and lure it down with the light of the Druid's Eye. I'll swing it again.'

The dragon balanced right on the brim of the ledge, elongating its neck to its full stretch, an angry rush of air hissing out through its nostrils. Caspar quaked at the sound. It was like a pit full of snakes churning in the monster's stomach. Though precariously perched on the rock, it whipped its arrow-head tail back and forth viciously across Brid, tearing the remains of her tattered dress and lashing her body. She was flung like parchment helplessly against the rough surface of the rock.

'Morrigwen, stop! He's killing her,' Caspar shrieked. The small youth took a brave pace towards the huge leviathan. 'Worm, you base beast of the underworld, pick on a man not a maiden. Pick on me.'

Brid lay in a crumpled heap and his desperation for her scattered the youth's senses to the harsh Vaalakan winds. With the double-bladed cleaver above his head he hurtled forward with the Torra Altan battle-cry pealing from his lips. A furious snarl was his dog's battle-cry, the hound moving awkwardly but with equal purpose to attack the dragon. Wartooth stood faithfully by his master. The youth was too small and light to brandish the war-cleaver. But within five paces he was against the beast's hindlegs, behind its vast quarters. With a scream of determination he hacked downwards. The first blow glanced off the rigid scales, twisting Caspar off balance. His momentum flung him into the wall of stone, bruising his shoulder.

He jerked himself onto his feet, held the axe low and charged again, this time chopping low, aiming for the beast's toes. There was a satisfying crunch like the sound of a holly log being cleaved in two as a giant claw split away from the three-toed foot. The dragon reared up onto its hindlegs, beating the withered stumps of its vestigial wings, and howled with its neck upstretched. It curled the long neck round, flicking the forked tongue over its wound and thrusting its face at Caspar.

The roar hit Caspar like a solid fist punching him in the stomach, bowling him backwards away from Brid. He felt his shoulder crack as he jarred against the pumice and gelatinous saliva coated his face, clinging to his skin. Raising a claw the dragon raked open his chest, then his thigh. Caspar couldn't breathe. The great maw was hungrily pressing closer. He could see down into the colourless mouth beyond the cord of the tongue that whipped back and forth, lashing across his face. He was aware of nothing, not even the pain of his wounds, except the enveloping throat and the flap of skin dangling down at the back of the cavernous mouth.

But then he heard Brid. Her screams reached a terrible pitch and the dragon whipped its head round, its tongue tasting Brid's scent to precisely place her. It froze solid almost as if staring. Caspar realized that it had to keep still to feel the vibrations of the girl's movements. Then its forked tail punched into Brid, sweeping her towards the edge of the precipice. The youth could no longer see her beyond the bulging flanks of the monster. He could only hear her high-pitched scream and the sound of rubble grinding across solid rock. Suddenly he could hear boulders crashing on rocks far below. He lurched to the left, trying to reach towards Brid but the weight of a leviathan claw punched into his back and pinned him to the ground. Squirming helplessly, he watched Brid being swept inexorably towards the edge of the cliff.

Her fingers snatched and grappled for a hold on the vast tail, but they slipped over the polished surface of the plates. A foot from the edge, one of her slender hands hooked onto a pointed fin near the end of the tail and she swung her other arm underneath, wrapping herself around the beam-like appendage. The tail swung out over the ledge and Brid's legs dangled in mid air. Her screams ceased. Caspar caught a glimpse of her white face and gritted teeth as she desperately tried to hold on. The dragon thrashed its tail as if trying to shake her free, but still she had the strength to grip on. In its irritation, the monster whipped its tail back to beat it against the sandpaper sides of the volcano's pumice walls until Brid's body was limp and exhausted. An arm fell loose and now she was barely grasping hold with one slipping hand. The dragon flicked its tail out over the precipice again whipping it back and forth over the lethal drop.

Trying desperately to throw up her free hand to grip onto the tail, Brid's feet swung limply back and forth like a doll's. She was slipping slowly at first and then with a rush she plummeted. For the briefest moment Caspar looked into her eyes as they stared with horror and her mouth opened to scream. The dreadful hollow wail plunged into Caspar's heart. The dragon's claw pinned him to the bedrock. He shut his eyes to block out the unimaginable pain of losing Brid.

But then . . . Yes, he could still hear her. A thin desperate whisper, a plea for help drifted up from just below the lip of the ledge. He could just see two of her fingernails hooked into the rock. Her voice was frail and thin as if she were losing strength. For a moment there was silence. Then Morrigwen's wavery voice called from below, 'Brid. Hold on!'

Still struggling, Caspar kicked and lashed out, wriggling like a worm as he tried to twist out of the dragon's grasp. For a moment he thought only of Brid and how he could rescue her, until the weight of the great beast pressed more heavily down on his ribcage. He was slowly suffocating, wondering when his ribs would crack and splinter under the crushing weight of the three-toed leviathan. The great jaw was open wide again, hissing, its rigid tongue jutting straight forward. Only the very tip of the forked end twisted and curled. Abruptly the snout lurched backwards. The dragon drew up and arched its neck as it prepared to strike.

'I can't hold on.' Brid's quivering voice filled the silence as the great blind beast reached the zenith of its height and paused for that split second in preparation.

The air was suddenly filled with a sound like the wind whistling through an arrow-slit in a castle. Caspar's horrified eyes fixed on the dragon's gaping mouth but he shut them as the spray of purplish blood spurted from the studded row of wounds that sprang from the bluish-grey underside of its neck. The blood splashed onto his upturned face and dribbled round the contours of his eyes. He blinked furiously to clear his vision. The shafts of six quarrels nailed the scaly beast and, as he looked, another two in unison pierced its skin. But as the dragon's great body shuddered in shock, three of the barbs clattered to the ground. They had caused as little irritation as pine needles to a forest bear. Another pair of arrows whistled through the air, one missing the target completely and the other one at last plunging into the soft palate inside the dragon's gaping mouth.

In his frantic state of near-asphyxia, Caspar was vaguely

aware of something out of place about those arrows. The quills were of grey goose feather . . . Torra Altan arrows, Caspar thought in bewilderment.

The last arrow, lodging deep in the inside of the dragon's mouth, distracted the beast. It drew up its front claws towards its jaw, reeling back onto its hindquarters and suddenly Caspar was free.

He rolled away from the dragon and found himself slumped against a pair of black leather boots.

Chapter 25

Caspar looked up at the unshaven face of his father.

Without taking his eyes off the dragon, Branwolf spat the words, 'Get behind me, Spar.' With a deft movement he reached over his shoulder, instinctively feeling the goose quills to search out two arrows crafted for short flight and deep penetration. They were not, of course, designed to slay dragons. No fletcher in a thousand years had troubled himself with the skill needed to make such arrows. But the angry long-nosed barb was specifically wrought to pierce horse armour and could disable the hardiest destrier. With great battle-skill he slotted two arrows at once to the bow, drew back the massive draw-strain of the string and let them loose.

One was deflected, clattering uselessly to the ground, and the other slid the barest of inches between the beast's scales. There was no reassuring sign of blood, but at least the dragon had released Caspar from its claw.

Branwolf wondered helplessly how his ancestors had killed these monsters? This one didn't even have wings. Many of the tapestries that draped the central halls of Torra Alta's keep depicted the ancient leviathan lizards, their wingspans casting great shadows across the battlefield as they circled above the slaughter of their race in the Dragon Wars. It was thought they had all been killed, or died, finally. To discover they were not extinct as he had thought was a great shock to the leader of Torra Alta. And what remained of the legendary dragon was a hideous wingless and blind monster, more crazed and dangerous as it was more ugly.

Caspar was too bruised and crushed to stagger to his feet.

His father was here, he didn't question why or how, but if Branwolf had found him everything would be all right. For a split second he let all his fears, all his responsibilities slip from his mind, content that his father would destroy the beast in a matter of seconds.

Brid! Her cries were frantic. Caspar could see only the bone-white fingers clinging to a lip of pumice. 'I can't hold on.'

He couldn't get to her. The dragon barred the way, its great angry bulk filling the ledge. He tried to burst forward, still half on his hands and knees but Branwolf's firm hand caught his collar. 'You can't do anything,' he growled. 'That dragon will eat you the second you get within ten feet of it.'

'Brid!' the boy yelled in utter despair.

Branwolf rapidly released arrows in a succession of pairs. His quiver was emptying fast. The arrows met a steel-like plating of overlapping scales. Even the vulnerability of the purplish grey underbelly was deceptive. The scales were merely smaller and more tightly packed but they were just as effective a shield against his arrows as the huge plates that clad the beast's back. The dragon was slowly approaching, slashing angrily at the rocks as it passed. The trident claws tore away loose boulders that bounced from ledge to ledge towards the plain far below.

Branwolf aimed for the wounded eye. Though the dragon was hit and shrieked with anger and pain fit to crack open the heavens it still advanced, the tail thrashing wildly as it drew up its neck to strike.

'Its throat,' Caspar yelled. He too remembered the tapestries covering the cold stone walls of Torra Alta. He remembered the bright gold threads woven through with emerald, and scarlet. The dragons of old were coloured by the ugly green of a storm-tossed sea and their tiny eyes like studs of ebony gave away no hint of emotion. Unlike his father he had been caught up in the fantasy of the ancient legends and he had been drawn into the pictures to walk with his ancestors through the brightly threaded worlds. Around each dragon a dozen brave and heroic knights were slain with gruesome injuries wrought by fang and claw. But each slain dragon had been felled in the same fashion: the upward thrust of a lance into the throat of the beast, reaching to its brain. The hearts were unreachable. The aim had to be sure to pierce the only weak spot in the thickly skulled brain. The arrow needed to track upwards through the soft tissue at the base of the skull where the spinal cord joined the brain. It was a difficult stroke.

'Upwards under the throat,' he urged his father.

The dragon held its head tightly coiled, arching its neck so that the underside of its gizzard was protected . . . and its flaring nostrils spat noxious stomach acids into their faces. At least there was no fire, Caspar managed to think as he gagged.

The noise of his own choking deafened him to the sounds of the Maiden as she kicked and scrambled for a foothold. Her skirts were blown like a battle-torn standard in the wind. With one hand she groped futilely for a purchase on the rock while she hung painfully from the other which was stretched up above her head like a taut rope. Blood trickled from around her fingernails as she clung on bitterly to the very last.

It was then Hal arrived, breathing hard, a terrible urgency in his eyes. Hal took in the scene, his heart still thumping in his chest from hurtling along the coiling ledge of the volcano, recklessly traversing the gullies that broke its course. His olive eyes were immediately drawn to Brid. He sprinted up the last stretch of the ledge to be faced with the angry lashing tail of the dragon. The pointed fins snagged at rocks that bounced and hurtled over the precipice, skimming past Brid's head. Hal flung himself to the ground, slapping his palm over the Maiden's wrists and crushing her bones in the fierceness of his grip. He dug his fingernails into her flesh, determined never to let go.

Her head turned upwards and her beautiful forest-green eyes stared deep into his soul. 'Hal! Thank the Mother.'

He could feel her grip slipping from the rock and his stomach tensed to take the strain as her whole weight dangled from his arm. The shock of the barbed tail slashing across his back jerked his body and for an instant Brid slipped half an inch through his fingers. She didn't scream but their eyes met, weaving an unbreakable thread between them.

The noise of boulders tumbling around them and the pounding beat of the dragon's tail as it shook the earth were blocked from the youth's mind. He dug his toes into the rock and reached his other hand over the ledge to lock onto Brid's forearm. He dragged himself backwards onto his knees, hauling the Maiden's light weight with him so that her half-naked body lay slumped on the ledge. The barbed tail tore at Hal's shoulder as he protectively covered her body with his own. He grimaced but turned his head to hide his pain from the girl and crawled at last beyond reach of the dragon's lethal tail, dragging Brid with him as gently as he could.

He pulled her into his arms and she slumped against his chest, clinging tightly. 'Hal,' she murmured over and over again.

After a brief moment he pushed her away and curtly ordered, 'Get down the ledge and out of harm's way.'

She looked fearfully towards him and then towards the dragon and Caspar. 'Spar!' she protested.

Hal shoved her behind him.

'Get out of the way, Brid.' Resolutely he drew the sword, which flashed shafts of light across the plain as it caught the rays of the morning sun. He braced his legs and held the sword high in readiness to strike at the barbed tail. He had to distract the monster.

'Attack the throat, Father,' Caspar cried again.

'Get out of range, boy,' Branwolf bellowed as he reached for another pair of arrows. His quiver felt light and still the dragon showed no sign of backing off. Its albino snout lunged forward with its serrated lips peeled back to reveal the rows of dagger-like teeth that gnashed within its jaws. Two more arrows spat from Branwolf's bow, glancing harmlessly off the warty nodules that studded the dragon's nose.

The dark shape of Wartooth leapt out from the shadows. Snarling viciously. With his hackles like spines along the length of his back, the faithful hound threw himself at the monster and latched onto the beast's lip. In a frenzy of snapping jaws, growls and yelps Wartooth sank his canines into the monster's scales. The dragon raised its head and whipped its neck from side to side in an effort to rid itself of the irritation. Nobly, Wartooth clung on.

Tears flooded across Caspar's cheeks as at last the old dog's strength failed him. The dragon flipped the hound's body up into the air, caught it, tossed it again and with a single snap of its vast jaws silenced Wartooth's howls. Branwolf loosed arrows against its exposed throat but the dragon was a frantic moving target. It flipped the limp body of Wartooth aside and it crashed into the rock-face to slump in an impossible tangle of limbs.

In disbelief Caspar stared at the body of his faithful hound, but he had no time for grief. The dog had brought them only a few seconds of grace. The ground shook as the dragon lunged another step forward to strike again.

Caspar ran to his father. 'I won't let you stand between me and the dragon like Wartooth did.' He looked past his father's shoulder as more arrows spat from the Baron's bow in rapid succession and Branwolf shouted in fear for his son, 'Get back!' But a pair of hands suddenly grasped the youth firmly from behind. Caspar struggled but the arms that pulled him backwards were strong and powerful like his father's. 'Come on, son,' a voice growled between gritted teeth in an accent that instantly marked him as a peasant from northern Torra Alta.

The dragon's head was arched. The short horns at its poll pointed heavenwards as its foul smelling breath enveloped Branwolf's body. He had spent the last of his plate armour arrows and was rapidly firing off the less useful barbs. The dragon was unflinching, the flickering tongue reaching out to taste him. It froze for the split second in preparation for its strike. Branwolf braced himself. Reaching for his throwing knives, he hoped that in the last crucial moment before the dragon struck it would expose its throat and he prayed that, when its jaws closed about his neck, he would have the remaining strength to thrust the blade into its brain and save his son.

The dragon's head jerked aside, distracted by the movements of Caspar's flailing arms. Wystan flung the boy to the ground and covered his small body with the breadth of his own.

A horrible scream filled Branwolf's ears. He turned to see the dragon's jaws rake across Wystan's massive back, shredding the flesh from his ribcage and exposing the bright pulsing muscles that covered the woodsman's torso. His bulging eyes turned to look at his master.

'Look after my May!' His lasts words were crushed from him as his ribcage splintered and the dragon spat him aside in frustration. The monster reared up to strike again but this time its face jerked sideways and it froze as if suddenly struck by a thunderbolt.

Bracing himself with widespread legs, Hal carefully judged the rhythm of the dragon's tail as he wielded the sword. With the sword high above his head, he slashed at the beam of the tail, praying that the beautiful white metal would slice through the dragon's armour as it had shattered the Vaalakan steel.

The weighty shock of the dragon's beating tail flung him to the ground. A rain of foul-smelling, purplish blood sprayed out, coating the pumice with a glistening liquid, like molten garnets. As the splattering droplets hailed down the ear-splitting roar from the depths of the dragon's maw turned to breathless silence. Its head snaked round so that the sensitive tongue could taste for its attacker's presence. Its tongue flickered once over bright steel and recoiled sharply. With the sudden grace of a mountain lion the great beast turned and swarmed up the rock to a ledge thirty feet above their heads, leaving a trail of rich dark blood. With the sound of scales grating against the coarse pumice, it slithered away into the crater and disappeared into the labyrinth of crevices that riddled the walls of the volcano.

Hal drew deep uneven breaths as he staggered to his feet,

his eyes first falling on his brother who stooped over the broken body of a woodsman from the Boarchase.

Though tattered and torn and despite the angry gash gouged into her shoulder, Brid rushed to the man and looked deep into his eyes. But it was only a few seconds before she raised her head and shook it sorrowfully at the great Torra Altan nobleman. He raised his eyes heavenward, muttering the words of a prayer. 'So brave and honest a soul.' The words were catching in his throat. 'We cannot bury him but we must build a cairn.' He knelt silently by the man, grasping his hand. 'I will look after your family, Wystan; I will do everything in my power for them. You have saved mine and I owe you the world.'

His dark olive eyes glistened with emotion when at last he turned towards his son but Caspar shrank back in anticipation of his father's renowned temper. Branwolf said nothing. He drew himself up and tenderly reached out a hand, searching Caspar's body for wounds. It hurt as his father crushed him against his chest, but it was a sweet joyous pain. The youth felt the tears rising in his throat, tears of relief and tears of thankfulness as he was swamped in his father's protective embrace. But finally he was overcome as bitter tears of grief flooded over his face as he sobbed for his faithful hound and anguished over the brave woodsman. Never once did the great Baron murmur one word of reproach.

With one arm still grasped firmly around his son, he stretched out towards his younger brother. Hal stumbled forward coated in dust, his lips dry from thirst and his eyes sunken with lack of sleep. The irrepressible glint of arrogance still showed in his smile as he stepped eagerly forward and grasped the broad hand. But the moment of emotion was too intense for words even from Hal.

Gradually Caspar became aware that Brid was staring at them. She cradled her right arm in the crook of her left as if nursing an injured shoulder. Her hair fell like rags from where it had been ripped from the braid and her skin was a dull grey from the dust off the plain. The once green robe hung like sacking from the point of one shoulder, revealing the rising bulge of her breast and the soft gentle curve of her shoulder. The angry wound on her shoulder was oozing but still Caspar saw only her beauty.

She stood proudly, angrily before the great Baron. 'So at last,' she almost spat, 'the great Baron.'

There was something sinister in the looks that the pagan priestess and the Baron exchanged, something that Caspar did not understand. They examined each other with the curiosity of strangers who had heard much about one another but were shocked at how their presumptions differed from reality.

'Father,' Caspar coughed, feeling uneasy at their gazes. Brid almost stared with contempt, and Branwolf, he couldn't tell, almost with recognition, dreamlike. 'Father, this is Brid.'

'Eyes like dew on the evergreen forest,' he breathed. To Caspar's utter astonishment the great Baron bowed low and courteously as if kneeling before a queen. 'It is an honour to greet you, Maiden, One of the Three and Daughter of the Moon.'

Hal's voice was raised high with astonishment as he exclaimed, 'She's a witch.'

Both Branwolf and Brid ignored the two youths and continued to stare into each other's eyes, Brid's eyes searching coldly.

'I don't know how to greet you, Branwolf of Torra Alta. Your guilt remains in question. We do not know whether you drove her away; whether the threat of desolation lies at your feet.'

'I know not myself.' The Baron's voice was heavy with sorrow. 'I know not whether it was at my deed or at my word; but truly it was never the will of my heart. I would die a thousand times to bring her back.'

Brid nodded as if accepting his words. As her stiffness relaxed Caspar saw her sway slightly on her feet. He pulled himself away from his father's grasp and ran to catch her but Hal was already there and scooped her up in his arms.

'Where's Morrigwen? Brid needs her.'

'On the ridge below,' Caspar answered quickly.

Hal turned to lead the way while Branwolf stopped to grieve over Wystan. 'As soon as I've seen to their wounds,' he promised, 'I will build a cairn over your brave body and when we return to Torra Alta I will build a monument in the very heart of the great keep. Your name will live on.' The raven-haired nobleman moved to stoop over the twisted carcass of the deer-hound, gently rearranging his legs before soothing his pointed ears. 'Gwion says there is no place in God's heaven for the beasts but I pray you will forever chase across the heavens, happily hunting the great white hart in the sky.'

Morrigwen immediately swooped on Brid, gently pressing her shoulder and examining her eyes. 'It's not deep,' she reassured her, 'but a wound from a dragon will fester and draw the strength from the body. Its blood must have mingled with your own.'

'It burns,' Brid murmured.

'Burns with the heat of the dragon's fire. I can mend it, child. We will borrow some of Vaal-Peor's own power. The boy touches on the terrible cold when he explores the Druid's Eye alone.'

She scooped the orb out of her shawl and handed it to Caspar. 'For her sake,' she whispered, 'seek out the cold and draw it to her.'

As he took the moonstone he was aware of the old woman addressing his father before his mind was absorbed into the trance-like depths of the world sealed within the skin of the magic orb.

'So, old woman, it's been a long time.'

'A long time of sorrow and despair,' her thin voice wavered. 'And now the Vaalakans have come to fill the void as the faith of the Mother dwindles from the land. The insipid God of peace from the south has no strength to protect us from the natural cruelty of the God of Ice. This new ethereal God is far too removed from Nature. My son, you have grown older and greyer in the long decade. Let us hope you have gained wisdom. I have something to tell you.'

As he slipped into his trance, Caspar could still feel the intense presence of his father. He was silent but he could hear the thick steady breathing and the power of his pulse beating faster now as he anticipated the words of the Crone.

'We have found her. The boy found her image in the moonstone.'

'Is she alive?' The Baron's voice was weak and desolate.

'It might only be the image of her ghost, the last energy of her dying body still trapped within the stone unable to be reborn. If she is dead we must release her so that her soul can return to the everlasting bliss of Annwyn, but I pray she is alive. For if she is dead we will never turn back the tide of half-starved Vaalakans and in years to come the beautiful land of Belbidia will be no more alive than the harsh Dragon Scorch.'

'Does the boy know?'

'No. To give him any hope when she may be dead seemed cruel. Also the shock . . . You have brought him up in the civilized ways of the God from the south, the faceless deity. The Great Mother is our provider and nourisher: we cannot allow the people of the world to turn their back on her. We need the Mother . . .'

The words echoed in Caspar's mind as he sank beneath the skin of the crystal. He felt he had been gliding . . . no swimming on the surface of the winter sea and suddenly the breakers had swept over his head and dragged him down into the airless depths and the suffocating cold. He was floating under the waves at first, his arms stirring through the liquid only he couldn't swim back up for air. A hand gripped his head and pressed him down into the ice-cold water. He struggled desperately, wrenching at a hand and grasping a black sleeve. The garment tore free, revealing an ugly forearm, where his fingernails made wet red tears across the black striations scarring it. Frantically he kicked with his legs to reach for air above, to the bright white light coruscating off the crystal blue of the water's surface.

Dots of sparkling white crystal, like points of stars, burst into life around his body. At first the crystalline points of light, which caught the unreachable sunlight above, were brilliantly beautiful, but gradually they joined together in tendrils to form a cancerous network about him. The hand above pressed him deeper. He tried to stretch up but something from within the half-frozen water grabbed his right arm.

Like the brittle hard bones of a skeleton, the fingers hooked around his wrist, tightening and squeezing in an ice-hard grip until he was fused to the presence that he felt beneath him. His head turned very slowly and stiffly through the thickening water. He no longer remembered that he couldn't breathe but felt compelled to meet the face that he knew was down there with him.

'You bring me life; you bring me warmth. You and I are one again. Do not leave me, Spar.'

There was an overwhelming sense of great beauty. All his fears and troubles were being soaked up by the will he felt next to him. He was absorbed into an emotion of magical closeness, as if he belonged to the presence. Yes, he belonged to the soft voice, which like a lullaby rejoiced in his ears, soothing him, lulling him . . .

He could no longer feel his arm, nor could he move it. The limb was frozen solid as the presence sucked like a parasite at his heat, drawing on his life. And yet he gave freely, and his mind was freed. With his own will he was desperate to sustain the life of this creature trapped within the icy core of the moonstone. The bright silver face of the moon, he had been told, had a dark side turned forever away from the Earth. He felt that although the orb appeared bright and impossibly beautiful he was now touching on the forbidden side, hidden from the eyes of man and only reachable through the imagination, through the soul.

His head was still turning imperceptibly, with the growing thrill of anticipation that soon he would look into the angelic face that was trapped beside him. He knew she was beautiful, more beautiful than any creature on Earth because of the depth of love in her voice. A smile of greeting was already on his lips as he turned to meet her eyes, but his lips stuck fast in frozen horror. A swirl of hair drifted around her face like tentacles around a poisonous jellyfish. Where the tresses were fused into ropes by the ice they were like vipers spawning from a central nest. Her mouth was a silent gaping scream and her eyes, frozen balls of azure, bulged out at him in agony. The beautiful mind that had lovingly reached out to him was trapped within a frozen carcass that had died in terrible pain as a thousand needles of ice had crystallized within her veins like a million minute spears tearing apart her body from within.

He felt tragically alone like an infant suddenly abandoned on a bleak mountainside in the cold mists of autumn. The sensation of her warm heart was suddenly snatched away as if a door had been burst open by a snowstorm of mid-winter. The cold was terrible. The pain of it ate through his flesh and buried into the core of his bones. His hand seemed to be crumbling away. His fingers were being snapped from his body like icicles from the eaves of a snow-laden roof.

He turned his face to beg her to release him from her torturous grip that fed like a parasite off his heat. Almost imperceptibly her eyes glistened with the hint of life as two brilliantly blue windows on her soul opened up to him. Caspar felt her acute need and willingly gave of his bodily heat, praying that what he could give her would ease her pain and sustain her in the clutches of Vaal-Peor's world.

But something fiercely hot now burned through his other wrist. He thought the contrast in the two extremes would split his body. It was like night and day filling the same sky at once, producing an impossible imbalance.

He was being dragged upwards. The cruel hand that had pressed him beneath the surface of the ice world was gone and friends, he was sure they were friends, were hauling him upwards to the surface. He resented it. Suddenly he wanted to stay down here with the woman and her beautiful eyes to sacrifice his life to sustain her in the unbearable misery of her frozen prison. Is this the love one gives to a Goddess? he thought dizzily? Is this what we have done to her by disturbing the balance of nature? Is this the great power that Brid and Morrigwen supplicate before? If so he understood the fierceness of the priestesses' devotion. He would do anything for this wonderful presence.

Suddenly he was aware that he couldn't breathe. The shock came to him in a rush of fear. He gasped, wheezed, trying to inflate his lungs. It hurt with the sharpness of frost. Every inch of him felt unbearably cold except for his right hand, which burnt with an acid heat. A deep familiar voice was demanding in his ear that he return to that other place . . .

Then Caspar knew it was his father calling. Branwolf's voice held a tremor. 'It seems to me that his mind does not want to come back to us.'

Morrigwen's instantly recognizable words followed, full of age, wisdom and the frailty brought on by a burden borne over many sorrowful years.

'Nor would you if you were with her in the depths of the crystal; but he's very strong; he'll be perfectly all right. The cold passes.'

Caspar was pleasantly aware that his right hand, which still throbbed with a pulsing heat, was resting against Brid's shoulder. Still mesmerized by his trance he wondered if anyone would notice if he slid . . . No, that was a terrible thought. He turned to look at Brid's quiet face, feeling her steady breathing against his palm and the reassuring thump, thump of her heart. But she did not respond to his look. Her face was brightly flushed and her skin was damp with sweat.

'Will Brid be all right?' he asked Morrigwen quietly.

Morrigwen hid her pleasure in Caspar's return to consciousness and nodded reassuringly at him. 'When you feel the hot and the cold balance within you then so it will be balanced within Brid. We must always look for the equilibrium, just as summer balances winter.'

Caspar watched with bewilderment as his father turned from him to stare angrily into the moonstone. The creamy patterns of the stone stormed furiously at his touch, blackening around the pressure where his fingers gripped the orb savagely. Morrigwen tugged at his arm.

'It won't yield for you: you belong too much to the new ways and your mind searches only for logic. Spar is the only one close enough whose mind is open to the mysteries of the old ways. You and Gwion might have taught his mind to pray to your God but no one has ever reached his soul.'

Branwolf had no answer. Surely his father wouldn't put up with any of their mystical talk, Caspar thought. 'Are we going home now?' he asked innocently, assuming that his father's presence would override the wishes of the two high-priestesses.

To his amazement Branwolf frowned at him quizzically. 'Haven't you been listening to the old woman? We must find her, find the woman in the moonstone.'

Branwolf had collected up any arrows that lay fallen on the ground and his quiver was now more than half full again. But there was more work to be done on the ledge. Caspar and Hal went with the Baron, leaving Morrigwen to tend Brid's wounds.

Just as he turned to limp after his older kinsman, Brid caught Caspar's arm. 'Bring back the dragon's claw. We can't leave behind such a potent talisman.'

They returned hours later with grazes on their palms from building two cairns; one for Wartooth and one for Wystan. Dutifully Caspar collected the dragon's claw for the priestesses, wondering what magical properties it was meant to possess.

They gathered the horses and towed them behind them. Wystan's placid draught horse calmly plodded into line but Conqueror chafed and snorted beside the cream stallion.

As they rode away the earth shook with the deep throated roar of the dragon somewhere in the belly of the most westerly of the three volcanoes.

'We didn't kill it,' Hal remarked bitterly.

'No, but it's severely wounded.' Branwolf sounded confident though Caspar noticed that the Baron's hand involuntarily sought out the hilt of his sword. But his eyes, like those of a true general, were already searching the level plain ahead.

Under the shadow of the dormant volcanoes the Dragon Scorch now blended into the dark crisp green of the steppes. 'Where are they? No living soul for tens of miles could possibly have failed to hear that beast roar. It should have drawn our enemies like a magnet. Hal, watch the rear. Keep your eyes skinned.' He thumped his heels into Conqueror's side and cantered twenty paces ahead of the rest of the party, scanning the horizon.

Even in this desolate place so far from his homeland, Caspar felt safe. His father, the great Baron Branwolf, led them and under his care there was no doubt that all their enemies would flee before them. He knew the thought was irrational, knew that Branwolf was no more than a man, but even so, he felt secure in his presence.

By evening they had reached the edge of the steppes and their eyes feasted on the fertile ground, supporting coarse-bladed grasses and low scrubby trees. The sound of water trickling across their path was music in their ears and they charged forward to throw themselves into the fresh running stream. The water in their canisters had tasted thick and stale and Caspar longed for the taste of pure water. It was cold, unbearably cold, as he cupped his hand and dipped it under the surface. His legs ached. He yearned to sleep for the night by the comfort of the stream.

It was clear however that the old woman was stubbornly refusing to give in to her aches and pains as she turned to remount her horse.

'We still have an hour of daylight left,' she muttered.

It took Hal's hand on her bridle to halt the cream stallion and put an end to the day's discomfort. 'Only a few minutes. Now that we've stopped we might as well rest for the night.'

Branwolf nodded in agreement.

Morrigwen did not waste energy on arguing. Once halted, she collapsed onto the ground and ordered the youngsters off to find dry bracken or, if they were lucky, brushwood for the fire. 'It might be dangerous to light a beacon, but we will certainly die of cold if we don't have a fire through the northern night.'

Obediently Caspar searched beyond the horses who blew and sucked at the running surface of the stream, flank by flank, for a brief moment forgetting their personal quarrel. It wasn't long, though, before the cream mare snaked out her neck to strike with blunt teeth at the strange black stallion.

Brid smiled. 'Men always think it's the stallion that leads the herd but as with wolves it's the matriarch that keeps them all in place.'

'Huh!' Hal objected, stretching out his legs.

'And dry, I said,' the withered old hag snapped irritably after Caspar. 'Dry wood only. We don't want any smoke, child.'

'Don't worry.' Brid laid a soothing hand on the boy's arm. 'She's old and fractious and her bones pain her. She doesn't mean to be short-tempered.'

Nodding in understanding, Caspar went in search of a choicer selection of kindling and returned to Morrigwen without showing any signs of reproach or defiance. The Crone conceded a brief smile.

The fire was most appreciated by the red salamander. It had slid out groggily from the saddlebag but now was greedily drinking in the warmth of the flames, its eyes mesmerized by the flickering light which it reflected in its big, black pupils. Caspar had the eerie thought that the miniature flame he saw in those unblinking eyes was the animal's soul burning brightly within. He looked at the fire-drake and thought of his beloved hound.

Hal was examining a number of cuts and bruises across his arms and shoulders. The young Maiden produced her leather herb-scrip and searched for the appropriate salve for his wounds.

'Nothing cures ills quicker than the loving attention of a beautiful female,' Hal joked as if that were a situation he was well accustomed to. Caspar, however, doubted that any woman had ever comforted the youth through a malaise, except perhaps for their old nurse of course. Elizabetta had never believed in mollycoddling her son through an illness and had declared that a stern heart and no sympathy were the quickest way to recovery.

'There's nothing loving about this,' Brid said acidly. 'If I had salt it would work just as well only you wouldn't be quite so smug.'

Branwolf gave a quick sharp snort as if stifling his laughter.

Indignantly, the dark-haired youth nudged a stick that was poking out of the fire. One end was glowing brightly. Black bark peeled away in concentric circles as it charred into cinders whilst the other end was cool and untouched by the flames.

Morrigwen whacked at Hal with a birch branch that had been lying idly in her lap but he flinched away in time. 'Don't meddle with my fire.'

'Thought you were asleep,' he muttered.

'Of course I'm not asleep. How could anyone sleep out here while there must be a thousand Vaalakans within striking distance? How can anyone sleep while we are just lying here in the open waiting for them to attack?'

'Where are they?' the youth suddenly exclaimed, spinning round to search out the Vaalakan plains. 'Yesterday there were plumes of dust just to the east where the Vaalakan columns marched southwards – southwards on Torra Alta,' he added bitterly. 'Guth-kak warned me that Kullak and Scragg were tracking us northward and today, there is no sign of anything. Not one single miserable Vaalakan.'

Caspar held his breath to listen and wondered why he hadn't noticed the unnatural silence before. They turned back to scan the brown scorched earth rising to the Three Black Devils, the flat crown of each just poking up above the southern horizon. Even from here they could hear the rumble of the dragon's roar like thunder rolling across the plains.

Morrigwen suddenly began to laugh, a shrill humourless laugh. The others turned on her expectantly waiting for her to explain herself. 'Don't you see? We can see three dormant volcanoes and know we are hearing the roar of the injured dragon that shakes even the very bones of the Mother. The enemy know of no dragon. They feel the shudder and hear the roar of an angry earth about to spill open and pour fiery lava onto the crust. They expect to be swallowed in the molten rock and buried beneath tons of sulphur raining out of the sky. They have turned as fast as an army can move away from the Three Black Devils. Kullak will never draw near while the dragon roars.' She laughed. 'Even the birds think the mountain will blow a cloud of burning rock into the air.'

Suddenly Branwolf was laughing too, though his mirth didn't last long. He drew himself away from the rest of the group and stared down at the ground. Scooping his cloak over his head, he hunched his back, looking as if the fate of the whole world rested on his shoulders. Caspar wondered whether he should go to him and sit at his feet but then he decided that the man might still be angry with him.

He wondered what had happened to the wolf, but Brid was unconcerned. She nodded towards Branwolf. 'I saw her a while back but she slunk away. No wolf would stay close while a man from Torra Alta is in our midst.' There was a note of bitterness in her voice.

As the sun dipped behind the horizon, Caspar dragged the bearskin up around his body, thankful for its insulation against the bitter cold of the north.

'So who's Guth-kak?' he asked wearily. No one, he noticed, had rebuked Hal for deserting them several nights ago. He for one was so glad to have his uncle back that he certainly wasn't going to mention it.

Hal was obscure. 'A Vaalakan. I met him alone in the Scorch.'

'And?'

'And, nothing. I cut his hand off.'

'Did you kill him?' Caspar asked in awe.

Hal nodded but there was no sense of glory or pride in his face.

Caspar didn't understand. His uncle was being very unforthcoming.

'He had a troll. I hate trolls.'

Caspar nodded. They were on common ground again. 'I hate trolls too.' The simple words meant very little; they were more a statement of the mutual bond of their friendship.

Hal began his description of the troll and how it had eagerly gnawed at the severed hand of its master.

'I don't think I want to hear,' Caspar said, nodding towards Brid. He was concerned that such gruesome details might upset the Maiden.

'They're not really trolls.' Brid turned her head without showing any signs of offended sensibilities. 'They're an abomination. Mutants, aberrations of nature.'

'And what does that mean?' Hal spoke softly to the girl, as though he were alone with her.

'Can't you see it in their faces?' Brid asked mysteriously. 'In their eyes?'

Caspar was suddenly struck with the answer and it turned his stomach. 'No, they're not human, I can't believe it.'

'According to the Great Book of Names,' she told them, 'the Vaalakan troll is a mutant cross between a bear from the tundra and a human girl-child born with a certain brain deformity.'

'That's absolute tripe,' Hal laughed, putting forward the side of reason and logic. 'You can't crossbreed different species.'

'I don't know how they do it,' Brid shrugged, 'but the Book says they have and I believe it: like Spar I can see it in their eyes.'

'It wouldn't work.' Hal shook his head. 'I'm telling you it's not possible.'

Reflecting on those haunting eyes, which Caspar felt spoke to him in a way that no ordinary animal had ever done, he shuddered. They were like the eyes of a drowning man trapped beneath the surface by a sheet of ice, only able to make out the outside world as a blurred unreachable existence. They had the tortured eyes of a confused creature whose base instincts were in continual turmoil as the separate natures trapped in the one body fought against each other. Caspar believed it: he did not know whether it was possible or not but he believed those eyes.

'What do you suppose a real troll is then?' Hal asked still sounding sceptical.

'The Book of Names tells us that the natural troll is an ancient caveman of the mountains. A man, but an ancient man that must have died out, unless one or two still live in the unexplored and wild places – like the dragon under Torra Alta.'

'The problem with these unnatural trolls,' Morrigwen sighed, 'is that nature cannot control them. They are anti-nature and without a name they are hard to manipulate with runespells.'

'Names are important then?' Caspar surprised himself at the sudden interest he felt in the runespells.

'Names are everything. Always look for the name . . .' Morrigwen lectured sternly as she cut into their conversation.

'What was that man's name, Father?' Caspar suddenly asked.

Branwolf looked at him steadily for a moment rather than immediately replying. 'Wystan, a woodcutter from the Boarchase. We owe his name much and must honour his family.'

Chapter 26

'Why is it?' demanded Caspar, 'that whenever goat-tracks look like they're really leading somewhere, they always suddenly peter out and stop? I mean where do the goats go? One minute they must be trotting along nose to tail merrily cutting a path for us and the next second – gone – vanished.'

Hal laughed. 'Well, unlike your theory on trolls, that I do believe – but I still don't understand it. All goat-tracks are like that. Always.'

'These are reindeer-tracks, anyway,' Morrigwen corrected. A large print of a splayed cloven hoof was pressed into the soil between the scrubby red birches that leant uniformly eastwards with the prevailing wind.

'Well, they think just like goats,' Brid reinforced the youth's argument, as they stared out across the undulating ground of the steppes. A strip of fertile sward stretched east and west as far as the eye could see, but to the north they could glimpse the strange glow of the sun glinting on the northern ice-cap.

'A day's hard ride,' Branwolf declared, urging his solidly muscled destrier onto a steady canter, the great hooves pounding like rolling thunder on the firm sod.

Give me Firecracker and I'd be there by noon, Caspar thought, frustrated by the flat lumbering strides of the mountain horses compared to the pace of his hot-blooded colt. And Wystan's draught horse, which was too uncomfortable to ride without a saddle, was towed behind them, stubbornly slow. Still they made good progress across the lands of the nomads. The steppes, however, seemed unaccountably deserted now that the three crests of the volcanoes had disappeared behind the southern horizon and the pipe of birdsong filled the air.

Branwolf still took the lead, something in his troubled soul making it unbearable for him to stay with the company of others. Morrigwen had relinquished the cream stallion to Caspar, finally conceding that the brute was too difficult for her to handle while it chafed to outrun Branwolf's heavy war-stallion. Brid had chosen to ride with Hal, though Caspar couldn't imagine why. She clung tightly to the youth's waist. Her loose hair was the only standard that the Belbidians unfurled as they penetrated deep into the heart of Vaalaka.

To their west climbed a low, scrub-covered slope and beyond that the rolling steppe-land. At first Caspar thought that the sward had been stripped bare, presuming that he was looking at brown earth rather than grass . . . only the earth was moving, stirring gently. Suddenly he realized that what he was seeing as the blur of brown earth was a herd of reindeer so vast that it covered the broad-bottomed valley, and so tightly packed that not one blade of grass could be seen.

'Come spring,' Morrigwen murmured, 'there will be no grazing left and they will starve.'

'You might have expected to see the odd nomad watching over the reindeer herds,' remarked Caspar.

He had caught a glimpse of the short velvet-coated antlers of a young stag poking out above the leafless branches of the scrub that flanked the left-hand side of the softly sloping valley. The thought of a stray nomad alone out here didn't trouble him at all. Hal had the great broadsword and Branwolf was now there to protect them. Still it was odd.

'What's driving him?' Hal nodded at Branwolf's back and the flowing cloak, now a dusty indeterminable shade, which billowed out behind him.

Brid said nothing and Caspar shrugged his shoulders. 'I don't know. He's not telling me. I feel I've been shut out in the dark as if I were the last person on earth he would confide in.'

447

Brid smiled kindly. 'He has a lot to worry about: responsibility for the mighty fortress of Torra Alta sits heavily on his shoulders.'

'He will have left the Captain in charge, though,' the taller youth reasoned. 'He'd know what to do.'

'The Captain, and Gwion of course,' Caspar added, not forgetting his kinsman.

Hal snorted dismissively. 'Maybe Gwion is in charge in name, but he is a man of peace. The Captain will make any necessary decisions.'

Conqueror's black shape rose up ahead of them on the skyline and Branwolf pulled him to an abrupt halt. Caught in mid-stride the destrier sank back on his haunches and threw up his head in a half-rear. Caspar thumped his heels into the cream stallion's side, urging him to a gallop, fearful that his father was facing danger.

As he approached, Branwolf signalled him to slow down so that when he broke over the rise he was walking calmly. Staring down at the scene below, it was all too obvious why they had met no nomads tending the reindeer herds.

'We have to help them,' Caspar whispered in a horrified voice.

'They are Vaalakans: the enemy. They have been abandoned by their own men, why should we, their enemies, help them?' Branwolf retorted, though he sounded unconvinced as if he were arguing with himself.

'Because we are Belbidians,' Hal declared proudly. 'And what are we fighting for anyway if not to save our country from barbarians? If we do not help them surely we are savages ourselves.'

Below them, marauding trolls paced covetously around a camp, a frightened group of women, girls and young boys brandishing burning staves in a feeble attempt to ward them off. Their circle of felt tents was huddled around a smoking fire that spat tongues of blue and red flames high into the cold air. A terrified scream stabbed the air as a young girl was snatched from the group by a triumphant troll. Around the perimeter of the camp lay a scattering of broken and gnawed limbs from the bodies of small children.

'I hate trolls.'

The bitter words formed simultaneously on the lips of Branwolf and Hal. They looked at each other in resolve.

'Morrigwen, Brid, stay here. Spar, you guard them,' Branwolf ordered, handing his son a knife to brandish alongside the Vaalakan axe.

'No, I'm coming with you,' the freckled boy argued.

'Do not disobey me twice, Caspar.'

With these words, the Baron and Hal thundered down into the shallow valley, Hal brandishing his sword above his head so that the bright metal flashed out shards of sunlight. Branwolf stood high in his stirrups so that the lower tip of the bow cleared Conqueror's withers. He let four arrows fly before they were within fifty strides of the snub-nosed trolls.

The Torra Altan war-song was deep and fearless in their throats.

Caspar did his best to sit tall and manfully on the back of the cream stallion, ready to repel any attack if necessary. Brid didn't seem even to notice him.

The assault was over quickly. Branwolf's aim was faultless and three trolls lay dead or dying at the edge of the camp. Two trolls reared up on their hindlegs, towering high over the heads of the horses and threatening them with broad sideways sweeps of their front claws. They squealed like stuck pigs as Branwolf's arrows pierced their ribcages. The remaining three trolls turned and lumbered away in that awkward rolling gait that looked cumbersome and slow yet still covered the ground with huge strides and a clean pace. One wheeled back up towards the ridge and Caspar manoeuvred the stallion out in front of the women. The troll approached, its small beady eyes focusing on him and a trail of thick saliva slobbering from its yellow tusks. Caspar shrieked his native battle-cry. The troll was unwavering in its stride.

A grey streak sped out from behind the horses and launched at the beast's throat, snarling and wrenching at its jugular.

The troll's short-lived scream of pain was deep and grating like a bear's as the wolf's throttling grip on its snub muzzle dragged its ungainly bulk to its knees. Caspar leapt from his horse and stood over the troll's head staring down at the beast, then tried to plunge his dagger into its brain. It took three attempts to pierce the coarse hide and the small eyes stared at him with bewilderment before finally he severed a main artery and the troll's blood gushed out over his feet. He carefully wiped his boots on the grass before lifting Brid up onto the saddle and leading the women down towards the circle of tents. The wolf vanished.

Shrieking and tearing at their hair, several of the nomad women ran to the murdered boy children who lay beyond the perimeter of the tents. A huddle of two dozen women clung closely together, gaping fearfully at the Belbidians.

'They think they've been saved from one terror only to suffer at the hands of the next,' Morrigwen mumbled. As Hal approached the women backed off as one. 'Stand still, young man,' she ordered stiffly. 'You might be better at chasing off trolls but leave this to me. We must see if we can heal any of their wounded.'

'Get my arrows, lads,' Branwolf ordered gruffly.

It was a messy unpleasant business pulling the arrows out from the trolls' carcasses especially when they needed to be twisted to avoid dislodging the barbs as they scraped between the rib bones. Caspar wiped away the sinews and shreds of muscle that still clung to the shafts before returning them to his father's quiver.

Morrigwen had made some progress with the nomadic peasants. There was nothing that could be done for the mothers who wailed with frenzy over their dead children, but at least they had saved two dozen people from the mindless trolls. The women were pressed together in subdued silence. Brid was already tending their wounds with a salve of calamine and yellow loosestrife. Not wishing to waste her herbs unnecessarily she had cleaned and bandaged the minor cuts to heal on their own. The women shuffled noiselessly across the ground.

Their feet and legs were so thickly bandaged with reindeer hides that they were entirely shapeless. Only the curve of their high ruddy cheekbones could be seen poking above their fur-lined collars, framing pale, deep-set, lupine eyes.

They kept their wary eyes fixed suspiciously on Branwolf. If he so much as put one foot towards them, they raised their arms as if anticipating a blow, cowering away and muttering in their guttural language. 'Is it because I'm a Belbidian or merely a man,' he said bitterly, keeping his distance. 'Come on, we've done what honour demands. We must go.'

'A minute, only a minute longer,' Morrigwen hurriedly begged as she eased away the thick layers of hide that had failed to protect an old grey-haired woman. The troll's tusks had ripped upwards as she had tried to drag away a child from its savage claws. Her eyes were darker, more like the blue of a sky glimpsed through the mists of mid-winter. She gazed into the Crone's face, studying her features and coming to rest on the mark of blue woad that stained Morrigwen's wrinkled brow. Feebly the injured woman half-raised her hand as if trying to reach the esoteric sigil. Her eyes sparkling with tears, she seemed to search deep into Morrigwen's soul, a look of hope, a look of wonder flickering across her face. Her lips parted in a toothless resigned smile. Unable to reach up to the Crone's face, she let her hand slump to her chest, knotting her bony fingers over Morrigwen's arthritic joints.

'She's an old, old woman. She remembers a time . . . she remembers a time even in Vaalaka when the sign of the Goddess meant fertile life and the hope of reincarnation.'

A younger woman knelt by her as the old woman muttered some unintelligible words and her younger kinswoman looked up uncertainly at the Torra Altan high-priestess. She spat contemptuously on the ground and pointed northward at the great white ice-cap gnawing southward through the steppes. The old woman hissed angrily and let loose a torrent of words that Caspar thought would serve as excellent abuse for those occasions when Hal really annoyed him. The younger woman tossed her head in a gesture of disrespect and the hag snatched at her hand, speaking coldly and calmly. Even the ice-voice of Vaal-Peor couldn't have been so coldly terrible, thought Caspar as he deduced that the old tribal matriarch was invoking some Vaalakan custom that gave her authority over her younger, stronger kinswoman.

'Here, Hal, Spar, lift this poor woman into the tent,' Morrigwen ordered. 'She needs warmth.'

Spitting and snarling, the younger women of the tribe growled at the Belbidians as they shuffled forward, bearing the weight of the ancient matriarch. She spat back at them and they grumbled more silently.

'You'd think they'd be more grateful to us for saving them,' Hal spoke bitterly.

'Would you be grateful to your enemies or consider it a disgrace?' Brid asked.

'A disgrace,' he replied, thinking of Guth-kak. 'But these are women.'

'And women do not have a code of honour?'

'I – well, I –'

'Of course they do. They owe us a debt, a debt they cannot repay because we are the enemy.'

Caspar looked pitifully at the sorrowful group of women who were about to face the deprivations of a northern winter alone. The grazing grounds were now no more than a day's ride across. The sward around the camp was already threadbare. 'Are these people really our enemy?'

Morrigwen shook her head. 'No, these women are not our enemy. These poor miserable creatures have been left behind by the enemy and their great war machines marching on Torra Alta. The Vaalakan men are closer to the trolls than their women.'

The distant hollow blast of an ibex horn mournfully sang out across the steppes. The Torra Altans froze. The thin reedy note underlain by a wailing howl, as the air spiralled through the twisted horn, was unmistakable. Immediately Hal felt for his sword. Branwolf had an arrow slotted to his bow.

'There may only be a handful of them,' Hal suggested.

'And here in the heart of the Vaalakan steppes there may be a hundred of them,' his nephew argued.

A few of the heavily clad women drew bone knives, hissing at the strangers and pushing them out of the tent.

'You'd think they'd show more gratitude,' Hal snarled.

'They're afraid, afraid of what the men will do to them if they suspect they've been harbouring us. We must face the enemy,' Branwolf declared loudly, drawing in a deep breath. The raven-haired youth took a quick sideways look at his brother. 'I'm ready, my Lord.'

The old woman, still lying on her bed of furs, snatched at Morrigwen's wrist, agitatedly shaking her head. She cupped her hand to her ears and then patted the ground.

Brid stared at her, perplexed for a brief second, before realizing what she meant. Flinging herself to the ground, she pressed her ear against the soil. 'The ground is trembling with the thunder of scores of feet,' she murmured, looking anxiously up at the Crone.

'I have no runes that can protect us from that number. I have runes that will protect us from evil spirits and from fools and thieves but not from this. They have been lost as the tide of the southern religion has swept across the countries of the Caballan Sea. A God of peace and mercy has left us defenceless and open to the butchery of the marauding hordes.'

'We will outrun them,' Caspar cried but all eyes turned on him in despair at his youthful innocence.

'They are on troll back, son. We must think of something else.'

Groaning, the old Vaalakan matriarch pushed herself up onto her elbows, breathing heavily with the effort. She pointed at her chest and then spread her arms wide to embrace the rest of her tribe, before pinching her lips together between thumb and forefinger. She repeated the gesture several times before Brid exclaimed.

'She means that they will keep quiet.'

The woman gave them an uncertain look as if unsure that they had understood her before continuing with her sign language. Thrusting her fingers at them she waved them away, stabbing the air forcefully in front of them and then pointing eastwards. Caspar felt like laughing as she made a low groaning sound and flapped her hands above her head, thinking that she must really be mad.

They looked at each other speechlessly.

'The reindeer,' Morrigwen said at last. 'She's making antlers with her hands. She means they'll say nothing if we hide amongst the reindeer.'

Without wasting any time they snatched up the horses' reins and led them across the near-frozen soil to blend into the stirring herd. The noise was numbing and the constant rattle of horns disconcerting. The reindeer were untroubled by the human presence, treating them like their normal herdsman as they closed flanks, swallowing them into the herd. After only a few minutes, Caspar had lost contact with the others, surrounded by the steamy breath and the hot sweet smell of closely packed animals. They munched at the grass and, as if drawn by the instinct of the herd, the cream stallion lowered his head and joined in. In this cold, he thought, the grass will never regrow. From somewhere to his left Caspar heard his father's solemn command. 'Whatever happens don't raise your head. Keep low beneath the level of the reindeer and then maybe we'll be lucky. Spar, did you hear me? Don't get separated. Make your way towards us.'

'Yes, Sir.' The youth felt chafed that his father no longer trusted him to instantly obey without question.

When the Vaalakan force broke over the hill, the boy had the unnatural feeling that he had become fully absorbed into the herd, which seemed to behave as one organism, one entity. He had groped his way through the tightly packed flanks of the reindeer but he could no longer work out where Branwolf's voice had come from. He didn't dare call out now that the Vaalakans were in the valley. The world all about him became a disorienting mass of stirring reindeer. Their heads lifted and turned in unison. Clouds of hot wet breath snorted through their stretched nostrils, as they strained to catch the scent of whatever predator had broached their valley. The separated youth struggled to see between the interlocked antlers that were like the tightly packed branches of coppiced crack willows. At last he glimpsed more than three dozen spears stabbing at the sky and the metal bosses of leather shields reflecting the pale red glow of the winter sun. A sharp shrill blast on the ibex horn announced their approach. They galloped down towards the tight circle of felt tents.

For a moment the herd stood still. There was a sudden silence. He could feel the air thick with life and the almost touchable tension before a squeal from a young stag shattered the quiet. Fear rippled through the herd. Almost like an army following set orders, the herd wheeled slowly at first and then started to run. Antlers clashed about Caspar's ears, knocking his face and he covered his eyes to protect them from the points. He must run too or be trampled beneath the flat of their cloven hooves.

The herd wheeled left and right in meaningless patterns and Caspar's heart burst with the effort of keeping up with them. His horse was gone, absorbed into the thick of the herd, and he ran on alone. The reindeer, once his protection and shelter, now became the enemy. They squashed and bumped him between their flanks, crushing the breath out of him as they hurtled forward in panic.

Brid, thought Caspar helplessly, where is she in all this? She's too small to take the blows. He sprinted on, thankful at least for the smooth short grass that made running easy, though the pain in his chest from gulping in lungfuls of cold, stinging air dragged at his stamina. If he stopped he would be trampled underfoot or even left behind by the herd and exposed to the Vaalakans.

'Brid, where are you?' he cried, now no longer worried that his voice would lift beyond the thunder of the herd as a thousand hooves drummed the ground. 'Brid!'

He thought of the Maiden struggling helplessly through the thick of the horned beasts. But Morrigwen . . . He didn't feel the same depth of emotion for the bitter old Crone but she would be in more peril than the young girl. If he was struggling the old woman would never have the strength to survive. He must find her. Snatching at the withers of a reindeer as its speckled hide flashed past, he launched high into the forest of antlers rattling above the running deer. He snatched a look around him, vainly trying to see the old Crone in the thick of the herd.

He slipped as he landed. Stumbling to his knees, he felt something punch into his back and he sprawled to the ground. Feeling the brush of hooves snag through his hair, he pressed his face into the earth as the reindeer skimmed over him, nimbly side-stepping to avoid him. He yelled as a hoof sliced into his arm. Get up! he told himself. But as he stumbled to his knees, trying immediately to break into a run, the spindly leg of a hind caught him in the back and sent him sprawling again. He rolled into a tight ball, feeling himself being knocked and kicked from all sides as the deafening roar of the cloven hooves beat out their rhythm on the frozen ground.

As quickly as it had started the herd stopped, returning immediately to the steady munch of their endless grazing. Slowly, stiffly, the youth unwound himself, wincing as he uncurled his back and pushed himself to his feet. His arm felt numb where the hind had cut his forearm but his fingers still flexed and stretched. Only bruising, he told himself firmly; nothing to get upset about. He lifted his head painfully, wondering if he would be alone in the herd and whether the others would be lying trodden into the soil lower down in the valley.

Behind them, what once had been green sward was now a churned mass of earth where the galloping hooves had torn up the grazing. In the distance he could hear the heavy unrhythmical beat of the trolls. He craned his head up to see their riders lurching awkwardly as they set off at a good pace due east out of the valley. They were safe at least from the Vaalakan men.

'Well, the old woman stayed true to her word.' Hal's familiar voice wended through the heaving sides of the reindeer and

Caspar beat a determined course towards him. 'One good turn deserves another, as Catrik would say. We saved the women and despite themselves it looks like they are repaying the debt.'

'Where's Brid? Where's Morrigwen?' Caspar begged, thumping the belly of an obstinate hind who refused to give him space to squeeze past.

'My God, Spar, what happened to you?' his uncle's voice exclaimed.

Branwolf reached out an anxious hand and pulled his son towards him. 'I *told* you not to get separated.'

The boy needn't have worried, they were all there together. The long-maned wolf was slowly circling them, keeping the reindeer at a comfortable distance. A stag lowered his antlers and scraped the ground threateningly every time the wolf drew near. She must have kept the trampling hooves and gouging antlers well away from the running humans. Evidently the herd didn't know quite what to make of a single wolf in the company of humans but now that they had ceased running, the reindeer drew nervously away from the wolf in their midst. As the crisp frosted grassland opened up before the Torra Altans, they stepped forward and pondered the difficulty of retrieving the horses.

Caspar dipped his hand into his pocket. 'It's not fresh but I still have some alfalfa shoots.'

He quickly caught the blue roan and the cream mare, handing them to Brid and Morrigwen to hold, but the wayward glint in the eyes of the other three horses made Caspar fear that they would be more difficult. Since the draught horse and the cream stallion were both heading keenly away from the humans, he offered to go after them while Hal and Branwolf stalked Conqueror, who was nonchalantly grazing close by. But it wasn't often that the black war-horse had been let loose in open pasture, having been stabled his whole life in the castle keep, and he found his new freedom too precious to relinquish. By the time Caspar had caught the draught horse, Hal had lost his temper and was swearing bitterly at Conqueror.

Fortunately, Branwolf managed to conceal his own irritation. 'Now, old boy, there's a good fellow,' the Baron said mildly in his deep tones as he twirled a spray of alfalfa between the fingers of his outstretched hand. He clicked his tongue encouragingly while the sleek black stallion tossed his head and showed the rebellious whites of his eyeballs.

'Look, Conqueror, I've trained you up as a war-horse; that means obedience. Any more of this –'

'And we'll have you cut,' yelled Hal angrily, picking up a loose flint from the earth and flinging it at the horse's hooves. 'You won't like being a gelding. Now just come here, you stupid ignorant troll of a horse.'

Conqueror bucked, flinging his huge hooves into the air and cantered out of reach.

'You'll never catch him like that,' Caspar chided his kinsmen as soon as he had caught the cream stallion. He handed the horse over to Brid and mounted the blue roan, which had come eagerly forward for the promise of one single wisp of wilting alfalfa, since he knew Conqueror would be more convivial towards a mare. Working his way in a wide circle through the reindeer, he approached at a different angle, ambling forward at a slow nonchalant walk. His hands were quietly on the reins and he deliberately refrained from looking at the great war-horse. Conqueror had his head down grazing but his tail twitched and the youth could feel the big black eyes studying him. He loosened his grip on the mare's reins, letting the animal stretch out to graze while all the time nudging her very gently in Conqueror's direction. Even when the destrier was within reach he didn't lunge for the reins, still thankfully looped over the pommel of the saddle, but waited until he could gently stretch over without any abrupt movements.

The war-horse was displeased as he suddenly realized that he had been deceived by the boy's nonchalant air and lunged away, snorting furiously. Caspar kicked his stirrups away and launched himself at the war-horse's back, fearing that the black stallion would pull away from his grip. The instant he landed on Conqueror's back, the stallion was submissive, curving his neck and taking the bit like the schooled war-horse he was. 'There.' Caspar warmly slapped the thick crest of his arching neck. 'That wasn't so bad after all, now was it?'

Branwolf tossed a thank you to his son and impatiently took the reins. 'We've wasted too much time. Come on.'

The Baron rode solemnly ahead and Caspar thought with distress that he'd never known his father so distant and irritable. It shocked him deeply as they rode on at a steady jog across the steppes, always keeping to the higher ground, avoiding any contact with the scattered tents that nested in the valleys. Caspar had no fear of being attacked; it was quite clear that all the Vaalakan men were absent, having marched south to join Morbak. He did, however, fear his father's mood and whatever burden was forcing him to such sullen isolation, always twenty or thirty paces ahead of the rest.

He confided in Hal. 'It's as if there's some horribly deadly secret that he doesn't want me to face.'

'I doubt it,' the taller youth replied lightly. 'He's probably just still cross with you for being so irresponsible.' But Hal's grin showed that he was only teasing and he looked at his half-brother's back with concern.

From behind the dark youth, Brid smiled sympathetically. 'Morrigwen is the same, always staring into the Eye, though she can see nothing.'

'Is it the power of Vaal-Peor? Is he really a God and is it his terrible presence that we can feel? Is that why everyone feels so bitter and cold?'

Hal laughed derisively. 'There is only one God. Hasn't Gwion ever taught you anything? Vaal-Peor is merely an idol of a backward race.'

Caspar clutched at the thought, trying to draw comfort from it, though he found the bitter cold of the northern steppes deeply oppressive. The cold seemed almost to have a tangible presence; he wouldn't find it hard to believe in an Ice-God. Realizing his thoughts had turned to heresy he imagined Gwion's chanting voice ringing out from the pulpit. But his memory found the words empty of meaning.

He looked at Brid and Morrigwen, proud, serene, the total conviction of their deity giving them an inner peace that he had never seen in any of those who worshipped the one true God. No, the men of the New Faith didn't have that single-mindedness of purpose. They were like Gwion caught up in the internal politics of the church. Who would be bishop? Who would stand before whom in the King's procession? Who could raise the most taxes to build the most lavish cathedrals to prove to their God the worth of their infinite love? If there is one thing that these women have shown us, he thought, it is that true, pure love needs no proof. They worship at the simple places, amongst the streams, stones and groves and it is enough. The love of God is not shown in gold chalices, ermines and scarlet threads, nor in cathedrals, which take generations to build, but within the inner peace of the soul.

He looked sadly at his father. And then he realized that the man was consumed by a grief and . . . and guilt. Surely that was what made him so stern and unapproachable.

Branwolf fidgeted with his reins, as he marched sternly northward. He wanted to gallop but he knew his horse was tired, not from that one day but from the long days of their terrible journey. Branwolf, also, was as tired as if he had endured a siege without hope of reinforcements or was wearily beating his way home after a long and unsuccessful campaign in the crusades. He had never ridden south to the holy lands but his nearest neighbour, Baron Bullback, had in his days before he inherited the Jotunn Barony. Though Branwolf believed in and worshipped the one true God he had found the crusades so distant and remote and his imagination had never been fired by them. Perhaps he should have gone and then in that long hot summer, fifteen maybe sixteen years ago he would never have met that beautiful peasant girl . . . ? Her hair had been like fire rippled with gold and streaked with burnished horse chestnut. He had been bewitched then and forever.

But if I had never met her, I would never have suffered this terrible loss. He couldn't bear to look at his son, still fresh-faced, with that same auburn hair. He couldn't look at those deep, deep blue eyes with their mystical imagination that leapt to the stars. And those high chiselled cheekbones, like an elf, he thought in dismay, small and fine-boned like an elf. What sort of an heir to Torra Alta have I produced? He could no longer stand to look at his wife's child.

Had it been his fault? He should have listened to her. His eyes scanned the frosted horizon with its short tufted grass bent over by the persistent winds. Keridwen, I'm sorry; I didn't mean to yell at you. Branwolf knew he had a bad temper – a temper just as wild and unreasonable as Hal's – but as he had watched his half-brother grow he had recognized his own faults mirrored in the boy and had striven to curb them. He now prided himself in being steady and calm, which he hoped he had achieved. But *then*, when Keridwen had publicly defied him, he knew he had been unreasonable. The next day she had gone. Is it really all my fault? He threw back his head and searched the wisps of high cirrus clouds that streaked the sky, drawn out in long mares' tails by the fierce winds.

'Oh God, oh great almighty Father, is it really all my fault?'

There was no reply save for the sighing breath of the wind.

He knew Caspar was looking at him. He could feel those searching blue eyes burrowing through his shoulder, but he couldn't look round. He loved his boy with all his heart but he couldn't look into those eyes any more. Not since he had seen them glazed over and still as sapphires as Caspar fell into the trance of that infernal moonstone, that Devil's crystal, he thought. He had seen Caspar stop breathing as the cold magic claimed him. It made him sick to the very core. He should turn back, turn away from this witchcraft, but he could not. He had to know, had to know the truth.

He drew up short, roughly snatching at Conqueror's bit as he broke over a long low rise. There at last before him languished the heavy layers of the ice-cap. It wasn't flat, as he had imagined, but rose steeply from the ground like an escarpment. It didn't start suddenly, of course. Tongues of snow feathered the edge, licking at the frontier of the steppes. Northwards as far as he could see the sun sparkled off the brilliant white snow that shrouded the compacted blue ice. But closer at the bottom of the valley it was a dull lifeless grey. Like the Yellow Mountains, he thought, which from afar glistened with the promise of gold but close up were no more than a mixture of pale buff and ochre earth between lichen-coated boulders, gorse and birch.

Between the black rocks and fields of snow a solid slab of ice spat forward into the steppes marking the most southerly frontier of Vaal-Peor's inner kingdom. It was the colour of molten pewter where the blue ice had trapped the wind-blown dust on its surface. Like a bitter old man its face was wrinkled and deeply fissured. At its very tip the cavernous mouth gaped at him, gouged out by the meltwaters of warmer springs of the past. The earth of milder years had warmed the ice from beneath. The thawed underbelly of the glacier had bled water from its core, spewing the meltwater from its mouth and so giving back some of the frozen territory to the steppes. Now the mouth merely growled its toothless yawn as if intending to swallow up more and yet more of the grassy plains. A cairn lay just to the west of the glacier.

Without waiting for the others Branwolf spurred his heels into Conqueror's sides and thundered down into the valley.

Caspar was hot on his tail, straining to catch up with his father who had already dismounted at the foot of the glacier and was examining the snow-fields to either side. The dark man swept the greying hair back off his temples and shouted something that was snatched away by the wind and drowned out by the drumming hooves of Caspar's mount. Breathlessly he reined in.

'What?'

'Hoofprints.'

Hal and the two priestesses were now there beside them.

'And I don't mean reindeer hooves either; I mean horse.'

'But there are no horses in Vaalaka,' Brid whispered as if mulling the idea over to herself. 'They say the northern tribes hunted them to extinction many generations ago.'

'I know,' Branwolf replied. 'That's what bothers me.'

Chapter 27

By nightfall they had reached the foot of the glacier and were faced with the steep climb over the rocks that cradled the ice-bluff. The cream mare, with Brid on its back, paced just ahead of Caspar. The Maiden's hair swished to and fro to the rhythm of the mare's gait, mesmerizing him. He yearned to touch the girl. Suddenly he felt ashamed that he should be seduced by such thoughts at a time like this, when he should only be concerned about the welfare of Torra Alta and the woman in the moonstone.

'We'll make camp here,' Morrigwen decided as they reached a point that looked down on the head of the frozen tongue of ice. 'By these stubby mountain oaks. They should give us protection throughout the night. Hal!' she ordered, provocatively fixing the youth with her eyes as if daring him to disobey. 'Fetch me some dry tinder or anything you can find that will burn.'

'Yes, my Lady.' He saluted her cheekily but nevertheless went off in search of firewood, muttering quietly to Caspar, 'I just haven't got the energy to explain to the old witch that she shouldn't speak to me like that.'

Caspar smiled, feeling inwardly gratified that, at long last, someone had won a battle of wills with his stubborn uncle.

'There's enough daylight left to start looking,' Branwolf objected.

Morrigwen shook her head. 'This is an evil place. There is no moon tonight, because of the thick cloud. We must stay by the fire within a circle of protecting runes. Vaal-Peor's breath is thick and foul in this place,' she shuddered.

'Old woman, your head is full of superstitious nonsense,' the Baron snorted.

'Fool man, you lack the sensitivity of your son,' Morrigwen replied stiffly. Caspar had never heard anyone speak with such daring to his father before and he sucked in a sharp breath. 'I know you are impatient.' Morrigwen suddenly softened and put her hand in a motherly gesture on Branwolf's arm. 'Torra Alta needs her. The very bones of the Great Mother shake with the marching beat of enemy feet and Torra Alta needs her. But there are more things afoot than you can know of tonight up here in Vaal-Peor's kingdom. I will carve the runes of protection.'

Caspar could almost feel the phantoms that stalked through the blue shadows created by the rays of the sun slanting across the crevasses in the glacier. The cloud had broken.

Branwolf sat with his back to the fire, staring out over the grey plains of the glacier, which now in the evening sun blushed with gold and crimson. 'I'm getting old,' he muttered, 'older than I thought I could ever feel.'

Caspar pulled his thoughts away from his father, finding him too strange and distant, turning instead to the warming glow of the fire.

The salamander croaked contentedly as it warmed its gills by the flames and the boy thought he almost had some affection for the single-minded creature. Brid was sitting apart, half her face in shadow; the other half aglow, bathed in the warm firelight. The effect reminded Caspar of the Maiden's divided nature. On the one hand she was just a simple girl, bright and cheerful but on the other hand her character was abstruse, hidden behind the exterior, like the dark side of the moon. She was no more than a young girl but still she was a high-priestess bearing the wisdom of years of accumulated knowledge handed down through generations. She was intriguing and delightful just to look at.

'Don't, Spar.'

Caspar jumped as he felt Morrigwen's cool bony hand rest on his shoulder. He had been so intent on watching the exquisite face of the girl, so lost in his dreams, that he had not been aware of the old woman as she crouched down beside him. 'Don't what?'

'Don't fall in love with her.'

'Who said I was?' The boy flushed with embarrassment.

The Crone's laugh crackled in her dry throat though she was teasing rather than being derisive. 'It's written all over your wide-eyed face.'

'But I don't . . .'

Waving aside his objections, Morrigwen's tone became serious. 'I know you won't take the advice of an old woman like me. I know you'll rashly follow your emotions until you get burnt – youth always does – but I'll tell you just the same. She's a free spirit and her religion will always come first. She needs someone less sensitive than you.'

The boy shrugged nonchalantly. 'Makes no difference to me.'

'If I were Hal, I'd be readily betting my hunting knife that it made an enormous difference to you, but –' Her words faded out into a shrug and she pushed herself stiffly up onto her feet. 'The young have to make their own mistakes.'

Feeling despondent, Caspar pulled the furs down over his head to shut out the sight of Hal sidling up to the young girl and sitting down easily beside her. Both stared wistfully into the firelight. Caspar muffled his ears to block out the sound of Brid's rippling laughter. Why did Hal have to chat to her like that? Hal was always grizzling on about Brid being a pagan and being haughty and difficult and then he goes and chats to her for hours. Why can't he stay away?

But soon Brid was busy. The circle of runes proved difficult to carve into the bare rock, though Brid and Morrigwen worked hard with the sharp points of flints before they were satisfied with the finished circle. Morrigwen warned sharply, 'Don't put even one finger beyond the circle.'

Just before he went to sleep, Caspar had a niggling thought at the back of his mind as if there were something he should know.

'The cairn, Morrigwen. Why is there a cairn here?'

Hal interrupted. 'How on earth should she know? We are in Vaalaka now.'

'How on earth?' the Crone sneered at the dark-haired youth. She took one of her sticks with which she had been prodding the fire and used it to goad Hal further away from the young priestess. 'And keep a seemly distance from Brid. How on Earth –' she mumbled. But then her voice became shrill and angry. 'I know because the Great Goddess, the Great Mother Earth doesn't bow down to the political boundaries of man. Vaalaka is still as much a part of the Great Mother as Belbidia, Ophidia, Glain and the Caballan Sea. Before man took to new Gods to further his own political ends, She was worshipped throughout the whole world, and there was peace and harmony. There are certain points on her mantle that have great power, where lines of energy converge. The cairn marks such a point.'

'A cairn, is that all? That isn't much of a cathedral to your Goddess,' Hal snorted.

'No? Would a cathedral, a mere man-made edifice, make the place of power any more significant? The cairn is there only for those who lack the sensitivity to tell them that they have reached the point of power.'

'Are there any other such places?'

'Confluences of power lines?' Morrigwen merely nodded before pulling her bearskin rugs up to cover her head. It was too cold to leave a single part of the body exposed through the northern night.

Caspar slept, though a voice in his dream troubled him. He knew the voice, but there was something different about it, as if it were carried before a storm, torn and rent by high winds until it became unrecognizable. A feeling of cold dread filled his dreams; a feeling of unutterable hatred focused on him, or was it through him to the woman in the moonstone? He couldn't tell. He could only feel the pure hatred. The hand was clawing at him, raking across the ground to try and reach him. The voice was terrible, filled with cold murderous hatred. Beneath the bitterness he could almost sense the person but not quite, so altered, so twisted was the personality of the voice as it mingled with the power of Vaal-Peor blowing across the tundra. The fingers of a hand clawed out of the night. The arm was ugly and shrunken as if it had been dead for a great many years. Grasping towards him, it sought his soul.

Dawn on the morrow was a laboured happening as an amber, half-hearted sun clambered wearily into a dull sky. Grey clouds precipitated a soft relentless drizzle of snow: it did nothing to lift Caspar's spirits. Brid was already awake, pacing the inside perimeter of the runic circle. She signalled Caspar to her side as she saw him stir. 'Look at these.' Her lilting voice was puzzled.

Tiny scratch marks raking towards the circle completely circumscribed the runes. Angry, hungry marks, Caspar thought with a shudder. 'What are they?'

Morrigwen stood beside them. 'Let us hope they were tundra foxes,' she whispered doubtfully.

The wolf though rarely visible was always near. Surely no fox would have come near with a wolf prowling the night. He shuddered as he remembered the sinister black hand that had clawed at him through his dreams.

'Tundra foxes,' Hal asserted with his own unique brand of self-confidence.

Branwolf stood tall and protective in the centre of his group of feudal subjects. His eyes were dark and heavy-lidded as if he'd slept little that night. 'We'll move up onto that west ridge.' He pointed at a grey peak rising above the left-hand side of the glacier. 'We'll get a better view of the whole ice river from up there and then we can plan how to search for her . . . if she is –'

The sentence died on his lips as if the Baron was unable to voice his inner thoughts. Caspar, however, was reassured by his father's presence. He was the linchpin of Torra Alta, and his natural authority subdued even the two women, just a little.

Morrigwen complained that the damp made her joints ache and she sat stiffly in the saddle as they made the slow climb to the snow-free rocks. By the time they reached the ridge the surrounding air was thick with moisture. Further north all the ice-peaks were caped in a shrouding mist that made the snow-mountains look even taller. It was impossible to distinguish mountain from sky.

'I've got a bad feeling,' Caspar spoke quietly to his uncle as they stared down at the gloomy surface of the ice river, which was deeply stained by the reflection of the oppressive grey clouds. 'My hazel pendant has a cold aching feel to it.'

'You've got a bad feeling! I can't think what we're doing here in this godforsaken place with these half-witted females. We should be in Torra Alta with a reliable bow and a quiver of the fletcher's best arrows. But Guth-kak made me certain that if we find this woman the superstitious Vaalakans will be terrified by the power we will then supposedly wield. Then they will turn back. They believe that Torra Alta is weak only because we have forsaken the worship of the Old Faith. It seems we need her.'

Caspar wasn't as cynical as his uncle: he had felt the power of the woman in the moonstone and he *knew* that Torra Alta needed her. 'I've got a horrible feeling that we won't be able to find her.'

'You and your feelings. Well, I've got a bad feeling too and it's nothing to do with any jiggery-pokery. Only a fool marches up into the ice-peaks with a mist like this one coming down.' He sounded irritated and concerned. 'We don't even know where to look. It's madness.'

When they reached the strategic vantage point that Branwolf had selected, the mists had drawn in about the glacier as if it were trying to shroud its secrets. They were only aware of a dull white mass looming out of the mist. There was nothing pure or virginal in the whiteness of the glacier. It was stale with age, an ancient river whose bubbling life had been sucked away into frozen silence. Only on the very fringes where the summer melt had nibbled at the dormant monster were there any signs of change in the glacier. The escaping meltwater had cascaded over surrounding boulders and then refrozen with the onset of autumn into a smooth opaque frosting.

The mist began to crowd in on them and Caspar felt the first snowflake land on his cheek, melt and dribble down onto his jaw-line. He wiped it away with a distracted sweep of his hand. 'Where are we going to look?' His eyes cast a despairing look across the rocks surrounding the plain of ice. 'It's vast.'

'And forbidding,' Brid agreed.

'Nobody could survive up here.' Hal's scepticism did nothing to raise their spirits. 'I'm sorry, but you've all got to face it. I mean, it's just too cold.'

'There could be a hut or a cave where she's been held prisoner. Those Vaalakans know about surviving in the very north,' Morrigwen pointed out as if she were trying to persuade herself rather than the youth. 'Right, we'll start the search along the western edge of the glacier. Somewhere hidden at the foot of one of these couloirs we'll find some shelter of sorts – somewhere – and she'll be there. She has to be. We just have to look.'

They dropped down towards the tongue of ice to begin the search, picking their way around the ragged edges of the glacier, stumbling across the scree and crunching through the belts of snow that lay in the hollows. The snow had decayed into grey slush, patterned with animal tracks of fox, rabbit, deer, ibex and even the occasional mountain cat. On exposed slopes, the snow was polished from the wind and was made treacherous by the glazing of ice over its surface where the snow had thawed and refrozen. The horses slipped and stumbled so often that in the end the travellers had to dismount and lead the animals, as they continued to scour the slopes. They could see nothing except the creeping mist that slid down the mountainside towards them. There were no signs of life other than the tips of two horns disappearing behind a rise.

'Goat.' Brid pointed.

'Or a horned helmet?' Hal's pessimistic mood had not

improved. 'Kullak could have tracked us down again.'

They searched on in silence, the crisp beat of the horses' hooves ringing through the ice-clogged valley. Listening to the sound, Caspar thought again of the hoofprints they had seen in the snow by the cairn. It was a puzzle he couldn't solve.

They marched on, crossing beneath scree slopes formed in the unstable spring weather of years past. Today Brid was riding the draught horse so that Caspar didn't have to envy his uncle's cosy proximity to her. The Crone had pursed her lips at Hal and austerely insisted that her ward should ride alone. Her frosted blue eyes spoke a thousand words of disapproval at the young dashing nobleman who grinned back, impervious to her displeasure. But that wasn't the worst of it, thought the younger youth resentfully. Brid probably wasn't that special to Hal, certainly no more than any other girl. He just had that certain way with all girls. He glared at his uncle's back. You don't even know how exceptional Brid is: you don't deserve her.

Branwolf suddenly called a halt. An ice-flow blocked their route ahead. Once it must have been a small tributary bubbling down the slopes to greet the larger river that carved out the main valley but now it was a treacherous strip of ice. No more than a dozen feet across, it was all the same impassable to the smooth hooves of the horses. The gentle slope of the ice-flow made it certain that they would slip on the glossy surface. Caspar searched up and down the slope for a safer place to cross while his father dismounted and scuffed at the ground with his heels.

'Hal, Spar, give me a hand. We'll grit it.'

With the planning of a garrison leader, Branwolf had thought of a way round their problem. Using the Vaalakan axe they chipped at the frozen ground, digging up flint chippings, earth and grit, to sprinkle over the treacherous surface of the ice-flow. They toiled tirelessly until they had scattered enough dirt to form a causeway suitably wide for the horses. Nevertheless they led the animals across. The horses picked their way tentatively on quivering limbs with their noses close to the ground, blowing clouds of steam anxiously at the manmade path. 'It's an unnatural place for a horse,' Caspar sighed.

'Or man,' Hal added but his eyes were searching lower into the valley and his voice trailed away as a frown knotted his brow. 'Branwolf,' he called sharply in the tone of a sergeant-atarms addressing his captain with urgent news. 'Branwolf, to your right, fifty foot below you.'

'My God,' the Baron exclaimed then cut a sharp glance at the others. 'Wait here, all of you.'

As the Baron flung Conqueror's reins into his son's hands he plunged down the slope with his sword already drawn. Caspar was still telling himself that he must learn to obey his father's commands when Hal took one quick look at him and plunged down the slope after his elder brother. It was too much for the younger boy and he dropped the reins and slid after them.

'I told you –' Branwolf began but fell silent as his eyes cast over the bright chestnut carcass.

'But it's Sandstorm,' Caspar cried as he noted the small diamond star on the horse's brow and the single white sock on the off-hind. 'I'd recognize him anywhere with that light fawn coat. Father, it's Sandstorm,' he repeated helplessly, not knowing what to think.

The horse was dead, already half frozen and they deduced that it must have fallen on the ice-floe, sliding thirty or forty feet to its death.

'Someone,' Branwolf muttered, 'someone has got here before us.' He looked up and down the slope for any hint of a footprint. 'How? How and *why* would anyone from Torra Alta be *here*?' His eyes sprang wide with a look of sudden realization. 'I didn't think much of it at the time, but Sandstorm was already gone when I went to fetch Conqueror. Whoever took him had already set out ahead of us, straight here. But why and who?'

They didn't have to wait long to answer one of their questions. A strip of dark cloth flapping in the wind caught their attention. Twenty feet further down the flow they found the broken body of a man dressed in the dark robes of a priest. Branwolf lifted the down-turned head and looked silently into the face.

'My God, it's Curate Dunnock.'

At his side was a Vaalakan scythe-sword. Branwolf rifled through his clothes and pulled out a crumpled roll of parchment. He looked at the strange indecipherable characters but instantly recognized the insignia of the Vaalakan crest stamped in wax at the bottom.

'Stolen or given to him for safe passage through the Vaalakan lines?' Hal posed the questions that were racing through Caspar's mind. 'Are we looking at a traitor or a hero?'

Stooping over the body, Caspar ripped back the man's sleeve, half expecting the skin to be scarred with the black ugly tears from fingernails. The skin was white and unmarked. He let the hand thud to the ground. 'But why would Dunnock, a man of the cloth and Uncle Gwion's curate, have stolen Sandstorm to ride up here, of all places, to exactly where the moonstone has guided us?'

Branwolf stood upright though he seemed to have shrunk under the weight of his troubles. 'We'll tell the old woman. She's not such a fool as she seems.' He led his young kinsmen back up to the two priestesses waiting expectantly.

Morrigwen was silent for many moments as she struggled to pierce the hidden meaning of the dead curate. She peered at the unscrolled parchment, twisting it a half turn as she tried to make more sense of the characters.

'Tree runes,' Brid declared looking over her shoulder. 'I can read the individual characters, though they are crude, but they don't form any recognizable words. I presume it's Vaalakan.' Her mouth formed contorted shapes as she moved her lips around the letters. 'V-a-a-l-a . . . It mentions Vaalaka.' Her eyes rapidly scanned the rest of the page. 'And Torra Alta and two names. The rest makes no sense to me.'

'What names?' Branwolf demanded.

'Morbak. It's signed Morbak at the bottom and at the top,'

she looked steadily at the Baron's eyes, 'it's addressed to some-one called Dunnock.'

'Traitor!' the Baron bellowed, his cheeks reddening and his eyes blackening in rage. 'Never has there been a Belbidian traitor.'

Caspar felt a deep sadness. The parchment could not have been stolen, not with Dunnock's name at the head of it. It could only have been written for him as a passport through the Vaalakan lines and given him by the chief barbarian, Morbak himself. A traitor from the very heart of Torra Alta: it was unthinkable. At least, he thought bitterly, he is already dead.

'Guth-kak wasn't lying,' Hal gloomily moaned. 'I thought he was trying to goad me into killing him, but he wasn't. He was trying to bargain. In exchange for telling me about the traitors, he had expected me to repay him by sparing him the shame and humiliation he would receive from his country-men.'

Traitors, Caspar thought in dismay. But Dunnock is only one man.

'Why?' Branwolf demanded.

'Why Dunnock?' Brid asked. 'Or why is he here?'

'Both.' It seemed ridiculous to Caspar that the great bulk of his father should be looking to this tiny young girl for answers, but there was something about Brid that made her rise to every occasion.

'Why Dunnock, I don't know. Greed for money, for power, discontent with his position?'

'Dunnock? Never. He was a little harmless man, devout, a sincere worshipper of the ways of the new God, always preach-ing of His benevolence and mercy. He travelled my northern frontier to bring word to the woodsmen.'

'And the Vaalakans, so it would appear. But if he is as devout as you say,' Morrigwen croaked after a moment's thought, 'then, I'd say he was here for his God. He's a man of the new God you tell me, a man sworn to peace, to love his neighbour and to uphold the word of his Lord. Such a man doesn't do these things for worldly gain but for his soul. Somehow he must have discovered the whereabouts of the Mother and feared that if ever she came back to Torra Alta the old religion would rise again. He has come here to find the Mother and see that she is destroyed for all time. Let us pray he has failed.'

'But how did he know she was here?' Branwolf demanded, his face contorted as if he struggled to understand what the Crone was telling him.

'I don't know the answers to everything, my son. He has taken the answer silently with him to his death. But if he knows then may be so do others. We must find her. We must pray that she is still alive.'

'Shouldn't we bury him?' Caspar asked distractedly in the stunned silence. His mind had already moved away from the curate. He could sense the energy of the moonstone throbbing out as if the woman trapped within its heart were forlornly trying to reach him. He sensed the violence of desperation as if she were balanced on the knife edge between life and death. His life would be as desolate and meaningless as this frozen land if he couldn't find her and release her from her torment.

'Bury a traitor! Never!' roared Branwolf as he led them on to their painstaking search of the edges of the glacier.

After many hours of diligent and fruitless scouring, Hal began to grumble. 'It's useless. The light is failing and if the clouds lower any more we'll get lost in the fog.'

Morrigwen sighed reluctantly. 'I have to admit that for once you are right. The next gully along will provide shelter from the wind and we'll make camp there.'

The other four, even Branwolf, nodded wearily without voicing any protests and they plodded on to the shelter of the next couloir. Caspar took one look up the snow-filled gully and shook his head. 'I don't care how tired we are, but we're not sleeping here.'

'Another one of your feelings?' Hal mocked.

'No.' The younger boy pointed to the footprints in the snow

near the foot of the gully. 'Look. There's still all the deer tracks but not a sign of any ibex prints.'

'You're right,' Hal admitted. 'I'm not sleeping under any slope that's going to avalanche, either.'

'Strange how the ibex know about avalanches and the deer don't,' Caspar said as if thinking out loud.

'Not really,' the weary old high-priestess contradicted him. 'Ibex have always lived up here in the far north and in the high peaks of the Yellow Mountains, but the deer's natural habitat was in the lower foothills of Torra Alta and the warmer steppes of Vaalaka – until man forced them to hide with the mountain goats.'

'I'm too tired for lectures,' the older boy grumbled.

That night they banked the fire high and cocooned themselves in furs but it was still miserably cold. They had dug a shelter in the lee of a rock, just managing to keep the chill of night at bay, but when dawn broke they were all eager to get moving again. The fog still roofed over the valley and sealed them into the glacier's domain. Everywhere was grey. By noon the mist sank lower and further searching became impossible.

'I'm sorry, Spar, but we have to stop looking. You couldn't see a hut or a cabin if it were ten paces away and in this choking mist you could walk straight over a cliff and not know it till you hit the ground,' Brid reasoned with the younger boy.

But Caspar was still determined to keep searching. 'But we've got to find her. We've got to keep looking,' he protested fretfully. 'She needs me.'

Hal gave him a look that seemed to say he thought his senses, always slightly unhinged, had finally left him completely.

'When the mist clears.' Morrigwen's decision was final.

The fog did not lift until mid-morning of the next day, by which time Branwolf was fractious with frustration. The muscles beneath his coarse growth of stubble twitched anxiously but he agreed they had to wait until they could see a little way ahead. The clearer skies, however, made little difference to their quest. By mid-afternoon they had not only completed their search of the western side of the glacier but had also scoured the eastern fringes as well.

'We can't search forever. It's beginning to look pretty hopeless,' Hal said matter-of-factly.

'No! She has to be here,' his nephew protested again. 'I saw her. I saw the cairn and this valley. Can't we look in the moonstone again and see if it'll be any more revealing.'

But the magical orb remained as grey as the shrouding mist and no amount of imploring thoughts raised to the Great Goddess would entice an image from its heart.

'There are too many evil forces about,' Morrigwen sighed. Lately she had grown more and more withdrawn as if resigning herself to failure. The sadness dragged at her wrinkled face. 'The spirit of Vaal-Peor is very strong in this ice-choked valley. If there is anything here for us to find, he is hiding it from us.'

'There's nothing here. No cabins, huts, caves, shelters or any sign of life. Nothing but the old glacier covered in cracks and crevasses. She isn't here.' The older boy spoke realistically and with rising impatience. 'Isn't it time we went home?'

Something gnawed at the back of Caspar's mind, a tentative suggestion just out of grasp of understanding. It was as if he knew where the Mother was, as if he had been shown or told but never realized at the time: there was so much confusion of thought surrounding her.

'I'll try the sprig of silver-fir again,' Brid volunteered. 'Perhaps the far-seeing tree will show us something.'

'Not again. Do you have to?' Hal complained but Brid was already entranced, her eyes rolling over and white. The youth looked away in disgust. 'Girls just shouldn't do that sort of thing: it's not pretty.'

When Brid was sufficiently recovered from the drug, though still pallid and taking sips of water from a flask to wash away the bitter taste, she shook her head at her companions.

'Nothing. Everything was just frosted over and cloudy.' The girl shivered. 'Just a sensation of cold; that was all there was.'

'The glacier,' Caspar suddenly shouted. 'She's not around the edges, but she's somewhere hidden in one of those crevasses.'

'Spar, you're being ridiculous. You can't hide in a crevasse: all you can do is die,' Hal pointed out bluntly.

'A cabin built in a crevasse?' Caspar suggested, grasping at any hope.

'We'll have to try,' Morrigwen decided.

'Of course we have to try. We have to try everything,' Branwolf thundered as he looked bleakly across the frozen river. 'Set the horses loose. We're going out onto the ice.'

Even the thin heat of the day had melted the top layers of the glacier, turning the ice to slush, but at least that made the going less slippery than expected. The persistent glare of the sun reflecting off the white surface, however, quickly made their eyes sore as they began their systematic search, sweeping back and forth across the tilted slope of the land-locked iceberg.

'I don't like this place.' Morrigwen shivered. 'It stinks of death, of Vaal-Peor. It's like a huge cathedral to that twisted God.'

Indeed, each crevasse that they tentatively peered into was a pit of broken carcasses where the unsuspecting deer had slipped and fallen into the open grave. Even if they had not died in the fall, the sheer ice walls made escape impossible and the creatures died of cold or, eventually, starvation.

As Brid craned her neck over the edge to search the deep fissures in the ice, Caspar thought about warning her to be careful, but he felt the advice would only annoy her. She would only rebuke him for trying to tell her what to do, so he remained silent. The boy's blood flushed hot, reddening his cheeks as he watched Hal simply take the Maiden's hand and tug her gently and protectively backwards.

'We don't want to lose you too,' he grinned at her.

Brid smiled appreciatively.

They stalked the shelving slope of the glacier with painstaking thoroughness until the sun slipped behind a conical peak and a grey finger of shadow lay across the sheet of white ice. The surface slowly began to glaze over where the slush refroze and each step became increasingly treacherous.

· 'Careful of snow bridges,' Morrigwen warned, pointing to the fresh white snow that lay in a bluish shadow. 'Look at that. There's nothing supporting the snow. It's just a thin layer bridging over a crevasse.'

'She's dead,' Caspar suddenly declared in despair. 'I can't feel anything but cold and what I saw in the moonstone was just a memory, the awful memory of her death.'

'Come on,' Hal tried to comfort him and to everyone's surprise added, 'We've looked this far so we might as well finish the job properly.'

'Don't give up now, Spar,' the young girl urged in encouragement.

The old Crone said nothing but nodded her head towards the higher slopes of the glacier as if ordering them all to continue the search. Something suddenly snapped inside Caspar and he felt he could no longer stand any more advice or take any more orders from any of them. All he wanted to do was to be alone and nurse his unbearable disappointment. Over the last few days he had grown sure that the wonderful love of the woman of the moonstone was still alive but now the hope was crushed by reason and logic. He felt nothing but a cold evil. Perhaps the icy hatred of Vaal-Peor had reawoken the chill in his neck from the black touch of Cailleach. Even the healed wound in his ankle began to ache with cold pain. He just wanted to escape from the others and be alone with his suffering. He started to run.

He sprinted, as fast as was possible on the treacherous slope and the icy air stripped the inside of his lungs. As he pushed himself to a muscle-tearing pace the pain of physical exertion eclipsed the pain of his loss. He slipped and grazed himself on the ice but scrabbled to his feet and ran on upwards, frantic to get as far away from the others as he could. He slipped again, catching his fall with his bare hand and a line of blood sprang up on his palm.

At last he stopped. Fighting back tears, he turned to look at the others below him. Pivoting on the smooth-soled heel of his worn-out boot, he slipped on the refrozen snow. He felt his foot skid out from under him as, with a cry, he started to fall.

Chapter 28

He slid head-first on his stomach over the refrozen snow, gathering momentum so that the ice skimmed past his face at a faster and faster rate. At first he spread his arms wide over the glacier, hopelessly scrabbling to catch onto anything that might break his fall, but the surface was unrelentingly mirror-smooth. On and on, he accelerated towards the blocks of ice lower down the slope, which threatened to cleave his skull in two.

A bump in the surface lifted him into a spinning heap. Unable to do anything but surrender to the power of Vaal-Peor's glacier, he curled up into a ball, scrunched his arms over his head to protect his skull, and prayed. This time the prayer came naturally and he pleaded for the protection of the maternal Goddess. A lifetime of indoctrination into the ways of the New Faith was banished in an instant. Driven by fear, he instinctively summoned the help of the woman within the moonstone, who seemed all the time to be silently calling him.

He bounced like a skimming stone over the ripples and mounds on the glacier's surface, thumping down hard on the solid ice and bruising all the points of his body, hips, knees and elbows. Miraculously his head remained unscathed. Another lip in the ice tossed him into the air, twisting his body. His arms flayed out uncontrollably. This time he landed awkwardly and his face smeared over the surface. He felt the skin being torn away as it grated against the raw glacier. The speed was too horrendous even to let him cry out in pain. Yet another bump catapulted him upwards and he braced himself for the diamond-hard impact of the frozen river. His stomach seemed to float above him as he became weightless for a second in flight before he smashed down again with a sickening jolt.

The slope briefly levelled out and he spun across it. Just before the white sheet started to tilt again he careered into a boulder of ice, his limbs folding around it as if they had no bones, and here at last he came to rest. Unable to draw breath, he lay face down on a stretch of the blue, translucent ice.

His breath came back with a painful rasp. His collapsed lungs heaved in all at once a great volume of ice-cold air that seemed to strip the moist warm lining from his throat. He felt he had been skinned both inside and out. He waited for the pain in the rest of his body to make its presence felt, but after a moment he began to circumspectly move his arms and legs. Tentatively he explored the flesh on his face, checking how much of his skin he had left behind, thinly spread over the ice for a hundred yards above him.

His right shoulder was numb at first and unresponsive but suddenly it screamed into life. He gingerly rotated his arm through its full range of movement, thinking with relief that at least it was not broken but wincing with the pain and screwing up his eyes to block it out. He blinked as swirling black and red patterns spangled with starry lights dazzled and spun before his eyes. Trying to concentrate on anything but his shoulder, he refocused on the crystalline ice beneath him, seeing at first only a hazy blur. Apart from the occasional stab of red light, his vision gradually cleared and he found himself scrutinizing the unfathomable depths of the ice-river. Nursing his right shoulder, he drew himself back to rest on his heels, gradually becoming aware of a dark shadow lurking beneath him.

The distorted blur of the shadow drew together into one picture and slowly he began to believe what his eyes were telling him. A growing realization emptied his mind of all else. He saw a face surrounded by a halo of dark hair – a face he recognized – screaming up at him through the impenetrable layers of ice. Suddenly everything fell into place and Caspar screamed back in horror.

He shrieked curses at whatever God hid behind the grey clouds above him. Why had he never before understood the moonstone's response to his touch. The woman within it had cried out for his warmth and his help and he had never given her either. Now he had found her buried in solid ice and at last, without understanding how, he knew her. In anguish he fell to his knees and beat his fists against the solid stone-hard ice. 'Mother! Mother!' he wailed.

An instinct deep in his heart yearned for her and all the love and protection he had been denied through his childhood. He longed for the depth of her love; he longed to be free of the anguish he felt at her loss. All the pain that had festered in his inner soul now welled up into his heart. Gone was any thought of the mythical priestess they had sought as the key to Torra Alta's salvation. He looked on his mother, his own flesh and blood, and his heart burst with unbearable grief.

Her face was contorted with agony. She was dead. She had died alone and friendless up here in the wilds of Vaalaka. Her soul was trapped beneath the ice, forever unable to reach its resting place beyond the slow torture of her death. 'My mother,' he shrieked as he slumped to his knees in despair, his head bowed over in surrender to his grief.

He became dimly aware of his companions as their caring hands anxiously prodded his bones and manipulated his muscles, testing for injuries. But the reality of the blurred, contorted face buried in the glacier consumed him. She had given him her love through the moonstone and he had not known her. Now he would never know her. The truth was that she was dead.

'My mother, she's dead!' he screamed, throwing himself again onto the ice.

'He's hit his head,' Hal said helpfully.

But then the others saw. Realization clubbed them into momentary silence before Brid's voice broke into a wail of lament.

Caspar swallowed his own tears, his throat aching. 'Father, she's dead. Entombed in the ice. Entombed within the cathedral of Vaal-Peor.'

But Branwolf's face was as hard and as white as the ancient glacier. He stared down past his son at the body of his wife. His tight fists uncurled like a dying man letting go of life. He didn't blink but stood stiffly, swaying on his feet, as if he were looking inward on an empty soul. At last a muscle twitched in his jaw and his teeth clenched hard in anger, anger at the death of hope grown over a dozen years of waiting for her return. 'My Keridwen,' he whispered.

'I really thought she was alive . . .' Morrigwen said as tears rolled freely down her cheeks, silent tears of grief. Dragging at her hair and tearing away white wispy strands with her bent fingers, the broken old woman continued to weep without sobbing. 'We'll have to take her home,' she said. 'I can't leave my foster-child here in this forsaken corner of the world, where the warmth of the Mother does not –'

Hal interrupted brusquely, 'She's under solid ice. We'd die of exposure before we could get her out.'

'Leave us alone,' stormed Morrigwen. 'She might not be my true flesh and blood, but in my heart she is my daughter. You intrude on my grief. You, boy, you don't understand.'

Abashed, the youth recoiled from the Crone's fury. 'I'm sorry, I didn't think.'

Caspar's quavering voice was added to the Crone's. 'We have to take her home and build a monument over her, in memory. We have to do something. Father? How do we get her out?'

Branwolf was locked in a bitter silence, staring down at his wife's agony-in-death. Taking a deep breath, he looked up at Caspar. His face softened but he could find no words.

Humbled by his own cruel lack of tact, Hal was the first to make a practical move, raising the Vaalakan axe above his head and pelting blows with its blade on the ice. A web of splinters fanned out across the ice and a shiver of fractures frosted the surface, but the blade was deflected, jarring Hal's arm. In disgust, he worked the weapon back and forth in a small fracture in the ice, staring down at the shadowy shape of the woman buried an arm's length below the surface. 'This is hopeless. If the axe makes no impression on the ice, there's nothing we can do.'

Wearily Morrigwen sighed. 'It's going to take more than brute force and a brave show of strength to make Vaal-Peor relinquish his prize. We're going to get her out of here and give her body some respect. We must free her soul. It is all that is left. All else is lost to the cruel-hearted Vaal-Peor.'

She closed her eyes. When she opened them again a moment later she had drawn the cloak of her vocation over her soul. She was no longer an old woman but a fearless and dedicated high-priestess, One of the Three to the Great Goddess. She no longer had emotions, denying herself such a luxury. A hardness focused her eyes, making her remote from all other creatures. 'I just need a moment to think.' Morrigwen's tone was calm and subdued. 'Brid, get that boy's face cleaned up and a cloak round him to keep him warm. The sun's going down.'

Caspar hardly noticed the Maiden's gentle touch as she wiped away the smeared blood. Oblivious to all else he mournfully studied the shadow within the ice. A tight knot seemed to close around his heart, squeezing out all the emotion. A gnawing void tore at his insides. She's abandoned me again. He tormented himself with the thought. She's left me. Brid ran her fingers along his collar bone. A nerve-splitting pain shot up his arm through his shoulder to his neck and jolted the boy back to his immediate surroundings.

'It's not broken,' she informed the boy. 'Just a good-sized bruise coming up already.' Her voice was as calm and distant as the old Crone's. She was no longer a girl but the embodiment of her Goddess.

Caspar drew strength from her cold, steely denial of emotion. He sucked in deep breaths of ice-cold air and shut his mind to his pain. 'I know. I'll live,' he said matter-of-factly. His eyes were drawn to his father's solitary grief.

'Hal, fetch me that great claw from the dragon,' Morrigwen suddenly demanded. 'The cold of the glacier might yield to the weight of a dragon's claw.'

When Hal returned with the old Crone's saddlebag his shadow lanced out like a long needle across the glacier as the last rays of the sun fled from the frozen world. Morrigwen ordered him to take up the tusk-like claw and strike again at the solid ice. She was bitterly disappointed when the surface of the glacier remained completely untouched and fell to muttering to herself for a while. 'I'm missing something . . . the glacier, ice, frozen water . . . water. Of course we must balance it with the element of fire. How many elements of fire do we have here, let me see? The dragon's claw, the moonstone, the salamander, the sword . . .' She then fell silent again and busied herself in the saddlebag. 'Brid,' she ordered gruffly, 'hold the light from the Druid's Eye over me: it's too dark to see now.'

'What sort of mumbo-jumbo is this?' Hal demanded. 'If the axe won't smash the ice nothing will.'

'You're wrong,' snapped Morrigwen. 'The axe is a thing of the enemy and so dedicated to the service of the Ice-God. Fire is the opposite element. Therefore to counteract the ice we need as many objects as we can find with the properties of fire. All very logical and simple. Now, what else? Brid, get thinking, girl. I want Keridwen to rest at peace.' An emotion flickered briefly across the Crone's disciplined face and her upper lip curled in anger, anger at the whole world.

'Blood,' the Maiden blurted out, staring at Caspar's raw cheeks. She searched around her looking over their belongings and then her eyes fell on the older youth. 'And Hal, of course. Fire governs his nature.'

'What are you talking about?' The boy sounded perturbed and indignant.

'Fire is a masculine element, so it rules you but not me or Brid. Your hot nature means you are more under its influence than Caspar, who is ruled by the more fluid, sensitive elements, or even the great Baron. Although he has much fire in his nature he also has much of the underlying solidity of earth.' She looked towards the dark shape of the Baron who was kneeling on the ice away from the others, nursing his grief. 'Also,' Brid turned back to look at Hal, 'you were born in a fire month, the month of hawthorn: Ostara in the old calendar; April, they call it in the new calendar. That means that, like the ram, the element of fire is very strong in your veins.'

'What do you want me to do?' Hal stood straight and looked smug. He was pleased to be credited with this masculine element of fire, though he still let an uncertain glance slide towards the frosty shadow in the glacier.

'In good time.' Morrigwen's eyes, red with weeping, told the boy to wait out of her way. 'Now give me the sword.' She stretched out a hand for the hilt.

The old Crone etched a line in the ice, drawing a circle around Keridwen's shadowy form. She then carved a sigil in its centre, directly above Keridwen's unbeating heart, and again carved the same sign at four points around the circle, pointing towards the four winds.

'I carve Kano's rune, the rune of fire. Great Mother, hear your daughter,' Morrigwen began to chant. As she continued with her invocation she seemed to swell in size until she was huge and powerful, like a magnificent empress at the head of her legions. 'These are the runes of fire. We offer the Druid's Eye whose heart is of fire; we offer the salamander whose thoughts and love are fire; we offer the ancient broadsword forged in fire; we offer our blood.' At this point she took the sword and slashed her forearm letting blood trickle out from the gash onto the ice. Brid also held out her arm and without flinching let Morrigwen cut into the flesh. 'We offer blood, the fire in our veins. And we offer Hal, born in the fire month. Help us to break the lock of ice that binds our sister. These are the runes of fire, let them burn our enemies. Let them burn.'

Brid and Morrigwen stepped out of the circle, leaving Hal standing bewildered and alone in its centre.

'What do you want me to do?' he asked, looking worried.

'Wait for a sign from the Goddess,' the old Crone explained.

As he looked at his uncle holding the sword above the ice, Caspar suddenly remembered the trance induced by the moonstone, when he had felt he was trapped within ice. In his nightmare Hal had freed him by striking the ice with the sword. 'Hal, use the sword to strike straight at her heart.'

Raising the sword as if it were a sacrificial dagger, Hal stabbed at the centre of the circle. He thrust straight at the etched rune of fire, only to hit his jaw on the hilt of the sword as the blade failed to penetrate the ice. His angry eyes swivelled and with equal force stabbed at his nephew. The scarlet fire-drake stiffened its ruff, like a snarling hound raising its hackles, and hissed from its gaping mouth.

'Of course the sword won't crack the ice. It hasn't got the weight, you fool.' The boy's lip was evidently smarting and it put heat into his anger.

'Help him channel it,' Morrigwen murmured to Caspar, but it took the boy a few seconds to realize what the high-priestess meant.

'Hal, listen to me,' the younger boy pleaded. 'Believe in the sword and channel that fiery hot temper of yours on the ice and not at me.' Caspar's understanding of his uncle's mercurial nature was deep enough to know that the raven-haired youth could flit from one target to another with ease. He was not surprised as Hal's stabbing eyes softened into a look of realization only to refocus with hardened hatred at the ice. His face twisted from sombre determination to pure aggression and, with the fiendish howl of his battle-cry, he smote the ice.

Collapsing onto his knees, Hal hunched over the hilt of the sword. Two feet of the blade's steel were swallowed by the glacier.

'It was just as if I'd thrust it into a pool of water,' he tried to explain as he stared with a dazed expression down the length of the sword. The glacier had remained undamaged except for where the thin blade had penetrated the ice.

Brid stepped out of the dark and into the circle lit by the pale light of the moonstone. She placed her hand on the hilt of the sword. The moment she touched the metal, her green eyes danced with brilliant sparkling lights as they filled with tears of joy and relief. 'She's alive!' Her words were like the beauty of a rainbow shining through a black storm. There was something so assured, so calmly convincing in her voice, all eyes were drawn intently towards her. Their minds, devoid of thought, were filled only by the single emotion of hope. 'She's alive,' Brid said again, wonder in her voice. 'I can feel her life-force pulsing up through the blade. Pitifully weak but it's there. The Great Mother is alive!' Brid spread her arms wide and threw back her head so that her soft curls floated around her waist. She laughed heavenwards with thankfulness.

Branwolf was galvanized. He snatched up the Vaalakan axe, strode determinedly into the circle of wan light and began chopping at the unyielding ice. Thwarted, he tried to wrench the sword free so that he could use it to pierce the ice once more, but it was resolutely claimed by the glacier. Pinched between a million tons of block-ice he could not move it. He looked up pitifully.

Caspar did not know how to ease his father's pain. Brid's words of hope had at first filled him with an unbelievable joy, but then the realization struck with horror. She's alive: the nightmare in the moonstone is real. She suffers the pain of her near-death second by second. The crystals of ice, like shards of metal, rip through her veins, pierce her nerves, tear her apart from within . . . For twelve years she has been in perpetual torture. It was too much to bear. Caspar wept.

Seeing his son's anguish, Branwolf at last came to himself and left the circle to comfort him. Morrigwen spoke gently to both of them. 'It is not a physical force that binds her in the ice but the work of a God. You will not break the spell with your bare hands. But our magic is strong and we will save her. Now stand back and let me work.' Her words were kind and confident. 'Trust me. Here at a confluence of power, we have much hope. The Goddess is not vanquished. While there is life . . .'

There is hope, Caspar thought. He took a deep breath and drew his father back into the cold night to let the priestesses do their work. Branwolf was there beside him and they clutched at one another.

Both priestesses, one in green, one in blue, touched the hilt of the sword, their eyes closed, their minds focusing inwards. 'Great Goddess, help us release the Mother from the ice-tomb. By rune of Kano, spirit of the fire, release her.' The concentration and effort were visible in their rigid muscles, which shook with the strain. But they both fell away in defeat.

'She's not strong enough,' Morrigwen said quietly. 'We cannot invoke the Great Goddess without the power of all three of us. It is the power of the trinity that focuses the holy might of the Mother.'

Caspar remembered the terror of the snake-filled fog in Cailleach's forest and the green demon mocking them: 'Two is not enough!'

As if turned by the same force, Brid and Morrigwen both looked towards him. 'All along only Spar has been able to reach her through the moonstone. She is the Mother: her greatest bond in all the world is with her child. Only you can help her, Spar.'

It became clear all at once. Caspar remembered the fierce heat of the dragon's blood that had boiled through Brid's veins. For twelve long years Keridwen must have been sustained by that fiery heat as it was transmitted through the moonstone. He remembered the terrible cold as his own warmth was sucked from him, his own life feeding her, sustaining her, keeping her alive, but barely. He looked at the moonstone now and the bright scarlet salamander with its foot anxiously pressing against the white globe. And now it is the fire-drake that keeps her with us.

'Come, my boy,' Morrigwen ordered. 'Put your hand on the hilt of the sword and feed your strength into her. Give your mother your strength.'

Willingly, Caspar stepped forward to make the sacrifice. Without hesitation, he firmly grasped the hilt, but was unprepared for the shock that penetrated his heart.

He knew the voice, remembered through his subconscious from the earliest years of his childhood, soft and clear with the same singing beauty as Brid's mountain lilt but with a deeper, mellow note of calm. 'I will not harm you, Spar, my child. I will take only what is enough and I will not hurt you.'

Caspar's arm snapped as taut as a rigid, brittle bone and he gritted his teeth against the depth of the pain. The healthy pink of his flesh turned a sickly ice-white and then the blue of death. He closed his eyes against the pain, willing to give more, his noble heart pumping the heat from his body as he focused the warmth at his mother. Suddenly he was thrown back and he staggered away, weakened by the effort.

Brid and Morrigwen replaced their palms on the wrought hilt, their fingers covering the large ruby over which the two metal dragons struggled in perpetual combat. Their faces contorted with pain but Caspar watched in despair as they released their grip and looked back at him. 'It is not enough, child, you must give more.'

Bravely he clutched again at the hilt with his numb fist, using his other hand to force his fingers closed.

'No, Spar, you cannot give more.' He heard his mother's voice whisper softly, so softly. He kept his grip in place and shook his head at the two pagan priestesses to indicate that he had failed. They stepped forward and closed their fists over his.

'Keridwen, you must take more from him. To save us all, you must.'

'I will not harm my son.' The words were final and not even Brid or Morrigwen could argue with the strength of the emotion behind them. 'Vaal-Peor can take the whole earth but I will never harm my son.'

'We must find another power,' Brid whispered.

'There is no time,' Morrigwen cried down at the crystalline surface of the glacier. 'The powers of Vaal-Peor march even now on Torra Alta. We need you now. All will be lost.'

Caspar kept his hands taut on the hilt of the sword and felt his mother's voice tremble up through the metal. 'You must find the Druid's Egg. Locked in its shell are all the secrets of the ancient lore, all the spells of witchcraft, enchantment and magic. The Egg holds the seeds of power and its might will split open the glacier.'

Morrigwen called back in despair, 'We will be lost before we can find the Egg. It has been kept in secret for thousands of years. We do not have the time to find it.'

'We must pray for time,' Keridwen answered resolutely.

Morrigwen threw back her silvery head and gazed up into the black heavens. The night was devoid of the mercurial light of the moon. 'We must pray for strength!'

A bolt of lightning slashed the starless sky; white faces leapt out of the startled night. With the shattering rage of warring Gods, a growl of thunder clashed against the distant peaks and shuddered the roots of the Vaalakan glacier. The ice hissed and crackled and an acrid smell of burning clogged the air.

The ancient Crone stalked the eyes of her companions. The mysterious power in the bent old woman eclipsed even the massive age and might of the glaciers around her. The force of life itself seemed to burn through her pupils. She raged. She spoke in riddles and chanted spells. She drew back her hands from Caspar's and crawled on the ground, carving a myriad of runes across the glacier. She commanded silence. 'We await the Sun God himself and the first light to bless the spell.'

Jagged lightning split the sky, sundering the black heavens with blazing white energy that empowered her words. A last clap of thunder shook the earth, but still the ice kept its cold jaws closed around the body of the Mother Keridwen. They waited through the black stillness of night, sustained by the electric force of the spells wrought around them, whose energy sparked off the mirror surface of the ice-river.

At last, the ghostly light of the northern dawn slipped between the teeth of the eastern mountains and tiptoed across the crystal surface of the glacier. The pearly light warmed to the blush of a ripe peach as the sun caressed the ground, blessing it with hope, the promise of life, a new beginning. Inch by inch the sun crawled into the hazy sky, its rays carelessly scattered by the splinters of ice and icicles that hung like daggers from the overhanging rocks. Inch by inch the power of the great Sun God crawled out of the east, spreading his cloak of warmth to embrace the Torra Altans, and at last touched upon the hilt of the sword.

'At last!' cried Morrigwen. 'The spell is wrought.'

All hands withdrew from the grip of the sword and Hal stepped forward as though he had been asked. He braced his legs and sought the eyes of each person standing around him, gaining their strength. Then he wrenched the sword from the ice.

It snatched at the sunlight, flashing golden rays across the ice-grey valley. With wide eyes he slowly lowered the sword. Where yesterday the central groove of the broad surface of the blade had been flawlessly smooth, now a stark pattern of pagan runes was scorched into the hard metal.

Morrigwen ran her gnarled fingers across the mysterious carvings, reading them. She raised her flecked blue eyes towards her liege-lord, Baron Branwolf of Torra Alta. 'These are the runes of war. You will carve them into Torra Alta's heartstone and they will protect the fortress from the ravages of Morbak's mighty army. Score these runes in the heart of the ancient fortress and you will stave off the assault from the land-hungry Vaalakans whose vanguard now laps at the frontier of your lands. But, because the lords of the fat and handsome land of Belbidia have betrayed the Great Mother, she gives us the power of these runes only for the turn of three seasons. The runes of war will hold steadfast in Torra Alta's heartstone until the rains of next spring erode their form and dull the contours of the etching. The mountain winds and the passage of careless feet will smooth the whinstone. In that time the magic in the runes will gradually fade and, like the dust of our bodies, their power will revert to the Goddess.

She gives us the grace of three seasons so that we can make recompense for our faithlessness and find the great talisman of power that will release Keridwen from the clutches of Vaal-Peor. We must find for her this talisman of immense and deadly power. If we fail, we will be at the mercy of Morbak and his butchering hordes. And Keridwen will die.'

The Maiden pushed aside the bony hands of Morrigwen, the Crone of Death, from the hilt of the sword, and with intense care fingered the ruby knotted between the claws of the forged dragons.

'Your sickle,' she demanded.

With nimble skill, she prised the stone from the dragons' grip and held it up to the light so that the sun shone blood-red through its heart. 'Look,' she cried in wonder. 'It is the rune of the Mother. She has given us her blessing.' Caspar looked into the heart of the stone and saw a perfect circle divided into three.

'The rune of the Mother.' Branwolf held out his hand to grasp the jewel. 'I will set it in the very centre of Torra Alta's heartstone so that it can pass the blessing on to my people. It will show the world that I wish to lead my people back to the Old Faith and restore the worship of the Great Mother to my lands.'

A look of dark shock clouded Hal's face.

Caspar turned to place his hand on the ice above his mother's heart. 'We will return for you, Mother, we will return with the Druid's Egg.'

Branwolf added his vow. 'We will find this pagan talisman of power and return for you, my Keridwen. With the runes of war I will hold off our enemies until the Druid's Egg is brought to free you.'

In the new light of day, the bleak plains of the Dragon Scorch lay before them and Branwolf stood straight. 'We will return to defend our castle.' His eyes skimmed with wonder over the bright sword etched with the power of the runes of war.

But first, he thought to himself, there is a family in the

midst of the Boarchase forest with a small and lovely daughter. I have to break them some sorry news.

Caspar thought only of his mother's pain as she lay entombed within the ice. His heart went out to her, and would stay with her locked in the ice until she was freed.

A

B

C

D

E

F

G

H

I } same

J

K

L

M

N

O

P

Q

R

S

T

U } same

V

W

X

Y

Z

Th

Ea

Ng

St

THE LORD OF THE RINGS
J. R. R. Tolkien

Part 1: The Fellowship of the Ring
Part 2: The Two Towers
Part 3: The Return of the King

The Lord of the Rings cannot be described in a few words. J. R. R. Tolkien's great work of imaginative fiction has been labelled both a heroic romance and a classic of science fiction. It is, however, impossible to convey to the new reader all of the book's qualities, and the range of its creation. By turns comic, homely, epic, monstrous and diabolic, the narrative moves through countless changes of scenes and character in an imaginary world which is totally convincing in its detail. Tolkien created a new mythology in an invented world which has proved timeless in its appeal.

'An extraordinary book. It deals with a stupendous theme. It leads us through a succession of strange and astonishing episodes, some of them magnificent, in a region where everything is invented, forest, moor, river, wilderness, town, and the races which inhabit them. As the story goes on the world of the Ring grows more vast and mysterious and crowded with curious figures, horrible, delightful or comic. The story itself is superb.'
– *The Observer*

'Among the greatest works of imaginative fiction of the twentieth century.'
– *Sunday Telegraph*

'The English-speaking world is divided into those who have read *The Hobbit* and *The Lord of the Rings* and those who are going to read them.'
– *Sunday Times*

The Lord of the Rings is available as a three book paperback edition and also in one volume.

THE HOBBIT
J. R. R. Tolkien

The Hobbit is a tale of high adventure, undertaken by a company of dwarves, in search of dragon-guarded gold. A reluctant partner in this perilous quest is Bilbo Baggins, a comfort-loving, unambitious hobbit, who surprises even himself by his resourcefulness and skill as a burglar.

Encounters with trolls, goblins, dwarves, elves and giant spiders, conversations with the dragon, Smaug the Magnificent and a rather unwilling presence at the Battle of the Five Armies are some of the adventures that befall Bilbo. But there are lighter moments as well: good fellowship, welcome meals, laughter and song.

It is a complete and marvellous tale in itself, but it also forms a prelude to *The Lord of the Rings*.

'*The Hobbit* belongs to a very small class of books which have nothing in common save that each admits us to a world of its own. Its place is with *Alice* and *The Wind in the Willows*.'
– Times Literary Supplement

'Has the air of inventing nothing. He has studied trolls and dragons at first hand and describes them with fidelity.'
– The Times

'One of the best loved characters in English fiction . . . a marvellous fantasy adventure.'   *– Daily Mail*

Magician
Raymond E. Feist

New Revised Edition

Raymond E. Feist has prepared a new, revised edition, to incorporate over 15,000 words of text omitted from previous editions so that, in his own words, 'it is essentially the book I would have written had I the skills I possess today'.

At Crydee, a frontier outpost in the tranquil Kingdom of the Isles, an orphan boy, Pug is apprenticed to a master magician – and the destinies of two worlds are changed forever. Suddenly the peace of the Kingdom is destroyed as mysterious alien invaders swarm through the land. Pug is swept up into the conflict but for him and his warrior friend, Tomas, an odyssey into the unknown has only just begun. Tomas will inherit a legacy of savage power from an ancient civilisation. Pug's destiny is to lead him through a rift in the fabric of space and time to the mastery of the unimaginable powers of a strange new magic. . .

'Epic scope . . . fast-moving action . . . vivid imagination'
Washington Post

'Tons of intrigue and action' *Publishers Weekly*

ISBN 0 586 21783 3